MAINELY POWER

MAINELY POWER

A Goff Langdon Mainely Mystery

MATT COST

Encircle Publications, LLC
Farmington, Maine, U.S.A.

Mainely Power © 2020 Matt Cost

Paperback ISBN 13: 978-1-64599-093-2
E-book ISBN 13: 978-1-64599-094-9
Kindle ISBN 13: 978-1-64599-095-6

Editor, Encircle Publications: Cynthia Brackett-Vincent
Book design and cover design by Deirdre Wait, High Pines Creative, Inc.
Cover photographs © Getty Images

Published by: Encircle Publications, LLC
PO Box 187
Farmington, ME 04938

Visit: http://encirclepub.com

Sign up for Encircle Publications newsletter and specials
http://eepurl.com/cs8taP

Printed in U.S.A.

ACKNOWLEDGMENTS

If you are reading this, I thank you, for without readers, writers would be obsolete.

I am grateful to my mother, Penelope McAlevey, and father, Charles Cost, who have always been my first readers and critics.

Much appreciation to the various friends and relatives who have also read my work and given helpful advice.

I'd like to offer a big hand to my wife, Deborah Harper Cost, and children, Brittany, Pearson, Miranda, and Ryan, who have always had my back.

I'd like to tip my hat to my editor, Michael Sanders, who has worked with me on several novels now, and always makes my writing the best that it can be.

Thank you to Encircle Publications, and the amazing duo of Cynthia Bracket-Vincent and Eddie Vincent for giving me this opportunity to be published. Also, kudos to Deirdre Wait for the fantastic cover art.

And of course, thank you to the real Coffee Dog, his namesake bookstore, and the inspiration he provided.

Dedication

To the Coffee Dog Bookstore, which was short-lived, but gave birth to the Mainely Mystery series, and so, lives on.

Prologue

Harold Dumphy crept through the shadowy corridors of the power plant's records department, the only sound the hum of the ventilation system. He was looking for something, something he had to know. For some time, he had felt that something was wrong. He couldn't quite put his finger on what it was, or who might be involved. As a matter of fact, Harold had no real evidence whatsoever, other than a slip of the tongue by Clayton Jones, the man who was assistant to the governor—and perhaps one of the men sleeping with Harold's wife. Harold had been in the security business for twenty years and had never run into a predicament of any import. But this time there was the suggestion of, not just a scandal, but a potential catastrophe that could rival Three Mile Island.

It wasn't hard to access the building at night after everybody had left, especially when you carried all the keys on a chain at your waist and carried a master key to open any door the keys wouldn't. It wasn't as if he was doing anything illegal. He was, after all, head of security for the plant, just trying to do his job. He wouldn't dare walk into the senior manager's office without something concrete, some sort of evidence, something tangible, for who would believe the hunches of a middle-aged nobody?

Harold wasn't sure what it was that had given them away and first kindled his suspicion that something was amiss. Perhaps it was the tightness in the face of the inspector from the Nuclear Regulatory Commission, the doors that only recently he'd found locked, or the addition of extra guards to Harold's staff without his input. It was not any one thing, but a multitude of bits and pieces the sum of whose parts added up to a whole lot of questions that screamed for answers—and urgently.

If he had been a smarter man, Harold thought ruefully, maybe a different kind of man, he would turn a blind eye, take another job and be far from here. He paused at the door to the Safety and Standards Room, where the weekly, monthly, and yearly inspection reports were housed, pausing to give himself one final opportunity to turn back. He sighed, knowing that was not an option. Certain safety standards were not being met, of this he was certain, just as he was certain that he could not be the only one to have noticed this.

He was 41 years old, balding on top, and, to compensate for what had gone missing above, he'd grown a thick mustache, drooping from his upper lip like a brush. Harold had always been fit, but just in the past year the food he ate seemed to be stopping at his midsection, pushing his belly out like some surprise growth and accusing him each morning when he stepped out from the shower and looked in the mirror. There were dark circles under his eyes, on his face a worried, haunted look. Not very long into his 10-year marriage, Harold had noticed the bored look in his wife's eyes when they made love, and soon after that social obligations had begun to demand more and more of her attention. Perhaps if he took a stand here, now, showed that he was a man of principle, maybe then his wife would desire him again.

He eased into the room and approached the rows of drab, gunmetal gray cabinets. There were dozens lining each wall, all locked, naturally. It took him some moments to find the right file drawer and then the right key, but find it he did. There was no going back now. He worked with his small flashlight clutched between his teeth, sweat dotting his brow and staining his armpits.

Harold had been 30 years old when he had taken the job as assistant head of security at DownEast Power. Then, he was a rising star known for his hard work and diligence, even if he wasn't exactly a genius. He'd moved to Maine from New York and almost immediately had begun dating Janice. One year later they had gotten married, and he was on top of the world. Of course, he reflected bitterly, when you're on top there is only one way to go, and not too many years later he had indeed found himself on the downward slope.

Day by day his bureaucratic job seemed to mire him in longer and longer hours of tedium, while night by night he seemed to be losing his wife. They had not made love in three years, a sad situation that Harold was certain represented a failing on his part. But that was about to change, because he was not going to be a doormat anymore. First, he was going to uncover the creeping evil in his workplace, and then he would confront his wife about her infidelities. His blood was racing in his veins, the adrenalin rush reminding him of being young and taking chances. For the first time in many years, Harold felt that he was taking a real step toward turning his life around.

He had worn skin-tight latex gloves for the job, and they made it easier to flip through the pages and pages in the files. He was looking through one of the most recent safety inspections, this one from just a few months previous, when he heard the whisper of cloth on cloth, and turned his head. And then he heard nothing at all. It would not be the fall followed by the cold shock of the water, nor the blow to the back of his head that would kill him. It would be those gloves, wrapped tightly around his throat that accomplished the grisly task. Death would find him next to a file cabinet in the early morning hours in the records department of DownEast Power, the nuclear power plant. His body would be found elsewhere.

Harold Dumphy had finally taken a stand.

Chapter 1

"Damn!" Goff Langdon cursed under his breath at the harsh sound of his alarm. His ex-wife had compared this very noise to a garbage truck backing through the bedroom at 5:00 a.m. When properly riled, Amanda would draw this metaphor in great detail, the churning wheels, clanging metal, and general all-around torment that had become the room they shared. It crossed Langdon's mind from time to time that all of his marital difficulties could be traced to this simple clock and that he should have gotten rid of it long ago. But he also knew that was pretty much crap and, besides, he was partial to the digital timekeeper.

Though his wife had left him six months earlier and wouldn't be haranguing him over the blaring alarm, the momentary peace was shattered by the arrival of another creature quite ecstatic for the new day. Langdon reflexively covered his face as a dark shadow came flying through the air with an eager whine and a clack of nails on the edge of the bed, just before burying him in a tsunami of fur and wet tongue kisses.

"Coffee Dog, get off me, you worthless mutt," Langdon said with a groan. "Enough." He wrestled with the canine, trying to pin him to escape the tongue lapping, and as the dog twisted loose, Langdon rolled away into the clear, and felt nothing for a brief moment, before the floor came rushing up to meet him.

This entire early morning ritual, from the still-clanging alarm clock to the all-star canine wrestling, had taken no more than 15 seconds, but already the downstairs neighbors were banging on their ceiling, his floor. Langdon never knew just how the Beans could get a stick into position so quickly, unless of course they waited poised for the opportunity. With a deft movement that bespoke of years of experience, Langdon, or maybe it was the dog, unplugged the clock and the infernal noise ceased.

Langdon lay without moving, as did Coffee Dog, whose teeth remained clasped around his master's ear lobe for almost a minute before Langdon conceded defeat. "Okay, okay. I'll give you the canned food for breakfast." With one final wrench, his trusty chocolate lab twisted the man's head to prove his superiority and then raced to the kitchen, his butt wiggling in anticipation of the breakfast to come.

Into this calm in the eye of the storm came the sudden ring of the phone. Both man and beast froze—for this was truly a strange occurrence. There weren't many calls interrupting them these days, not unless of course it was one of those infernal sales machines. It took a pretty lonely person to wait past the recording for that human voice to come on the line trying to sell weed whackers or whatever the hell was the item of the day. But it was too early even for those talking headaches just doing their jobs. This had to be something real.

On the fourth ring, Langdon plucked the receiver from the cradle and croaked a greeting in an early morning rasp.

"Is this Goff Langdon?" a voice asked sharply, almost derisive in tone.

Langdon found himself angry. "Sorry, this is his cleaning lady," he said.

"Is this Goff Langdon?" The voice was patient and flat, without emotion.

Langdon stirred uneasily in his hardwood chair, wanting suddenly to be free of this moment. "Sure, this is Langdon."

There was a pause before the voice continued, "I know where you live." The phone went dead, an insistent buzzing in his head.

"Big deal, you jerk-off," Langdon said in the silent darkness of the Maine morning into a dead phone. "I'm listed under L in the phone book." Nonetheless, a foreboding of bad things to come filled the kitchen, at least until Coffee Dog reminded him that he was owed canned food for breakfast, and the spell was broken.

With the eerie voice resonating in his head, Langdon went about feeding the dog and climbing into the shower. He took an ice cold shower every morning, both to get his blood flowing and to clear the cobwebs from his mind. He never quite rinsed all the shampoo out of his hair. The result was dandruff. He decided he could put off shaving for another day. It was not that he was lazy, not about important things, but rather that he struggled to accomplish what he considered the more mundane chores of life.

He was a private detective. Bookstore owner. Environmentalist. Football fan. Red meat eater. He voted Independent, sometimes Democrat, never Republican.

By the time Langdon made it to his car, he had all but forgotten the early morning call. It was hard to impress much less frighten a man who had become disillusioned with life at the tender age of twenty-eight.

It was late November in Maine which meant the temperature was somewhere near freezing. Maine was a place of pristine beauty—summer, fall, or winter—there was really no such thing as spring. It was the cold that kept the rest of the United States from moving there. If you could overlook the cold, then there was really no better place to live in the entire world. It was a reasonable enough trade-off, Langdon mused, and he had long been thankful that the climate provided a barrier against the spread of civilization to his backyard.

Langdon rode with the top of his convertible down. The car was a Chevy Impala or something like that, he could never quite remember. He did know that it was an early 1970s model. The day was still dark and his hair, still wet from the shower, froze, but he hardly noticed, although he sometimes wondered if this would kill the dandruff. Langdon had never been one to embrace fully the adult requirements of life, but rather, appreciated the intrinsic rewards granted to those who paid attention to what mattered—like the image of Coffee Dog with his paws balanced on the front windshield as his ears blew backward in the rushing wind.

The two of them, man and dog, went directly to the diner, as breakfast was the most important meal of their day. The waitress greeted them both by name, not commenting on any number of things—such as the wind-blown redness of Langdon's face, the icy spikes of his hair, nor the fact that his companion was a dog. They were regulars.

"Hey Langdon, did you catch the game last night?" This from the large woman working the cash register, her ruddy face already warmed by the ovens and beaded with sweat.

"Watched it at home with my buddy here. You see Danny T., you tell him he owes me five bucks." He slid into a booth that overlooked the street and smiled up at the waitress. "Alison, has the paperboy gone and gotten himself sick?"

"Sorry, Langdon, the gentleman over there has the paper."

Without turning his head, Langdon chuckled. "What gentleman? You mean Bill? He can't read, so maybe just give him the advertisements from the middle, maybe the women's lingerie section to finger through." Normally, this would have caused Alison to blush, but a certain stillness in her face caught his attention. "Not Bill, huh?" A nod. "Probably not even somebody I know would be guess number two."

With deliberate calm, Langdon rotated his head 90 degrees to the left and right smack into a face he'd heard recently. It was the face that went with the cold, derisive voice on the phone earlier this morning. Before the man even opened his mouth, Langdon had no doubt of this. It was like knowing that John Wayne's voice would be gravelly, or that Keanu Reeves would speak like a surfer dude. Sometimes, the brain just intuitively filled in the blanks, one sense anticipating, as it were, information not yet provided by the others.

The man was slender, dainty, even foppish, but by no means soft. His head was narrow, oddly like a banana, protruding slightly at the forehead and the chin. He had no facial hair to speak of, almost as if it had been waxed away. His eyebrows were so sparse and lightly colored that it took careful scrutiny even to see them. He wore a dark jacket and nondescript red tie. The man grinned at Langdon, his smile filling his face but never reaching his steel gray eyes.

Langdon smiled back and said, "So, I know where you eat your breakfast now, don't I?" He waited for a reaction, any change in expression, but was disappointed.

"Good morning, Mr. Langdon." Coffee Dog growled deep in his throat, more a vibration felt in the table than a sound. "It would seem that I have taken the paper usually reserved for you. Please accept my apology."

Langdon held his gaze. "Perhaps you could let me have the sports pages, and maybe 'Calvin and Hobbes'?"

"Of course, my dear man, help yourself." The words were polite, but the manner was more of one throwing down the gauntlet, more like the opening move of a game of chess than one side of a polite exchange in public.

Langdon rose, stretching to his full height of six feet, four inches, momentarily pausing to consider how Easy Rawlings would handle this situation. More than likely the Walter Mosley hero would have been overcome with rage at what he would have deemed a racial power play and would have escalated the situation to raw violence until the opponent was a spent and useless puddle on the ground. But then, Langdon wasn't black, this wasn't about race, and he wasn't about to escalate over something he couldn't even prove. Which only left that little question of "why?". Why was the man provoking him?

"In that case, I may just take 'Big Nate' as well." Langdon had his own style, and it was not his way to ask questions.

Though the opening move of a chess game is often the one that determines the outcome, Langdon well understood the value in keeping his powder dry. When this silly-looking guy with the phone manner of Oscar the Grouch and the dress of Groucho Marx was ready to come through with what this was all about, well then, Langdon would be more than willing to listen.

Half an hour later, Langdon was in the middle of his weight lifting routine, today being his day to work shoulders and arms. The gym was something Langdon greatly enjoyed, the physical equivalent of the cold shower, a hard workout, tuning up his body and mind before embarking upon the day's work. If one were to eat poorly and imbibe too much—both sins not unknown to Langdon—then exercise was crucial.

A few minutes before nine o'clock, Langdon, freshly showered and in a crisp, dry-cleaned shirt, arrived at his bookstore. It was actually more a much-loved hobby than a hugely profitable business, though it did pay most of the bills and keep Coffee Dog in quality kibble. Thanks to his crazy Aunt Zelda—who had had a special affinity for her nephew, Goff, and had left him a legacy to match—Langdon was able to supplement his unreliable private investigation business with a mystery bookstore that had no outstanding loans. This was a godsend, as the book business was pretty much suicide. Langdon had quickly discovered that the margins of an independent shop were razor-thin, no match for the megastores and this new thing called Amazon. But with no debt and a small payroll, Langdon found he could get by.

The population of a small Maine town like Brunswick—about 25,000—couldn't wholly support a venture of such limited and specific interest as that of a mystery bookstore. Yet, by the same shortsighted logic, his day job as a private eye in rural Maine should have curled up and died before it was born. Langdon had always gone his own way in life, and he held to the philosophy that, if you liked your work, then you didn't need much else. It seemed to be the trend of the present generations to slave 40 to 60 hours a week at jobs they didn't like just to make enough money to take a yearly two-week vacation in the Virgin Islands, or to buy a jet ski to ride on Sunday afternoon for two months of the year, or to drive a Volvo—living the American capitalist dream. This was not a mentality that Langdon understood.

His father had once told him, "Goff, do whatever you want in life, but make sure that you do it correctly. If you're going to be a ditch-digger, well then, be the best damn ditch-digger there is." This is how Langdon had lived his life thus far. Once he dug his teeth into something, he didn't let go until it was done.

The glass door he now pushed open had two inscriptions, the top of the door reading, THE COFFEE DOG BOOKSTORE, and the bottom, GOFF LANGDON, PRIVATE DETECTIVE. The store sat right on Maine Street; the only truly Maine Street in the state. Brunswick as a town was very much a throwback to the way things used to be in rural America, with small local stores owned and operated by people who lived in town. Maine Street was the widest main street in the state with two lanes going each way. Brick sidewalks stretched luxuriously in front of numerous and varied businesses—a natural food store, two bakeries, a coffee house, a video store, a restaurant or two, and here and there, a doctor or dentist's office—all of the owners local, fixtures in the neighborhood who not only greeted customers by name, but asked after their spouses and kids, too.

The Coffee Dog Bookstore sat right in the center of all this. It had expansive picture windows displaying a sampling of what lay inside—the most extensive collection of mystery books in all of Maine. These books had shaped Langdon's life, starting with Encyclopedia Brown, the Hardy Boys, and the Great Brain, before progressing with time into James Lee Burke, Dashiell Hammett, Raymond Chandler, James Crumley, Stephen Greenleaf, and John Dunning, amongst others. He was not always sure that the deep impact these books had had upon his life had been a good thing.

After all, it was more than likely the reason for his wife leaving him.

Langdon banished this from his mind and set himself the task of opening the store, turning on the lights, making coffee, booting up the computer, stocking the cash register, and picking some good jazz for the morning sound, choosing Louis Armstrong to start the day.

At 9:30 a.m. on the button, two things happened. Langdon flipped the open sign up and opened the door for Chabal. She was his sole employee, a mother of three, though only 31—she still had the figure of a college coed. Wisps of blonde hair poked out from under her navy blue beret, framing the delicate composition that was her face, the green fire of her eyes, and the spray of freckles that stood out in this morning's chill. Her cheeks bulged slightly, like a squirrel with a nut in each side, a trait that Langdon had come to find adorable. She was two inches over five feet, about eye-level with Langdon's upper ribcage. "Pert" is the word that came to mind when describing her, but he knew better than to voice it.

Just when the bookshop had become busy enough for Langdon to hire his first employee, Chabal had walked through the door as if sent by some divine fate. A conversation about a book had evolved into him asking her if she wanted a job, and she'd shrugged and said sure. When he asked about her exotic name—pronounced "Sha-ball"—she'd told him that her mother had grown up in the town of Chautauqua, in upstate New York. The next town over was the childhood home of Lucille Ball, and so she'd closely followed the career of that star, and in many ways, closely identified with the TV series "I Love Lucy." When her only daughter was born, she morphed her hometown with her hero, and came up with Chabal.

He knew that Chabal had been up since five to get her kids ready for school, just like he knew she came by her teeming energy without the benefit of coffee. In fact, he reflected, he knew quite a lot about her, though less about her home life, as she was a private person.

"Yo, Langdon, what up?" she asked.

Langdon liked how she rolled his last name off of her tongue. "Glad you could make it, sweetheart," he said with the inflection of a film noir character. His wife would have taken offense at this, but the woman in front of him merely grinned mischievously back, sending hot flashes up and down his spine. "The store is yours," he said. "I'll be in the office. When some lady comes in looking for me, just send her back."

"Okay, boss," she mocked.

Langdon—or was it Spade?—merely waved his hand over his shoulder in dismissive fashion, pretending exasperation with this woman who was his friend, his associate, his secretary, his teacher, and his secret desire. Of course, he'd never act upon this last inclination, for sometimes the wanting is better than the having. And then there was the small matter of his marriage—intact in law only—and her marriage, and her kids, and her husband… so many "ands" that admiration from afar (or up close, as it were) seemed best.

He had to stoop to fit through the small door to his office, and took the opportunity to steal an appreciative look back at the lithe figure now bent over the books on the coffee table.

Chabal felt his eyes on her backside and smiled to herself. The best streets in the world went both ways. Langdon had such an easy confidence, a trait that her own husband totally lacked. John Daniels needed constant reassurances that Chabal loved him or he would be a complete basket case, whereas Langdon seemed to amble along not caring what anybody around him thought.

Langdon's office was a small room with no windows and limited lighting. Along the right-side wall was an old leather couch where Langdon had taken many a nap, and even slept the night through a few times. His worn and beaten mahogany desk was perched in back, mostly clear of debris except for a few papers and a small lamp. On the right was another desk with his computer and printer, while the left had two tall gray filing cabinets.

Business was slow, for what crimes really happened in small-town America?

There had been the case of the lost dog back in August—but that canine had turned up on his own, having found the hunting life to be a little harder than the domestic life. Violence—from bar fights to personal vendettas—was generally settled in Maine without outside intervention, as neither the victim nor the antagonist tended to want attention brought to their plight, which was usually the result in one way or another of the demon drink. It was the cheating hearts of the local population whose spouses constituted Langdon's regular clientele.

Most of his time as a detective was spent with a camera in hand, following people on their lunch hours to secret rendezvous, where they lived out their fantasy that the grass was always greener on the other side of the fence. Small town life made this a very delicate matter, for on more than one occasion, Langdon knew at least one of the partners in lust and had thus faced a real conflict of interest in bringing the evidence he'd gathered back to the spouse. He also got the occasional background check on new employees at Bath Iron Works when their own internal investigation had red-flagged something.

Of course, there was the recent run-in with the mill up in Clinton, Maine, that had brought him front-page celebrity status. The Family of the Forest was a small, radical group led by a man with the unlikely moniker of Rasputin Snow, who appeared to have come straight out of a B-grade horror flick. His long black hair was wrapped into a tight ponytail, his nose, having been broken a time or two, flat and crooked, cheekbones that threatened to burst out of the skin, all perched atop a body that was short, squat, and sturdy. When he smiled, though, the initial impression of horror was dispelled and warmth radiated forth.

There were seventeen members of the Family of the Forest, including five well-loved children of undetermined parentage. The group had cohabited since the 1970s, dwindling in numbers from a high of fifty-one, as many of them tired of the whole hippie thing and returned to mainstream civilization, succumbing to society, the desire for their own families, houses with gas heat and running water, and monogamous relationships.

In an effort to stave off the inevitable, Rasputin had mobilized the remaining members into activists, allowing these hippies to flex their considerable talents, their intellectual prowess, while remaining true to their heartfelt ideals of the simple life, rejecting technology and the modern world.

Just down the river from the commune's compound was a paper mill, and it was Rasputin Snow's contention that this mill had been leaking chemicals, polluting the water, and killing the fish downstream, and thus posing a health risk to anybody who came in contact with its murky water. Rasputin had hired a lawyer friend of Langdon's, Jimmy 4 by Four, to get a restraining order to prevent any further illegal dumping.

4 by Four had accepted the case *pro bono*, this being the type of work he had left New York City to take on. He had lived there long enough to remember when the Androscoggin River had been second only to the Cuyahoga in pollution from all the mills that lined its banks. Though it had never caught fire like the Cuyahoga, he knew, like any freshwater fisherman, that you never ate what you caught, unless you craved dioxin and heavy metals. His first step had been to engage the services of Goff Langdon, private investigator.

While 4 by Four prepared an injunction against the paper mill, Langdon had worked to gather proof of the ongoing polluting. The lawyers representing the corporate suits were not about to see their clients' profits vanish due to some dirty water, however, and they had stonewalled both.

Sometimes, Langdon had told 4 by Four, you have to fight dirty, and that is what they did. One night, Rasputin and Langdon stole a cow from a local barn while the lawyer kept watch. They let the bovine work away on a salt lick for the better part of an hour before leading the poor beast to its slaughter. Sometimes, in a war, sacrifices have to be made. The next morning, the cow was found dead next to the river, poisoned by the polluted water, and somehow, newspaper reporters were present, as was a veterinarian taking blood samples.

The Family of the Forest had prepared signs in advance and began protesting immediately outside the gates of the mill. Langdon had made the front page of newspaper, being quoted as saying, "I'm just glad that it was a cow that discovered the water was being poisoned and not the farmer's kids." The mill was never brought up on formal charges, but public opinion forced them to change their practices and generally clean up their act. Four by 4 had made sure the mill compensated the farmer generously for his loss.

Langdon was not proud of having killed a cow, but he couldn't abide the fact that human beings were being poisoned every day and nothing was being done about it. He'd butted his head against this powerful corporation to no avail, but it was not in him to give up. Out of other options, he had resorted to this drastic measure. He'd comforted himself with the thought that, if it were his own daughter in danger, the point would have been moot.

As the private detective business didn't reliably provide enough money to make a living, his Aunt's timing in leaving him a parcel of money to open the bookstore had been impeccable. Except that this store was the straw that had broken the back of his marriage. Amanda, who had been a much better girlfriend than wife, had been hoping that Langdon would finally concede defeat, and that they could move to her hometown of Atlanta, where, she argued, investigators were making money hand over fist and were never, ever, short of cases. Unfortunately for their wedded state, Langdon had chosen to be dirt poor in Maine over a life of filthy riches in Georgia.

At this point in his thoughts, a light knock at the door caused him to hurriedly pick up a *Publishers Weekly* as if busy, bidding the person to come in. The woman who entered the room was, to use a Sam Spade descriptor, zoftig, her body full of contours. She wasn't overweight, but was a very curvy lady, her too-tight clothing struggling to confine the ample flesh. Her perfume instantly filled the small office, and a glance at her face revealed a heavy hand with the make-up brushes. She wore gold pendant earrings that were bookends to her well-tanned cheeks, and high heels that drew attention to her shapely ankles and muscular calves.

"Mr. Langdon?"

He didn't rise, just nodded his head, taking everything in, lost in the first impression that was so crucial to his understanding of people. A nervous man was liable to hedge the truth, a confident woman would not give out any more information than she had to, and a guilty person would be stuck on claiming their innocence, while a truly innocent person would be lost in fascination over what had actually happened, and so on.

Langdon did not know why the woman was here, only that she'd called and set up an appointment. His guess would be, based on her appearance, that it was a sexual offender case, the offender being her husband and the sex taking place without her, which was fine with her as long as she could leave the union with a large paycheck.

"You are Mrs. Dumphy?" he asked.

"Yes."

"Goff Langdon," he replied, holding out his hand. "What can I do for you?"

"I want you to find who killed my husband," she said calmly.

Langdon twitched. "Please have a seat, Mrs. Dumphy."

"Janice. Please call me Janice," she said, her voice tickling his ears with small, insistent caresses. She settled into the chair in front of him, leaning forward ever so slightly, her blouse open one button too far.

"Killed, you say? Please, start at the beginning."

"You don't know who I am, do you?" she asked. "My husband was Harold Dumphy who died two months ago, yesterday. Do you read the papers or have a television set, Mr. Langdon?"

The name triggered a dim recollection. Harold Dumphy had been found in the river near the old railroad bridge, floating facedown and quite dead. It had been a suicide, or so the media said. Whether it had been his job or personal stress didn't really matter, only that he'd offed himself.

"Of course I know who you are," he replied. "Why do you think your husband was killed, Mrs.... I mean, Janice?"

"He told me things about work, things that were going on that weren't right. He wasn't sleeping nights and wasn't eating."

"What things?"

"Harold had been working security for plants all over New York and New England for the past twenty years. He knew there should have been inspections that weren't happening, that regular maintenance was being ignored, that people in suits were suddenly no longer talking to him. He said there were strange faces showing up for meetings behind closed doors he could find no minutes for, and Harold, being so long in the security business, knew his way around paperwork."

Langdon stared at the woman as she shared her husband's suspicions. "And what was it that he suspected was happening, Janice?"

"I don't know."

"Yet somebody killed him?"

"Yes."

"What could be so bad as to make someone commit murder?"

Janice Dumphy stifled a sob, no more than a low guttural intake of breath, but it was this that brought the rest of the story rushing back to Langdon. Harold Dumphy had worked at the aging nuclear power station up the coast, DownEast Power. He hadn't been some lowly security guard, either, but in fact the Head of Security there.

Chapter 2

Once the Widow Dumphy had left, Langdon cursed himself for not talking money with her. Perhaps it was the blouse open one button too far that had clouded his judgment? Oh well, nothing to be done about it right now. Langdon eased out of the small office with a slight whistle to his sleepy dog who lumbered to his feet and jogged irritably along. He took a minute to put the top up on his convertible, as there was an icy mist in the air, and lunch was going to be at Hog Heaven, which was a drive-in restaurant. Several signs proclaimed 'Lights On for Service'. The food was cheap and greasy and tasted great, making it a regular destination for Langdon, even if the waitresses weren't on roller skates and they didn't serve alcohol.

He was meeting Sergeant Jeremiah Bartholomew, who he'd called after Janice's departure, to see what information he could pry out of his friend about the Dumphy case. With this in mind, he stopped to buy a six-pack of Geary's. Why, just because Hog Heaven didn't serve alcohol didn't mean he had to deny himself a couple of cold ones at lunch, and he knew that Bart would feel the same.

Langdon was usually no more than a social drinker, but certain periods in his life had manifested in him a darker, more alcoholic side. The latest disruption in the cosmos was his wife leaving him, causing the gloves to come off and the sauce to go down way too easy. He'd been in some state of drunkenness for too much of the past few months. He had a philosophy in regards to this, or perhaps it was a rationalization? He believed that with a few beers sloshing around in his gut, jokes were funnier, television was bearable, McDonald's tasted good, and the crap of everyday existence melted away. Sometimes—like when your wife took your daughter and disappeared—life was so much better with the edges dulled.

Langdon pulled into Hog Heaven and with an unsettled pleasure, popped the cap off the bottle of beer and took a swig. The fine taste equaled, and then overcame, his self-contempt. A rapping on the canvas roof startled him and he looked up to see Bart at his window, so he rolled it down. "Will you be my waitress today?" he asked.

"About time you put the top up. You know, we have people calling the station to report sighting a crazy man driving around town."

Langdon grinned at his friend. "Sounds like Brunswick P.D. is pretty busy saving the world from catastrophe."

Bart shambled around the car and pulled open the passenger door, easing his tremendous bulk into the seat. "Beats being a home wrecker," he said, implying that Langdon's work as a private investigator led to break-ups and divorce, but then his face reddened, as he remembered Langdon himself had recently split from his wife.

"I see myself as a facilitator of love," Langdon replied. "When people start cheating, it's like a cry for help. I help provide the information to let all parties move on with their lives."

"Facilitator of love? Fuck me," Bart replied, a slight grin creasing his weathered features.

The window that Langdon had only just rolled back up again resounded with knocking. He rolled it down with a solemn face. "Hi Bess, what can I do for you?"

The waitress shook her head and sighed. "Goff Langdon, you're sitting here with your lights on, which means you must know what you want to order. I am the one who will take your order, and stop drinking that beer, you're going to get me into trouble." The girl was only 19, a little bit high-strung, and Langdon enjoyed yanking her chain.

Bart, on the other hand, had little patience. "Girl, stop your yapping and bring us some fried clams, a couple McDonny burgers, and two orders of onion rings."

There was not a chance that Bess would sound off again. She wouldn't have in the first place if she'd seen Bart in the car. Everyone with any intelligence was terrified of the bad-tempered man with the badge. Langdon was one of the few who knew that his bark was much worse than his bite—though Bart's hot temper had actually been a large part of how they had become friends so long ago.

As a high school student, Langdon had, like everybody else, steered a wide berth around the bear of a policeman. There were some cops you might sass, even some you might blatantly defy, especially when you were the captain of the state championship football team, darling of the town, cock of the walk. But Sergeant Jeremiah Bartholomew was not one of them.

Langdon had had his first proper introduction to Bart after his junior year in college, when he'd worked the summer as a bouncer for Goldilocks Bar downtown.

Bart had come into the bar one night in jeans and a stained and faded t-shirt. He was quite obviously drunk, the first and only time Langdon would ever see him so, as his tolerance for alcohol seemed limitless. "Hey, college boy," he'd snorted by way of letting Langdon know he had his number.

"Yes, sir," Langdon had replied. He wasn't supposed to allow any intoxicated person to enter—but Bart was the police, and a large, drunken, and angry policeman at that, so Langdon was willing to make an exception.

"I'm here to kick the shit out of some druggies who've been dealing to high school students," Bart said. "I think you know who I mean."

Four young men had recently adopted Goldilocks as a hangout, men in their early twenties, handsome, polite, and well dressed. It was the '80s and the entire town knew they were the biggest suppliers of cocaine in Brunswick. They were sitting at a table in the corner. Langdon looked uncertainly in their direction before leaving his post at the door to find the owner of the bar. He'd not taken two steps when he saw Bart swinging a bar stool over his head and crashing it into the head of one these dealers. The man—who bore an odd resemblance to Don Johnson—crumpled to the floor with a whimper. A melee ensued—tables, chairs, pictures, and dartboards knocked to the floor in the swirling mayhem.

The owner, Goldilocks, suddenly appeared, leaping over the bar to help Bart. Langdon didn't want to get involved, least of all in a knock-em-down, drag-em-out fight between a drunken cop, a bartender, and a gang of drug dealers, but suddenly there was Bart, pinned down. Without really thinking, Langdon's feet took the two forward steps necessary to tackle the nearest drug dealer before he could stick Bart with a knife.

The next day, the police chief had paid a visit to Langdon, investigating a complaint about Bart's off-duty vigilante work. Langdon had smiled and said he hadn't seen a thing, effectively ruining any case against the rogue cop. From that point forward, Bart had expressed his gratitude, not in so many words, but by watching out for Langdon like a gruff, beer-bellied, ill-tempered fairy godmother. On the one occasion when he'd mentioned that night, Bart implied that he believed the chief had willfully turned a blind eye to the drug dealing in town.

Currently, Bart was wolfing down the food that had been delivered, and Langdon was wondering if any part of the large order was his to eat.

"Okay, what do you want?" Bart asked, still chomping on the remnants of a fried clam and an onion ring.

"The Harold Dumphy suicide," Langdon replied, "and maybe a burger and some fries."

Bart dutifully held out the tray, and a brown head suddenly appeared from the back seat, snatching a mouthful of fried clams from one basket and leaving dog slobber over the rest. Bart eyed the remaining clams for only a brief second, before continuing to eat, having deciding that a bit of dog saliva did not adversely affect fried food, and cop and dog noisily kept trucking through the meal.

"What do you want to know?" Bart asked, wiping his mouth.

"Who killed him?" Fifteen minutes earlier, Langdon would have phrased this as a question, but Bart's tone had diminished his doubts.

"I don't know."

"It was murder, then?"

Bart sighed and looked away, tapping the passenger window lightly with his fingers. "There were a lot of loose ends to be looked into, and then the case was closed. Suicide. Officially, I wasn't part of the team, but it sure as hell didn't seem so cut and dried to me."

"Details?" Langdon asked, prodding his crusty friend along.

"Tommy—it was his case—said there were some strange bruises around the corpse's neck. There were bruises all over the body, jumping off that bridge and hitting the water and all, but a ring around his neck? Didn't make much sense."

"Like he was strangled?"

Bart stuffed a few more onion rings in his mouth and chewed while he reflected on the question. "I don't know. The investigation was closed, and they buried him."

"What else?" Langdon tried to contain his excitement, as he realized he might truly be working a murder case.

"He had none of the classic suicide indicators, no signs of depression. Although his life wasn't all peaches and cream."

Langdon's beer was forgotten in his hand. "So, why does the case get closed?"

Bart took a healthy haul off his own beer, finishing half of it in one gulp, then paused for a loud burp before continuing. "Three days before he bought it, he took out a large life insurance policy."

"From what I've heard so far, Dumphy doesn't strike me as a stupid man. He'd know that the policy would be voided if he offed himself."

"Rumor around the station is that maybe he didn't actually want his wife to collect. Like, he was snubbing his nose at her, knowing she wouldn't see a dime of it after his death."

"Any special reason for this blissful matrimony?"

Bart yanked another bottle out of the cardboard Geary's box, his third in twenty minutes, and he was on duty. Langdon hurriedly finished his own beer so he could grab a second before they were all gone.

"This is all speculation," Bart said. "Nothing you can quote me on, but the word on the street is that the Dumphy widow was hauling more ashes than just her husband's."

"She was having an affair?"

"Not just *an* affair. The woman's a goddamn franchise. She's got more men in her life than you had beers in this car, and neither was enough."

Langdon took the last bite of his McDonny burger, staring at the attractive figure of a waitress across the way. "So, the theory goes, the husband finds out about the wife's little dalliances, and takes out a life insurance policy just to spite her before jumping off a bridge to nullify her ability to collect? Sounds pretty thin."

"It doesn't smell right at all." Bart finished the last of the clams. "Hey, flick your lights back on, I want a sundae."

"Who was Mrs. Dumphy making it with?" Langdon asked as he turned on the lights.

"Nobody who's ever admitted it."

"Who was rumored?"

"Greg Carr from the appliance store right down the road from here. Stan Jacobs from the town council. Some clam digger lives out to the trailer park on Maquoit Road. Pick a name, chances are you'll be right." He took a swig of beer and then glanced at Langdon. "Been awhile for you, hasn't it?"

"For what?" Langdon asked. Bess came back over and took Bart's sundae order. His eyes might have lingered as she walked away.

"Since your wife left you," Bart said diplomatically.

Langdon ignored the intrusion into his personal life. "You said that Dumphy showed no signs of depression, even though his wife was screwing everybody in town? Sounds like reason enough to me for the man to be a bit… despondent."

"Yeah, Tommy said that Dumphy had been acting real strange the last few days, according to the people who knew him, like something was tearing him apart."

"Who told him that?"

"Some of the guys at the plant, the neighbors, the paperboy—who, by the way, was making it with the widow."

"Sounds like cause for depression to me, anyways."

"Yeah, if you think killing yourself over the fickleness of some woman is a good idea," Bart said, his face again reddening at his indelicacy, given Langdon's current plight. There had been the rumor that Amanda, Langdon's wife, had been having an affair with Jackson Brooks, a handsome state trooper out of Augusta, but then she'd run off with a professional golfer, and was now somewhere down south.

Langdon shrugged awkwardly, wondering if the man was drunker than he looked, then changed the subject. "But what about the marks around his neck?"

Chapter 3

As Langdon drove back into Brunswick, his cell phone rang. He wrestled the phone from the holster on his belt and barked a hello into it.

"Goff Langdon?"

"Yep."

"This is Abigail Austin-Peters from DownEast Power, returning your call."

Langdon had left a message earlier inquiring about Harold Dumphy. This was a quick response indeed. "Yes, Ms. Austin-Peters, I am looking into the death of Harold Dumphy and was wondering if we could meet. I have a few questions, if you don't mind."

"The police closed that case months ago, Mr. Langdon. What is your connection to any of this?"

"His widow has hired me to investigate his death."

"Why?"

"She has some question in regards to his demise. I can assure you that it won't take long. Is there a time I might come by and ask you a few questions?"

The phone was silent long enough for Langdon to look at it to make sure the call hadn't been dropped.

"Where are you now?" she asked finally.

"Brunswick."

"I'll come to you. I have business down there later this afternoon, anyway. Can you meet me at the Wretched Lobster in half an hour?"

Langdon agreed and hung up. He pulled in behind the bookstore and parked, passing through the shop to check in with Chabal on his way to the Wretched Lobster, which was just a block down the street. She said there had been a steady flow of customers, but she was keeping up fine, so he continued on, thinking he was ready for another beer while he waited.

The bar was down in the restaurant's basement. Langdon settled onto a stool and laid his elbows atop the bar. Richam, the bartender, finished drying the glass in his hand, inspecting it briefly before hanging it up on the rack. He eyed Langdon, calculating, based on years of experience, how many drinks had already been consumed.

Richam Denevieux was one of the few black men in Brunswick, a rake-thin man with a military bearing, even though he'd never served. As Maine towns go, Brunswick had its share of ethnic diversity, between the naval air station and the college, but Richam was more than a migratory figure. This had been his home since he'd fled a Caribbean island with his wife and young son, looking for a better life. The only thing left from that place was the faint accent that tinged his sentences, a soft lilt that made the listener want to lean closer, as if secrets were hidden among the sing-song syllables.

"Cup of coffee?" he asked.

"New study says too much caffeine is bad for you. I'll stick with a beer just to be safe," Langdon replied.

Richam pulled a Geary's from the cooler, twisting the top and pouring the beer into a glass. "You've been drinking too much of late." Richam was also a friend.

"Yeah, probably," Langdon agreed.

"How many you had already?"

"It's a phase."

"It's a weakness."

Langdon smiled, uneasy at the turn the conversation had taken. "You probably won't understand this, but I'm striving to reach the moment of crystal clarity that occurs somewhere between sobriety and a drunken stupor."

"Where's your mutt?" Richam knew when an argument with a drunk was a waste of time.

"Ah, he's still upstairs terrorizing the restaurant patrons. They sure do love him up there, but I can't imagine it is very good for business having a beggar making the rounds at the tables."

"You got a reason to be here other than day drinking?"

"As a matter of fact, I'm meeting a lady."

"A date, I suppose?" Richam asked with a straight face.

Langdon chose to ignore the jibe and instead took a slug from the beer. "What can you tell me about the Dumphy suicide?"

Richam considered the question. "Do you know that in olden times the newspapers would send people to the taverns to find stories to write? When the news was slow, they'd send a man down, tell him to 'go sip a beer' and keep his ears open. Over time, this got shortened to gossip."

Langdon nodded. "Drinking establishments are certainly the center of a community," he agreed.

Richam flicked his eyes over the almost empty room. "His wife spends a considerable amount of time in here," he said quietly.

"That's my client," Langdon replied.

"Use protection."

"I'm still a married man."

"Yet you're meeting a woman for drinks?"

"Business," Langdon said. "Tell me more about the widow."

"She goes home with a lot of different men, but my saying 'use protection' was a double entendre. She is also one tough lady. You don't want to get on the wrong side of her or you'll end up hurt."

Though he certainly trusted the man's knowledge of people, Langdon played the morning meeting with Janice Dumphy through his mind, judging the accuracy of Richam's words. The man was the kind of bartender who watched and listened, spoke rarely, and made his own interpretations only after mulling over what he knew.

"What are people saying about the suicide?" Langdon asked.

"What does she say?"

"That it was murder," Langdon said.

Richam smiled humorlessly. "She tell you who did it?"

"No. You doubt it?"

"The man didn't commit no suicide." Richam generally spoke like a well-educated man, but, like every good barkeep, adapted his speech to fit in with his customers, lobstermen being as rough on English grammar as they were on traps and rope.

"People keep telling me that," Langdon muttered. "But who would want to kill him?"

Richam paused, as if considering something, before shaking his head.

Langdon frowned, knowing there was something the man wasn't sharing, but decided to let it rest for the moment. "I'd better go see what my dog has gotten into before they call Animal Control on him." He rose and crossed the room to the stairs, taking a huge gulp of his beer once he was out of Richam's sight.

Coffee Dog had his head perched on a navy-blue skirt that belonged to a woman sitting at a table just inside the upstairs door. "You must be Mr. Langdon," she said as he approached to retrieve his dog. She was fit, well-dressed, tan, and had an intelligent gleam in her eyes. Langdon felt, in that instant, intensely jealous of Coffee Dog.

Ms. Austin-Peters smiled across at Langdon. Her dark eyes were hidden behind jagged eyelashes above prominent cheekbones. Her body matched her face in hard angles: elbows that jutted out, defined shoulders, and breasts that poked their way forward as if trying to pierce her blouse.

The restaurant had a crisp whiteness, in direct contrast with the rough-hewn bar downstairs. Fresh tablecloths adorned the finely-crafted tables, atop which were designer pottery dishes and eclectic bottles with a solitary flower in each. No two bottles, or flowers, were the same.

"I know it's a bit forward, but would you like a drink?" she asked, raising her hand and beckoning a waitress over. Ms. Austin-Peters appeared to be woman who got what she wanted. "Wild Turkey on the rocks for me." She looked at Langdon with an eyebrow raised like an arrowhead.

"Sure," he said, shrugging. "Why not?"

"Oh, I know you," she said suddenly. "You own that mystery bookstore."

"Are you a reader?"

"I love books. I'm reading *Dangerous Liaisons* right now. Have you read it?"

"I've seen the movie," Langdon said. "I think I actually own it."

"Maybe you can invite me over to watch it some time?"

The woman was very attractive in a carnal way, and Langdon felt his ears redden. He certainly had enough on his plate right now with one wife and one woman he desired. "Perhaps we can get down to business?" he asked.

"You're here on behalf of Janice Dumphy?" she asked.

"She's my client." Langdon was suddenly not quite sure why he'd set up this meeting. What had he hoped to learn from her, a PR person? He regretted the beer buzz clouding his mind and slowing his thoughts, but there was nothing to be done about that now. Ordering a Wild Turkey on top? Now *that* had been a bad idea. "Do you know the Widow Dumphy?"

"I remember meeting her at a Christmas party, but no, not really. She seemed to hit it off with several of my male colleagues." This was said with a slight edge of sarcasm. "What does the widow of a suicide victim want with a private investigator?" There was no hint of a smile on her face. Langdon liked that.

"As I said on the phone, she has asked me to look into her husband's death."

"And what am I doing here?" She tapped her nails on the table next to her glass, drawing attention to the fact that her drink was almost gone.

Langdon wasn't even aware they'd arrived. He gamely took a mouthful of the brown liquor, almost gasping at its burn. "To eat lunch?"

"I don't eat lunch," she replied.

"Drinks, then."

"Is there a point to all this? I am a busy woman, Mr. Langdon." Nonetheless, she raised two fingers to the waitress, who soon returned with two fresh glasses brimming with drink.

Langdon sat patiently, waiting her out. He definitely sensed a glimmer of something—impatience? nervousness? fear?—behind that chilly exterior. Why had she agreed to come? He casually leaned forward in his chair. "I wasn't sure why I called you, other than to get a clearer picture of who Harold Dumphy was, but the fact that you returned my call so quickly and immediately agreed to meet with me?" He looked her straight in the eye, challenging her. "That makes me think one of two things: either you have too much free time on your hands, which you've just professed to be not true, or you have concerns about someone digging into the death of Harold Dumphy. Someone like me."

The lady didn't miss a blink. "Are you saying that you don't think Harold committed suicide?"

Langdon shrugged. "What do you think?" he asked.

She tipped her glass sideways, swirling the ice cubes in her now-empty second drink. "I would have to say that there were some discrepancies in the police report, but what does that have to do with DownEast Power?" With a sort of carelessness that was wholly sexy, she chewed the ice cubes while raising two fingers for more drinks. She rolled the split cubes over her tongue while keeping her eyes locked steadily onto his.

"What I'm thinking..." Langdon said, picking each word with great care, his tongue now thick with drink, "is that if Harold Dumphy didn't commit suicide, than his death must have been an accident, or murder." The last word hung heavy in the air between them.

"I still don't understand what your unfounded suspicions have to do with DownEast Power?" She took a slug from her fresh Wild Turkey, looking at him doubtfully over the rim of her glass.

Langdon plugged doggedly onward. "Dumphy was your head of security, yes?"

"Yes," she said in a bored tone, her lips absently chasing a drop of liquor down her chin.

"Do you think that it's possible that he found something that he shouldn't have, or was maybe involved in something, got in over his head with the wrong people?" Even as he spoke, he realized how lame he sounded.

"Like what, Mr. Langdon? What people? This is Maine, not Manhattan." she said, a rolling of the eyes accompanying her arrogant tone.

"I don't know," he admitted. "But I do know that nuclear energy is a potentially devastating power source."

She glanced at her watch. "What is it that you are trying to say?"

"I don't really know," Langdon replied through the black cloud that had settled over his brain. "Aren't you in the least bit worried that your head of security may have been murdered?"

"No. The official report is that he committed suicide. Probably because his wife was sleeping around, if you want my opinion." This she said with an air of finality, signaling the end of her interest in the conversation. Abigail Austin-Peters had taken his measure and found him wanting. He could almost see her mentally writing him off as a harmless buffoon. Still, he took one final stab. "So why are you here, then?"

In response, she looked at her watch again, the motion waking Coffee Dog, who had drifted off, his blocky head still on her lap, and stood up. Her voice was polite, but tinged with annoyance. "I really have to be getting back to work now." As a final insult, she placed two twenties on the table. "Here, this should cover it. Goodbye, Mr. Langdon." With a stoop to pat the dog's head, a step, and a flutter, the lady who was all sharp angles and words disappeared out the door.

It was only mid-afternoon, and Langdon was completely soused. He started to stand up, stumbled, and quickly sat back down. Coffee Dog gave a low whine, and then disappeared out the door, while the waitress across the room was suddenly very intent on wiping down a clean table. Langdon counted to three and then pushed himself to his feet and staggered towards the door. How many Wild Turkeys had he drunk? He was counting them in his head when an arm draped itself over his shoulder.

Sensing that Langdon was in need, Coffee Dog had gone to get Richam. Before Langdon could argue, resist, or even reply, he found himself sitting on a barstool downstairs, drinking coffee and spilling his guts to his friend. In some part of his mind, he knew he'd hate himself the next day. But now, in his weakened state, his sadness and anger at losing his wife and the open wound that was his absent daughter roiled his stomach, the confession of his pain underlining its piercing agony but at the same time bringing cleansing relief, however momentary.

~ ~ ~ ~ ~

When Chabal arrived at six, obviously summoned by Richam, two hours of black coffee had brought Langdon some clarity and a clearer head, and the bartender knew more than he cared to about Langdon's personal life.

With one look at Langdon's red eyes, the mother in Chabal kicked in, as if one of her kids had scraped a knee on the playground. She was all business, pulling him from his perch at the now-crowded bar.

"Thanks, Richam," Langdon said, too embarrassed to make eye contact. "Sorry to unload on you like that."

"Why don't you come over this weekend," Richam replied. "I know Jewell would love to see you."

"Sure," he replied, turning to go, but then pausing. "Do you know many women who can slam three Wild Turkeys in half an hour and not even blink?"

"Who are you talking about?" Chabal sounded annoyed.

"The PR Director at DownEast Power," Langdon said, his eyes seeking out Richam.

"Yeah, I know a few, but none as good-looking as the hostess upstairs claimed your lady was," Richam said, his eyes on Chabal. He'd heard a note of jealousy in her tone and wondered about its source.

"She was a looker, for sure," Langdon concurred. He kept it to himself that she was a bit too bony and hard-edged for his taste.

"Can we go?" Chabal asked irritably. She pulled her keys briskly from her purse. "I don't have time to play nursemaid to a grown man."

Langdon turned red, his cheeks nearly matching his hair in color. "Sorry. I can take a cab."

"Don't be silly," Chabal relented. "I work for you, remember?" she joked. "Just as long as you don't expect me to do your laundry."

Chabal drove a Volkswagen Beetle, an oddity in Maine, but one that fit her personality to a T. She drove recklessly, zipping around corners, zooming up behind people, and quickly accelerating from stops. It was a good thing the car was a bright yellow so that others could see her coming.

"Thanks for bringing me home, Chabal," Langdon said as he got out of the car. "Just one of those days, I guess."

"Langdon," she said, looking expectantly at him, a small part of her willing him to ask her up. "Take care," she added, and before the door had quite closed, she rocketed away.

It came as no real surprise that the Widow Dumphy, as Langdon had come to think of her, was sitting on his stoop. He silently thanked Richam for the countless cups of coffee, which had left him sober enough to deal with the flirtatious, overbearing woman.

"Hello, Mr. Langdon," she said. "I've been waiting for you." She was dressed all in black. Black jeans. Black sweater. Black boots. What else, he wondered, might she have on that was black? Mourning did not seem to be on her mind. "When I missed you at the store I looked you up in the phone book."

"Let me feed my dog," he said. "And then maybe we can go grab a coffee?" This was meant to be a statement, but it came out as a rather limp question.

"Do you mind if I come up while you… feed your dog?" Her voice was teasing, somehow making his simple question sexy and erotic. She was a woman who knew the effect she had on men.

"Sure," he replied. He'd always had a weakness for women, though usually only those who wanted nothing to do with him. He was cursed with this strange affliction, that the females he found to be interesting, enticing, and intellectually challenging pretty much thought him a lazy, useless dope. Chabal was an exception in that she put up with him. Then again, she was married, and thus, unobtainable.

There was no light on over the stairs, so the widow found it necessary to hold onto his waist, her breasts rubbing against his back, causing him to fumble with the key ring to open the door.

"Did you find out anything today your client might want to know?" Her voice was slightly husky.

"Did you give your husband any reason to kill himself?" he asked, more abruptly than he had intended. He pulled away and went to the closet for Coffee Dog's dinner, not that he hadn't gotten plenty of food begging in the restaurant.

"What would it take for you to kill yourself, Mr. Langdon?"

"We can't keep asking each other questions, Janice," he said, feeling like he was in a bad Peter Sellers movie. He knelt to pour the food into the dog bowl. "What would really help at this point would be if you could tell me the truth about your relationship with your husband." Coffee Dog attacked the food as if he hadn't eaten in weeks, the noise of the heavy bowl moving this way and that with his enthusiasm the only sound in the suddenly quiet room.

"My husband was a strong man. If he was angry with me, he possibly could have killed me, or one of my lovers, if that's what you're getting at, but he wouldn't have committed suicide."

"Fair enough," Langdon acknowledged, hearing the doubt in her voice.

"Are you a strong man, Mr. Langdon?"

"I can't imagine ever killing myself, even if my wife were cheating on me," he said, knowing in his head that, technically, she was.

She put a warm hand around his bicep. "You seem to be very strong. You must work out?" she asked, her eyes wide, inviting him to make the next move. It wasn't difficult to understand how easily she picked up men. More difficult to understand was her compunction, what she might be looking for other than raw sensation. Maybe it made her feel alive?

"Strong?" he asked, pulling away and sitting down at the kitchen table, motioning for her to sit down opposite him. "I tend to eat poorly, drink too much, not sleep enough, let salesmen walk all over me, give to every charity that asks, and even my dog has my number."

Janice sat down, not opposite him, but next to him, pulling the chair close. Her eyes were very dark, and she smelled of some exotic perfume. Wind whistled around the eaves of the house, carrying a crisp ocean breeze, but inside, it was cozy and warm. Coffee Dog sensed the tension and looked up from his empty bowl, curious what new excitement might be coming into his life.

"I need to know who you've had relationships with over the past couple of years, Mrs. Dumphy. And how you left it with… them." He was trying to move the conversation back to firmer ground. It wasn't every day that he got offered a murder case to solve. And even though he was, for the moment, a single man, he wasn't going to blow the case just to sleep with a woman who, as his upper brain had instantly recognized, would only leave him wanting the real thing.

"Relationships? My parents? My brother?" she asked. "It's warm in here. And please, call me Janice." She pulled her sweater over her head, revealing a V-neck blouse unbuttoned below her large breasts, a cavern of cleavage threatening to escape its flimsy confines at any moment.

"Let's keep our relationship professional, Mrs. Dumphy. As a matter of fact, we have not yet discussed money." His formal tone seemed to have an effect, and she drew a deep breath, her eyes downcast. "My normal rate is $250 a day plus expenses. I'd like $1,000 up front to get started."

"That's fine," the Widow Dumphy said. "I'll bring the money by your office tomorrow. Now, what do you want to know about my brother?"

There was still enough Wild Turkey in Langdon's system for him to dish out the next low, but necessary, blow. "I am more interested in the paperboy who was delivering more than the paper, or the clam digger who wasn't just raking the mud flats, or…"

"Okay, okay! I get the point," she interrupted him. She leaned back in her chair and cast an appraising glance at him. "Do you want details or just names?"

"Just the details that matter," he said. "But none of the bedroom antics, please."

"The last man I slept with was Greg Carr. He owns the appliance store on Bath Road. He lives with his wife and two kids in a house just down the road, but he has a lovely summer place out to Bailey Island. I've gone there with him four or five times over the past six months. Is that what you mean?"

He nodded. "When was the last time?"

"Last night."

Some grieving woman, Langdon thought. Before Greg Carr, it emerged, there had been a long list of men. In the past year, thirteen to be exact, ranging from a one-night stand to extended affairs that sometimes overlapped. The woman certainly kept herself busy. The youngest was sixteen at the time, now seventeen, and a junior in high school. He'd probably told all of his friends about his escapades with a married woman—with none of them believing a single word.

"I know what you must think," she said. "But I get so lonely." She leaned into him again, giving him an eyeful no matter how hard he tried to look away, her hand on his knee, her scent in his nostrils.

He gently removed her hand from his knee. "Mrs. Dumphy, I am very much a man of weakness, weaknesses, actually. I go through cycles. Most of the time I amble through the routine that is life. Then, every once in a while, the devil rears its ugly head in me and I drink too much, smoke cigars, chew tobacco, gamble, go to strip clubs, and generally make a mess of my life. Usually, a good drunk erases those other desires, and I'm able to return to the routine. That's where you've caught me today. I'm not interested in sleeping with a recent widow. Though I'm separated, I am still married. If you want me to do some investigative work for you, fine, but please, let's keep a professional distance."

It was only after the widow had slammed the door, stomped down the steps, and driven away in her Camaro with a squeal of tires that Langdon realized he could really have used a ride back into town. Oh well, he thought, Coffee Dog could use the exercise.

No sooner had they stepped out the door then it started to snow, making the two-mile walk to Bowdoin College a slippery ordeal. The wind was gusting, the visibility poor, but neither man nor beast noticed, one caught up in his thoughts, and the other finding the cascading snow a delirious game. It took forty-five minutes to make the trek, during which time the dog became disillusioned with the novelty of the storm, pausing occasionally to gnaw at the clumps of snow clinging to his paws.

It wasn't often that a nearly-frozen Neanderthal of a man walked into the library of a small, preppy, liberal arts college with a hulking canine beast at his side. The young student at the entrance desk, almost ogling Langdon as he proceeded to the computers to search the library's catalogs, was so intrigued by this sight that she decided not to enforce the no pets rule. Besides, what was the man supposed to do with the dog, tie him up outside in the storm?

After a few minutes, with information scribbled on an index card, man and dog disappeared into the stairwell.

It was hours later, midnight to be exact, when the young woman, a stocky college sophomore from Texas, approached Langdon in the upstairs stacks. "Excuse me, sir, it's closing time." His head jerked up from the books he'd been bent over, as if he'd been caught in some inexcusable act. "We're closing for the night," she repeated.

Langdon smiled warmly to show he was no threat. "I'm sorry to hold you up." He paused momentarily, looking for a foothold. "But could you help me out?"

She wondered if perhaps he had a hearing problem, but she was indeed intrigued by this bedraggled man, or maybe it was the dog, and liked to avoid conflict at any cost. "What can I help you with?"

"I've been doing research on nuclear power, but have found very little recent information on DownEast Power."

"Did you try periodicals?" she asked in a whisper.

"No, I didn't think of that."

She eyed him quizzically. "What exactly are you trying to find?"

Langdon frowned, his confusion obvious. "I'm not really sure."

She said nothing. Patience was her strongest asset.

"Let me level with you," a weary Langdon said. The day had begun with a strange and threatening phone call, progressed into a murder case after a bibulous lunch with the local lawman, followed by a drunken stupor induced by a gorgeous but chilly PR person, on the heels of which he'd fended off the advances of an oversexed widow, and the whole day was topped off by hours of fruitless research into the nuclear power plant just up the road. "I'm a private detective working on a murder investigation, and the victim was head of security at DownEast Power."

"You mean up in Woolington?" She was beginning to wonder if the man was sane.

Langdon pressed on. "I'm thinking that the man was murdered because he stumbled upon something that others wanted kept secret."

"We're not talking hydro power," she said, thinking aloud, caught up in the moment. "I mean," she paused again. "We're talking about the same process that is used to make nuclear bombs."

When somebody else said it, it sounded more ominous than crazy, Langdon thought. "If somebody was trying to hide something at a nuclear power plant, something that was so horrendous they'd kill to keep it a secret, what might that something be?"

"Nuclear waste storage problems? Maintenance issues? Leaks? Radiation leaks? Sabotage? Safety issues?" she replied without a moment of hesitation.

Chapter 4

The coed hesitated, shifting back on her heels. Her face was caught in a pose of indecision. Langdon had just asked her out for a drink. He wanted some simple sanity in his corner for a few moments, which she seemed to represent. "Maybe," she murmured, afraid that this was just another cruel joke of the kind that members of the male sex seemed to like to play on girls like her, making them feel important and popular, and then pulling the rug out from under them.

He held out his hand to put her at ease. "My name is Langdon."

"Patti Smith. My friends call me Peppermint Patti."

"What should I call you?"

"We'll see." By this time, Patti had moved to a seat across the table, smiling shyly. Her brown eyes had nothing to hide, young, innocent, and very much alive, dancing without movement. Her hair was deep amber, pulled back into a tight bun, probably her attempt to fit the image of a librarian. Freckles were scattered across her nose. She was not actually overweight, just a big boned girl, probably—judging from her drawl—right off of a Midwestern farm.

"Shall we go?" he asked.

She looked away, embarrassed. "I'm not old enough to get into any bars."

Langdon smiled. "I have friends in low places."

They stopped so she could log out on the computer at the front desk, where she grabbed her jacket and hat and gloves. "You mean to walk all the way downtown in this weather?" Peppermint Patti asked.

She gave a casual wave as they passed an elderly lady ushering the last students out the library door.

Now, it was Langdon's turn to be embarrassed. "Do you have a better idea?"

"Don't you have a car?"

"Yes, but I left it downtown. At least I can give you a ride home later."

Peppermint Patti refrained from asking why. "Why don't we just take my Jeep?" she asked sweetly.

"That seems like a splendid idea," Langdon said crossly, "if you're afraid of a little snow."

"I could meet you there if you'd rather walk." Peppermint Patti was enjoying herself, for once confident in front of this shambling man with an easy manner.

The Jeep proved to be a brand-new Cherokee, fully decked out, black and silent looking in the night. The girl was not hard up for money, Langdon thought, appraising the cool splendor of the vehicle.

"So, where are you from that you're afraid of a little snow?" Langdon asked lightly, feeling more at ease now that they were actually on their way.

"Texas. Lubbock, Texas," she replied.

"What the hell's in Lubbock, Texas?"

"No snow, for one," she said. "But not much else either, or I sure as heck wouldn't be up here in some province of Canada, trucking around with some Eskimo and his wolf cub, who claims he can get me into a bar that probably closed long ago due to the storm."

"Hey, don't get me wrong," Langdon replied. "I don't have anything against the South. I just wouldn't want to go there for more than a week, and not at all in the summer. I even named my daughter Missouri."

"You know Missouri is not in the South, don't you?" So the man had a daughter, she thought, even though there was no ring on his finger.

"Of course I know that," he said, though he'd had no idea when he and his wife had named her.

"What's your last name?"

"Langdon."

"Oh, silly me, I thought that was your first name."

Langdon grinned in the darkness, thinking that perhaps he had bitten off more than he could chew with Peppermint Patti Smith. "Goff Langdon. Pull into that parking lot right over there."

"You're taking me to Goldilocks?" Peppermint Patti stared skeptically at the sign, barely discernible through the snow.

"Something wrong with that?"

"Bowdoin students don't ever go there, and the few that do usually get beaten up."

"You've got the wrong idea about the place."

"So I should leave my blackjack in the car?" Peppermint Patti smiled, her nervousness fading in his calmness, but then there was the sound of a car horn, and her face froze with fear. "Oh, shit. That cop is staring right at us."

It was Bart, sitting in his parked cruiser, fairly certain he'd spotted Langdon in the passenger seat of the Jeep. "Wait here," Langdon said, whistling for the Coffee Dog to follow, but the mutt remained rooted to the seat in back, eyes wide, a pleading whimper to stay in the warm car rather than venturing out into the frigid violence that Mother Nature had whipped up for the residents of Brunswick this evening.

"I thought that was you," Bart said, rolling down his window. "But I couldn't quite figure out what you'd be doing in a Jeep with Texas plates with a girl who's young enough to be your daughter."

"Tutoring," Langdon replied dryly.

"Can I talk to you for a minute?" Bart asked, gesturing to the passenger seat.

"Sure." Langdon walked around the car and climbed into the cruiser.

"What's with the girl? Is she as young as she looks?"

"Peppermint Patti? She's old enough to know better than to get caught up with me. She's just helping me do some research."

"Yeah, right, *research*. I had a girl help me with my homework when I was in high school. Boy, did she ever help me out, but at least she was my age."

"It's not what you think. Really. Now, what'd you want to talk to me about?"

"Bowdoin student?" Bart was happy to see Langdon out with a female, even if she wasn't legally old enough to drink in the bar he was about to take her into.

Langdon wasn't interested in chatting. "Bart, for Christ-sake, what do you want to talk to me about?"

The big man withdrew momentarily in reaction to Langdon's sharp tone, betraying the fact that his gruff exterior only served to cover up a more fragile inside. "The Harold Dumphy thing," he finally said. "I talked to Tommy, the officer working the case."

"Yeah, he was the one who decided it was a suicide, wasn't he?"

"That's just the thing. That ain't how it happened. I got him off in a corner tonight after he'd tipped back a few, and he spilled the beans."

"Beans?"

"Word came down from up top for him to drop the case and go with a suicide ruling."

"Up top?"

"The chief himself. Brooked no argument. He even threatened to fire Tommy if he didn't deep-six the whole thing, and fast."

"Is that all?" Langdon was now certain that something fishy was happening.

"Is that all?" Bart blustered, and then realized Langdon was smiling, and that his buttons were being pushed. "Get the hell out of my car and back to your date."

Langdon opened the door and stepped out, leaning his head back in before shutting the door. "Thanks Bart, I owe you one." He walked back over to the Jeep and rapped on the window, which after a few seconds, slowly lowered halfway. "You coming?" he asked.

"So I can be arrested for underage drinking?" she asked, fear and irritation contorting her face.

"Oh, Bart? He's a friend. He just wanted to say hi."

The window went back up and the Jeep lurched forward, and then made an awkward three-point turn at the back of the lot, before accelerating towards the entrance. When it reached the road, it paused, and then slowly backed into an open space. Peppermint Patti got out and opened the back door to let Coffee Dog out. "I was all set to leave," she said. "And then I remembered I had your dog."

Langdon led the way down the steps into the bar, bantering with Peppermint Patti in an attempt to dissipate her anger. They chose a table at the front and had barely sat down when the bartender delivered a pitcher of beer. Coffee Dog was caught between jumping up on the man and sitting down to show how good he could be, his entire body quivering with excitement. Goldilocks, the bartender, quietly produced a dog biscuit from his pocket and walked away from the dog, whistling absently with the treat dangling in his hand. Coffee Dog followed a close step behind, eyes glued to the biscuit, his head going up and down like a yo-yo with the movement of the treat. Suddenly, Coffee Dog struck, snatching it from the man's hand. Goldilocks laughed, and proceeded to fill a bowl with water for the dog.

"So, let me get this straight: you were angry because you thought you were being arrested for pulling into a parking lot outside of a bar?" Langdon poured her a half glass from the pitcher on the table in front of them. She'd put away the first two in record time, maybe trying to drown her awkwardness, he thought. For his part, he was still nursing his first one after drinking his afternoon away.

Peppermint Patti's displeasure was finally beginning to subside, leaving her feeling a little silly at her naiveté, but hey, what did it matter? "Tell me about your daughter," she said.

"What do you want to know?"

"Why'd you call her Missouri?"

"I'm not sure." Langdon said. "My wife and I went to St. Louis for a vacation during college. It was a good memory, I suppose."

"Your wife?"

"My ex-wife," he corrected.

"Not for long, one would think, if you're still making that slip."

"Just about six months now."

"Separated for six months or divorced for six months?"

The girl didn't miss a trick. "Separated."

"So, you're still married?"

"Technically." Langdon squirmed, uncomfortable with the conversation, the split still raw.

"What happened?" She covered her mouth as soon as the words escaped. "Sorry. Bit personal."

He looked at her and shrugged. "S'okay. We discovered we were different people," he replied.

"So, who does Missouri live with?"

"Not the guy who is out in the wee hours of the morning drinking beer with a college student."

"So, where are your daughter and wife, presently?" Missouri made sure to emphasize wife.

"Amanda took E and ran off to Florida with some golf pro."

"You call your daughter E?"

"Yep."

"Why?"

"I suppose it was because my wife started calling her Missy, and as I said, we are two different people, so I started calling her E."

Peppermint Patti shook her head. "You are one fascinating man, Goff Langdon."

"Can we talk about DownEast Power, please?" he asked, tired of having his sorry life analyzed and found wanting by yet another person.

The alcohol had warmed Peppermint Patti's face so it shone like a burnished cherry, and her flaming hair had escaped its bun and now cascaded down around her shoulders. "So, Mr. Private Detective, tell me about the case."

She listened attentively as he told her, drinking steadily from her mug, a new pitcher arriving before the old one was even finished. At one point, Langdon persuaded Peppermint Patti to give up her keys if she was going to continue working the grog. Langdon omitted the details of what had happened earlier in the evening with the Widow Dumphy, saying only that they'd scrapped and that he wondered if he still even had a case.

When he'd finished, he summed it up. "There you have it. This morning I was threatened, offered a real live—no pun intended—murder case, got drunk under the table by a nuclear power plant public relations director, and then fired—I think—from the case by a sexually overactive grieving widow, all before I ran into you."

"You think you might have gotten fired and the first thing you do is go to the library to research the case?" she asked, perplexed.

Langdon didn't hear the question, as his attention was on a tall, gaunt man with a thin, graying mustache. He'd caught the man stealing glances in their direction, and recognized him as Ellsworth Limington III. The man owned most of the town of Woolington, including a ski resort, several restaurants and hotels, and who knew what else.

"Earth to Langdon?"

"I'm sorry, what did you say?" He shook his head. He was probably just imagining things.

"Why persist in researching the case if you no longer have a client?"

"I'm sorry, but can you excuse me for just a moment?"

Langdon eased out of his chair and over to the small corner table where Ellsworth Limington III was drinking a martini.

"Mr. Limington, do you mind if I join you for a moment? My name is Goff Langdon."

Limington gestured at the empty chair across the table. "Help yourself. I know who you are."

"Thank you," Langdon said, sitting down. "Were you meeting somebody?"

"What can I do for you, Mr. Langdon?"

"I was hoping to ask you what you know about DownEast Power?" The nuclear power plant was located in the town of Woolington, where this man was the largest property owner by far.

~ ~ ~ ~ ~

Peppermint Patti stole a glance over her shoulder at Langdon and the man he was sitting with. She wondered if he was an old friend, or if it might have something to do with the case.

"You fixed for drinks?" It was the bartender, discreetly checking up on Langdon.

"I think we're fine," Peppermint Patti said.

"You known Langdon long?" Goldilocks asked, wiping idly at a few drops of spilled beer with a rag.

"Just met him tonight," she replied. "I'm Patti Smith, by the way."

"People call me Goldilocks." The man reached out and shook her hand.

"This is your place?" She should have guessed. Blond curly hair flopped around his head in perfect disorder.

"Sure thing."

"How about you? Have you known Langdon long?"

"Yep. Since he was no taller than that barstool you're sitting on."

"Tell me about him?" With any less alcohol in her system, Patti would never have been so bold. "I mean, he seems so fragile and strong at the same time."

"He is a gentle soul, but don't mistake that for softness."

"There is something maybe not exactly indomitable but certainly relentless about him," Patti said. "Like his dog with a bone, I imagine."

Goldilocks went back to the bar to fill a drink order, but returned after just a minute. "When Langdon was just a youngster, his no-account father left their family. His mother was a good, decent woman, but a few years after Goff's younger twin brothers were born, the father, Donny Langdon, up and left all four of them."

"That's terrible," Patti said, thinking of her own privileged upbringing. It must have been hard to grow up without a dad.

"They didn't have much money. The twins weren't in school yet, and Sharon, the mother, couldn't afford childcare, and thus was unable to work. So Langdon got a job working on a lobster boat. He got up at 3:30 every morning and got a ride to Harpswell with one of the crew. They'd pull their traps in Maquoit Bay around eight in the morning, and drop him off at Nate's Marina, and he'd hitchhike to school by nine."

"He worked on a lobster boat before school? How old was he?"

"You don't want to know. Too young."

"Whatever he's telling you is a lie," Langdon said, sitting down with a grin.

"What'd you want with Limington?" Goldilocks asked.

"Oh, it's a case I'm working on," Langdon said. "I'm looking into the death of the guy that was head of security out at DownEast Power."

"You should have stuck around over there, then. You know the fellow that he's leaving with?"

Langdon looked over his shoulder where the two men were preparing to leave. "He introduced him to me as John."

"Johnson Halperg," Goldilocks replied. "CEO of Casco Bay Power." He went to take the order of a couple who had just sat down at the bar.

"So, before you ditched me, we were talking about why you are still looking into the case if you think the lady, or the widow, dumped you?"

"I guess I'm sort of interested in the whole thing. It's like starting a puzzle and then having it taken away from you. It nags at you."

"So, you're going to investigate the death for free?"

"Unless I can find somebody willing to pay me."

Peppermint Patti pursed her lips. "Like maybe DownEast Power?"

"That would be a good place to start," Langdon agreed. "But if Harold Dumphy found something they want to cover up..." He trailed off without finishing the thought.

"Such as?"

"According to what I found earlier in the library, the inspection of nuclear power plants is pretty intense, as you can imagine. There are actually three inspectors from the Nuclear Regulatory Commission who go to work every day at DownEast Power. Then, annually, there is a records and procedures audit by an outside team of 20 people who spend a couple of months there."

"If the plant itself is covering something up, maybe the utility company that owns them might be interested in hiring you."

"Casco Bay Power is the majority stockholder," Langdon assented. "It looks like I just missed my chance at speaking with the CEO." He said it casually, but inside he was kicking himself for not recognizing the man.

"Although," Peppermint Patti thought aloud, "CBP wouldn't be too hot on you finding something wrong there, either, now would they?"

"Not if it meant shutting it down," he agreed.

"How about some sort of environmental movement?" Peppermint Patti asked. "I know a couple of students at Bowdoin who are involved with this group called Flower First. They supported Harper Truman and certainly helped him get elected governor last year." She went to take a large gulp of beer, and in her inebriated state, dumped the entire contents of the glass down the front of her blouse. It was a lacy, white material, and Langdon suddenly found himself staring at the young Texan's bosom through her transparent shirt, not without some enjoyment.

She froze for a moment, her boldness and playfulness disappearing as she reverted in her mind to an awkward, overlooked, overweight outsider. A tear formed in the corner of one eye, followed by another. She rose to her feet, knocking against the table and spilling the half-empty pitcher onto the floor, and then fled, leaving her pocketbook and jacket behind.

Langdon gathered her things and whistled for Coffee Dog, who was already in hot pursuit, thinking the girl was playing a game with him. They caught up to her just as she reached her Jeep and realized that it was locked, and she had no key. Adding insult to injury, it was frigid, her blouse was doused, and she had no jacket.

"Let me give you a ride home." He draped her jacket around her shoulders and unlocked the doors.

"I can drive myself," she all but yelled.

"You have two choices," he said patiently. "Either I drive you, or we call you a cab."

She eyed him apprehensively. Coffee Dog looked at both of them forlornly.

"Me or the cab?"

She stomped around and got into the passenger seat. Langdon slid into the driver's seat and eased the Jeep out of the lot through the blinding snow. Once again, he was leaving his own car behind, which most likely meant another walk in the storm once he'd delivered Peppermint Patti safely back to her dorm.

"We've all spilled beer before," Langdon said gently.

She merely glared at him, so he shut up, only speaking to ask for directions to her dorm. When he pulled into the lot she directed him to, he turned the ignition off and handed her the keys. She shook her head. "You take it. This weather is not fit for man or beast to be out in. If it ever stops snowing, park it back here and leave the keys under the mat." Coffee Dog pleaded with him to accept.

Langdon drove Peppermint Patti's Jeep the few miles to his apartment, his head stinging from the smoke of the bar and all the accumulated alcohol, and his body aching from the day's stress. Janice Dumphy, Abigail Austin-Peters, and Peppermint Patti all in one day was a trifecta of women, each one completely different from the

others. He smiled at the thought of Peppermint Patti, and wished her
a silent good night.

~ ~ ~ ~ ~

Langdon was not surprised to find the slender, sallow faced man
sitting at his kitchen table reading his afternoon paper. It was just
after 3 a.m. This day might never end, he thought with a sigh.

"Mr. Langdon," the fop sneered, his voice crisp and proper.

Coffee Dog growled, the hair on his back sticking straight up.
Langdon told him it was okay if he lay down, and the dog agreed, but
kept his sleepy eyes on the stranger in his kitchen.

"Where have you been?" the man asked. "I've had a long wait for
you."

"Out making snowmen."

"How do you expect us to get along with that kind of attitude?"

Langdon filled a glass with water. "I've had a long day. Could you
just deliver your message and be on your way?"

"Who says I have a message?"

"Your kind always works for somebody else, Mr....?"

"Shakespeare."

"Shakespeare. You're no more than an errand boy, a lackey—a
messenger, if you will. So, what is the message? I want to go to bed."

Shakespeare's mild manner morphed to sudden anger, his lip curled
at the disrespect. His eyes narrowed, hard and unforgiving. "I came here
to ask that you stay away from the Dumphy case, Mr. Langdon. I have
even brought a sum of money to compensate you for your troubles."

"Just tell me one thing, first," Langdon said with exasperation.
"What is the Dumphy case? I would probably be passing it off as the
greed of a not-so-grieving widow trying to get insurance money if
some strange-looking sort of chap wearing undertaker's clothes and
named Shakespeare didn't keep popping up in my life."

"I am trying to nip an embarrassing situation in the bud, Mr.

Langdon." Shakespeare took a deep breath, tucking his anger away for the time being. "There has been no crime, and as a matter of fact, this has nothing to do with DownEast Power. My employer is a gentleman here in town who would like to keep his relationship with Mrs. Dumphy a secret, for his family's sake. When she told him of her plans to hire you, he tried to dissuade her, knowing that your first order of business would be to interview everybody who had had an affair with her. Sadly, he failed in his attempt. That is all. No espionage. No crime. Just a desire to keep private affairs private."

That was the link, Langdon thought, his tired mind jolted into overdrive. That was why he'd been warned off the case before he even had the case. The Widow Dumphy had told one of her lovers that she planned to meet with Langdon. He doubted that further conversation would get him anywhere now—so he slammed the man in the face without warning.

Shakespeare went over the back of the chair into the wall without a sound. He lay without moving. Langdon had thought it was only in movies that people could be knocked unconscious with a single blow. He reached down and felt for a pulse to make sure the man was still alive. He was.

Langdon quickly set about searching his pockets. There was a long black pistol, worn and dangerous looking. There was a driver's license with the man's picture—Lawrence Shakespeare, from New York City. Langdon copied down the license number and the address. There were six $50 bills. No credit cards. No pictures of family or friends. An inside jacket pocket yielded a bonanza in the form of a yellow manila envelope with $10,000 in it. This, then, was the amount being offered to drop the case.

Langdon took this money and put it in the oven, which as far as he knew, had never been used. He pulled the man's boots off and discovered a long and tapered blade, which he took and put in the knife drawer. He emptied the bullets from the pistol, and put it on the table, before filling a pot with cold water and dumping it over the inert figure on his floor. Shakespeare stirred, jerked, and then reached for the empty holster at his chest. There was a large welt on his jaw. In degrees, his composure returned, but never calming the seething fury so obviously boiling inside him, his eyes flashing deep and dark.

"I will kill you," he finally said, the comment's import somewhat compromised by the fact that he was putting on his shoes.

"Not this morning."

"Where's the money?"

"Safe."

"You accept the offer then?"

Langdon opened the door, letting the storm in. "I'm thinking it over. In the meantime, I'll hold onto the money. Goodnight, Lawrence."

Chapter 5

For the second morning in a row, Langdon and Coffee Dog were jolted out of sleep, only this time it was the phone. He'd purposely not set his alarm, realizing he needed to catch up on his sleep, and that getting up early for the gym was not in the cards. He scrambled out of bed, tripping over the dog, twisting loose of the blankets, and made his way across the room to pluck the receiver from the cradle. As he struggled with the dog, who wanted to play, the Beans from downstairs began banging on their ceiling, his floor. By the time he barked a hello into the mouthpiece, there was little trace of sleep left in his voice, even though he'd only slept about two hours.

"It sounds like I caught you sleeping," the voice of 4 by Four laughed into the phone. "Thought you were an early riser?"

Langdon let loose a string of obscenities that faltered only when he realized that his lawyer calling him this early was unusual, indeed. "What's up, 4 by Four?"

"I got you visitation rights to your daughter," 4 by Four said.

After making plans to be at the lawyer's office twenty minutes later, Langdon sat very still in the middle of the floor where he'd ended up at the end of an all-star canine wrestling session. Amanda had just disappeared one day with Missouri in tow, a short note claiming they were done with the cold and were going south. Rumors drifted back that she'd taken up with a professional golfer. It was one thing to leave him, another to leave him for another man, but completely unacceptable to have taken his daughter. Langdon had been considering closing the bookstore and going in search of them to at least retrieve his daughter but had consulted 4 by Four first. Now, it seemed, this problem might be resolved.

~ ~ ~ ~ ~

4 by Four had grown up in New York City, in the Bronx, and fought his way into Rutgers University, his ambition driving him like a train, never slowing to pick up passengers or baggage along the way. Graduating seventh in his class, he'd been accepted into Yale Law School, and worked nights and weekends at any job he could during school to pay off his monumental student loans.

He got a job with a prestigious law firm in New York City, becoming a partner in just four years. He worked fifteen hours a day, seven days a week, and billed for most of them. He was a legal genius, without a doubt, the rising star of the firm. Along the way he picked up some bad habits, smoking two packs of cigarettes a day and sucking down coffee like others drew breath. His home was an opulent brownstone on the Upper East Side, but he couldn't have told you the color of the kitchen walls or what grew in the back garden, so rarely did he spend more than a few hours there, and those in darkness.

One morning, Jim Angstrom, as he was known then, woke up and said "Enough!" By 11:30 in the morning, he was driving north in his BMW. At two in the afternoon, somewhere outside of Hartford, he traded his car straight up for a Volkswagen Vanagon that sat in the furthest corner of a used car lot. The dealer thought he was taking a real chance with what he assumed was a stolen car, but his greed got the better of him, particularly because the van wasn't worth much. The rest of the trip was like molasses rolling uphill, the top speed 45, but Jim was content. He broke down in Topsham, Maine, which apparently had a silent 'h', and never made it to the true backwoods that was his destination. Sometimes fate intervenes in these matters.

He rented a house in Bowdoinham, the next town up the pike, sat for and passed the Maine bar, then took on just enough work to pay his minimal bills, the easy rhythm of his new life allowing him to breathe again. He smoked a considerable amount of pot, grew a beard, lived in a house with no electricity, did some painting and sculpting, and had a series of live-in girlfriends his mother would have called hippies. He didn't give a shit.

Now, fifteen years later, he'd begun to emerge from his self-imposed isolation. His cocoon had gradually opened to reveal a confident and deeply contented man who enjoyed the practice of law on his own terms. The therapy had not been quick, but he was now a fully recovered workaholic. He could put in a day's work and leave in the middle of an uncompleted project without taking any of the stress home with him. Somewhere along the way he'd become 4 by Four. Langdon had asked him many times where this odd moniker had derived from, but had never got an answer.

~ ~ ~ ~ ~

"What's the deal?" Langdon asked, striding into 4 by Four's office in Fort Andross at the appointed hour.

4 by Four struck a match, studied the flame, pondered the fate of this unlit cigar for a moment, and carefully lit the end, inhaling deliciously. It was just past six in the morning. "Your wife's in Philadelphia right now," he said. "She's staying with her sister."

Langdon sat down, knowing better than to press for details, for hurrying 4 by Four only slowed the man down. 4 by Four had come from a world in which there was never enough time to do all, say all, or be all that he wanted. Now, if he wanted or needed time to stand still, well then, time stood still.

"I believe that she would welcome a break from being the mother of a three-year-old child, maybe for even as long as a month." This was a summary of what had been a long phone conversation.

It was relevant that she'd called 4 by Four, and not Langdon, with this information, but what did it really matter? If she'd been after reconciliation, well then, she'd have called him, but it was Missouri who Langdon most wanted to get back. Later, in the car, he would ponder the implications of the situation, but right now, it didn't matter.

"I'm on my way," Langdon said, doing some internal calculations. "I'll be there in about seven hours."

"You can't get there that quickly, my friend." 4 by Four said softly. It was an easy nine-hour trip doing the speed limit, not including stops.

Langdon paused at the door. "Just call her and tell her I'll be there by two."

It wasn't until Langdon reached his car that he realized his lawyer was right behind him. "It has been awhile since I've seen Philly," 4 by Four said.

"But I need you to call Amanda and tell her I'm on the way."

"I called her back right after I spoke to you on the phone and told her we'd be there by three," 4 by Four said. "Besides, you forgot to ask me for an address. Philadelphia isn't exactly like Brunswick, country boy. You can't just pull into town and ask the first pedestrian you see if they know some blonde named Amanda and her spitfire daughter, not without risking getting shot anyway. So, quit your bellyaching, and let's go."

Langdon did as he was told. After all, the man had a point.

~ ~ ~ ~ ~

It wasn't until Portsmouth that any conversation passed between them, prompted by Langdon cursing under his breath.

"What?" 4 by Four asked, coming out of a half-sleep.

"I was supposed to return somebody's Jeep Cherokee this morning." Langdon had driven to his own car, dug it out, but had neglected to return the Jeep as he was in a hurry. Now he was leaving New England, and he didn't even have her phone number.

"Who?"

"Somebody I just met," Langdon replied warily.

4 by Four smiled knowingly. "New woman friend?"

"Why do you say that?"

"Just how you're acting, is all."

At that moment, 4 by Four's beret disappeared into the backseat. Coffee Dog had come awake. With a quick move that took the dog totally by surprise, the lawyer went over the seat in a flying tackle and pinned him down on the seat, holding his head down by the collar, and with the other, deftly snatched the hat, dotted with only minimal slobber, back from the wily canine.

Sprawled in the back, his feet sticking over the front seat, his face being eagerly licked, 4 by Four continued the conversation as if nothing had happened. "Not to mention that she probably sent you off in her Jeep so you wouldn't have an excuse to stay at her place."

"She's twenty years old."

4 by Four's smile deepened. "Bowdoin student?" Langdon's astonished face in the mirror was all the answer he needed. "It's pretty elementary that only a Bowdoin student could afford a Jeep Cherokee at the ripe age of twenty."

"Brand new," Langdon admitted.

"What were you doing with some girl who can't get into bars?"

"What's that supposed to mean?"

"I mean, she may be old enough to fool around with an old geezer like you, but she still can't legally participate in your favorite activity, which is going to bars."

Langdon ignored the barb. "I met her at the college library when I was researching a case." He didn't add that he'd then taken her to a bar where she'd proceeded to get drunk and make a bit of a fool of herself.

"The Widow Dumphy's husband?" 4 by Four kept the smile from his face only at great effort.

Langdon swung his head around in surprise, despite the fact that he was cruising along at close to 90 miles an hour. "Now, how the hell do you know that?"

"Richam stopped by last night," 4 by Four said. "He seemed a little worried about you."

"If this is the point at which you tell me that I need to start going to AA meetings, well then, you can just skip it."

"That's not what he's worried about," 4 by Four retorted. "And by the way, if you think having your lawyer in the car is going to get you off of going to jail for driving to endanger, think again. Slow the fuck down."

Langdon steadied the rumbling beast down to a dull 80—which in his exasperated state, did not feel nearly fast enough. "What is the bartender worried about, then?"

4 by Four sat up in the back seat, hugging his knees, speaking more cautiously as he read the annoyance in Langdon's tone. "Well, he was talking to Bart."

Langdon rolled his eyes, secretly happy that it was not about his drunken ramblings of the previous afternoon. "Go on."

"The thought seems to be that this Dumphy guy was killed for something he knew, something you seem to be stirring up. It doesn't take Sherlock Holmes or even Watson to know who the next victim will be."

"Oh, come on! This isn't some dime detective novel with guys and gals being shot up with gats left and right. This is real life. There ain't nobody gunning for some private dick in small town Brunswick."

"It's not just in cities like Boston that people get killed for no reason. Not anymore, anyway," 4 by Four said, taking care with each word. "Big city crimes—and criminals—have rippled outward, first to the suburbs, and believe it or not, to even rural places like Brunswick. But you wouldn't have been paying much attention to any of that, right?"

"What's that supposed to mean?"

"Maine is changing fast, dude, if you haven't noticed. The computer age, technology, and the shit that comes with it. Twenty years ago, displaced, disgruntled Americans like me moved here to escape all of it, but it has come and found us. Faxes. E-Mail. The Net. Don't kid yourself. Civilization and all that comes with it has found Maine." The lawyer leaned back and lit his cigar. Coffee Dog, sensing opportunity, grabbed the hat back from 4 by Four's lap. That was the thing about the dog—he was patient, biding his time, and then striking when attention flagged. When he realized 4 by Four wasn't going to put up a fight, he tried to egg him on, jabbing the hat against the man. 4 by Four, lost in thought, absently patted his head. "And that includes the bad with the good."

"What are you saying? That my business as a private detective is going to be picking up?"

"Look at Brunswick and who lives there now. Do you know who lives out on Mere Point? How about Harpswell or Bailey Island? It's not just fishermen anymore, but rich, influential people who like the lifestyle and plan to exploit that very lifestyle to further their aims."

"What do you mean by that?"

"They will hurt anybody and anything to make themselves happier."

"Don't you think they're bringing something with them as well?"

"Like what?"

"Money for the economy, culture for the mind, work for the contractors and house painters. I don't know, but they seem like good enough people. I don't buy this theory that you have to be a third generation Mainer to be considered a local, to be worthy of social acceptance."

"It's not really their fault," 4 by Four said, picking his words with care. He'd given this a great deal of thought. "But the kind of people who move to Maine are usually upper-middle class. They believe in the American Dream: progress, the digital age, and all that stuff. They no sooner move in than they notice there isn't a Walmart, and instead of thinking that's nice, a place littered with small businesses, they see opportunity. Bigger is better. Strip malls reign over most of the country, and there's a reason for that. It's called convenience, but that doesn't mean it's better."

Langdon felt that Maine was changing as well, and agreed that it wasn't all for the better, but those people from away were often the best customers at the bookstore. "What else did Richam have to say?"

"Not much. Tell me about your new case."

Langdon filled him in on the previous day's activities, including his aggravated assault of the strange man who'd been following him, as well as drinks and conversation with Peppermint Patti. The only part he kept quiet about was the sense of loss he felt with his wife and daughter gone missing for the past six months, and how alcohol seemed to be the only cure, however temporary.

4 by Four listened thoughtfully, rolling his cigar in his mouth before speaking. "That's too bad you missed out on your opportunity to speak with the CEO of Casco Bay Power. What'd you say his name was? Johnson Halperg? I have a friend who works for CBP in the head office. He might be able to set something up for you."

"I should probably follow up with DownEast Power first," Langdon said. Admittedly, there was that underlying urge to see the mystery lady, Abigail Austin-Peters, again, she who had so unsettled him.

"If, and I stress the if, there is something odd going on at DownEast Power, there's a real good chance that the plant managers know about it." 4 by Four tipped ashes from the cigar out the window. "I mean, how could they not? So what do you think is happening there, anyway?"

"Beats me," Langdon said.

"Come on, I know you better than that. You at least have some sort of hypothesis, no matter how stupid." 4 by Four had worked cases with Langdon before, the most recent one of substance being Rasputin Snow and the Flower of the Forest hoping to find evidence of river pollution by Maine factories. 4 by Four had come to appreciate Langdon's instincts and ability, as well as his stubborn persistence.

"Well, Peppermint Patti did come up with one possible scenario, but I'm still not sure about it."

"Come on, let's hear it."

"She suggested that perhaps it has to do with nuclear waste."

"Nuclear waste?"

"Sure. Why not? These plants generate all kinds of waste, from low level contamination of gloves and work clothes, to spent control rods and what not. What happens to all that shit? Believe me, the place isn't treated like a missile silo. What security there is, well maybe it's pretty minimal." Langdon thought about Harold Dumphy being killed before going on. "It wouldn't be that hard to slip radioactive waste out of the facility."

"Sounds pretty far-fetched to me."

"Yep."

"And why?" 4 by Four asked, wondering aloud. "I mean, what's the point."

"Terrorism?" Langdon suggested.

4 by Four laughed. "You think somebody is collecting radioactive clothes to fill a truck and then park it outside the White House with the doors open?"

"Why not?" Langdon asked. He was not smiling. "What if you dumped a load in the water supply of a major city?"

4 by Four considered this. Terrorism à la nuclear waste seemed a stretch, but he trusted Langdon's knack for getting to the heart of a matter. "Don't you think it more likely that there's some kind of corporate cover up thing going on, like, I don't know, safety issues being ignored there? Perhaps the reactor is damaged, or something's happened just because it's aging. I mean, it's what, like, twenty-five years old already? Pipes corrode, cement walls crack, stuff breaks, right? And the top brass is covering it up so they don't get shut down?"

"Could be," Langdon agreed.

~ ~ ~ ~ ~

It was a good thing that 4 by Four had come along for the ride, for their destination wasn't actually Philadelphia, but Williamstown, New Jersey, 30 miles outside of the city. 4 by Four tried to decipher the directions he'd scrawled down while referring to a map spread across his lap. Williamstown was a result of the 1980s boom in condominium developments, neighborhood after neighborhood of cookie cutter dwellings looking like eggs in a carton.

Langdon observed it all in wonder, imagining it to be a capitalist utopia, every single person living in identical homes, probably working in cubicles, driving four-door SUVs of conservative colors. In order to provide all the amenities for this mass of people, strip malls had sprung up with generic signs dotting their facades, each and every one promising the fulfillment of some necessity with as little social interaction as possible. If, and when, automation replaced humans, this would be where it started. It wasn't as if the shops were bad in and of themselves, as everything a person could possibly need was here, from groceries to donuts to drugs to liquor to movies to dancing girls. He was certain there must be a neighborhood of quaint and fancy—and probably older, super expensive—houses, but so far, they were nowhere to be seen. It simply was what it was.

4 by Four was doing his best to decipher his own scrawled directions, looking up only when Langdon jerked the wheel to pass a car or slammed on the brakes to avoid running a light. Pedestrians were much safer in New Jersey than in Maine, for they knew better than to even attempt crossing a road.

"This is it, right here, on the right," 4 by Four yelled. Langdon continued on without slowing. "Hey, whoa! You deaf? We didn't come all the way to Condo-Mall World just to turn around and go back without stopping, did we?" 4 by Four asked, noting the panicked look on his friend's face.

"What if she doesn't want to see me?"

"Missouri? That girl loves you, Langdon. One of the saddest things I've ever seen is the two of you apart. You might be bad at a lot of things, but being a father is not one of them."

"I'm just not sure I'm ready to face my ex-wife," Langdon said.

"She's not your ex-wife unless you got another lawyer to file the paperwork, buddy-boy. Not that your marital status is the issue, or even seeing Amanda for that matter, is it?" He looked at Langdon and realized maybe he was wrong. "You're scared to face Amanda?"

Langdon forced a smile. "I've always been terrified of my wife."

4 by Four chuckled. "Remember that time we had the poker night, took a break to go bar-hopping, and then returned to the table until six in the morning and you never called her to let her know?"

"She does have a certain bite to her when she's angry," Langdon said, grinning. "But this time it's not me who's been missing for the past six months, so maybe I'll get the easy side of her tongue."

~ ~ ~ ~ ~

After the briefest of stiff greetings at the door, it wasn't long before Amanda's true colors—red-hot and on the boil—emerged. She was, Langdon reflected, even more beautiful in her anger. "You needed your lawyer along to pick up my daughter?"

Before Langdon could lash back, a tiny voice shrieked, "Daddy!" A small body ran full tilt into his legs and hugged them fiercely. Missouri was tiny and delicate, but strong and seemingly untouched by the chaos of the adult lives around her.

As Langdon stooped to pick her up, she was bowled over by the Coffee Dog, who then stood over her, licking her face, enormously pleased. Screaming with laughter, she tried to kiss him back, but was unable to as he was in the middle of his happy dance, his entire body gyrating to the rhythm of his wagging tail.

"Daddy, Coffee's got serious butt wiggling going on," Missouri yelled ecstatically.

The dog found the ponytail band holding her hair in place and somehow managed to whisk the elastic off without pulling her hair. He trotted away with his prize, happy with his achievement, and

Missouri gave chase, the two of them running into the next room of the condo.

For all of his brave talk of facing the music and paying the piper and all the rest of that bull that 4 by Four had used to convince Langdon to return to the generic condo—he had proven to be more meek than anything else as he skulked down the walkway at the rear of the car.

"He came along as a friend," Langdon replied in defense of his now tongue-tied attorney. "Somebody to help with the directions in this land of traffic, highways, speed traps, and stop lights."

Amanda leaned against the wall by the door, her arms folded across her chest. "Do you want to come in and have some coffee?" The words were civil but the tone was more of an invitation to do battle, like drawing a line in the sand and daring the boy in front of you to cross it.

"Sure," he replied, and followed her in.

"Still take it black?"

"Yep."

The living room was small, but tasteful, with stairs leading up on the right side to a balcony. There were mood lights illuminating walls covered in artwork. An occasional crash from upstairs suggested where Missouri and Coffee Dog had disappeared.

Amanda handed him a cup of coffee, and once the burning liquid was safely in his hand, he ventured a conversation starter. "I guess I have to ask. Where have you and my daughter been for the past 6 months?"

Amanda sat down on the sofa, and the anger that had held her rigid since they'd arrived, abruptly dissipated. She seemed suddenly fragile and bewildered by a life that hadn't quite worked out the way she'd planned. "I got swept off my feet by a professional golfer. Not that I ever saw him golf. All he wanted to do was go to cocktail parties and get smashed, and then try to seduce any female that looked twice at him. He ended up sleeping on the floor by mistake more often than not. I finally drew the line when he hit me."

For a moment, Langdon felt an overwhelming sadness for her. He remembered the first summer they'd dated, and how confident and happy she'd been, but then, a more sobering question struck him. "Where was Missouri during all of this?"

"She was around for a bit of it, when not with the babysitter." Amanda hung her head with the shame of it all.

"You had my daughter in the middle of that garbage?" Langdon asked in a voice so low it was barely audible. "When you could have just left her with me?"

"One thing just led to another. I didn't mean for it to turn out that way." Amanda began to cry, tears streaking her cheeks without a sound.

Langdon spoke in a calm and precise voice, unmoved by the tears. "I'm going to take her with me now. I don't think you'll be getting her back, not if my lawyer is worth half what he charges."

Amanda nodded her head once, and then again. "Let me pack a bag for her and get you the car seat."

"Mommy, what's wrong? Aren't you happy that Daddy's back?" Missouri stood at the bottom of the stairs, one hand resting on Coffee Dog's head.

~ ~ ~ ~ ~

4 by Four drove back with the dog in the navigator's seat, while Langdon and Missouri rode in the back, she chattering away, flitting from subject to subject until she dropped off to sleep. When he was certain that she was sleeping, Langdon broke the silence. "She looked healthy, if not happy, didn't you think?"

"Who?" 4 by Four was surprised out of his hypnotic driving state.

"Amanda."

"Sure."

"Even through the sadness, she seemed to be comfortable in her own skin."

"If you say so," the lawyer replied cautiously, inwardly thinking, *Yeah, for someone who just lost the man she once loved, and said goodbye to her daughter, probably for some time to come.*

"I was pretty angry about her bringing my daughter into the middle of her mess," Langdon said.

"I guess sometimes those things happen. Aren't you worried about bringing her back into the middle of *your* mess?"

"What do you mean?"

"Well, just twelve hours ago a man with a pistol and a knife paid you a visit in the middle of the night and you knocked him out. What if Missouri had been there?"

"Yeah, well, he was just trying to buy me off the case, not hurt me. I'm not sure I believe his story about wanting to keep his employer from being dragged through the muck for having an affair with the Widow Dumphy, though."

"You think he had another motive?"

"Maybe," Langdon said. "Not that I know anything, certainly not enough to be offered $10,000 to drop the case."

"You do have a successful track record. Your celebrity status may have opened the piggy bank."

"What are you talking about? That dog I didn't find, or the pictures of Belinda Belanger with her lawn boy?"

"It was only six months ago that your picture was on the front page of the Portland newspaper breaking that story about the paper mill."

Chapter 6

Langdon woke up in a crowded bed. The whole night, he seemed to recall, had passed with Coffee Dog, Missouri, and Langdon all fighting for space and covers. Missouri, who had won the battle, slept deeply, arms thrown carelessly over her head, a little smile kinking the corners of her tiny mouth. On a normal morning, the dog would have leapt out of the bed at Langdon's first movements, butt wiggling and quivering with excitement at an impending breakfast. This morning, however, due to a lack of quality sleep, Coffee Dog took the opportunity to snuggle further under the covers into the warm space Langdon had vacated.

~ ~ ~ ~ ~

When Langdon emerged from the shower, his ears were tickled by the suppressed giggles of his daughter, a sound that had been sorely lacking in his life for too long. He poked his head around the corner of the door, making sure the towel was securely fastened around his waist. There had been the time right before Amanda had left when the two-year-old Missouri had come into the bathroom just as he was getting out of the shower. She had giggled, pointing, and asked him why he had a thumb on his belly button. He had been more careful since to cover himself up.

Currently, Coffee Dog was diligently lapping any vestige of sleep from Missouri's face. Missouri was not your typical child who shot out of bed at first light, exhausting all the slower-risers around her with her endless energy, but more like a teenager in her morning routine, sullen and cranky. The Coffee Dog was the only one who'd found a way to make her rising a happy event, it seemed.

"Coffffeeee," she squealed in delight, for she truly loved him and he her, two beings with no accumulated clutter to cloud their true emotions.

Langdon reflected that it wasn't a bad way to wake up, smothered with kisses by the one true love of your life. Missouri had been telling people for over a year now that she and the dog were married. Well, maybe in a way, they were.

"Morning, sweetie," Langdon, now dressed, tested the waters to see if Coffee Dog had banished her normal morning crankiness. "How did you sleep?"

"Daddy, Coffee's licking my face," she replied. She was not known for answering mundane questions.

"What do you want for breakfast?"

"Bagel with cream cheese and some juice," she yelled. She was not wishy-washy about her food choices.

"Sorry, there aren't any bagels," he said.

"Toast and cream cheese."

"Actually, we don't have any toast and before you want cream cheese on something else, we don't have any cream cheese either." Langdon went to the kitchen and surveyed the contents of the refrigerator with disdain. There were eggs, but he didn't feel like making them. That left days-old Thai food, and a mostly-full case of beer. Predicting that her next request would be something other than what there was, he returned to the bedroom with a new suggestion. "How about we go out for breakfast?"

"Yay," Missouri said, standing up on the bed and jumping up and down.

"Just let me make a few phone calls first." He called Jewell, Richam's wife, to see if she would be up for watching Missouri.

"Goff, you know I love that darling girl of yours," she said. "Bring her right on over whenever you want. I'm home all day." Jewell's accent was Caribbean, a beautiful mix of African, French, Native, and English, each word spilling from her mouth like waves lapping the shore.

"And Jewell? Could you tell that husband of yours to not go stirring things up that are none of his business?" Langdon thought of Richam talking to 4 by Four behind his back.

"Sure, honey," Jewell replied, a bit taken aback. "But that man's instincts are generally on the money, you know that."

The next call was to ensure that Chabal could and would open the bookstore today, which she agreed to readily enough.

He then called Bowdoin information to get Peppermint Patti's number. She came to the phone sounding like a Grumpy Gus, like a college student after a frat party, but Langdon managed to make plans with her to meet that afternoon so he could return her Jeep and follow up on her further research on DownEast Power.

The last call was the one he'd been putting off, but finally he dialed the number for the widow Dumphy.

"Hello." Her voice was a throaty purr, almost caressing through the phone.

"This is Langdon." He paused, expecting her to hang up. When she didn't, he cleared his throat tentatively. "I just wanted to make sure you were still retaining me to investigate the murder of your husband."

"Of course," she replied. "And I do notice that you said murder, and not suicide or suspicious death or some such."

Langdon was not in the mood to play cat and mouse, especially when he was the mouse. "I do need to talk with you again. Some things have come up since we met. Can I come by in an hour?"

"Sure," she replied. "I'll put something on."

He hung up the phone. "I'm all done, E, we can go," he called into the bedroom. There was no answer, so he went to the doorway, a twinge of fear poking at him to find the room empty. "Missouri?" This time, Coffee Dog came bounding out from under the bed, a dead giveaway that his daughter was hiding under there, but Langdon played the game anyway. "Where are you?" he sang out playfully. "Are you in the bathroom? Noooo. Are you in the kitchen? Noooo." All the while, Coffee Dog energetically wagged his tail and stood by the edge of the bed, emitting a low whine from deep in his throat, as if to say—right here, stupid! Missouri finally sprang from under the bed screaming, "BOO!" He was properly frightened, she was appropriately happy, Coffee Dog was sufficiently disgusted, and they were on their way to breakfast once Missouri was dressed.

"Where are we going?" she demanded as he buckled her into the car seat.

"The diner for breakfast, and then out to see Will and Tangerine."

"Yippee," she yelled in his ear, excited to see her friends.

~ ~ ~ ~ ~

Rosie, the hostess and owner, greeted Missouri with a false look of sternness. "Isn't this the girl who pulled the fire alarm in here about a year ago?"

Langdon had quite forgotten that, and Missouri looked uncommonly shy.

"Everybody had to pile out into a freezing snowstorm, all, that is, except for old man Rodgers who never heard a thing and was sitting hidden down in a corner booth."

Missouri eased behind Langdon's legs to hide.

"Don't worry, darling," Rosie said, laughing. "I'm just teasing you. We needed a fire drill anyway, so we know to check for old man Rodgers if the real thing comes along." She led them to a booth, past a glaring couple from away who seemed to have been waiting for a table for some time. Langdon shrugged—there were perks to being a local and a regular and one who brought a lovely little girl into the bargain.

The waitress returned with coffee and an orange juice with a smile. "That man is in here again," she whispered.

"Can we get a bagel with cream cheese for Missouri, and I'll take the two eggs over easy special, please," he replied.

"Pancakes," Missouri said.

"You want pancakes instead?" Langdon asked. "I thought you were set on a bagel and cream cheese?"

"I want both," she said.

Once Alison, the waitress, had returned to the kitchen, Langdon's eyes drifted around the diner, coming to rest on Shakespeare, who was reading a newspaper at the end of the counter, a glass of water in front of him. The man sure did like to read the newspaper, Langdon mused. As if aware of the sudden attention, he looked up, catching Langdon's eyes upon him.

He dropped the newspaper and walked over. "Good morning, Mr. Langdon," he said.

"Good morning, Mr. Shakespeare. Is that a bruise on your jaw?"

His eyes narrowed and got real tight and hard. "Have you given further consideration to my offer?"

"And that is…?"

"Mr. Langdon, if you continue to play childish games, I will have to take an alternative route that might not be so pleasing to you. And then I would retrieve the money from your oven."

Missouri took this moment to peek her head out from under the table and yell, "BOO!"

Shakespeare flinched and stepped back off balance, before regaining his composure. "My, what a pretty little thing you are. Is this your girl, Mr. Langdon?" Shakespeare asked, his voice sickly sweet, the words dripping with evil.

Langdon didn't answer.

"And what is your name, little girl?"

"Cinderella," Missouri replied.

Langdon pulled her over to him and held her tight, his eyes

locked on Shakespeare, as she squirmed to get free.

"It was very nice to meet you… Cinderella," Shakespeare said. "I hope you don't lose your slipper." He turned and walked out of the diner as Langdon struggled to respond to this thinly veiled threat.

~ ~ ~ ~ ~

Jewell and Richam lived in a stylish ranch house out on Simpson Point, a quick drive from the diner. Though not far from downtown, the area was secluded, and best of all, on the water. The driveway was a dirt path weaving through pine trees, which shielded the house from the road. Richam had built the place with the help of a few friends, including Langdon. The outside was stained wood with large picture windows facing the bay, a lawn covered with snow rolling down to the water.

Langdon and Missouri entered through the open garage and made their way into the house with just a quick knock. Missouri immediately went skittering through the house looking for Tangerine and Will, more than comfortable in their home. The hardwood floors were partially covered by bright, Caribbean-style rugs, and the furniture was simple, yet elegant. Plants hung from the ceiling, soaking in the sunlight that streamed through the windows.

Missouri came back, telling him that everyone was outside, and could she go, too?

Indeed, they found Jewell on the back deck, a vast expanse twenty feet wide and running the entire length of the house, taking a picture of her children. She was dressed in a ski jacket with a bright-green headband that not only kept her ears warm, but also held back her rich, dark hair from getting in her face. She was model-tall, with well-defined features, and had a generous nature—but you wouldn't want to get on her bad side.

Tangerine, age four, and Will, age seven, were in the spacious, snow-covered yard. A wooden picket fence kept the children from spilling into the ocean, now at high tide and just feet from the edge of the yard. The two children were building a snowman, the sunny day having transformed the snow into the perfect texture.

Missouri whooped when she saw them, but then hid behind Langdon's legs.

"Missouri!" Will yelled, bounding over and dancing around her.

"Missouri!" Tangerine shouted, falling into a snow bank in her excitement.

"Hello, Goff," Jewell said, stepping off the deck and pulling her four-year-old out of the snow.

It didn't take long for Missouri to disappear into the white wonderland of their backyard, egged on by Will and Tangerine into ecstatic, squealing delight as they all wrestled.

"Will it be okay for Missouri to spend some time here over the next few weeks?" Langdon asked. "Or should I look around for a daycare?"

"Of course she can stay here! You're not going to put that child into a daycare," Jewell said. "She is more than welcome here. Besides, having her makes it a lot easier on me. Tangerine and Will get tired of each other and start bickering, but Missouri brings a new element that keeps everybody happy."

"She's always loved coming over here," Langdon agreed. "Plus, she needs to be around other kids more than she is." Langdon chose not to say goodbye to Missouri and turned to go.

"You be careful, Goff," Jewell said. "Richam told me a little of what's going on, and it sounds like a real powder keg."

Langdon looked at her a moment before replying. "You tell Rich to stick to bartending and I'll stick to investigating."

"He's worried about you on this one, Goff," she said, with a mother's protective tone. "And you know he doesn't worry easy."

Real or imagined, Langdon felt a sudden chill in the air. He paused and looked at the yard. Missouri was on her back making snow angels, vigorously flapping her arms and legs. Langdon took three large steps over to her through the snow and picked her up, smothering her with a great big bear hug and kissing the rosy cheeks glistening with melting snow.

~ ~ ~ ~ ~

The widow Dumphy was draped in a multi-colored silk bathrobe that did nothing to hide the fact that she was naked underneath. The robe wasn't transparent—rather, it somehow hinted at bare skin tickling the underside of the fabric. For somebody who had just supposedly rolled out of bed, her hair was amazingly primped, her make-up abundant and finely applied, and her manner sharp.

"Hey, Janice, good to see you," Langdon said. "I'm glad you decided not to fire my ass."

"I suppose you thought I was trying to seduce you the other night," she replied. "But you were quite rude."

Langdon decided not to apologize. "One thing we seem to have forgotten was the matter of my retainer?"

"A grand?" she asked.

"Yep."

She found her purse and handed him an envelope, already having written the check, her touch on his hand lingering.

"Can you tell me who your husband was friends with?" Langdon asked.

"His best friend in the whole world was Bob Dole, not the presidential candidate, mind you, but just some schmuck that Harold knew from school." She went on to give him a list of eight or nine other names.

"I know this is difficult, but how exactly did you hear about the… death… of your husband?"

The widow uncrossed her legs and leaned back in her chair. "I might get a cup of tea. Would you like anything?" The offer seemed to truly suggest *anything*, but Langdon wasn't going to be tempted and merely politely declined.

While she prepared the tea, Langdon took the opportunity to survey his surroundings. His attention had been focused on Janice Dumphy, and not just because she was barely clad. The living room furnishings, where he sat, had come straight out of a catalog. Every piece—and knickknacks littered every surface—had obviously been purchased from Tupperware-type parties—more of an excuse for women to get together and drink lots of wine, but usually with a mandatory purchase attached.

The carpet was thick lavender shag, the walls a soft but distinctive pink. The room was a perfect square, not much larger than an office cubicle. There were several wall hangings saying things like, "Jesus Loves" and "God's Footprints". Langdon did not fit in the space, his frame too large, the décor too fragile, and the room too clean for his boots.

Maybe Harold Dumphy *had* committed suicide.

The widow swayed back into the room, her silk bathrobe matching the walls, the carpet, and the floral displays perfectly. It was almost as if she were in camouflage. "Where were we?" she asked.

"I asked you how you heard about the death of your husband."

"Oh, yes, that's right. It was the chief, Gaylord Thompson or something like that."

"You mean Guyton Lefebvre?"

"Yes, that was his name. He came over with some other officer, I don't believe I ever got his name."

"What did Chief Lefebvre say to you? Exactly, or as close as you can remember."

"He told me that my husband was dead."

Langdon leaned forward, careful not to break anything. "Tell me exactly what he said. Did he say, 'dead' or 'there's been an accident,' what exactly were his words?"

"Well, he asked if I was Mrs. Harold Dumphy, and I said yes. And then he told me that he had very bad news, and that my husband had been killed, and—"

"Killed? He used that word?" Langdon interrupted.

Widow Dumphy looked at him with large eyes, her face serious as she thought back, and her manner sincere for the first time since he'd met her. "Yes. He said killed."

~ ~ ~ ~ ~

When Chabal arrived to open the bookstore, Langdon was in his office attempting to organize all of the names into lists. It was time to start talking to Harold Dumphy's friends and co-workers, as well as Janice Dumphy's man-friends. The first thing that stuck out was that Janice had been making time with one of her husband's co-workers—and *two* of his "friends."

"Morning, Langdon," Chabal said, popping her head through the door.

"Morning, sweetheart," he replied, speaking in his best Sam Spade voice. "Did you happen to open the shop yesterday?"

"Sure thing," she replied. "And closed it, too. All by my lonesome and certainly no thanks to your worthless ass. 4 by Four called to let me know you were picking up your daughter. Did you get her back?"

"Yep." There seemed to be an entire network of people working to keep him from screwing up his life.

"How is the little imp doing?"

"She seems fantastic."

"Did you see Amanda? Of course you did. How is she?" Though unspoken, Langdon could hear the vitriol and was pretty sure "that bitch" was what Chabal was thinking.

"She's fine," he said. "Could you get me Abigail Austin-Peters on the phone?" He thought he'd test his theory on people bending backwards to help keep his life on track, but Chabal merely laughed at the ridiculousness of the suggestion as she turned and went back to the business of opening the bookstore.

With a wry grin, Langdon picked up the phone and dialed the private number the angular woman director of public relations at

DownEast Power had given him. She answered after three rings, and he stumbled through a greeting. "Abigail... Ms. Austin... this is Goff Langdon. Can I ask you a few questions?"

"I'm awfully busy right now." She tried to brush him off. "But I can make a minute or two for a man with such a cute dog."

"I was hoping to speak with some of the employees at DownEast, Harold's co-workers? Is there a day that might work...?"

"Sure. How does next Friday sound?"

"I was thinking more like this afternoon, or maybe tomorrow morning?" He was actually planning on tracking the people down at their houses, not really thinking that she would invite him down to the plant, not if she thought he was chasing his tail, and certainly not if there was something suspicious going on.

"Any earlier than next week is impossible, Mr. Langdon. You have to realize that we have a schedule to maintain, and that a nuclear power plant is not the same as a grocery store."

Langdon put his feet up on his desk. "Well then, maybe you can explain exactly what it was that Harold did for your company."

"Mr. Dumphy was in charge of security," she replied patiently.

"And what docs that cntail?"

"I'm sorry, Mr. Langdon, but it would takc somc timc for mc to explain all the responsibilities security has at a nuclear power plant. I could set up an appointment for you to interview our new director of security for next week as well, if you want."

"Was Harold good at his job?"

"Meaning what, Mr. Langdon?"

Getting anything out of this lady was like pulling porcupine quills out of Coffee Dog's nose. "Meaning, was DownEast Power happy with the job that Mr. Dumpty... Dumphy did?" Langdon winced at the slip, but he hadn't been able to get the nursery rhyme out of his head since taking the case.

"That is not my domain, Mr. Langdon."

"And whose domain would that be?"

"I would think the personnel director, Avery Quimby."

"Do you have a number for Mr. Quimby?"

"I believe he is on vacation for the next two weeks," she said. "I am sorry, Mr. Langdon, but I really must go. I am sorry that I can't be more help."

"On the contrary, Abigail, you have been a great help." It was true. Langdon's real reason for the call had been to see if the company would help, hinder, or, as was most often the case, string him along until he got tired and went away. DownEast Power had certainly been less than helpful, but Langdon had no plans to go away.

~ ~ ~ ~ ~

Langdon came out of his office to find the bookstore surprisingly crowded for a weekday morning. Of course, it was filled with his friends. Richam, Bart, 4 by Four, and even Peppermint Patti, were milling about the store chatting. Langdon set his irritation aside, for there was nothing to be done about his friends sticking their noses into his life.

"Is it my birthday?" Langdon asked. "Or an intervention?"

"Your birthday was last month and we got good and drunk and ended up stuck in some mud hole in the woods wondering why your ragtop wasn't four-wheel drive, you schmuck." Bart often did not pick up on subtle sarcasm.

"Don't tell me you all needed a new book at the same time?" Langdon asked.

"Thought maybe you wanted to go do some more day drinking," Richam replied.

"You know I don't drink when my daughter's around, Mr. Butt Yourself In Where It's None of Your Business."

"Kind of like me calling Chabal yesterday to make sure somebody was here to open your bookstore, and then navigating your sorry ass down to get your daughter?" 4 by Four asked.

His tone was a bit too smug for Langdon. "Listen, you yuppie wannabe Indian Zen philosophizing yoga pretzel load of warm fuzz balls, I can get along just fine without your interference."

Peppermint Patti had stopped her conversation with Chabal, and was now standing stock-still with her mouth agape.

"Now that we have all that settled," Langdon continued, his eyes sweeping the room. "Are you all here to lend a hand? Or do I have to put it in writing?"

Even Bart smiled at this, and things soon fell into place. Peppermint Patti was the one most suited to do research on nuclear waste, DownEast Power, reactors, and all of that technical junk that left the rest of them perplexed. Richam knew most of the people on the lists that Langdon had created of friends, co-workers, and lovers, and thus took on the task of asking them some basic questions to try to get to know Dumphy or perhaps glean some hint of what he'd gotten himself into. Even the minister from Harold Dumphy's church was a regular at the Wretched Lobster.

4 by Four, having heard of the icy beauty of Abigail Austin-Peters, offered to see what he could dig up on her using his lawyerly skills. "She'll talk to me or get slapped with a lawsuit," he said brashly, even though they all knew, except maybe Peppermint Patti, that it was an empty threat.

"Okay, we will let you go undercover with Ms. Austin-Peters," Langdon said with a straight face. "But, be awful careful. She is some sort of beautiful sorceress who seems to have sold her soul to the demons inside the Wild Turkey bottle. Make sure she doesn't eat you up and spit you out—or get you so drunk you get popped for OUI."

4 by Four smiled, enjoying some image conjured in his mind.

"I guess I should go over the case with Tommy," Bart said. "It sounds like there are some real discrepancies, but don't think I'm going to lose my pension over this. If Chief Lefebvre tells me to lay off, then I'm going to lay off," Bart hesitated, before continuing, "and crack him right upside the head, that little pretty boy suit that calls himself a policeman. He's nothing more than a politician with a gun."

Chabal grinned at Langdon. "Sounds like all the bases are covered, Langdon. Looks like you can go take a nap, and we'll come wake you when the case is solved."

"Yeah," Peppermint Patti chimed in. "You keep out of our way and we'll take care of the rest." She immediately clapped her hand over her mouth, astounded and shocked at her brash words, and in front of all these adult strangers at that.

Chabal laughed while the others chuckled, their eyes measuring this new voice in their midst, not accepting her instantly, but definitely leaning towards making room for one more in what was a very select group.

"Don't you worry about me," Langdon interjected into the sudden silence. "I think I may look up my friend Shakespeare and see if I can't *shake* some information out of him." No one even groaned in reply. "Okay, Richam is going to start working on the list of names, 4 by Four has the lady with two last names, Bart will check in with Tommy, Peppermint Patti is on the research. If anybody finds anything, report back to Chabal here at the store."

The group broke up, mission(s) launched if not yet accomplished— Langdon getting the much-needed help that only friends can supply, and said friends getting a chance to live out the fantasy of being Philip Marlowe, Sam Spade, or V.I. Warshawski.

Chapter 7

Peppermint Patti left the gathering a little bit disillusioned with the whole private detective business. She had summoned every drop of courage twenty years gives a Texas girl and had shown up out of the blue at the Coffee Dog Bookstore, discovered a gathering of his friends, bantered with them—and now she found herself returning to the Bowdoin Library to do research. If research was what she wanted to do, dammit, she could be preparing for her term paper on Lenin.

"Hi, Patti," the elderly receptionist at the front desk called out as she came through the door. She was thin and wore dowdy clothes, with slightly powdered, tightly-curled white hair, and had brown horn-rimmed glasses perched upon her nose—in short, your stereotypic small-town America librarian.

"Hello, Mrs. Bostwick," Peppermint Patti replied, taking a moment to stop and trade pleasantries. "How is it today?"

"Busy. Very busy."

"I guess the end of the semester is coming before we know it."

"It's nice to see everybody getting an early start on their studying," Mrs. Bostwick agreed. "What are you working on?"

"I'm actually researching DownEast Power, you know, the nuclear power plant up in Woolington?"

"Oh? Really?" Mrs. Bostwick perked right up. "If you need any help, my husband, bless his soul, worked there for twenty-two years before he died of a heart attack."

"What did he do there?"

"He worked in security. He never had any health issues, but the stress of being responsible, even in part, for watching over such a potentially dangerous facility wore on him, and one day, right in the middle of the night shift, he dropped dead."

"I am terribly sorry," Peppermint Patti said.

"It was years ago," Mrs. Bostwick replied, waving her hand, but there might have been a catch in her voice.

"I didn't even realize it had been around that long." Peppermint Patti shifted the topic away from the husband and back to the plant.

"Oh, yes, they started building the plant right after the big blackout of '65."

"The big blackout?"

"There was some sort of electrical overload in the grid, something shorted out somewhere, causing a chain reaction of blackouts whizzing all over New England and Canada. It knocked electricity out all over and scared the dickens out of everybody. It was as if the end had come. Some people thought the Russians had finally dropped the big one. So the state government decided they needed an alternative energy source, one that was cheaper, easier, and safer. They built DownEast Power, and all of our problems were solved."

"And your husband worked for DownEast Power from the very beginning?"

"He sure did, right until… that day," Mrs. Bostwick replied, her voice husky. "They found him lying peacefully in the middle of the break room."

"Do you live in Woolington?" Peppermint Patti realized how little she knew this elderly lady she'd worked with for over a year now.

"We bought a house there in '67, and that is where I plan to live out the rest of my days."

"Isn't it a bit of a drive to get here? Especially in the winter? Why don't you move closer to Brunswick?"

"I couldn't afford to leave Woolington, my dear. Why, my taxes are almost nothing, with the plant picking up so much of the burden."

Peppermint Patti wondered how many people traded the dangers of living next to a nuclear power plant just for the tax relief. She excused herself, and retrieved several books on nuclear power, and then secreted herself in a carrel in a corner of the second floor.

An hour later, Mrs. Bostwick appeared with a stack of articles she'd printed off from the microfiche. She plopped them down, suggesting that they might be useful, that she was going to get some more, and that this was just to get her started. Peppermint Patti considered telling Mrs. Bostwick that she didn't have to do that, but refrained, realizing that the lady liked to be kept busy with a project instead of just sitting at the front desk, bored. Helping others seemed to truly make her happy. More than likely she had taken care of her husband's every need before his death, and now there was a void in need of filling in her life.

After almost eight hours of research, the only breaks coming when Mrs. Bostwick delivered books, notes, photocopies, and the occasional suggestion, Peppermint Patti wasn't sure what she'd learned, only that she had a crushing headache.

She had discovered that the plant used Uranium-235 that was shaped into fuel pellets about a half-inch long and no thicker than her finger. Two hundred of these pellets were packed into a tube, and 179 of these fuel rods were bundled together to make a fuel assembly. These fuel assemblies were delivered to DownEast Power and placed in the reactor located in the containment building.

This building was made of reinforced concrete and surrounded by thousands of gallons of water as a buffer, and set to automatically seal tightly if anything went wrong, preventing anything from escaping. The center of the reactor was where the nuclear fission—the splitting of the atom—took place, which was the necessary factor in the creation of power. Water was the key to this process, by slowing down the neutrons and forcing them to collide and split.

Control rods, made of material that absorbed neutrons very quickly, were kept at the ready to be lowered into the reactor should the fission process somehow get out of hand. The water surrounding the fuel assemblies inside the reactor was a further safety check, cooling any pellets that got too hot.

In the next stage of the process, a large pipe moved water past the fission taking place, heating it, but not quite to a boil. The water then flowed into a steam generator, where it met water from a secondary pipe system, turning it into steam before sending it into the turbine, a cylinder-shaped machine whose purpose was to convert other forms of energy, such as heat and kinetic, into electricity. The turbine was shaped like a fan, the steam causing the blades to turn large magnets, thus creating an electric field.

Science was not really Peppermint Patti's thing, but she thought she had a general grasp of the project. She had also studied the layout of DownEast Power, but now needed a break. "Ach," she said aloud, shaking her tousled red hair to clear the cobwebs. "I've had enough of this crap."

"What's that, dear?" Mrs. Bostwick asked, appearing around the corner of the stacks with yet another armload of material. Her shift had ended an hour earlier, but helping Patti sure beat returning to an empty house.

"I was just asking you if you wanted to go get a beer." Peppermint Patti said with a sheepish smile.

"Oh, no thank you, dear, I don't drink." Mrs. Bostwick said. "But you go right ahead. I've been telling everybody that Ms. Smith is too serious, always working, never smiling. You should go and have some fun."

~ ~ ~ ~ ~

Perhaps her roommate, Anne Spelling, would tip back a beer with her, Peppermint Patti thought, walking down the hall of her dorm. As she went to put the key in the lock, she heard an unusual sound and stopped to put her ear to the door. There was the sound of heavy breathing, a bed creaking, and then a squeal of pleasure. She smiled, turned, and walked away, happy for her friend, who, like her, seemed to have a hard time meeting nice boys. Good for her.

The two girls had decided to room together not because they were such great friends, but because of the simple fact they had had no other options. Being lowly sophomores, there was little chance of either getting a single room, and out of necessity, they'd agreed to share. Peppermint Patti's thoughts drifted back, starting with often eating lunch alone in grade school, being the last one chosen for a team in fifth grade gym class, even though she was a fairly athletic girl. It was this that turned her to individual sports such as tennis and track. By the time she entered high school, Peppermint Patti had become a confirmed loner—attending movies by herself, studying and reading to fill her time, and constantly daydreaming about what it would be like to be popular.

It looked like she would be going to have that beer alone, but that was nothing new, and she certainly didn't hold it against Anne. Rather, she was happy for her to find a little bit of companionship in this lonely world. Her Jeep seemed to find its way to Goldilocks all on its own. She was a bit embarrassed to go in, having run out a couple nights earlier covered in beer and stumbling drunk, but she figured, what the hell? She was going to turn the page and create a new Peppermint Patti Smith, one who worked with private detectives and dallied with bartenders.

It was the bartender from the other night, but this time he asked her for identification. "I didn't bring it," she replied, staring him straight in the eye.

"No identification, no service. I'm sorry, but I can't get busted for serving underage coeds." He went back to polishing glasses at the bar.

"I came in here with Langdon a couple of nights ago," she said. "And I'm meeting him here tonight." A small fib, but he might show up. Goldilocks carefully set the glass down, looking up and reassessing this plain girl. She flashed him a smile of victory, relishing her new strength, and the power of friends. "Bring me a beer." She did not ask.

"You were drinking Geary's," Goldilocks said. He took the defeat easily, admiring the girl's backbone.

"My name's Peppermint Patti," she reminded him as he set the beer on the bar.

"Goldilocks."

"You were telling me about Langdon working on a lobster boat when he was eight. Was that true?"

"Sure enough."

"What's good to eat here?" she asked.

"The lobster roll."

"Is it fresh lobster?"

"I hauled it this morning."

"You did?"

"Yeah," Goldilocks replied. "When I got my stake working on the water, I opened this place up, but I still keep a few traps. This time of year, the critters are moving out to deeper water, so I'll haul 'em all in soon, put 'em on the lawn, and wait for spring."

"I'll take one."

"Sure enough," he said, setting her beer down in front of her.

"Thanks for the beer."

"No problem," he said, moving away to take other orders at the end of the bar from a couple frantically waving their hands as if in horror at the thought of their drink running dry before they could get another.

Peppermint Patti was just finishing her lobster roll when a man who'd been eying her from across the room chose to make his move. Somehow, she knew that he was coming for her, even though she was a novice with men. He had a very powerful body, but at the same time, walked delicately, light on his feet. His face and hands were weather beaten, his face with just a hint of scruff, almost a Brad Pitt look. The man took his time, working slowly through the tables, chatting with people as he went. He seemed to know everybody there.

"Buy you a beer?" he asked when he'd finally reached her.

"Sure."

She saw that his knuckles were scarred as he laid his hands on the bar. They were the hands of a man, and not a Bowdoin boy. "Haven't seen you in here before," he said.

"Only my second time."

"New to town?"

Peppermint Patti suddenly did not want this man to know that she was a Bowdoin student, a rich kid from the hill, somebody who had had it easy all her life, with parents who spent many thousands of dollars a year just so she could read books and go to parties. She didn't want him to know that her *high school* graduation present had been a brand new Jeep Cherokee, and that Christmas would be spent in Paris, and then the Caribbean for Spring Break. "I just moved here," she said, instead.

"Where you from before?"

There was no use trying to hide the South in her speech, not even from this man, whom she would guess had only been out of the state when he was in the military, if at all. "Texas."

"Well, I'll be. All the way from Texas." He was in his early twenties, but oh so much more mature looking than the college boys she lived among. "What brings you up to our neck of the woods?"

Peppermint Patti noticed the man was missing a tooth, a not uncommon sight in Maine. He looked like he'd probably been involved in a few scuffles in his time, and had likely enjoyed them all immensely, won or lost.

With a start, Peppermint Patti realized this man was flirting with her. She fumbled for words, her mouth opening and closing like a fish out of water. Then for no apparent reason, she blurted the first thing that came to her mind. "I got a job working for Harper Truman."

The man whistled low in his throat. "You work for the governor? And all the way from Texas? What's the matter, he couldn't find nobody local willing to work for him?"

"That I do, yes, and I don't know," Peppermint Patti replied. "Can I get you another beer?" From his surprised look, she realized that it wasn't her role to be buying *him* beer.

"Sure," he said. "I'm Josh, Josh Martin."

"Patti Smith." As she spoke, Goldilocks ambled down the bar, and she signaled for another round by pointing at their drinks and lifting her eyebrows.

"So, Patti, what do you do for the governor?" The beers arrived, and he tipped his fresh Budweiser at her, clinking the Geary's draft in her glass.

"I'm the assistant to his secretary," she said.

"I've got some grievances that you might bring to his attention," Josh said. "If you wouldn't mind?"

Peppermint Patti had always heard that the problem with lies is that the first begot the second, then the third and so on, but she'd never lied before, so had no way of knowing how this lie might morph and take on a life of its own. "Sure," she said weakly.

"The town has decided to hand out clamming licenses like candy on Halloween, while at the same time, the damn state keeps adding restrictions on where we can rake." One of Josh Martin's favorite pet peeves was the government and everybody who worked for it, but he'd make an exception for this young woman with the shapely figure.

"You clam for a living?" she asked. "We don't do much for clams down in Texas. Oysters in the gulf, sure, but not clams. Tell me all about it." He was happy to talk about his work and yammered on about his job out on the flats. Oddly, this man who dug clams for a living intrigued her.

It was another beer in the telling, and Peppermint Patti pushing her half-full glass away when she realized she was getting buzzed. Josh Martin had his arm around her as he continued to talk about clamming, embellishing what he did with every sentence, making the job romantic. To a girl from Texas, it was certainly exotic, if not quite romantic, much like being a cowboy to somebody from Maine. The truth of the matter was that both jobs were filled with long tedious hours of brutally hard work. Of course, probably due to the popularity of westerns, cowboys had become strong romantic figures—John Wayne and Clint Eastwood and Roy Rogers—while clammers had gotten the short end of the stick.

What the clammers needed, she mused as Josh talked, was a movie hunk to take up their cause. Peppermint Patti could just imagine Brad Pitt taking the role of the man she was talking to, working his clam flat, saving up for a lobster boat or something like that, fighting back when a large seafood conglomerate tried to push him out of a job by buying up the waterfront. He'd be deadly with a clam rake, a poetry-spouting digger who bothered nobody except when pushed, and made all of the girls' hearts flutter, with a charged-up Ford F-150 into the bargain instead of a horse.

The bar had become increasingly noisy, and Peppermint Patti had to lean in to be heard, her lips brushing the man's leathery ear as she spoke. "I'm supposed to go out to DownEast Power tomorrow for the governor," she said. When had she become such an adroit liar? "I'm ashamed to admit I don't even know how to get there. Are there a lot of security clearances, gates, sentries, and things like that?"

"Phssst. Security?" He guffawed. "I hit the clamming flats out there sometimes when the tide is low and I'm right there. There have been times when I've looked up and realized I'm practically in the middle of the entire complex. They're not much worried about anything being stolen out there."

~ ~ ~ ~ ~

Bart walked away from the Coffee Dog Bookstore angry. He'd shown up to help out, but hadn't realized he would be one of many. He cursed 4 by Four under his breath, and Richam. What help could a hippie lawyer and a bartender be? And what had the college girl been doing there, and did Langdon call her Peppermint Patti? It certainly seemed that if anything were really going to get done, it would be up to Sergeant Jeremiah Bartholomew to make it happen. His bad mood was slightly eased by the sun shining on the snow, a brilliant early winter day, and in his mind, he tried to think what words he might choose to describe it. Not even Langdon knew that Bart liked to dabble with writing poetry.

It wasn't the grand things of life that Bart lived for, but rather something more ineffable, almost too small to label or grasp, glimpses of things that made waking up each day somewhat bearable. It was the smile of a baby, a young woman playing a guitar on the mall, a teenager riding his bike with no hands down Maine Street, and it was these molecular moments he tried to capture in the notebook he carried with him everywhere. He was not certain that he'd ever share his words with anybody, or if they would remain forever his alone.

Starting about seven years earlier, he'd been trying to capture the essence of life on paper. He was not so much interested in a fancy restaurant or a Broadway play—give him a picnic at Popham Beach or an eagle circling lazily in the sky over the Androscoggin River any day. No museum was as beautiful as a walk through the forest. He'd never liked cities, but feared they were creeping his way, sneaking silently up on him, and that suddenly he would find himself swallowed up in a concrete jungle populated by rude people drinking lattes and complaining that they couldn't get a good bagel.

This Harold Dumphy murder/suicide was just another sign of that creeping urbanization—why, it had the stink of big city corruption all over it. It had to be stopped, before Brunswick became North New Boston. That, and the fact that the word to drop further investigation of Dumphy's death had come straight from the chief was almost more than Bart could stomach.

It was a short walk across Maine Street and down Center, cutting across the rec parking lot to the police station. He passed by the receptionist with a casual wave of his hand and a gruff, "Hallo." The files were centrally located, so there were several other officers around as he pawed through them looking for what he wanted. The Dumphy file was missing. Bart double-checked—making sure it hadn't been slid into another one by mistake, or been replaced out of order. He suddenly became aware of the silence and looked up to see Chief Lefebvre standing over him.

"Looking for something, Sergeant?"

"Yeah, I'm looking for the Dumphy file, only there ain't no file."

"The Dumphy file?" The chief asked, but to Bart, it seemed too glib, contrived.

"Yeah, ya know, Harold Dumphy, the guy that got murdered and we called it suicide."

Chief Lefebvre rocked back slightly on his heels, and then dark clouds descended upon his visage. "Come into my office, Sergeant," he commanded. Guyton Lefebvre was a couple inches over six feet, his shoulders stooped as many tall and thin men's were, which gave him the look of a vulture on a perch scanning for carrion. Most of his hair had receded, leaving him just a crown of white ringing his head. His eyebrows were an anomaly, thick and bushy. His face was bony, the skin pulled tightly over harsh features, and at this moment, one of the mustache-like eyebrows was raised in question, as if professing ignorance to whatever it was that Bart was talking about.

Bart followed him into the jurisdiction of his office and now stood fuming in front of his desk. "What's going on?" he demanded.

"That's what I want to ask you," the chief replied. "What is this nonsense you're spouting?"

"Why was the Harold Dumphy case closed?"

"The case is more delicate than you think, Sergeant. It has not been closed at all, but rather, prioritized. That is all I am at liberty to say. I'd like it if you would give me the benefit of the doubt before you go around casting aspersions."

"I talked to Tommy," Bart said quietly.

"Really?" The chief breathed thinly through his nose. "I told him to keep his mouth shut."

Bart stared morosely at the chief. It was time to keep his big yap shut. It was one thing to jeopardize his own career, but now other possible casualties were springing up around him.

Guyton Lefebvre had been the chief of police in Brunswick for nine years now, and before that, in Beverly, Massachusetts. Bart had not been happy they'd brought an outsider in, and had disliked him from the start. The chief's appearance was just another instance of the creeping urbanization that was eating away at the foundation of Brunswick's small-town fabric.

The chief settled into the chair behind his desk, folded his fingers, and looked up at Bart towering over him. "Okay, Sergeant, I'm going to give you some top-secret information that is not to leave this room. Understood?"

Bart merely grunted.

The chief took that as an assent. "It looks like Harold Dumphy was murdered. I don't know the why or the how, because before we could more than get our feet wet, the Feds swept in and took it over. They asked that I downplay the whole murder angle and minimize the story to the media as much as possible."

"So, you called it a suicide to keep the papers quiet?"

"Yes, and to not tip off the killer or killers that we are on to them."

"The Feds are on to them, you mean?"

"Yes, that is correct. The Feds are on to them."

"Call me crazy, but isn't that illegal as hell?"

"You know as well as I do that sometimes we have to bend a bit in the name of ultimate justice," the chief said.

"What about his widow's feelings? What if she blames herself? And what about his friends? His family? Christ, man, you're tearing a bunch of people apart with your lie."

"You'll have to give me some slack on this one, Bart," the chief said with a beseeching look. "I'll make everything right as soon as I can."

"Interesting that I haven't seen any Feds crawling around," Bart said. "They usually stick out like a city slicker at hunting camp."

~ ~ ~ ~ ~

4 by Four returned to his second-floor office in the Fort Andross building on the Androscoggin River overlooking Maine Street, the river the dividing line between Brunswick and Topsham. From his desk he could see the length of Maine Street, capped on the far side by the First Parish Church, just this side of Bowdoin College. His thoughts were filled with the image of Abigail Austin-Peters that he'd conjured from the few tidbits that Langdon had shared with him.

4 by Four knew that he had an addictive personality, having spent the first part of his adult life obsessed with work, the middle with marijuana, and most recently, with the pursuit of women. He wasn't a one-night stand kind of guy, but neither was he a settle down and become domesticated fellow either. The movie *9 ½ Weeks* had been a strong influence, the flick with Mickey Rourke and Kim Basinger based upon the premise that this was the perfect length of time for a relationship. Any shorter and you might miss out on increasingly intimate experimentations in the carnal side, any longer and you were slipping into a boring routine. 4 by Four understood that a therapist might have some insight into this, but he didn't particularly care, as he was content with who he was.

He dialed the number Langdon had given him. "Is this Abigail Austin-Peters?"

"Yes." The voice was like a chill wind, cooling on a hot day, frigid on a cold day, thoroughly composed and dangerous.

"Ms. Austin-Peters, James Angstrom here. Listen, I'm a lawyer here in Brunswick, and I've been retained by Janice Dumphy in the matter of her husband's death. I was wondering if perhaps we could have a sit-down to discuss DownEast's responsibilities in the matter?"

"I'm not sure that I'm the person you need to be talking to. Legal issues aren't my forte, Mr. Angstrom. I'll pass you on to Legal, though."

"My interest concerns policy, and not legal action, at this point. I am merely gathering information as to what course DownEast Power has followed in regards to this death."

"My job is public relations, Mr. Angstrom, not policy, and not employee relations." Her voice was impatient.

"The suspicious death of the head of security at DownEast Power and a potential cover-up certainly seems to be a public relations issue, if not nightmare, to me, Ms. Austin-Peters."

An extended pause followed, and 4 by Four could almost hear the wheels turning in her head. But, nothing if not a patient man, 4 by Four waited her out. "I will connect you with my secretary to set up an appointment."

4 by Four knew that this meant sometime next week at the very earliest, and that was not soon enough, not by a long shot. It was time to get tough. "Let me get this straight, Ms. Austin-Peters," he paused, as if writing it down. "DownEast Power has no comment on the mysterious death of their head of security and the concerns of the community that there is some kind of cover-up, possibly relating to security lapses, operating irregularities, or—"

"There was no mysterious death," she interrupted, "and this is the first I'm hearing about any of the rest of it."

"I can see the headline in the *Bath Daily News* now, 'Dead Men Tell No Tales,'" 4 by Four said, wincing at his own corny words. "Or, I can meet you at the end of your day today just to get your responses to a few questions I have. Your office, perhaps?" It was blackmail, pure and simple, but he knew from experience that that was the only way to deal with corporate America.

"No. Not here." She sighed audibly. "A body has to eat, I suppose. Where, then, would you like to have dinner?" she asked, and it was 4 by Four's turn to go silent.

Chapter 8

Langdon had a few more things to do after the rest of the gang left the bookstore. He did own a business, after all, and while Chabal's hands were quite capable, he couldn't neglect responsibility. First, he had to take Coffee Dog out to do his business, it being time for his morning poop. The dog had a favorite flower bed he liked to utilize, and Langdon looked left and right to make sure nobody was watching him pick it up, before grasping the turds in a bag, reversing it, tying the top, and arcing a high skyhook into the bank's dumpster.

Once back inside, Langdon called Baker & Taylor to order some new releases, replacements for books sold, and special orders from customers. He was disheartened to discover that the latest James Lee Burke had been delayed, yet again. Langdon called his *Bath Daily News* advertising agent to check on a coupon he was hoping to run in a special section they were promoting, but was forced to leave a message. He called over to the Lenin Stop Coffee Shop, who roasted their own beans, and ordered more coffee for the store. He had to call back the artist that was having an opening in the store in a few weeks about the details of setting up the rock collages that were her specialty, and then he was done.

He stepped out of his office and went to the counter where Chabal stood and surveyed the store, seeing a single person browsing at the back. "Hey, if you get a chance, can you change the spotlighted author's tables, and get some Marcia Muller books in the front window?"

"Sure," she replied.

"We should be getting an Ingram order in today. The request sheets are in the folder."

"The request sheets are in the request folder? What a great idea."

"If anybody calls with anything important, I have my cell phone with me."

"Right-o, boss man," she said.

"If you have some free time, see if you can find a contact name at Casco Bay Power, would you?" Langdon was procrastinating, not wanting to leave Chabal's calming influence. Yes, Chabal, who, of all his friends, had been his rock during this recent difficult time in his life. Plus, he had little desire to confront the dangerous man called Shakespeare. Quite out of excuses, Langdon finally raised a hand. "Goodbye, then."

"Take care of yourself," she replied. There was more she wanted to say, but this would have to do. She was married. He was married. They both had kids. She worked for him. He was her boss. But, dammit, she couldn't stop feeling that warmth and comfort, that crazy spark of "what if" when he was at her side.

Langdon passed a few people, likely browsers, entering the store as he left. After a few years of selling books, he could immediately pick out the serious buyer from those just killing time. On the street, he looked back for a moment. It was hard to leave Chabal behind, but it was time to take the bull by the horns. Coffee Dog pulled him forward, anxious to get to wherever they were going next.

~ ~ ~ ~ ~

"Hey Rosie, how's it been?" Langdon asked as he entered the diner.

"Welcome back, Goff Langdon, where is that wicked pretty little girl of yours?"

"She's visiting with friends," he replied. "I'm working on a case." He knew that this would stir the pot, for this place, and Rosie, were gossip central in Brunswick. The slightest fluctuation in any regular's schedule created all sorts of talk. If you wanted the latest sports news, sleeping arrangements of married couples, or recent arrests, well, this was the place to find it out.

Rosie leaned over the counter, her large breasts getting a momentary respite from their ongoing battle with gravity. "Anything I can help you with?" she asked excitedly. Her short, pudgy forearms bespoke a strength that you didn't get in any gym.

"Cup of coffee, beautiful, and maybe a few questions answered?"

She grinned wickedly. "Coffee will be fifty cents, but the rest might cost you plenty."

It was now late morning, a good time to catch Rosie with a moment to spare. There were just a few regulars nursing cups of coffee at the counter, and all of the booths were empty, waiting for the lunchtime rush.

"You know that man that came over to my booth this morning?"

She nodded. "He sure is a strange fellow, don't fit in around here at all, and queer as a three dollar bill."

"You know anything about him?"

"Like what, does he prefer little boys over women, that sort of thing?"

"Anything you can tell me."

"He comes in every morning, just like clockwork, eats dry toast, drinks black coffee, and leaves a decent tip—better than you do, you cheapskate."

Langdon knew better than this, for he was a good tipper. "You know where he's staying?"

"No idea, hon," she replied. "He was cozied up to Sam and Jason after you left this morning. When I see them, I can ask what they know. What were you two talking about the other morning, anyway? Everybody's been trying to figure that one out."

"You ever seen two dogs pissing on a post?" Langdon smiled at Rosie, just a tinge of teasing in his voice. He gave her a chance to reply, but when she remained silent, he continued, "Well, the two of us were just testing each other to see who was tougher by pissing on a hypothetical post."

"Okay, I'll bite. Who was tougher?"

"Can't really tell by pissing on a post, now can you?" A hand slapped his back and Langdon whirled around with his fist raised.

"Shit, Langdon. I'm just joking around, give me a break," Danny T. said. He was a regular at the diner and a friend of Langdon's. He was as round as he was tall, with no other word for it than fat, but with an agile wit and a cunning mind. Danny had dropped out of school to go to work on a fishing boat, but an incident where he cut a $25,000 net to save a crewmate's arm had resulted in him being blackballed from the water. Now, with no diploma and few skills, he struggled at menial jobs to get by.

"You think I'm going to give a break to a guy who owes me money, and then sneaks up behind me?" Langdon asked. "I thought you were trying to bump me off to save yourself five bucks." Langdon's casual dismissal of his violent reaction didn't fool either Rosie or Danny T., but they let it pass.

"Double or nothing on Vikings-Bears this weekend?" Danny T. asked. "If I can't kill you, I might as well make my money back."

"Your Bears don't have a chance against my Vikings, Danny T."

"Do you really think the fact that you came of age when the purple people eaters were devouring quarterbacks makes them any good now? The Bears are Super Bowl–bound this year."

"Double or nothing it is, then," Langdon said.

He started to leave, tossing two dollars on the counter for his fifty-cent coffee, but he stopped by the door. "Hey, Danny T., do you know anything about the strange fop that's been hanging around?"

"You mean the one you got in a pissing contest with?" Danny T. asked. "Yeah, sure, I heard some things about that fellow."

Langdon walked back to the counter. "I'll give you seven points in the game," he said.

"I sure could use some food," Danny T. said in a pitiful voice, staring at a passing platter of eggs and bacon.

Langdon threw down ten dollars on the counter and took two premade egg and bacon sandwiches from the warmer. "Let's go," he said, Danny T. following behind more obediently than the Coffee Dog, who was behind the counter frantically licking every spot ever touched by food.

As Langdon impatiently called for his dog, Rosie began lobbing small pieces of bacon to alternating corners of the diner. Coffee Dog was forced to run back and forth across the small space, bowling into patrons, all regulars who soon joined in the fun. Langdon was forced to grab the dog, pick him up in a bear hug, and carry him out.

"Coffee Dog, don't you understand dignity?" Langdon struggled with the squirming dog, finally wrestling open the back door and stowing him inside. "They were laughing *at* you, not *with* you," he snapped and he slammed the door. As he walked to the driver's door, Langdon pondered whether dignity was actually more important than food.

As he pulled the car onto Pleasant Street, the seat all the way back so that Danny T. could fit, Langdon looked over at the man, who was gobbling down his breakfast sandwiches as fast as the Coffee Dog had wolfed down the scraps. Neither man nor dog made apologies for their love of food. Langdon waited impatiently for him to finish, knowing the man was incapable of concentrating as long as there was any food left in front of him.

The day was a real corker, and as the sun melted the snow on the sides of the road, Langdon realized it was December 1st. He waved to Jack Turgeon, the tall, gaunt man crossing the street with his eyes pinned to his feet, and beeped at Alice Renquist, who was coming out of the deli with several friends. Whatever else, this was Langdon's town, and the place he belonged. He knew people here, had friends, was respected, and fit into life here with an intimacy only those born and raised there knew. It was too bad that his wife couldn't understand that, or never would, it seemed. Amanda had wanted to take him south, dress him up, teach him polite manners, take him to the opera—well then, after all that, one day he'd wake up and no longer be Langdon, just some wannabee Southern gent.

Amanda had never been able to understand fundamental pieces of his personality, such as his friendship with the man currently sitting in his passenger seat. Okay, so the man was overweight, his clothes unkempt, and sometimes even malodorous. Danny T. worked at Cumberland Farms, and didn't have a car, much less a driver's license. There wasn't a lot of what people termed upward mobility in his life, but at the same time, there wasn't a mean bone in Danny T.'s body. For Chrissake, the man always had a smile plastered on his face and a kind word or little joke on his lips. Langdon was convinced that he was smart enough to go to college and make a better life for himself, but then, would he still be Danny T.?

"So, you're looking for the guy that took your paper the other day at the diner?" Danny T. finally spoke, having finished the two breakfast sandwiches. Langdon had turned off Maine Street and onto Route 1. "Seems a lot of trouble just because he took your paper."

"Yeah, well, I had an ad in the newspaper I wanted to see," Langdon said. "Former private detective and bookstore owner looking for quarterback job with NFL team, preferably in Minnesota."

"The way Moon is throwing the ball, you have a chance there, partner. Maybe you should actually give it a go," Danny T. said with just a touch of malice. He took his football very seriously, second only to food. "Besides, he's almost forty. I think the retirement age at Cumberland Farms is forty, let alone the NFL."

"Whatcha got for me?" Langdon asked.

"Your man, the fop, he's been around asking a lot of questions. I don't think he understands our small-town mentality. He acts like he wants to blend in, slip into the background. He buys the Cumbies gang coffee and cigarettes and hangs out in front of the store. But not only does he stick out like a sore thumb, then he starts asking all these questions, and that just puts people off more."

"What kind of questions?"

"Seems he's interested in Janice Dumphy, you know her?" Langdon nodded. "He's also been asking about DownEast Power. Where the dead hubbie worked?" Danny T. rambled on, finishing each statement with a question, taking his time and enjoying the spotlight.

"That's the case I'm working," Langdon said, choosing his words carefully. Maintaining 100 percent client confidentiality didn't exactly hold sway when it came to dealing with people like Danny T., whose stock in trade was rumors and gossip. If Langdon were too secretive, it would just cause the man to make stupid shit up and spread false gossip. "The Widow Dumphy has hired me to investigate her husband's death."

"Why's that?"

Langdon pondered the best way to answer this and decided to be a bit creative, not necessarily lying outright, but fudging enough to maybe generate some talk in the rumor mill. "This man Shakespeare might have had something to do with his dying."

"You mean Shakespeare killed Humpty Dumpty?" Danny T. asked, eyes wide, already anticipating the excitement this morsel would elicit at the diner.

Langdon wagged his head back and forth noncommittally. "You were saying…?"

Danny hesitated, and Langdon knew his hunch had been correct. The fat man always held something back, hoping for a little bit more, even if it was just another breakfast sandwich, a grin from a pretty girl, a pat on the back, such was the currency of the rumor mill.

"It's possible that Shakespeare did kill Harold Dumphy," Langdon said. After all, it was possible, wasn't it?

"Well, this should be interesting to you, then," Danny T. said, leaning towards Langdon as if to share a personal secret. "You know Randi Petersen? The young lady who nannies for the governor?"

"Yeah, I know who she is," Langdon replied. "She comes into the bookstore with the kids all the time. They got an open tab, and

Harper or Karol comes in once a month to pay up." Governor Harper Truman and his wife Karol lived in Brunswick. Langdon liked both of them, as they seemed to be regular folks who didn't put on airs like they were better than the peasants who cleaned their houses and raised their children.

"Well, Randi, she was in the diner the other day after you left, and that fop, Shakespeare, was still there. What kind of name is Shakespeare, anyway? Is it French?"

Langdon stared at him, shaking his head. The man might be street smart, but he was obviously not much of a reader. "I don't think it's his real name, but Shakespeare is English."

"English, huh? Go figure. Like Smith?" Danny T. looked out the window lost in the fog that was his inner thoughts. "I kind of remember the name from school, before I stopped going, but as I recollect, none of the words made any sense, so I figured it must have been French."

"Please, please, get to the point."

Danny T. turned his mournful eyes on Langdon. "Okay, so Randi is right next to me in the diner, and she turns to her friend, not that I was eavesdropping or anything, but I was just right there and all."

"Danny," Langdon said in a low growl of warning.

So Danny T. told him the story. How Randi had apparently been watching a movie after the kids had gone to bed when the doorbell rang. She'd answered the door, wondering who it could be at that time of night. Outside, with his back to the light, stood a man of elegant dress, his face hidden in the shadows. When she asked him what he wanted, the man had demanded to see Harper. When she told him that Mr. Truman had already gone to bed, the man had insisted. Finally, she'd gone up and awoken Mr. Truman, telling him that a man named Shakespeare was asking for him, waiting outside. Upon hearing the name, he'd leapt out of bed and followed her down, pulling a robe over his pajamas. He'd told her to go to her room. There had been a brief conversation on the stoop, she'd heard the front door close, and that was it.

Langdon tried to process this information. Shakespeare and Governor Harper Truman knew each other?

Danny T. was wiggling in his seat, reminding Langdon of an excited Coffee Dog. "Pretty good stuff, huh, Langdon? The guy who you think may have caused Humpty Dumpty to have a great big fall is having late-night conversations with the governor? The same guy who has been asking around about whether or not Missouri is your daughter or not, and what you do for childcare, and whatnot."

"What?" Langdon slammed on the brakes, the car behind screeching to a stop just inches from his bumper, and a whole host of cars suddenly honking. He didn't care. "Shakespeare's been asking about Missouri?"

"Just today," Danny T. replied. "He's been telling people he's her godfather, and that you and he go way back, but nobody really believes him."

Langdon's mind raced. He remembered the thin man's cold and dispassionate eyes, and he knew Shakespeare would have no qualms about using his daughter against him if necessary. He was also certain that there would be one big mouth in town, somebody who would tell the man how Langdon was close with Richam and Jewell, and that Missouri was friends with their children.

His cell phone was plugged into the cigarette lighter. He quickly punched the numbers in, then had to delete and start again, but finally the phone began ringing. After an eternity, it went to the answering machine. "Hello, you have reached the number—" Langdon was about to hang up when Richam's voicemail was interrupted by Jewell's impatient voice, "Hello? Hold on, just let me shut this stupid machine off." She was out of breath and sounding flustered, causing Langdon's anxiety to mount as the clicking noises continued.

"Jewell, is everything okay?" Langdon shouted into the phone.

"Goff, is that you?" Her voice was calmer now. "What's going on?"

"Is everything okay there?" Langdon asked, relaxing, even if his heart was still beating wildly in his chest.

"Everything's fine. I was just out back when I heard the phone ring." Jewell spoke in perfect clipped tones with just a hint of English accent. "Is something the matter? And what is that ruckus?" The cars behind Langdon had been laying on their horns for the past 30 seconds or so.

"I'm just in a traffic jam," Langdon said, easing his foot off the brake and continuing on with a wave over his shoulder to the cars behind. "Have there been any strangers around today, driving by or parking across the street?"

"Strangers? No. Missouri fell off a stool trying to get on the counter, but she's fine."

"Do me a favor, would you, Jewell? Go look out the front and see if there's anything or anybody you don't recognize on the street."

Jewell must have sensed his urgency because she didn't bother asking why. Langdon heard her set down the phone and could see her in his mind's eye walking to the front window.

"There's a car parked just down the street. No one parks there because we all have driveways." Now, her voice was anxious. "What's going on, Goff?"

"Jewell, listen to me carefully, do not hang up the phone, but make sure you get all of the children inside and lock the doors. Do not let anybody in. I'm on my way and will be there in five minutes." The phone went silent, and then Langdon could hear Jewell yelling for Will, Tangerine, and Missouri to come inside. Langdon handed the phone to Danny T. and then set to the task of breaking every traffic law in existence to get there as quickly as possible, hoping for once in his life that the cops would follow.

He just made the lights at Cook's Corner, flying through the yellow even as the red began to take its place. The car in front of him was, for some reason, actually stopping, and Langdon had to swerve into the other lane to get around him and then cut back the other way to make a right. They were weaving in and out of incoming traffic on Bath Road, flashing past cars as if they were parked, all the while

Langdon keeping a running monologue, the words pouring from him in his growing anxiety.

"This guy, Shakespeare, is the only real suspect I have in the murder of Harold Dumphy." Though he'd just minutes earlier been floating this as a rumor, it was, he realized as the words left his mouth, in fact true. "You following me so far?" He looked over at Danny T., who was white as a sheet, and looking strangely like the Pillsbury Dough Boy, if a very unhappy, perhaps even nauseous Dough Boy. "The police have closed the case and he thinks he's home free. But then Janice blabs to someone that she's hiring me to investigate, which gets back to him, so now he's kind of worried. He figures he can try to lay low or scare me off, so the other night he pays me a visit and does a little bit of both, and I punch him out. So now, he can't lay low, because I'm onto him."

"And you don't scare easy," Danny T. squeaked from the passenger seat.

"I didn't think I did either, Danny T. I didn't think I did either."

"So, this guy is after Missouri to get to you?"

"I hope not," Langdon replied. "I just don't know, and that's what's got me worried."

"You can probably slow this heap down, then," Danny T. said, trying to keep his voice level. "If Shakespeare *is* trying to scare you through your daughter, well then, he ain't going to hurt her or there wouldn't be no way left to get to you. He might want you to think he's after her, but if he's got any brains, he ain't touching her."

It was at moments like this that Langdon realized Danny T. had some smarts, even without book learning. Taking in the man's words, Langdon took his foot off the gas. As they came whipping around a sinuous curve affectionately known as Blind Man's Alley, they came upon a moose licking at the salt on the side of the road. Langdon swerved to avoid the thousand-pound beast, avoiding a collision that would have been like driving Langdon's jalopy straight into a brick wall. If they'd been going any faster, they would've rolled for sure.

The car went over a snowbank at a pretty good clip and slid into what was, luckily, a field and not the forest. Langdon cut the wheel back, the convertible struggling to gain traction, and then man and machine shot back onto the road. Lady Luck must have been attending, as the only injuries were to Danny T.'s strained vocal cords as he screamed in terror. That, and the phone, which had slipped from his grasp and was smashed against the dashboard, the charging cord acting as a bungee as they went up and over the snow bank. Not that big of a deal, Langdon thought, as they were almost there.

Chapter 9

Inside the house, Jewell had ordered the children upstairs. Missouri, not understanding the seriousness of the situation, hid under the kitchen table, and then ran through the downstairs of the house laughing—a true pain in the ass as only a three-year-old can be. At this moment, Jewell wasn't amused. The thin man had slid out of the car across the street and was looking towards the house. She yelled into the phone, but it had gone dead.

"Will, get Missouri, and take the girls up to Mommy and Daddy's room and lock the door. Now!" Will, at seven, was old enough to understand the time to rebel and the time to obey. Even Missouri paused at the fear in Jewell's voice and allowed herself to be herded upstairs.

"Damn that Langdon," Jewell cursed under her breath.

"What was that, Mom?" Will looked back over his shoulder from the top of the stairs.

"Nothing, honey. Get in the room and lock the door. Don't come out until I come and get you, no matter what." At that moment, there was a loud knock at the front door.

Jewell pulled open a kitchen drawer and fumbled through the junk, finally laying her hands on the small key she was looking for. In the front hallway closet, on the top shelf was a lock box, and she pulled this down, just as another, more insistent knock rang out. Her shaking hands unlocked it, and she pulled out the ancient Smith & Wesson pistol, a relic from their past life in the Dominican Republic.

She checked to make sure it was loaded, and then went to the door, as a more vigorous rapping echoed through the house.

"What do you want?" Jewell asked through the closed door.

No answer.

"What do you want?"

"Please let me in. I have a very important message for you from Goff Langdon."

Jewell took a deep breath, exhaled, unlocked the door with a quick twist of the hand, and then swung it open abruptly. She held the old pistol tightly down at her side, and once the door was open, she brought it up, her other hand clasping the grip to steady the gun. The barrel was no more than a foot from the man's narrow face. He seemed surprised that he hadn't found a cowering, submissive housewife, but didn't flinch or even take so much as a step backwards, which alarmed Jewell.

"Don't move, motherfucker!" Jewell had a fleeting thought of the various B movies that she'd stolen this line from.

"Calm down, lady," Shakespeare said in a soothing tone. "I don't have any money on me, I'm not the legal representative of your divorced husband serving papers, and I'm not the local crack dealer." He wondered if they even had crack up in this godforsaken place. "So, please, move the gun away from my head before it goes off."

Jewell held the gun steady. "You told me what you're not, now tell me who you are before my finger slips and I find out I just blew a Jehovah's Witness to kingdom come a bit prematurely."

"Mom? What's going on?" Will's voice drifted down from the top of the stairs.

What happened then played out as a slow motion nightmare. Jewell turned her head towards Will in surprise that immediately turned to dread as she realized that she'd fucked up. Shakespeare uncoiled and struck like some desert snake, his left hand snapping up and over, removing the gun from her hand. Will opened his mouth to shout a warning that never made it out of his mouth as the man smashed his mother in the side of the head with the pistol. Jewell spun sideways from the force of the blow, her hair knocked askew, her legs going wobbly underneath her, and the world went black and white. Shakespeare followed the first blow with a direct punch to her jaw, the crack ringing through the house.

Will ran to the inert form of his mother. Missouri and Tangerine came to the top of the stairs and stared silently down, paralyzed by what they were seeing. A car had come to a shuddering stop in the driveway, and Shakespeare turned to face this new threat just as Langdon came charging up the porch steps.

Langdon had been aiming for the vicious blind side hit—the blitzing linebacker who comes from the backside to take a chunk out of the opposing quarterback. Shakespeare neatly turned with a feral snarl, teeth bared, and smacked Langdon with the butt of his palm just as he came over the last step. The blow drove Langdon's nose back, and he teetered for just an instant before crumpling backwards off the porch.

"Bastard," Shakespeare said.

Langdon struggled to his knees, feeling like a freight train had rolled over his head, blood from his broken nose spraying onto the white snow, with just one thought in his muddled brain: he had to protect his daughter.

Shakespeare came to the edge of the porch and kicked Langdon in the face with a pointed boot, knocking Langdon over onto his back, and following him by taking two steps down, and stomping on his stomach. Langdon found himself suddenly gasping for air. He tried to roll over to his stomach, but his limbs had stopped obeying orders from his brain. He was aware of the redness of the snow next to his head and the sunny day had suddenly darkened.

"What we have here, Mr. Langdon, is a failure to communicate," Shakespeare ranted, his eyes barbaric and wild in his head. As he spoke, spittle flew through the air past his bared teeth. "I tell you to do something, and you ignore me—no, in fact, you do the exact opposite.

Yessir, a failure to communicate!" Shakespeare was pacing as he spoke, delivering sharp kicks to Langdon each time he passed by, to the chin, to the back, to the kneecap.

At this point, Coffee Dog, having leapt over the seat and escaped out of the driver side door Langdon had left ajar, came streaking across the short distance from the car like a bolt of brown lightning. The dog ploughed into Shakespeare, knocking him off his feet. Shakespeare raised the pistol still in his hand and pointed it at the dog, but with a supreme effort, Langdon rolled over and kicked out, jarring the man's arm and sending the bullet whizzing away into nothing.

Shakespeare retaliated in return, kicking Langdon in the crotch, just as Coffee Dog bit into his forearm. He flung the dog to the side, and when the mutt came at him again, punched him squarely in the head, toppling him into a heap in the snow. He turned and kicked Langdon again.

Danny T., watching all this with horror, was pinned to the seat with fear, finally pawing through the glove compartment and searching in vain for a weapon. His frantic eyes fell upon the keys still in the ignition.

Tangerine left Missouri frozen at the top of the stairs and went back into her parent's room. She picked up the phone and imitated punching buttons like she saw adults do, and in this case, she hit the programmed number for her dad.

Richam answered the phone in the bar, and was at first met with silence, and then a small voice said, "Daddy?"

"Tangerine, is that you?" Richam smiled, waiting for some innocuous request that he bring home ice cream or paper towels from the store.

"Daddy, there is a very bad man here. He hit Mommy." Tangerine spoke very clearly, before a sob came rippling over the phone that hit Richam in the guts as if he'd been kicked by a horse.

And then Missouri began screaming in the background.

Richam was stunned for just long enough to hear the screeching of tires over the wails of Missouri, and then there were several sharp loud pops that could only be gunfire. He was over the counter and out the door before the echoes on the phone had died away.

~ ~ ~ ~ ~

It took Richam nine minutes to reach his home. What he found there was exactly the kind of nightmare scene he'd moved to Brunswick to escape.

Langdon's car was resting silently against the living room window, gleaming shards of glass scattered in bloodstained snow.

Jewell was sitting on the porch with the children clutched to her, dazed and bewildered. Missouri was trying to pull free, to get to the driveway where Langdon was on all fours trying to stand-up. Coffee Dog was licking his face, urging him on. Danny T. was slumped next to the driver's side of the car.

The mist that had cloaked Langdon's consciousness for the last few minutes began to clear, and he felt a moment of stabbing panic before his eyes came to rest on his little girl. Tears streaked her face as she twisted away from Jewell and ran to her daddy. And, as if he hadn't known it already, Langdon knew there was nothing more important in the world than the safety of this two-and a half foot tall, thirty-pound human being.

The sound of sirens filled the air. Blue lights came flashing up the driveway. Two patrol cars pulled in.

~ ~ ~ ~ ~

Once he was certain that Shakespeare was gone, Langdon, with Missouri in tow, stumbled into the house and made three phone calls.

"Chabal," Langdon gasped hoarsely into the receiver. "I need you to meet me at the hospital."

"What's going on?"

"I had an accident, and I need somebody to keep an eye on

Missouri. Somebody she knows. Shut the store down. Kick everyone out. Please."

She would be there.

His lawyer was the second call. "4 by Four? I need you to contact Amanda. She needs to come get Missouri." Perhaps it was Langdon's voice, but 4 by Four didn't ask a single question. "And then come meet me at the hospital."

The last call was to Langdon's brothers. Lord and Nick Langdon were 24-year-old twins living in Colorado. "Lord, is that you? I need your help, you and Nick, can you come give me a hand?"

The booming voice of the eldest twin rang in Langdon's ear, asking for more details.

"They threatened my daughter, Lord, they threatened my little girl. Bring your guns."

Lord and Nick would be on their way.

Then, there would be hell to pay.

Chapter 10

"Nick, wake up, we gotta go."

"What?" Nick asked blearily. He was currently pressed facedown into a pillow, trying to sleep off the hangover from the previous night's bender, which had actually lasted until the sun was just coming up that morning.

"Goff just called. He needs our help."

Nick went cold. Their older brother had never asked for their help before. He was always the one who helped them. It was Goff who had driven them to their football games, delivered them to friend's houses, and helped them with their homework. It was Goff who rescued them when they did something stupid, who beat the shit out of the guy who had pulled a knife on Nick, who loaned them money he never expected to be repaid. In fact, he had bought them the Volvo they still drove. He was their mentor, their teacher, and their role model. He was their trust fund, but more than that, he was their best friend. When their father had left the family, Goff had stepped in and filled the role, filled it better than most real fathers could ever hope to, all without creating any resentment. In fact, Lord and Nick worshiped their older brother.

"He call from Brunswick?"

"Yep."

"Sound serious?"

"Yep."

"Bring the firepower?"

"Yep."

~ ~ ~ ~ ~

It was only a matter of minutes to grab a few items of clothing and their guns, and they were off in the car, headed for Maine.

"What'd he say the problem was?"

"All he said was that they threatened Missouri."

The speedometer shot upwards. "Did you remember the ammo?" Nick asked.

The twins had few real allegiances in life. They owned nothing that couldn't be left behind at a moment's notice. Their apartment would probably not be theirs when they returned—*if* they returned—as they paid month to month. They had stuffed their few clean clothes in a laundry bag, and just up and left. They did not bother calling in to work. The few friends they'd made would find out soon enough. For all intents and purposes, Lord and Nick Langdon were about to disappear from Denver, Colorado, without a trace.

When they reached the airfield, they found it mobbed with police, or, to be more specific, two police cars, an ambulance, and three fire trucks. It wasn't hard to guess that their friend, Crazy Larry, was involved.

In fact, there stood the man himself in front of a burning husk of a plane, arguing with a man who appeared to be the fire chief. Larry's only clothes were tight blue jeans with holes in the knees and butt, and black socks. His naked torso was skeletal, with pencil-thin arms sprouting from either side. His scrawny neck led up to a head that was too large for his body, dominated by a colossal hooked nose under a mass of thick, black curls.

When Larry spotted them, he waved Lord and Nick over. "This buffoon is trying to tell me that I can't burn up my own plane. What? Give me a fire permit then, and let me get on about my business. The damned thing don't fly, costs too much to fix, and is costing me money every day." He turned back to the fire chief. "If you want the goddamn thing, then take it, but don't tell me that I can't burn my own shit."

The fire chief shook his head in disgust and walked off, gesturing to the police and then Larry as if they might better handle this lunatic. Lord took advantage of this interruption to tell Crazy Larry that they needed a plane, ASAP.

A blink of sanity crept into Crazy Larry's eyes, and he cast an appraising glance at Lord and Nick Langdon, a look that took in their appearance, the tightness of their eyes, measured the clipped tone of Lord's speech. He nodded brusquely. "OK," he said, walking off, nodding his head slightly that they should follow.

When one of the patrolmen yelled for them to stop, Crazy Larry raised his arms to the heavens and let out a wail. "Christ, my Lord, has spoken to me and told me of the devil that would appear, dressed in shiny blue, and attempt to interrupt the doings of my work on earth. But first, I must take a shit, and then I will be back."

The patrolman determined it would be best to let him go take care of business, and perhaps by the time he got back, somebody else would have arrived and could take over.

Crazy Larry led them around a hangar, his body convulsing with suppressed laughter. "The religion thing scares the dickens out of them every time," he gasped, his face a mottled red from trying not to roar aloud.

Nick and Lord both had their pilot licenses and merely wanted a plane, not a pilot, but Larry had other ideas. "I'm not going to face that mob over there, not for just burning my own property, and I do hate to miss an adventure. You want a plane, you gotta take me too."

There was really no other choice. The boys nodded and Larry pointed out a gleaming Cessna 414. In seconds they had boarded the eight-seat, twin-engine aircraft. Larry immediately began hitting switches, thrusting levers, and going through a modified and hurried pre-flight checklist. Nick had barely sat down before they were taxiing down the runway towards the cluster of policemen, firemen, rescue workers, and the vehicles they'd all arrived in. A warning must have been passed, for all the figures turned towards them, waving their arms overhead, their mouths open, yelling. But of course, they couldn't be heard.

~ ~ ~ ~ ~

Langdon and Jewell had refused the service of an ambulance, and instead, Richam drove them to the hospital. Jewell needed to have her jaw checked for a fracture, and her ear looked at, as it was still ringing from Shakespeare's glancing blow. Danny T. had not been injured physically, but mentally he was a wreck, having fainted away after crashing the car. As for Langdon, he was fairly certain his nose and at least two ribs were broken, and seriously hoped there was no more internal damage than that. The three children were silent, shocked by the violence that had blown apart their world, three minutes of carnage coming out of nowhere. Coffee Dog was licking his bruises when not hovering at Missouri's side.

Chabal had been waiting at the doorway to the emergency room when the motley crew arrived. As they pulled up in front and tumbled from the car, her heart raced, especially when Langdon emerged carrying Missouri, crusted blood covering his face. Her questions died on her lips, as she realized what was most important now. She was relieved that they had showed up, as there were two hospitals to choose from in town and Langdon hadn't told her which was their destination. When the bloodied band of friends reached the front counter, Chabal held out her arms, and took a somewhat reluctant Missouri.

"Can I help you?" the ER receptionist said, her face impassive behind the thick glass of the triage window.

"Yes, I was wondering if this is where I might pick up a job application?" Langdon asked, his expression deadpan. Blood streaked his face, clotted his hair, and streaked his shirt. He had a wad of tissue stuck into each nostril of his broken nose, and more blood trickled down his face from his gashed scalp as he spoke.

After an awkward ten seconds of silence, Jewell chuckled, followed by a giggle from Chabal, and a huge guffaw from Richam—and then the whole group of them was standing in the emergency reception area of the hospital howling with laughter, Langdon gripping his sides in pain even as he roared.

This was the scene that 4 by Four walked in on, his face a mix of perplexity, concern, and then fear at his friend's condition.

"What is your name, sir?" the stern receptionist asked. She hadn't even come close to cracking a smile. Once she got his name, she pushed a clipboard at him. "Fill these out and bring them back up." She had obviously decided that he did not merit immediate medical attention.

Langdon turned to 4 by Four as Jewell was ushered into an exam room before her x-ray. "Did you get through to Amanda?"

"I left a message for her with her sister." 4 by Four eyed the bedraggled group. "What's going on, Langdon?"

"Jewell and the kids had a run-in with our friend, Shakespeare. Me and Danny T. showed up, and he sucker-punched me and kicked me around a bit. Danny T. scared him off by running my car into the side of their house." He shook his head, still marveling at the action. "Pretty brilliant maneuver, y'know. I never would have thought of something so, well, primitive, but it sure enough worked."

"He was shooting at me," Danny T. spluttered. He had finally done something brave, bordering on heroic even, and now Langdon was belittling his gallant charge of the enemy lines. "And he didn't sucker punch you. You ran straight into his fist."

"Mr. Langdon?" the receptionist called. "Is that your dog?" Her voice implied that dogs were *not* allowed in a hospital waiting room.

"I have no idea whose mangy mutt that is," Langdon said. "But I wouldn't go near it—look at the frothing at its mouth. I bet the thing's got rabies."

Coffee Dog turned his mournful eyes on Langdon wondering what praise he was being showered with.

"Just kidding, bud," Langdon said. "Chabal, will you take Missouri and Coffee Dog home with you?"

4 by Four shook his head. "I don't think home is such a good idea right now."

"Where, then?" Langdon asked.

~ ~ ~ ~ ~

By the time 4 by Four, Chabal, Missouri, and Coffee Dog got the key, stocked up on a few basic groceries, and drove to the vast mill building on the river, Langdon and the Denevieux clan were pulling in right behind them. The doctor had wanted to keep Langdon for further testing and suggested that overnight would be wise, but he'd refused, insisting he could manage between the ibuprofen and the tight tape wrap encircling his midsection. Missouri ran over to him and he swung her up into his arms, wincing with the effort. As they waited for the elevator, he mentally cataloged his aches and pains. After the adrenaline had worn off, his body was beginning to feel the beating it had taken that day. But Langdon shrugged, consoling himself with the thought that this was how the Vikings' forty-year-old Warren Moon probably felt every Monday after a game. Perhaps, he thought, professional football was not all that it was cracked up to be. Getting the crap beat out of you by a gun-toting maniac certainly wasn't.

As they entered the loft, Richam let out a low whistle that echoed through the gigantic rooms. "Man, oh man, I do believe we might stay in hiding for the rest of our lives." Fort Andross was a big old mill on the river, which had been transformed into commercial space for various businesses, restaurants, condos, and office spaces. The 'loft' was a space of at least four thousand square feet, with a fully furnished kitchen, living room, gaming area with a ping pong table, pinball, pool table, a fully stocked bar, and even a baseball diamond. It belonged to a wealthy author who summered in Brunswick. Langdon had done some investigative work for the man—namely taking pictures of his cheating wife—thereby saving him mucho bucks on the divorce settlement.

"A little nicer than my office," 4 by Four said dryly. His office was a fraction of this size in the same building. "I got to keep moving as I've got a dinner date with Abigail Austin-Peters."

"Good work," Langdon said. "See if you can weasel out anything about what DownEast Power has to do with the governor. Any contribution will be public record, but maybe it goes deeper than that. Danny told me that our fellow Shakespeare was visiting with Truman the other night."

"What?" Chabal said. "I'm pretty good friends with Karol. I can't say I know Harper very well, but I can't imagine him mixed up with that psychopath."

"I'll see what I can do," 4 by Four said.

"I'm sure you'll pump her for information," Richam said, a leer in his voice.

"Can you bring me back to my car at the hospital?" Chabal asked.

"Do you think that's wise?" Langdon interjected before 4 by Four could reply. He didn't like the idea of her at home while Shakespeare was on the prowl, and it was comforting to have her there, as well.

"My husband isn't too keen on me doing a sleep-over." Chabal made a face, but it was tough to tell whether it was mocking her husband for his controlling behavior or in jest at the concept of an adult pajama party. Once again, he thought, he was forcing her to choose a side.

"Just be careful," Langdon cautioned. She was an adult, and a married woman at that, so it was not his business to weigh in. Still, every part of him wanted her to stay. "Hey, if you get a chance, can you swing by the bookstore and put a sign in the window saying 'closed for a family emergency'?"

"Sure," she replied. "Anything else?"

"Yeah, actually. Do you think you can give Karol Truman a call? See what she may or may not know about the English bard?"

"Shakespeare?"

"One and the same. That's what I like about you, you're fast like a tractor."

Coffee Dog was doing his best at bounding around, but it was an effort as his body, like Langdon's, was apparently aching from the ordeal. Before the grumpy receptionist had been able to expel him from the hospital, a nurse had come along, a real dog lover, checking him over before salving his bruises. She had even given the mutt half of her ham sandwich.

Richam took it upon himself to cook the group a simple meal of pasta, hamburger, and tomato sauce with garlic bread and a salad. Of the children, Will was the only one awake when the food was ready. They ate hungrily and in silence.

Langdon and Jewell cleared the plates as Richam chatted with Will about what had happened that day. "Jewell," Langdon attempted the beginning of an apology. "I'm sorry to have gotten…"

"Let's not talk about it right now, Goff." There was no room for argument in her voice, also no reason to think that the morning would find an apology any more welcome. Langdon had put the kids in danger, and whether it was his fault or not, it was unforgivable.

Langdon understood.

~ ~ ~ ~ ~

If there was one thing that Langdon had learned as a parent, it was that kids were amazingly resilient, seemingly needing no more than a good meal and normal night's sleep to bounce back from just about anything. On some mornings, this resiliency was not necessarily all good. Before the sun had reached the eastern horizon, Missouri was doing a war dance on the pullout couch they shared, the early bedtime the night before having disturbed her normal slow-waking routine.

"Don't jump on me. Please!" Langdon managed to say, even if too late, as Missouri had already gone airborne, turning into a human cannonball, rising high into the air and then descending onto his cracked ribs. Langdon rolled to one side, but his attacker took this as a declaration of war, and now it was a fight to the death. With that agility gifted only to the very young, Missouri twisted out of his grasp and smacked Langdon in the shoulder, which he discovered was also bruised. His grunt of pain she mistook as acting.

Before Langdon could pin this whirling dervish, she delivered three more shots to his damaged body. He grabbed her arms and squeezed, his brow in a cold sweat, as he gasped in pain. There was no real way to explain cracked ribs to a young child.

"Let go, Daddy," she cried, struggling to get free.

Langdon held her at arm's length with one hand and tousled her head with his free hand while explaining that he hurt—and why— searching her face to see if she was yet comprehending the previous day's events. "Listen, kid, I gotta take a shower or I'm gonna be grumpy all day long. You don't want that, do you?"

Missouri's face became very serious. "You must be Grumpy," she said in her best Snow White imitation.

"I'll just be a minute," he said. The bathroom held the largest whirlpool tub he'd ever seen, and Langdon changed his mind about the shower and the "minute" he'd promised to Missouri. He set the tub to filling, squeezed in a few drops of bath gel, and peeked out at Missouri who was now pretending to be Snow White, conjuring dwarves from pillows while swanning around wrapped in a sheet. With a groan of pleasure, Langdon slid into the hot water and hit the button for the jets. His battered body enjoyed the soothing water therapy for about ten minutes until his internal alarm went off, and he rose with a sigh, knowing that Missouri would be up and about, venturing out into God knows what kind of trouble.

He dried himself off with the fluffy white towels, swearing he'd throw out his own thin, ragged specimens and pay a visit to JCPenney's in Cook's Corner for some new ones. There was a brush, lather, and a straight razor on the top shelf behind the mirror over the sink. Langdon liked the novelist more and more and wondered why his wife had ever cheated on him. Perhaps he'd have to stock his books in the shop, even though the man didn't write mysteries, but rather, fictional accounts of modern day cowboys on road trips discovering the meaning of life. On a clothes rack along the wall, Langdon found a pair of pants and a shirt that were a bit tight but still better than his ripped and bloody clothes.

"Okay, you little monster, let's go find some food," Langdon growled at Missouri. While he didn't feel quite as awake and alive as his daughter, at least he'd had some sleep, hours for his body to begin to heal from its beating.

They were the first two up, but Jewell and Tangerine were not far behind. The two young girls went racing off through the loft while Langdon poured Jewell a cup of coffee. He happily discovered that 4 by Four had thought to buy bacon, eggs, potatoes, some onions and other vegetables, and English muffins. Langdon began prepping while Jewell went to spell out the rules of this new space to the girls, the very first of which was to keep it quiet when others were sleeping.

The wafting aroma of food, especially the bacon, brought Richam and Will wandering into the kitchen area, and soon Langdon was calling out for the girls to join them at the table. Danny T. shambled over, almost drooling at the prospect of food.

Richam eyed the home fries dubiously. "Dang, Langdon, my kids won't touch these things. You got mushrooms, onions, and pepper all in there."

Langdon looked over at Will and Tangerine, who were both shoveling the food, veggies and all, into their mouths like they hadn't eaten for days. "There's Cheerios," he said.

"What time is 4 by Four coming back?" Jewell asked, methodically picking through her food, leaving the potatoes behind.

"Sorry," Langdon said, noticing that Richam had entered the fray, mixing his eggs into the home fries and going to work on them. "He called while you were off with the girls. He said he was coming by around ten and so was Bart, who has a surprise."

"Surprise?" Jewell asked.

Langdon shrugged. "Your guess is as good as mine."

"What's the game plan?" Richam asked. "We supposed to just sit tight? Not that I couldn't get used to that. Did you see the beer refrigerator? Packed to the gills with every beer I know, as far as I could tell, and I *am* a bartender."

"We'll talk it over when 4 by Four and Bart get here," Langdon said. "Don't worry, we'll come up with something. As for staying here, my friend the owner told me to take as long as we need, just leave it clean and replace the beer."

"More juice, Daddy, please?" Missouri asked.

"And, I really don't think it's safe to go home right now, not until this thing with Shakespeare is… resolved," Langdon said, pouring more juice.

"What about 4 by Four and Chabal?" Jewell asked.

Langdon winced inwardly, hearing the implied accusation in her voice. "I doubt that Shakespeare has made a connection between 4 by Four and me."

"And Chabal? It won't take him long to figure out she works at your shop," Richam said.

"Daddy, Coffee Dog's bothering me," Missouri complained. Coffee Dog seemed to have recuperated from his harrowing day, and indeed, was nudging at Missouri, begging for food.

"Coffee! Get over her," Langdon commanded. The dog hung his head and came to Langdon, plopping himself down on the floor with a weary sigh. "I made some calls yesterday. The cavalry's coming but I'm not sure when they'll actually arrive." He didn't think it would take Lord and Nick very long, but they weren't the kind to give an ETA. "My brothers are on their way." The others looked at him uncertainly, having heard the stories about the crazy-ass twins, not quite knowing if that was a good or a bad thing.

There was a sudden pounding at the door. "Open up! It's the police." The voice was the unmistakable baritone of Bart.

Langdon went to the door and slid the heavy dead bolt back and swung it open. Bart lumbered through the door, and behind him were the twins, Lord and Nicky, and some crazy-looking fellow. An untrained observer might not realize that Langdon's younger brothers were identical twins, or related at all. They were both an inch over six feet and quite muscular. Lord's physicality was more delicate, lithe and toned, whereas Nicky's arms and chest bulged with a brute force. Lord was dapper, clean cut, with short hair and a fresh clean-shaven face. Nicky's clothes were not so much chosen with care as thrown on from the clean pile, his hair and whiskers showing the same neglect.

Chapter 11

Chabal had just gotten her kids out the door and onto the bus when the doorbell rang. Of course she answered it, swinging the door wide just as she remembered that there was a villain on the loose preying upon Langdon's friends and family. In the doorway stood a thin man in an old-fashioned suit with a face pinched and creased in suppressed rage.

"Mind if I come in?" Shakespeare entered the house, forcing himself past a startled Chabal, who backed down the hallway as he slammed the door shut. "Nice house you have. Lived here long?" He moved like a snake, and his voice made her think of Kaa from *The Jungle Book* in its wheedling and insidious tone.

"What do you want?" she demanded.

"I am Mr. Shakespeare," he said, extending his hand. "And you are Mrs. Daniels."

"Don't touch me," she replied.

He looked her up and down with a leer. "Don't worry, I like my women a bit more leggy."

"I hear you like to punch women and scare small children."

"As I recall, I kicked your boss around a bit. Does he come under the heading of a woman or a child?"

"Get out of my house," she said, turning to make a dash for the back door.

Shakespeare's hand shot out and grasped her by the throat. "How is your memory, sweetness? I have a message for you to convey to

Mr. Langdon, wherever he is hiding his sorry, aching ass. Mind, lass, if your memory is poor, I might just have to carve the words into your skin for him to read. Think you can remember a simple message?" He pulled something from his pocket and brought it to her cheek. She heard a click and a blade popped out, its razor edge slicing her cheek so swiftly and unexpectedly that she didn't have time to react.

She tried to twist away, to escape the man, but he held her tight, his clammy fingers digging into her wrist, his wiry arm clasping her to him. "I'll do what you want," she said, whimpering. "Just stop!" Droplets of blood seeped from the wound and dripped onto her white blouse.

"Tell Mr. Langdon he can keep the ten thousand dollars. I will also leave you an envelope with two tickets to Hawaii. I suggest that Mr. Langdon take his daughter on vacation. Tomorrow."

He paused and she made to pull away, but he clasped her tight, pressing the blade once again to her cheek.

"Tell him that if this was tomorrow and he was still here, that you would be dead." Shakespeare pressed the blade a bit tighter to her cheek. "Tell him that if he is not on that plane, I will find him. I will cut off his hands and feet. And while he lies there, bleeding to death, I will slash his pretty little daughter's throat." He was clenching her neck more tightly, working himself into a rage, the knife now laid flat on the open wound, tiny flecks of spittle landing on her cheek as he spoke. "My employer will not see DownEast Power shut down due to a few minor cracks. Do you understand me?"

~ ~ ~ ~ ~

At 9:30, when 4 by Four came by, he found the door open and rushed in, finding Chabal slumped forward on the sofa, her head in her hands. She looked up with red eyes, and he saw that she was trembling from head to foot, one hand clasped to her cheek.

"What happened?" he asked, crouching down in front of her and taking her hands in his own, taking in the wound on her cheek and the droplets of blood on her blouse. When she didn't answer immediately, he went to the kitchen and came back with a damp hand towel and set about cleaning her face.

"A Mr. Shakespeare stopped by." Chabal said, her voice hoarse, almost cracking. "I have a message for Langdon." She looked at the envelope Shakespeare had dropped contemptuously on the coffee table before slipping out the door.

4 by Four looked at her questioningly but she shook her head.

She took a deep breath and sat up, squaring her shoulders. "I think that it'd better wait until the whole group is together to hear it," she said, a firmness creeping in and erasing the fear.

"Everybody's at the loft, even a few surprise visitors."

"Who?" Chabal asked, but in her mind she was still seeing the sallow demon holding a knife pressed to her face, his rancid breath in her nostrils. She wondered just how close she had come to death, especially after his inadvertent admission. She had watched his eyes measure her reaction to what he'd said, and she'd kept her face as impassive as possible, as if too terrified to understand the import of his words, with her life hanging in the balance.

"The twins showed up in the middle of the night. When Langdon didn't answer his phone—he said it got busted, I guess—they called Bart to pick them up outside of Lewiston, and they were all banging on my door first-thing this morning."

Chabal breathed deeply. Lord and Nick were here? From what she knew, that was very good news, indeed. "I hope they catch him and make him piss himself," she said with malice. "Will you stay just until I change my blouse?"

4 by Four stood uncomfortably in the living room as she disappeared up the stairs. He found himself staring at a wedding picture of Chabal and her husband. "Does your husband know any of what's going on?" he asked when she returned.

"We don't talk about anything important anymore, unless you count shopping, who's picking up the kids, who's taking the cat to the vet." Her voice drifted off, and he heard a whisper of regret, or maybe pain, he couldn't tell.

"So, you didn't tell him about what happened yesterday?"

"I don't ask about his work, and he sure doesn't want to hear that I'm in danger because of Langdon, who he suspects of having designs on me and has ever since I started working at the bookstore."

"I don't believe that." It was not clear whether 4 by Four meant the complete lack of communication with her husband or Langdon having designs upon her.

"It might be closer to the truth than I want to believe, too," she replied. It was true that she didn't ask him about his work, but also true that he was loath to even hear Langdon's name on her lips. "We'd better go. Shakespeare's message was pretty…" she grimaced, "urgent."

Once in the car, 4 by Four turned to Chabal. "We have one stop to make. We're supposed to pick up Peppermint Patti from the Bowdoin library."

"Man oh man," she said, shaking her head, "that girl shouldn't be part of this."

"You're probably right, but it's not our decision to make. She's an adult."

Chabal snorted. "Yeah, right. She's just a kid."

"She knows how to do research. And Langdon likes her insight into the case. I think she might have a bit of a thing for him."

"Langdon is in the middle of a mid-life crisis at age 28, and that makes it okay to endanger her life?" Chabal asked, her tone sharper than intended.

"Okay, we'll suggest she doesn't come with us, but we can't not stop and talk to her," 4 by Four said, relenting slightly.

"I'm going to talk her out of it," Chabal said in a civil tone. Inside, she was raging, the thought of anyone else having a thing for Langdon now a dark cloud coloring her thoughts.

~ ~ ~ ~ ~

When 4 by Four, Chabal, and Peppermint Patti arrived at the loft, Langdon was waiting at the door. His eyes went immediately to Chabal's cheek, and then to her eyes, before his arms enveloped her in a mammoth hug that made the universe stop spinning for just a moment.

"What happened?" he asked, his lips pressed to her ear.

"A Mr. Shakespeare came by with a message for you, um, for all of us, now that I think about it."

Langdon gripped her tighter. What was he doing, he wondered, putting everybody dear to him in danger? "So spill it."

"I don't want to have to repeat it, and I think, no, I *know*, everybody needs to hear it," she said.

"I'll get the gang together," he replied.

The kids had discovered a toy box full of toys and games and were busy creating magic worlds in the living room area, so the adults gathered on couches to one side of the gaming area, Richam and Danny T. shooting a plastic puck back and forth on the air hockey table until Jewell confiscated it.

Langdon had already related the previous day's events to Lord and Nick. Nick couldn't understand what there was to discuss. He was an intelligent man, but his mind worked in a very linear fashion. It was clear to him that they just needed to track down this Shakespeare dude and kick the living shit out of him before dumping him hundreds of miles away like a nuisance raccoon. He was currently flipping a seven-inch Bowie knife into the air and catching it. Lord, more of a strategic thinker led by logic, was considering the potential paths leading forward, brute force aside, to ultimately determine which one was best. He sat in a walnut chair behind a desk fit for a novelist, scribbling hypothetical situations, as well their potential pitfalls and possible outcomes, in a notebook.

Jewell and Richam had settled together on a love seat, their hands clasped tightly together on her right knee. She was sipping tea, while he was working on a cup of coffee braced with Jack Daniels. The ringing in her ear had mostly subsided, and ice had finally brought the swelling in her jaw down enough so that she no longer looked like "the elephant woman," as she'd just observed to her husband.

Peppermint Patti and Chabal sat slightly apart from the others in two low armchairs, a design perfect for Chabal's short and petite frame, but a little tight for the much taller Peppermint Patti, forcing her knees about as high as her head. Chabal was trying to convince the college student that it was time for her little adventure to end, and that safety demanded she go back to Bowdoin and return to her studies. What would her parents think if anything were to happen to her? Peppermint Patti, who generally avoided conflict with a passion, was strangely sticking to her guns and refusing to go.

What she did not tell Chabal was that this was the first time she'd ever felt she belonged, and even though she'd just met them all—even the stunningly handsome man writing in a notebook at the desk— she was willing to risk it all to stay part of the group. She'd asked Chabal who the man was, and when introduced to Lord Langdon, she felt her emotions tipping towards this younger brother of the man she'd thought she liked. Chabal had caught the lingering looks, which made her more inclined to drop her efforts to get the girl to leave.

Bart stood morosely by a column, drinking his second beer of the day, even though it was only ten in the morning. This room held all the people in the world that Bart counted as friends, no, more like family. The only living relative he possibly had left was his dad, who'd been in the Navy. Some thirty-odd years earlier, just before leaving his posting at the Brunswick Naval Air Station, he had met Bart's mother at a bar and coupled with her, and here Bart was. Neither he nor his mother had ever tried to track down the gunnery sergeant, so the man didn't even know he had a son in Brunswick, Maine. All Bart knew aside from his rank was his dad's first name—Jonathan—and that was okay with him. Two years ago his mom had died of liver trouble. He would not be taking the lives of anybody in this room for granted, that was for sure.

4 by Four was shooting pool, taking his time with each shot, knocking the balls in with the steady precision of an expert. Right after they'd arrived, he'd slipped into the bathroom to smoke a joint, somehow thinking the others wouldn't smell it, his nerves frayed from everything going on. The pot had settled him, and his mind turned, not for the first time, to the legal implications that might pop up as they moved forward—or didn't—with the matter at hand. Danny T. was eating peanuts and watching him play, and Crazy Larry was busy playing pinball.

Once they were all gathered, Langdon stood up from his seat. He looked around with a warm feeling. These were his people. The conversation dropped away as all eyes found him. "First, thank you all for being here. I know that for some of us, there was no choice, but thank you anyway." He let that sink in for a moment. "We are all here because some guy who calls himself Shakespeare threatened Jewell, her kids, and my daughter, and then kicked me around. From there, he moved on to Chabal, this time delivering a warning with a knife. All, we can presume, to force me to stop investigating the death of Harold Dumphy."

"He hit her," Richam said.

"Sorry, what's that?" Langdon asked.

"The fop struck my wife. Twice."

Langdon nodded. "Shakespeare whacked Jewell in the side of the head and then punched her in the face." Nick made as if to stand, his face red with ire, but then settled back.

"This morning that very same man delivered a message to Chabal for all of us." Langdon looked around, again feeling guilty at all the lives he'd endangered, his eyes finally settling on Chabal.

Chabal stood up and slowly looked around the group, the cut on her face red and angry-looking. "I opened my door this morning to find that queer-looking man standing there. He put a knife to my face and asked me to bring a message to Langdon. He gave me an envelope with two plane tickets to Hawaii and suggested that Langdon and his daughter should be on their way today, or that there would be… repercussions." She had spoken almost hesitantly, but then her manner changed, and a defiant look flickered across her face. "But, I say, fuck him." Chabal was not known for cursing.

"Is that what your husband says?" Langdon asked.

"I haven't told my husband about any of this and don't plan to."

Jewell pressed the point. "How about your kids, Chabal? Are you willing to risk their lives for Harold Dumphy? And do you trust this bumbling fool to somehow keep you—hey, all of us—out of trouble?"

Chabal hung her head, and then looked around the room. "There's more," she said finally. "Shakespeare let slip something about there being what he called 'a few minor cracks' in the reactor, and how his employer didn't want to shut down the plant just because of that."

Nick gave a low whistle as they all pondered this statement.

"Jesus Christ," 4 by Four said. "You mean to say that just up the road, we have a potential nuclear disaster?"

"I only know what he said," Chabal replied. "And after he let it slip, I could tell he was looking at me," she shivered, "looking at me as if deciding whether or not he was going to kill me."

"That must be what Dumphy found," Bart said.

"And what he was killed for," Richam added.

"So, to answer your question," Chabal continued, turning to 4 by Four. "This isn't just about some security guard that got murdered, although that should be horrible enough. The really appalling piece, the part we can't walk away from, is the threat of a nuclear accident. We know that a wrong has been done, and that it has snowballed into a calamity involving lots of people, some of them bad but most of them innocents. You ask, Jewell, how I feel about putting my children at risk? I say that the risk is that they ever find out that I hid from the truth, and that when push came to shove, I folded up my tent and ran away."

"We've risked our lives for causes that we believed in," Richam defended his wife, stung by the implication. "Causes we were willing to die for, if necessary. And when our side won, we discovered that those ideals we held so dear were merely an empty bag of words with no meaning."

"So you choose to no longer fight for what you believe to be right?" Chabal asked.

"There is only one reality here, and that is some dude slugged my wife and put my children in danger."

"And you choose to protect your children by giving up?" This was certainly a new Chabal, her brush with death having brought out her more aggressive nature.

"Survival is the most important lesson," Richam replied.

"I'm sorry," Langdon interjected apologetically. "This whole thing is my fault. But the die is cast. It is time to either leave town or get nasty. I have to face this, but I can't ask any of you to stay." He looked around the room, his eyes finally settling back on Richam. "If you want to take Jewell and your children on a trip while I sort this out, nobody will blame you at all."

"First of all," Jewell spoke up, her words dripping with anger. "Don't you think that somebody had better ask the 'little woman' her thoughts before her man packs her off with the kids?"

Langdon's face reddened. "Sorry, I was presuming like the backwoods Mainer I am." He put his hands in the air, as if in surrender. "What do you want to do?"

"Well, I don't know what they teach you rednecks in Maine, but it's one of the great black myths that the man is in charge. Just like you white folks, us women let the man huff and puff and make a lot of noise, and then we make the decision for him." Richam started to interject, thought better of it, and suddenly became very interested in a bit of fluff stuck to his pants. "It was me that that bloke with a funny name hit, and it is me who will decide whether to stay or go." She looked around the room, challenging anybody to say anything, and more than one set of eyes looked away from her fierce gaze. "And I say that I am staying."

"We will stick." Richam nodded.

"Next time I pull the trigger first, and *then* ask the questions," Jewell said.

"Anybody else?" Langdon looked around, his eyes this time coming to rest on Danny T.

"I don't want any part of this," Danny T. said. "I mean, I have no idea what is even going on."

"Well, neither do I," Langdon admitted. "It all seems to have started with Dumphy's death, probably because of what Chabal just told us." He went on to summarize the facts, as they knew them. That there might be 'cracks' at the plant, suggesting safety concerns at the very least. "And then yesterday, right before the incident with Shakespeare, Danny T. gave me an important bit of information, that Shakespeare has visited the governor on at least one occasion."

"Harper Truman?" 4 by Four asked.

"The very same," Langdon replied. "Perhaps Governor Truman isn't as squeaky clean as he presents himself."

"Of course he's not," Bart growled. "He's a politician."

"Langdon asked me to do a bit of digging into Truman's background last night," Chabal said. "My neighbor is one of those dyed in the wool Birkenstock Democratic activist types, so I invited her for a glass of wine. Turns out she's known Truman for quite some time, almost since college days. Afterwards, I went on the computer and filled in some of the missing bits."

"Truman is a twit," Bart said.

Chabal glared at him for interrupting. "The governor was one of the original founders of the Flower First Party. After graduating from Maine Law, he opened up a practice in Madison, north of Skowhegan, with two other lawyers, Jordan Fitzpatrick and Jonathan Starling."

"Madison is a mill town, isn't it?" Richam asked.

"Yep. Paper mill."

"Tough place to found an environmental group," Langdon said. "Walking around with signs saying 'save the trees' in a town that depends on the money created by turning those trees into paper."

"So, how does that connect to Shakespeare?" Lord asked.

"I remember reading something about Flower First," 4 by Four said, and then his eyes widened and he jumped up. "Didn't they have some pretty aggressive tactics?"

"They sure did," Chabal said.

"Aggressive as in lawsuit aggressive?" Langdon asked.

"Nope. More like sugar in gasoline tanks, spiking trees, even shooting out tires on the big rigs, that sort of thing," 4 by Four said.

"Bingo," Chabal said. "Apparently, there was a small offshoot of Flower First that thought that the situation required more direct action given how quickly the loggers were moving. That group called itself 'Terror First, Flower Second'."

"Now I remember," Bart said. "Didn't some guy get killed?"

"Yeah, that's right," 4 by Four said. "Planted his own chainsaw right in his head."

"One of the things they did was spike trees," Chabal interjected. "Pound foot-long spikes made for pinning retaining walls together and such right into the trees. Then they'd reveal this to the public. Of course, the paper company couldn't tell which trees in the forest were spiked without close inspection. Terror First was sure the company would just avoid cutting that old growth swath. At first, it worked, but then the loggers got frustrated, or some didn't believe it, or the company put lots of pressure on the lumbermen who are, after all, independents and need to feed their families, too. One poor fellow found a spike with the blade of his saw, and it kicked back and buried itself in his skull."

"And Harper Truman was part of that? How did he ever get elected?"

"There was never any connection proven between Flower First, which he helped found, and this underground group. Only speculation. Plus, he had enough money to squash any rumors, I guess," Chabal said. "And they're still out there. You remember that incident in Rumford a few months ago? When vandals poured sugar in the gas tanks of the skidders and sand in the oil?" Chabal looked around the room. "It seems that the mainstream media is avoiding giving credit to radical environmental groups and just passing things off as boys will be boys. But my friend made me curious, so I did an Internet search. There was a letter to the editor of a weekly that I found in which Terror First claimed responsibility, in so many words."

"I do remember thinking that the perpetrators sounded more like 'the Monkey Wrench Gang' than kids," 4 by Four said.

"How about the sudden resignation of the man in charge of bringing the cargo port to Searsport?" Chabal asked, looking around the room. "Terror First."

The cargo port at Searsport Island had been a major source of controversy over the past year. The paper companies had been looking to develop a market for their excess wood, or scrub wood. The solution seemed to be to turn it into wood chips, which in turn could be formed into cheap chipboard. There was interest from potential customers in Europe and Japan, leaving only one difficulty to overcome: how to get the material there. Searsport Island, on Penobscot Bay just below Bar Harbor, had been chosen as the best site for the distribution facility. It was a beautiful and pristine island that was quintessential Maine. The paper companies were going to have to dredge the harbor so that the large ships could access the port. On top of that, the entire business of wood to chips was messy, and created pollution.

"I thought it was just the NIMBYs that stopped that?" Langdon asked.

"It's certainly more difficult to put a factory in the middle of land owned by wealthy and educated people," Chabal admitted. "But working in the background and inciting unrest was the Flower First organization, if not their more militant branch. I'm certain that if the paper companies had gone forward with the plan, we would have then seen more radical measures."

"And you found all this on the Internet?" Bart was skeptical. While he'd heard of this Internet thing, he'd never actually used it.

"Yep," Chabal replied. "Or, at least, what Sally, my neighbor, hadn't already told me."

"Okay, okay, I think we're getting away from the point here. The long story short is that Governor Harper Truman was one of the founding members of Flower First, which seems to have a more radical offshoot called Terror First. And these members are militant and prepared to use any tactics necessary to achieve their aims. Finally, Shakespeare was visiting with Truman just the other night," Langdon said.

"So, are we thinking that Harper Truman's two law partners have continued on as leaders of the Flower First or Terror First organization, while he reigns at the Blaine House in Augusta?" Peppermint Patti did not at first realize she'd said her thoughts aloud, and reddened when everybody looked at her. She'd been quiet so long, most of them had forgotten she was there.

"Exactly," Chabal replied, her eyes taking the measure of the girl sitting next to her. "But, it looks like they've probably gone underground to pursue their agenda."

"What do we know about the two, Jonathan Starling and Jordan Fitzpatrick, right?" Langdon asked.

"Not much," Chabal admitted. "It looks like Truman and Starling were in law school together, and when they graduated, went straight to the battlefront to wage war against the paper companies."

"What about Fitzpatrick?" Lord asked.

"He joined the practice later. I didn't find much of anything on him at all," Chabal said. "But, I can keep digging."

"So what?" Bart asked. "Governor Truman used to be an environmentalist. What does that have to with anything?"

"Don't you get it?" Richam asked. "Terror First is involved in some sort of vandalism at DownEast Power. Harold Dumphy discovers it and they kill him. More than likely, this man Shakespeare does the killing."

"And when the police investigation gets a bit too close, Governor Truman pulls some strings and forces Chief Lefebvre to close the case and call it a suicide," Jewell said, excited as the clues seemingly plunked into place.

"The chief was acting real strange when I talked to him," Bart said. "He was definitely hiding something."

"Shakespeare is part of an environmental group?" Langdon asked, the doubt evident in his words.

"Maybe just a hired gun. He don't seem like no tree hugger, not from what I've heard," Bart said. There was now a neat row of empty beer cans on the table next to him.

"He's got a real city boy attitude and dress," Langdon agreed. "And you don't learn how to be a thug overnight. I bet he's got a record."

"We seem to be missing one ingredient here." Peppermint Patti, emboldened by her last comment, stood and walked to the middle of the room as if giving an oral presentation in class. "Why would an environmental organization, no matter how extreme, vandalize a nuclear power plant? This makes no sense for two reasons. The first is, nuclear energy is a clean energy. It is certainly more earth-friendly than coal or oil. The second problem with this whole line of thought is that the worst possible thing that could happen to the environment would be a disaster such as Three Mile Island or Chernobyl."

"Weren't you having dinner with Abigail Austin-Peters last night?" Langdon asked, turning to 4 by Four.

"She's the lady who works for DownEast Power?" Lord asked.

"Yeah, their public relations director," Langdon said, looking back at 4 by Four.

"What?" 4 by Four asked. "We had dinner."

"What did you learn?"

4 by Four thought back to the previous evening and realized that the conversation had mostly centered on him, and that he'd learned very little about the mysterious lady or DownEast Power. "Not much." He'd thought for sure that she was going to come back to his place

for a nightcap, but at the last second she'd claimed to be tired and left on her own. 4 by Four had thought of little else than this alluring and totally sexy lady since, and had been making plans to see her again as soon as possible.

Langdon shook his head in disgust but couldn't blame the man, as his own meeting with the lady had provided little information and left him hopelessly drunk in the middle of the day to boot. "Okay, so let's move forward. The first step would be for me to check in with Janice Dumphy and make sure she wants to move forward with this. The catalyst behind the entire thing seems to be the death of her husband. If we can find out what happened to him, who did it, and why—we'll be a long way towards unraveling this mess. Who is Shakespeare working for, and who has ten grand plus plane tickets to Hawaii to throw around? The police investigation into the death of Dumphy was abruptly shut down, and Bart says that Chief Lefebvre is acting strange. Why?"

Chapter 12

It was decided that 4 by Four and Bart, who had lots of vacation time due him, would go to Madison and see what they could dig up on Flower First or Harper Truman's old law practice. Nick and Crazy Larry, the pilot who'd arrived with the twins, were tasked with finding the elusive Shakespeare and following him. Danny T. decided he wanted no part of it, and had asked to be dropped off at his apartment, besides he had to work that night, and he couldn't afford to lose his job. Jewell and Richam would stay at the loft, make some phone calls, and keep an eye on the kids. Chabal was deliberating on whether or not to ask her husband to pick up the kids from school and take them to his parents' home for the weekend, but still insisted that she go open the bookstore. If anybody discovered anything, they were to call her, and she'd pass messages along as necessary.

Peppermint Patti was left sitting on the couch. "What about me?" she asked, half afraid at the serious turn events had taken and half angry that she'd been overlooked, or worse, purposely left out. When Langdon didn't respond at once, her anger won out. "You're not leaving me out of this thing. I'm in it now, whether you like it or not. I'm not a child."

Langdon was taken aback, for he had no intention of leaving her out. He'd been mulling over a plan in his mind, and she was a crucial part of it, having skills no one else had. "You're going with me and Lord," he said.

"Oh, okay." Peppermint Patti looked sheepish. "Where exactly, and what will I be doing?" Inwardly, she was dancing a jig: one, she was included; and two, she would have a chance to talk to Lord. The man had a cool confidence that excited her.

"We'll turn you into a journalist," he replied. "Hold on, let me say goodbye to my daughter."

Missouri was in the playroom wearing a blanket wrapped around her waist as a skirt, and her shirt was now wrapped around her head like a turban. She wore nothing else. It made Langdon want to jump right in and play dress-up, but that was sort of what he was doing anyway, play-acting at a game for which he knew only some of the rules. He knew that he was in way over his head on this case, but his life had a way of careening out of control, events that started out as merely disturbing, but then snowballed to unstoppable—and usually unhappy—conclusions.

"Daddy, play with me," Missouri yelled. "You can be the prince and I'll be Snow White."

Before Langdon quite knew what had happened, his entire persona of hard-boiled private detective came tumbling down. He found himself with a blanket tied around his neck as a cape and a hair net on his head as a crown.

"Dance with me, my prince, dance with me," Missouri yelled, a child who lived life at full volume. Will had turned the radio on and the Rolling Stones were belting out "Jumping Jack Flash."

Tangerine and Will joined in, and the four of them cavorted and tumbled around the room in something that may have resembled dancing. Peppermint Patti stood watching the performance with a smile lifting the corners of her mouth. She had never met a man as crazy as this Goff Langdon.

Lord Langdon came up behind Peppermint Patti, close enough that she could feel his warm breath on her neck. "He's always been like that," he said. "You know, he raised me and Nick, alongside our mom of course, but he was a father to us, and not even when he was the most popular kid in the high school was he afraid to act like he is now."

Peppermint Patti could feel her legs trembling slightly, and she eased backwards as subtly as she could, until she was almost touching the man behind her. "It sounds like he was a big influence in your life."

"He is the most important person in both our lives. There is nothing we would not do for him. Nothing."

"So, tell me, who are you?"

Lord leaned forward the few inches separating them, his lips brushing her thick red hair. "Me and Nick? We just bop around."

"So, you're boppers?"

Lord chuckled, his hand coming to rest on her hip. "We enjoy life, it's who we are. We don't hold with the whole notion of a career, a home, a white picket fence, a wife, kids, and the whole concept of the American Dream that was created by some marketing company in New York City."

"That sounds fabulous. My life has been mapped out for me since I was four years old." Peppermint Patti leaned back into the muscular body behind her and suddenly felt dizzy, but protected, as she felt the warmth of his chest.

Missouri wasn't very happy when her dad stopped dancing and told her he had to go. She threw a tantrum and her tears tore at Langdon's frazzled nerves. His very first priority in life was his daughter. But how could he be a good father if he chose to run from the first conflict that threatened his family? While there were many facets to being a dad, wasn't one of the most important to be a role model? Life—and life's problems—needed to be attacked head on. Chabal came in and picked Missouri up, holding her tight, and mouthing the words 'be careful' to Langdon over her shoulder.

Langdon decided to leave Coffee Dog behind on this particular mission, as that would help console Missouri, plus, he wasn't sure what the day was going to hold. He had noticed Peppermint Patti and Lord having a conversation that seemed to require bodily contact, and this made him smile inwardly. While she'd momentarily crushed on Langdon, and he did appreciate her beauty, his younger brother was a much better fit for the Bowdoin student. He silently wished them the best.

Peppermint Patti tossed him the keys to her Jeep Cherokee in the parking lot and suggested he drive, as he knew where they were going. Richam had called in a favor from a friend who owned a motel and got them a couple of rooms under false names. The motel was on Pleasant Street, the busy road connecting Maine Street to the highway. The plan was to present Peppermint Patti as a journalist with *Time Magazine* doing an exposé on DownEast Power, all in an effort to see what they could stir up. They stopped by her dorm room so she could pick up more appropriate clothes before setting Lord up in a room across the way and on the second floor. He was to be her protector, for Peppermint Patti would be out in the open, shaking the trees to see what might fall out.

The rooms had been left open with the keys inside. Lord went to his room, while Langdon and Peppermint Patti went to her ground floor unit.

"Are you staying here, too?" she asked.

"I was planning on it."

She nodded. "Is it okay if I take this bed?"

"Sure. You can have the bureau, also. I don't have anything to put in it."

There were two keys in the small table between the beds with a note attached, saying that any friend of Richam's was a friend of Jack's, who must be the owner, and a cell phone number to call if they needed anything else. Langdon opened the small fridge, revealing a bottle of Chardonnay, which Langdon looked longingly at. It had now been two long days since he'd had a drink—which hadn't happened in the past six months.

Peppermint Patti lay down on the bed, arms spread wide. "This is a lot more comfortable than a dorm bed."

"Are you all set with what you have to do?"

"Sure," she said languidly, stretching her arms overhead, her breasts straining the tight t-shirt. "My name is Cassandra Greer. I work for *Time Magazine*, and my editor is John Lavoie."

Langdon had called an old college buddy who worked at *Time Magazine* who had agreed to provide a cover-story in case anybody checked up on Peppermint Patti. "Okay, so you know who you are, but what are you doing?"

Peppermint Patti got up from the bed and brushed past him to go to her bag of things they'd picked up earlier. She rummaged through, before pulling out a hairbrush, and began brushing her luxurious red hair back off her face as she walked back to the bed. "I have a list of names from DownEast Power, and I will try to get them to meet with me for the story I am doing on nuclear power." She set the brush down, rifled through the papers, and held up one, and then another. "And then I ask them these questions regarding safety protocols, emergency plans, and oversight."

"Why don't you get started while I go take care of a few other things? I should be back in a few hours."

"I'll be fine," she said. "What room is Lord staying in?"

"He's in room 24 keeping an eye on you. So if you need something, don't hesitate to call him. There's not a person I trust more in the world," Langdon said. The motel was in a U shape, with a swimming pool, now closed, in the middle. Lord Langdon was across the way on the second floor with a clear view of their room.

"He speaks highly of you," Peppermint Patti said, already working on the reason she would call Lord later.

"You two seemed cozy back at the loft," Langdon replied.

She blushed. "He is very handsome."

"You know that once this is all over, he and Nick will be gone before the dust clears, right?"

"Yep." Peppermint Patti did not say that she'd already decided to live for the moment, and not the future laid out before her, for the first time in her life.

"Okay, then." Langdon walked to the door, but hesitated, his hand on the knob.

"What?"

"There's something that's been bothering me."

"What's that?"

"It's what Shakespeare said to Chabal. He said that his boss was not going to have DownEast Power shut down due to some leaks at the plant."

"I think she said cracks," Peppermint Patti corrected him.

"Yeah, whatever, the point is we seem to be acting on the premise that Shakespeare works for Governor Truman. But why would Truman, if he truly is working for Flower First, want so desperately to keep the plant open that he would kill for it?"

"That's what I was saying back at the house," Peppermint Patti reminded him.

"Yeah, I didn't get a chance to follow up on it, but it has been nagging at me. So, the question is, who would want to keep the plant open?"

"Maybe the owners or the employees? Isn't it owned by the state?"

"No. Casco Bay Power owns it, and they are a public company," Langdon said. "I suppose it might be worth it to track down some of the board members, even take a crack at talking to the CEO. I had my chance the other night when we were at Goldilocks, and didn't even realize who he was."

"He isn't going to be killing people to keep it open, now is he? I mean, it's no skin off his nose," Peppermint Patti said.

"Don't these top executives often own quite a bit of stock in the company? I can only imagine that if DownEast Power were to be shut down, CBP stock would take a pretty huge hit. It would quite likely lead to replacing the top brass, and the buck doesn't go any higher than the CEO."

"What'd you say the name of the CEO was?" Peppermint Patti asked.

"Fellow by the name of Johnson T. Halperg."

"What else can you tell me about him?"

Langdon chuckled and then pursed his lips. "Nothing. That's what that Apple PowerBook thing of yours is for, isn't it?"

She cocked her head at Langdon. "Dude, you might not *be* that much older than me, but sometimes it seems like you were born, like, a hundred years ago," Peppermint Patti said. "But I still don't think some guy making a few million dollars a year is going to jeopardize all that by suddenly knocking off his own head of security."

"So you think rich people all get that way by being decent human beings?"

"I'm not saying that, I'm just thinking we take it one step at a time. First, we look into any connections between DownEast Power and Governor Truman, and then we can move on to the parent company."

"Okay, okay," Langdon said, his hands up in surrender. "You're the boss."

"Get the heck out of here, Langdon. I've got work to get started on and you're just distracting me."

"Bye to you, as well." He smiled and stepped over and squeezed her shoulder. Then he left after a last look taking it in—her eyes, round with flickering lashes, burning with all the life and passion of being twenty years old and out to right a wrong.

Langdon pulled the Jeep Cherokee out of the parking lot and accelerated into traffic. He felt fully alive, the case challenging his prowess as a detective, the heightened contact with Chabal arousing him in a way that hanging at the bookstore never had, and the warmth of having his friends and brothers rally around him in his time of need. Even if there were miscreants creeping around in the shadows, weren't they prepared for them? Peppermint Patti was the only one away from the security of the group at the loft, but Lord was guarding her. There was not a man in the world that he trusted more than the slightly elder twin. Of course, Chabal was at the bookstore, but nobody would dare attack her in such a public place, now, would they?

With this thought, he picked up Chabal's cell phone, much fancier than his own, which had been smashed the other day when he went over the snow bank. The left lane stopped suddenly for a car turning, and Langdon had to pound the accelerator and shoot into a gap in the right lane to avoid it. He dialed the number at the next red light.

"Yes?" Lord answered.

"What about hello?" Langdon asked flippantly. He was certainly feeling on top of the world, even if he was not yet sure what to do when he returned to the motel room later that night. Perhaps he should send Lord down to share the room with Peppermint Patti while he stayed upstairs? "You sound like an English butler, all stiff and formal. Lighten up, man."

"Goff, you're married, separated, have a child, being threatened by a dead author, and investigating a murder, and you tell me I'm too serious? I used to live in Colorado with my twin brother drinking beer every night and chasing girls, not a care in the world until you drop me into this shit. And you're telling me to lighten up?"

"Sorry, I just need to be sure you got eyes on Peppermint Patti, that you don't get distracted by, um, other things."

"I won't take my eyes off her," Lord replied.

"I bet you won't."

"I think we have a chemistry together."

"She's a fabulous young woman," Langdon said.

"Yes, she is."

"She shines when she talks about you."

"Is there a point to this?" Lord asked.

"Make sure you protect her."

"I've got it under control, but you can't be bugging me with needless phone calls." Lord hung up the phone.

As he drove, Langdon reflected on the pieces of this complicated pie. He felt like he was missing something, that he didn't yet understand what was really behind the murder, yes, but all the subsequent violence. What was the point? Perhaps it was the Casco Bay Power angle, the one Peppermint Patti thought they should put on the back burner. He dialed Danny T.'s number.

"Hello," he answered after seven rings. Langdon could imagine the consternation the timid man faced as he tried to decide whether to answer the phone or not.

"Danny T., Langdon here, can you do me a favor?"

"I don't think so."

"Of course you can."

"I don't much like being shot at."

"This is a piece of cake. All I want you to do is ask around a little about Johnson T. Halperg."

"Who is Johnson Halberg?"

"Halperg," Langdon corrected him. Like any good salesman, Langdon knew that the battle was half-won once the customer started asking questions. It didn't matter if it was selling books or ideas. "He's the CEO of Casco Bay Power."

"I suppose they're the ones who own DownEast Power?" Danny T. asked with a dejected tone, knowing full well he couldn't refuse Langdon.

"Controlling interest, anyway. See what you can find out about him, who his friends are, if he has any hobbies, and most importantly, does he have an alibi for the night Harold Dumphy was killed."

"Cut it out, Langdon," Danny T. whined. "I don't want any part of this case."

"You can't let them scare you, my man. You gotta keep going, or else they win and you lose."

"Who are 'they'?"

"The world, Danny T., the entire world."

"Okay." He surrendered. "I'll ask around and let you know what I find." He hung up abruptly, and Langdon stared at the phone. Was this a trend, people hanging up on him? He knew that Danny T. didn't swing in the same circles as Johnson Halperg, but he was tapped into everything that happened in the Brunswick area. Halperg might not frequent the diner or Cumberland Farms, but the nuclear plant workers and power company linesmen most certainly did. Danny T. was nothing if not persistent, a real dog with a bone once he was hooked.

Langdon pulled into an all-day spot right behind Matt & Dave's Video Venture. The police station was just about a hundred yards behind him, and this was his next destination. He thought it might be wise to call first.

"Brunswick Police Department. How can I help you?"

"Is Chief Lefebvre available?"

"Today is his day off. Can I help you with something?"

Langdon took a wild shot in the dark. "Tommy DePaola? Is that you?" Langdon barely knew the man and would never recognize his voice, but sometimes you had to just throw the line out and see what you caught. And after spilling the beans to Bart, it seemed a reasonable guess that Tommy DePaola had been demoted to desk duty.

"This is Corporal Tom DePaola." The voice was cautious.

"Tommy, this is Goff Langdon. I need you to do me a favor. I'm working the Harold Dumphy case and I really need to reach the chief."

"I'm sorry, Mr. Langdon," Tommy said, his tone suddenly wary, "but I'm not aware of any Dumphy case, not one that is open. Anyway, I don't think you'd want to be bothering the chief on his day off, even if I was stupid enough to give you his home number."

"Maybe you can talk to me, then."

"About?"

"Why you called a murder a suicide."

"I did no such thing."

"I know that you were ordered to do it, but you must realize that it's your name on the report. It's your ass that is going to be taking the heat, not if, but when this blows up. You know that shit rolls downhill, Tommy."

There was a long pregnant pause on the phone. "Okay, I get off in half-an-hour. I'll meet you."

"I'm right outside. I can wait."

"Are you crazy? If I'm seen with you, my career is over. Hell, I'll probably go to jail."

"Okay, okay. I'll meet you in the back corner of Hog Heaven. Are you hungry?"

~ ~ ~ ~ ~

Langdon couldn't remember the last time he had gone to Hog Heaven without purchasing a six-pack first, but this was the new Goff Langdon—upright business owner, wily private detective, and most importantly, father of a three-year-old girl currently in his care. The stakes of the game at hand seemed to be life and death, and a few drinks might mean a daughter forced to grow up without a father, or worse, forced to call some idiot golfer, "Dad."

Instead of buying beer, he went to the Jenny Station and bought some fat cigars. Not the healthiest choice, but better than beer, and safer than bullets. A few minutes later he pulled into the back corner of Hog Heaven and turned his lights on. A girl he didn't know took his order, and then he lit up a stogie.

Ten minutes later, Tommy DePaola slid into the passenger seat. "Dammit, Langdon, I thought I told you I couldn't be seen with you? Why don't you just sound a siren and put up neon lights, let the whole world know that we're having a private conversation?"

This took Langdon totally by surprise. What in heck had he done? Langdon puffed on his cigar, the lazy smoke drifting up into the sky. "What are you talking about?"

"You said the back corner of the lot," Tommy said. "This isn't even close."

"There were no spaces," Langdon said calmly. "Probably a lot of trysting going on back there. This is the best that I could do."

"Whatever. What do you want to know?" Tommy was fidgety and his eyes darted from side to side.

"Tell me about the... death... of Harold Dumphy," Langdon said.

"Murder. Just say it. You know it. I know it." Tommy was on edge, his eyes sunk in deep pouches as if he hadn't slept in weeks.

"Tell me about the murder, then."

Tommy stared intently at his feet. "That's what I'm trying to do, don't you understand? I want to work together on this. It ain't right. I can't sleep. I can't eat. All I can do is drink to erase the guilt. I can't take it anymore, you hear me?"

Chapter 13

Bart brought his cruiser home, changing it out for his Cadillac for the drive to Madison. The Cadillac wasn't much to look at, rusting away at the edges and then some—with more than one deep dent in its rusting bodywork. The vehicle was brown, but yellow paint streaked the driver's side door where Bart had had the misfortune of meeting a gruff young woman who had lost control of her car on an icy hill, sliding sideways into him, their eyes locking briefly before their cars did likewise.

The jarring impact had been much like the relationship that had followed, though that link had long since been severed. There was something sexual about their car crash, a heightening of sensation, a helpless dependence, a tingling of fear and excitement fed by that initial rush of adrenalin. It was this emotion that had sustained their affair for several months.

There was a taillight out, and the front bumper was mangled from being used as a braking system. But, the tires were all brand new, top quality, and inflated to the correct pressure. The car's interior was black leather, soft, and lustrous. He'd removed the seatbelts, as they only seemed to get in the way of his bulk. Bart had the seat all the way to the back and didn't feel in the slightest bit cramped, not how he felt in most cars.

The Caddy was his baby. It was his pride and joy. This was one of the few places that he felt comfortable, on the open road, his foot on the accelerator and his hand on the wheel. So as to not wear out the pleasure, he only took the automobile on longer road trips, and he didn't often leave town. Most of what he needed in life could be found in Brunswick. With a smile, Bart turned the engine over, and its throaty roar enveloped him like a warm blanket as he eased it out of the garage.

~ ~ ~ ~ ~

Crazy Larry donned a sheepskin coat over his shirtless chest, one that he'd found in the closet, the type of jacket a man from Montana might own. He selected this particular coat for two reasons, the first being warmth, but the second being that it hung down far enough to cover up the twin pistols he wore crisscrossed at his waist. He still wore his lizard skin cowboy boots. His jeans were caked with dust from Colorado, and a black skullcap, pulled tightly over his ears, now covered his head. He was busy checking his appearance in the mirror, turning this way and that, and reached his hand into his jacket to check access to the pistols.

"There's lipstick and eye liner in the bathroom if you want to put your face on before we leave," Nick said. He had been growing increasingly exasperated with the endless preparations of the man.

"I got to make sure I fit in with Mainers before I go out on the streets. It wouldn't do to stick out like a sore thumb when going undercover," Crazy Larry replied.

"If you took every villain from all the cheap western movies ever made and molded them together—that would be you," Nick said.

"Uncle Nick, save us from the bad man," Missouri shrieked, running into the loft's main space with Tangerine at her side, and Will in hot pursuit with a cap pistol.

Nick looked around, suddenly on high alert, scaring Will half to death with the intensity of his gaze before he realized the kids were just in the middle of a game. There was a strained silence until Nick eased the tension with a boyish grin, but not before Will had fled.

"You scared the bad man away," Missouri said. "Thank you, Uncle Nick."

"That's what I'm here for, honey. I'm here to protect you from the bad man. Now, you be a good girl until I come back."

Nick and Crazy Larry left the loft with a brief goodbye to Richam and Jewell, who appeared to be in the type of serious conversation had by spouses when their lives were suddenly upended and their family threatened. Nick smiled broadly on seeing the keys to the author's Hummer still hanging by the door. They took the elevator down and found the yellow tank-like vehicle in the back parking lot. Nick slid the rifles into the back, and settled comfortably into the driver's seat, starting it up with a roar.

"Oh, Shakespeare, come out, come out, wherever you are," he said softly as he eased out onto Maine Street.

~ ~ ~ ~ ~

"They're blackmailing the chief," Tommy said, wedging an onion ring into his mouth.

"What? Who?" The further Langdon got into this case, the zanier it seemed to become. If this had been a mystery novel, he wasn't even sure what category he'd slot it into on the shelves of his store. This sort of stuff did not happen in Brunswick. "Speak up, man."

"He wouldn't tell me," Tommy replied. He seemed relieved to be unburdening his secret. "Only that they had him by the balls, and they were going to hang him out to dry if I refused to go along with the suicide ruling. He'd lose his job, his family, maybe even go to jail. I think he's sleeping worse than I am."

"Who? What are the bastards blackmailing him with?"

"Something about having made a mistake and screwing the wrong woman."

Langdon rolled that over in his mind to see how it fit in with everything else. An affair wouldn't send the chief to jail, unless he had used his badge to force somebody into it. Having sex with his hair stylist, say, would certainly cause some difficulties with his wife and children, and would most likely get him fired or suspended, for Chief of Police was a position of public trust, after all.

"Who is he sleeping with?"

"He wouldn't say, Langdon. And I didn't press him. It's none of my damn business."

"Where is the chief right now, Tommy? Does he really have the day off?" If Langdon could find out who the blackmailer was, well then, he would most likely know the identity of the person responsible for Harold Dumphy's death, or at least be a step closer.

"Yeah, he took a personal day. He's at home. I talked to him right before you called me."

"Yeah? What about?"

"He just called to apologize for everything. Said he didn't mean to put me in that position and that he was sorry. Asked if I could forgive him. That sort of thing."

"He called to apologize?" Langdon asked, this thought troubling him. He seemed to remember that this was a response common in suicide scenarios.

"Yep. He said he was real sorry he had me lie, but I didn't have to anymore. He said I could come clean. Said it was too late for him, anyway."

"Where does the chief live?"

"Why?"

"Tell me where the chief lives and get out of the car, Tommy."

Ten seconds later, Langdon was screeching out of the parking lot. Men like Guyton Lefebvre only asked forgiveness when they had made up their mind that it was all over. Langdon had never particularly liked the chief. Lefebvre was a man who ran things by the book, making sure to dot all the i's and cross all the t's. He was a very conservative man who believed in authority and brandished that authority whenever he was able. For all of that, Langdon had always considered him a strong man with rigid discipline and a total inability to admit mistakes. Men like him didn't call up an underling begging for forgiveness unless they were in an absolutely desperate mental state.

Langdon gunned the Jeep across the back roads of Brunswick, cutting through a laundromat parking lot at a red light, the car ricocheting onto Pleasant Street between an oncoming oil truck and a minivan. Langdon spun the wheel like a captain of a ship in a hurricane. When he turned onto River Road, Langdon opened the Jeep up, swerving into the left lane and leaving several cars in his wake.

Tommy had told Langdon it was a gray Cape, three miles out on the left, but there were two of them, side by side. This never happened in any mystery Langdon ever read. As he was about to choose the wrong one, he caught a glimpse of the unmarked cruiser in the garage next door, and cranked the wheel back and into the correct driveway.

A faint wisp of smoke rose from the chimney, coming out dark against the white backdrop and turning light as the tendrils reached the coming of night. A look at his watch told Langdon it was only 3:51 in the afternoon, even though the sun was already low on the horizon. A bike with pink tassels and training wheels lay next to the car in the garage, a promise of warmer days. The curtains were drawn tightly shut except for those in the kitchen, which Langdon peered through, trying to grasp whether or not his concern had been warranted. He felt silly rushing into this serene setting, having risked life and limb to get here.

The unmistakable sound of a gunshot suddenly spoiled the peaceful afternoon, erasing all doubt from Langdon's mind. The single report had come from inside the house. Langdon put his shoulder down and charged the front door, only to trip over the stoop and go sprawling against the door, which swung open, suggesting it had not been locked, or even closed.

As he stood rubbing gently at his aching ribs, Langdon drew the pistol that Lord had given him earlier. It was a .357 Magnum, with a six-inch barrel, and had a nine-round magazine. At eleven inches long and weighing four and a half pounds, it was more a cannon than a handgun. Lord had called it a Desert Eagle, and Langdon had chosen that one from his brothers' collection for the name, now second-guessing his decision as he hoisted the heavy weapon out in front of his body with difficulty.

Langdon had carried a gun only once before in his life, back when he'd been hired to dissuade some deer poachers from encroaching on private property. On that occasion, he'd forgotten to load the gun. This time, Lord had made sure the magazine was full, that Langdon knew how to use it, and that he had an extra box of the heavy caliber cartridges in the glove compartment. Not that Langdon could hit anything smaller than a house if he tried, but he could pull the trigger and scare the bejesus out of someone.

He stood in a kitchen with shiny silver appliances and marble countertops. With the cannon held in front of him, he eased through the room and to the opening that led into the dining room, which also proved empty. He worked his way through the house, room by room, in this fashion.

It was too quiet in the house for there to be any danger, Langdon realized, as he peered through an open doorway into a study. Guyton Lefebvre lay behind his desk with most of the back of his head missing, or not missing, as the bone fragments and goo that comprised his noggin were splattered all over the wall behind him. Langdon paused, his body frozen, as his eyes tracked the scene in front of him. He'd always been good in a crisis, somehow managing to banish the panic, assessing the trouble, not bothered by fear, emotional dismay, or revulsion, which would come later.

It appeared that the man had stood up, placed the pistol in his mouth, and pulled the trigger. There was no doubt that the chief was dead. After discerning what little he could from the scene, Langdon stepped forward to check the man's pulse, just to be sure. He was dead.

There was a note on the desk, and Langdon quickly scanned through the long rambling coward's goodbye. He felt little compassion for a man who would leave his children without a father. He made no mention of why he'd killed himself, only a vague illusion to depression and overwhelming anxiety. It was only then that Langdon noticed the thin tendril of smoke rising from the wastebasket. There was a single piece of paper and the remnants of a photo in the metal bin. They had been set alight but appeared to have gone out before fully burning away to ash.

The sound of sirens split the quiet of the suicide situation. They were a long way off, but he knew in his bones that they were coming here. Somebody else must have heard and reported the gunshot, or maybe Tommy had gotten nervous and called the station with a warning. He probably should've stayed, but the thought of being held for questioning didn't appeal to him much. And there was even the possibility they would think he'd shot the man, and he'd lose the time it took to clear his name. Langdon scooped the burnt piece of paper from the trash and walked out the door, patting the embers out against his pants leg.

He climbed into the Jeep and drove in the opposite direction of the sirens. He'd been careful to leave no fingerprints, except maybe on the front stoop, but he doubted they'd dust there.

Langdon knew that it was possible that a neighbor might have taken down his license plate number as he was leaving the chief's house. If so, it was only a matter of time until they traced the Jeep to Peppermint Patti. He clearly had to ditch it, but where? He wondered about the Hannaford parking lot, or maybe the busy municipal lot in town, but finally decided on leaving it at a friend's home. The man and his wife were retired, snowbirds who went south every winter, but still had their long driveway off Greenwood plowed so that the property manager could check in on it.

He had to trudge a hundred yards through the snow to reach the railroad tracks that would lead him to just behind the motel where

Peppermint Patti and Lord had a room each. He was halfway to the motel when his phone rang.

He heard Richam's voice, the words curt. "The police are looking for you in connection to the murder of Guyton Lefebvre."

~ ~ ~ ~ ~

Peppermint Patti set the receiver back in the cradle and then stared at it for a full five minutes, trying to come to some sort of decision. She made sure the curtains were pulled, and then stripped down, examining herself in the hallway mirror before putting on the panties and bra she'd bought from Victoria Secret down in the mall in South Portland. They were a forest green lacy material with plenty of clear spaces exposing her flesh underneath, and she turned this way and that, liking how it brought out her hair and eyes, causing her to brush out her rich red hair until it shone. In the bathroom, she applied just a tiny dab of lipstick and a hint of perfume.

She hadn't had a chance to pack much in her dorm room, but luckily she had grabbed her white pants, not the straight-legged type favored by the bulimics in her school, but ones that flared and gave her curves instead of thickness. Her blouse was yellow and low cut with a stitched-white pattern around the V-neck. She spent twenty minutes in front of the mirror, and given the opportunity, would have changed her outfit ten times, but she had no other options.

With a deep breath, she went back to the phone, picked up the receiver, set it back down again and went back to the mirror, and then with a curse, back to the phone.

"Lord? Can you come down here? I think I might be onto something but best if I run it by you face to face. Great. See you in five."

It was an excruciating five minutes until the gentle tap came on the door, and she let Lord Langdon into her room.

"You look stunning," he said. "I mean, wow. Did you set up a meeting with somebody?"

"I've set up several interviews for tomorrow," Peppermint Patti replied. She took his coat and hung it in the closet. "But I think it's getting too late to make any more calls this afternoon." It was just past four, so she might have been fibbing slightly.

"What did you want to discuss?" Lord went to sit in the rolling chair at the desk, and then realized this was her workstation, and sat down on the bed instead.

Peppermint Patti sat down next to him, her thigh touching his, her hand on his knee. "Do you think I'm pretty?"

"I think you're beautiful," Lord said.

"Would you kiss me?" She had never been so bold in her life, but time was limited, and after all, this was the new Patti Smith, wasn't it?

"I would love to," he replied, his eyes never leaving her eyes. "But, you know when this is all over, I'm out of here?"

"Let's let tomorrow take care of tomorrow," Peppermint Patti said. She leaned her face forward, lips quivering, and he came the rest of the way. His lips were firm but soft, gentle but rough, and his tongue flicked with insistent caresses.

They sank back onto the bed, he rolling so that he was on top of her, kissing her neck, nibbling her ear, and she moaned low inside, grabbing the back of his head. Lord Langdon was an experienced and patient lover, just what she desired for her first time. Later, when they were done, she felt sated for the first time in her life, at peace with her own body and mind.

"Let me take you out to dinner?" Lord asked.

"It's a little late for that, don't you think?" Peppermint Patti giggled.

"I'm starving. There's a fabulous Italian place down the street, Scarlet Begonia's."

"I need to take a shower," Peppermint Patti said. "Give me an hour to get ready?"

He assented, going back to his room to keep watch and give her privacy.

~ ~ ~ ~ ~

The cops were looking for him? Langdon paused on the snowy train tracks and wracked his brain how the Jeep could have been connected to him so quickly. What was Richam talking about? Maybe somebody had seen him? "Did you say *murder* of Guyton Lefebvre?" Langdon asked as the wrongness of the words finally sank in. "Don't you mean suicide?" His heart had begun hammering in his chest, not from the exertion of the trek, nor the cold, pure air, but from the knowledge that he was surely being set up somehow.

"So you know he is dead?" Richam asked, wanting Langdon to confirm what he seemed to be insinuating.

"I heard the gunshot. I saw the body. It appeared very obvious that he put the pistol in his mouth and pulled the trigger."

"Why?"

"He was being blackmailed for having an affair," Langdon said. "That's all I know. How about you tell me something?"

"Bart heard it on his scanner. He said there was an anonymous tip that placed you in the house at the time of death, and a neighbor verified seeing you leave."

"Okay, now, that is truly creepy. I feel like whomever Shakespeare works for might be tapped into the police department. And all of that adds up to one powerful person capable of putting a whole lot of hurt on all of us. Be careful."

Langdon signed off and began walking again, and then broke into a trot. His speed certainly wasn't going to impress the Viking scouts, but it was all his battered body could handle. As he jogged, his brain returned to the ever more complex puzzle that was Dumphy's murder. Langdon felt like a puppet, a twitch of the puppeteer's hand sending him first one way and then another, enmeshing him deeper and deeper into what he did not know.

In the dark it took him a few moments to locate the back of the motel, and a minute to climb up the icy slope through the brush, but finally he reached the top, lying on the ground for a bit, gasping. There was a fire escape that led up to Lord's room and Langdon took this to avoid being spotted. He found himself staring in the bathroom window, which was locked, so he tapped on the glass, wondering why he hadn't just gone up the front way.

An icy rain began to pelt him, and he tapped on the glass louder. The enormous barrel of a big game rifle poked its way into the bathroom, followed by a wary Lord Langdon. When he saw his older brother, Lord shook his head, stepped forward and unlatched the window and pushed it open. Lord set down the rifle to help pull Langdon through the small opening.

"Hello, Goff," Lord said. "Funny place to run into you. Still coming through the servant's entrance, I see." This was a gentle prod at Langdon's wife, Amanda, and her extravagant lifestyle. She had grown up in a mansion in Atlanta that had a separate servants' entrance, and Langdon, uncouth backwoods hick that he was, had often felt that this was the more appropriate door for him. Lord and Nick had visited him there once, and had, in fact, spent most of their time in the servant's quarters playing poker and drinking beer, and having, Langdon was certain, a much better time. He had been stuck upstairs, perched delicately on antique furniture, sipping white wine, and making polite conversation on the plusses and minuses of the neighbor's new flower bed or his father-in-law's golf handicap.

"I finally found my place in life, Lord. I now know who I am, and I am a man who enters residences through bathroom windows."

"Well, from now on, I'll make sure to install doorbells on my bathroom windows so as to not keep you waiting."

"How are things here?"

"Quiet. Peppermint Patti hasn't left the room, and her only visitor so far has been the Domino's guy at a little after noon." Lord did not mention that he'd just come from her room.

Langdon had doubted that she'd have any immediate success meeting with people, but was surprised she hadn't taken any breaks all day to go for a walk at least and get some fresh air. Hopefully, her day had been fruitful, and she would be brimming with information to share, the type of intelligence that would clear Langdon, expose Shakespeare, and lead to the people behind Harold Dumphy's murder.

"How about you? Anything more exciting to your day than the Domino's delivery man?" Lord deflected the conversation back to his older brother.

Where to begin? Langdon gave him a brief rundown of the day's chaotic events. When he came to the chief's death, he struck his forehead with his palm, reached into his pocket, and pulled out the charred paper the chief had meant to destroy. He sat down at the desk and smoothed it out as Lord looked over his shoulder. It had writing on it and the remains of a picture still stapled to the front of it. The picture appeared to contain a man and a woman, naked, and in bed. The profile of Guyton Lefebvre could be discerned still, if smudged by soot, his head resting on a woman's bare stomach. One of her naked breasts rested on his head, but her other breast and face were gone, casualties of the fire.

"That's some solid evidence for you. Our suspect is now a one-breasted woman with no face. I want to be there for the police line-up," Lord said.

"Well, it is proof that the chief was being blackmailed to steer clear of the Dumphy case, anyway, even if we can't identify the mystery woman." He stared at the picture—something about the woman tickled his subconscious mind, even though her face was gone and the chief's head covered her midsection, leaving only the one breast as identification. "Don't laugh. I can't place her right now, but I think I know who this woman is."

Lord refrained from snickering only with great difficulty. Langdon shook his head. He hadn't seen a naked woman other than his wife in many a year, so it was unlikely that he truly knew the identity of that boob. He carefully pulled the picture from the note and smoothed it out.

ton Lefebvre,

would like to encourage you to drop the investigation of the death of Harold Dumphy. The photo I have enclosed of you with Mrs.

is just the tip of the evidence that I possess of your infidelities. I have many more pictures of a much more carnal nature that I am sure your wife would be disgusted by. The police would also be interested in why you were having an affair with a mur   suspect. For these reasons, I suggest that you close the case as a suicide and continue on with your life.

—Your friend L

"It figures that the name of the woman is missing," Lord said.

"We know that she is a married woman, at least."

"And I would guess that this burnt part here is saying she is a murder suspect," Lord said, touching the paper gently with his finger. "I don't imagine you have many murders in Brunswick."

"Not so many."

"So, the chief was sleeping with a woman, not his wife, who is a suspect or person of interest in a murder? Was he aware of this? Is it the Dumphy murder? Or some other murder?"

"I don't know," Langdon said. He pursed his lips, thinking how strange it was the lengths that men would go for sex, putting their marriages, careers, their very lives in danger, and all for a few minutes of physical pleasure. He understood the urges, because he, too, had them, but to risk everything just because a woman made his blood race? "It's funny how a good woman can make a bad man good, but a bad woman can destroy a good man with just a look, a smile, a touch."

"So, we have a picture of a woman's boob and the first initial of the blackmailer. That's more than we had five minutes ago."

"Did I mention that I'm wanted for the murder of Chief Guyton

Lefebvre?" Langdon asked his brother, realizing he hadn't quite finished sharing the details of his day.

"No, you seem to have overlooked that," Lord replied. "What was your motive? Or are you still working that out?"

"I don't know, but an anonymous caller gave my name and a neighbor gave a description that made the police think it was me."

"Why did you leave?"

"I was worried they'd detain me, and that I'd be letting everybody down sitting in jail, just when Shakespeare seems to be on a warpath."

"We're on top of things," Lord said. "They wouldn't have held you for more than a few hours if what you say is true about it being an obvious suicide."

"Yeah, I was more worried about your intentions with young Peppermint Patti than Shakespeare, to tell you the truth." Langdon looked at his younger brother, who was staring at his shoes. "What? Tell me you didn't?"

"I tried not to," Lord said. "She asked me to come down, and one thing led to another. Believe it or not, she was the... the insistent party."

"Aren't you supposed to be watching her room?" Langdon suddenly remembered the danger they were all in, especially the young woman from Texas masquerading as a journalist.

Lord hurried over to the window where there was a chair pulled up, a spot he'd spent the day in before visiting with Peppermint Patti, and again until interrupted by Langdon's arrival and lengthy recounting of the day's news. There was no movement in her room, and a faint glow seeped under the door and past the drawn curtain, suggesting an inner light on. A few doors down, a man and woman emerged from their room and went to their car.

"Pretty quiet," Lord said. "She was going to take a shower and then we were going to go out to dinner. I imagine she's about ready."

Langdon sat down on the bed next to his brother. "Be good to her. She's pretty innocent."

"She's quite something," Lord agreed. "I was straight up with her that I wouldn't be around long."

"Pretty, smart, and witty. Maybe you should stick around for a bit and see where it takes you?"

Lord snorted. "Yeah, I'm going to rent me an apartment in my hometown and date a college girl. You know better than that."

"Yeah, I guess that wouldn't be such a good fit, and besides, who'd keep Nicky out of trouble if you stayed?"

"Enough about me," Lord said. "What's the deal with you?"

"With me?"

"Isn't it time for you to move on?"

"What do I need to move on from?" Langdon asked, already knowing the answer, as it was an issue he'd been struggling with. He did seem to be floating in some sort of limbo, and maybe that drove the heavy drinking. The problem: he wasn't sure, as the old song said, "Should I stay or should I go?"

"What do you want, big brother?" Lord asked.

"I guess I'm not ready to give up on my marriage, not yet, not right now, anyways," Langdon replied.

The room was silent for a few minutes as both men thought about that simple sentence with all it implied.

Finally, Langdon stood and put his hand on Lord's shoulder, a silent thank you for talking with him. "Why don't you let me go talk to Peppermint Patti about what she found out today before the two of you go out. Give me twenty minutes?"

Chapter 14

The road flew away beneath them, the landscape sliding past in a blur as the Caddy ate up the pavement like some hungry beast on the prowl.

Bart and 4 by Four contemplated the empty beer cans in their hands—the last of the six-pack they'd bought in Topsham right before getting on the highway. It was only mid-morning, but the beers had gone down smoothly. Now they were dry, still several miles from their exit in Waterville. 4 by Four was silent, knowing that it was his misjudgment that had caused the shortage. Although he'd only had two of the six, it was not the first time he'd traveled with Bart. He should have known better and laid in more provisions.

The car hovered in the passing lane at a steady 95 miles per hour. The Caddy was such a smooth ride that 4 by Four would've guessed they were only doing 60, except for the ease with which they flew past other vehicles.

"So, what's the game plan, anyway?" Bart decided to let 4 by Four off the hook for his rookie mistake. "We go up to Madison and poke around, looking for what?"

"Aren't you supposed to be the cop? I'm along to keep you out of jail if you get in trouble, but you're the investigator."

"Does Flower First have an office up there? I think they moved their headquarters to Augusta, probably to be closer to the governor."

"All I know about the area is, a few years back I went up to Starks for the annual Hempstock celebration. I brought a tent, stood around a fire in the middle of the woods, got really stoned, and left in the morning."

"You can be a real knucklehead," Bart replied. He took the first Waterville exit, even though this was not the one they wanted, but beer was calling. "You want me to go in this time so you don't screw things up?"

Luckily, the first store was a drive-thru beer store, and Bart merely had to pull up to the window and order. "I'll take a twelve-pack of Lite, some ice, better throw in some chips, how about Salt and Vinegar, and do you have any donuts? No, okay, how about cigars? Yeah, best give me two boxes of those and a lighter."

By the time they reached Madison forty minutes later, they'd sunk a few more beers. They decided that their first move—after a good, long pee, of course—would be to stop at a phone booth and check the local phone book for a listing for Flower First, Jordan Fitzpatrick, or Jonathan Starling. There, of course, was no listing for Flower First, nor for Starling, but seven Fitzpatricks were listed, none of them with even a first initial J, though. They called them all anyway, getting through to four, but nobody knew a Jordan.

"What we need to do is find some old codger," Bart said. "Every town has one, some guy who doesn't have a penny to his name because he spends it all on booze in the local dive, but knows more local gossip than anybody in town."

"Should we check the phonebook under O for Old Codger?"

Bart stared at him with contempt. "Let's find the dive bar."

Madison had three drinking establishments. The first was not yet open for the day, the second was too fancy, but the third one was just right. It was called simply, "The Pines." This name was hand painted on a four-by-six-foot piece of plywood leaning up against the wall next to the entrance. The door was slightly ajar, but swung open with only a tiny screech. Bart stepped in and immediately moved to the left, habit pushing him away from the light of the doorway. Thus, it was 4 by Four that the seven or eight people inside saw when they looked up, his figure illuminated and a nervous grin flitting across his face as he blinked rapidly, trying to adapt his vision to the dark interior. Once he could see again, he sauntered over to the bar and ordered a couple of beers.

After a few minutes, Bart joined him, pulling up a barstool. "You got any menus?" he barked at the chubby bartender. She waved her hand behind her, a broad sweeping gesture that encompassed bottles of alcohol, coolers, and a faded chalkboard with barely discernible offerings. "Give me four bacon cheeseburgers and some fries. You want anything?" he asked 4 by Four, who shook his head no. "Better bring us a pitcher of beer," Bart added. "And while you're at it, buy everybody in here a shot of tequila."

When the bartender was safely out of earshot bringing the food order to the kitchen, 4 by Four leaned over to Bart. "You notice anything missing in here? Like teeth?"

"I believe the people here have chosen to fund their booze habits over a dental plan," Bart agreed.

One of the pool players approached them. He was fairly young, maybe twenty-five, and did have a full set of teeth, flashing a smile to prove it. "Either you guys want a game?"

At that moment, Bart's food arrived, and he raised an apologetic hand and gently pushed 4 by Four out of his seat to play pool.

"How about we play for five bucks a game?"

4 by Four nodded. He was, after all, quite good at pool.

"I'm Jere," the man said, holding out a scarred and powerful hand.

"Jimmy," 4 by Four replied, noting that the man squeezed a bit too tightly.

"Where you from, Jimmy?" Jere asked, chalking his cue.

"Brunswick."

Jere wasn't actually a very good pool player, but he was always happy to engage a stranger in a game, most of the locals knowing better than to play him for money, which either resulted in them losing money or being goaded into a fight. Either way, it was a lose-lose situation.

"Nice shot," 4 by Four complimented the man on a fairly easy cut shot. "You live here long?"

"Just since I was born," Jere joked with a wink, thinking this was a strange question. Nobody moved to Madison. You were either born here or you were just passing through. "Hey, Gail," Jere shouted as 4 by Four was about to shoot for the eight ball, causing him to miss. "Send over a couple of beers with JD chasers."

Jere then ended the game with an easy tap-in of the eight ball. "Hey, why don't you pay for the drinks and we'll call it even?" Jere said.

4 by Four glared at the man in irritation, the beers making him bold. "Why don't we play for ten bucks this game?"

The two rough-looking men sitting at the closest table hooted and slapped their table. "This guy is hustling your ass, Jere, you best look out."

"Sure. That's fine with me." Jere smiled and slammed down his shot of JD.

If 4 by Four had been sober, he would have noticed that the game had become the center of attention for the small crowd in the bar, and he probably would have been aware that those sitting close to the pool table had edged their chairs away. The alcohol may have diminished his perception, but it didn't adversely affect his pool skills, and he easily whipped the wannabe shark.

"How about double or nothing?" Jere asked.

"Nah, I'm good," 4 by Four replied.

"Come on, just one more game." Jere was not smiling now.

"No, I'm done, sorry."

"You're gonna take my money and then quit?"

This was the first inkling that the lawyer from Brunswick had that he'd misjudged Jere's nature. "Look, tell you what," 4 by Four said. "We'll call it even. You won the first game and I won the second."

"You think I need some kind of charity from some dickhead out-of-towner?" Jere had now moved up close, his face less than an inch from 4 by Four's, his body twitching in anticipation. "Let's play for a hundred. Right now."

This was either an elaborate hustle of some sort, and 4 by Four would be out a chunk of change, or a foolish challenge, and Jere would lose his money and the last of his patience. It was not the first time 4 by Four had been hit, and he prepared himself for the blow before speaking in reply. "No."

Jere pushed him with a forearm, a gentle nudge. "I think you're a pansy." He gave another shove, harder, more persistent. "I'm gonna shove this pool cue right up your ass." He grabbed 4 by Four by the collar.

4 by Four knocked his hand away with a slap and the room froze. "You shouldn't have done that," Jere snarled.

Even though 4 by Four was prepared for anything, the swiftness with which Jere threw his first punch took him by surprise. But somehow the blow never arrived. Where his assailant had been, there was now only an empty space.

"Let me go," Jere's piteous voice came from across the room where Bart had him pinned to the wall with one beefy hand wrapped around the man's throat.

"I'll let you go when you settle down," Bart said.

"Go fuck yourself," Jere said.

Bart let him go, and Jere immediately swung a wide roundhouse blow at the gruff cop who ducked—then knocked him out cold.

The bartender, who'd shown little interest in them up until this point, filled a pitcher of beer and waved to Bart with a wide smile on her heavy face. "On the house," she said. "I've been waiting a long time for somebody to give Jere the business."

"Thanks," Bart replied, with what almost passed for a smile crossing his face. "I appreciate that." He took the pitcher, grabbed three glasses, and motioned for 4 by Four to follow him to a corner table. He whispered, or what passed for a Bart whisper, "I think I found our old coot." While the lawyer had played pool, the cop had surveyed the room and zeroed in on what he took to be an elderly man sitting in the shadows.

"Jonathan Starling, I would like you to meet my partner, 4 by Four."

4 by Four was struck dumb. Even full of beer and confused by what had just happened, the name Starling registered with him. This was one of the original founders of the Flower First group, along with Governor Harper Truman and Jordan Fitzpatrick.

But, while Truman had gone on to become governor, this man had definitely taken a different path. It had been many days since his face had seen a razor, the bristles on his face splattered with tobacco juice and saliva, while yellow phlegm hung from the corners of his mouth. His black hair was streaked with gray and cut short, most likely by his own shaky hands if the shaggy ends were any indication. The man was thin, frail, and beaten. He was dressed in a large green army surplus jacket, which hung from his body like an empty tent. Every once in a while he coughed, a hacking expulsion of spittle from somewhere deep in his body. With every shot poured from the Jack Daniels bottle Bart had purchased for him already, Starling's eyes flared brightly, a hint of the man he'd once been. The brightness was like a shooting star, gone before you were sure you'd even seen it.

"Mr. Starling used to be a lawyer here in Madison," Bart said delicately, easing the old man into his story without giving away the fact that Starling's past associates were what had brought them to town in the first place.

"Is that right, Mr. Starling?" 4 by Four asked. "I'm a lawyer as well. Do you still practice?"

"Of course not, you son-of-a-bitch," Starling retorted. "Look at me. I'm a drunk and a bum, but I'll still kick the shit out of you if you try to patronize me like I'm a fucking idiot."

4 by Four flushed. This was just not his day. He thought about an angry reply, but realized it was hard to insult a man who beat you to the punch in insulting himself. "My mistake, Mr. Starling. What kind of law did you practice?"

"I was just telling your friend, the jolly green giant, that I used to be an environmental lawyer." Jonathan Starling had that keen ability common to bitter old men of being able to insult at least one person with every sentence uttered. "As a matter of fact, Governor Truman and I had a practice together." He poured another shot and downed it, whether to refresh his memories or chase away demons, it was tough to tell. "Go ahead, ask anybody in here, they'll tell you. Truman, Starling, & Fitzpatrick Law Associates, just up and around the corner from here." He looked up into the shadows, seeing a distant past. "Right out of law school, we were full of piss and vinegar, wanting to make a difference, a *real* difference, not the false bullshit that so many others claim. We were going to shake up the system and kick some ass."

4 by Four was not sure what it was that gave it away, but he suddenly realized in horror that this man probably wasn't much over forty years old. He would've guessed well over sixty, his body so gnarled and twisted by alcohol and bad living. "What happened?" he asked.

"Ya know, I could probably use something to eat, sop up this whiskey. You fellows feel like treating me to a meal?"

"Whatever you want," 4 by Four said. "Tell me what you want and I'll go put the order in."

"Not here, Mr. Eager-Beaver. Even an old drunk like me wouldn't eat the slop this place serves. Riverside across the street has some pretty good barbecued ribs. And the fajitas appetizer with hot sauce will knock you right out of your socks."

Bart grinned. "Sounds good to me. I'm somehow hungry again. Let's leave this shit-box and go get some real grub."

"Riverside it is," 4 by Four said, feeling his own belly rumbling a warning of low fuel.

Jere still hadn't moved as they went to leave. Nobody seemed to pay him any mind, the bartender going on about her business, and other customers walking around him where he had fallen. It was almost as if he were just another piece of furniture. Bart walked over, checked his pulse. The man was alive, probably out from all the booze he had consumed as much as the blow. In a little bit, he'd come to and slink out the door. For a few days, he'd keep his head low, but then he would resume his bullying, and life would continue as normal.

The bartender gave Bart a big wink and blew him a kiss. Outside, daylight—cold and piercing—met them with an awkward embrace. It was as if they'd traveled down into Hades and returned with one of the lost souls—an action that was certain to have repercussions from the gods.

Chapter 15

Chabal stood behind the counter of the bookstore, tapping her green nails against the hardwood surface. Thelonius Monk wafted from the speakers on the walls. A gray-haired lady had been slowly wandering the aisles for the past hour. Chabal mused that the woman could have read an entire book in the time it took her to pick one, but maybe she found her enjoyment in the looking. Life seemed to work like that, Chabal mused. True appreciation was more often found in the striving for than in the actual having. Which led, somehow, to more musing on her marriage, which had begun to worry at her at odd moments, often here, in Langdon's presence, or surrounded at least by his personality as communicated by his bookstore.

Chabal's husband was an accountant down in Portland, good with numbers, gentle of manner, and sensitive to her needs, wants, and desires. He cooked two nights a week, helped with the kids when he was home, was a thoughtful lover, provided a comfortable income and a nice vacation every year, and frankly, she couldn't be more bored with her life. At some point, she had come to work for Langdon in the bookstore, and she had fallen in love. She was not sure why or how, merely that she had.

Getting Langdon to take out the trash required at least four reminders. He often showed up to work unshaven and uncombed. He was currently living in a trashy apartment and drinking too much. His diet was abysmal. But the man had charisma. He exercised, was attractive in an unflashy way, and certainly added an element of excitement to her life. She had never felt so comfortable talking to another person, for it was almost as if they had one mind they shared. Of course, Chabal was perfectly content with her crush from afar, enjoying her desire without having to act upon it. She was a mom and wife with three kids and a nice husband, and her family wasn't something she had any intention of walking away from. Except, of course, that these particular thoughts were not going away, and she sometimes felt like she was holding her breath, waiting for something to happen.

There wasn't much to do in the store that day. Chabal had cleaned, made displays, and completed her busy work. Customers had been sporadic, but what she was truly hoping for was the phone to ring with an update from the others, some juicy piece of info. She resented being left behind while the men roamed the state in search of information. To make it worse, that new college girl, Peppermint Patti, had just appeared in their midst. Did Langdon actually have a *thing* for her? Chabal wondered.

"Can I help you, ma'am?" she asked the elderly lady for the third time, knowing there was no need to rush her, but too bored not to.

Chabal had always been feisty, perhaps the result of having four older brothers, all jocks, football players and wrestlers who liked to fight and didn't cut her much of a break just because she was a girl, and tiny at that. She was eleven when she'd first fought back, dashing her mother's hopes that there would be at least one civilized being in her family. Eleven-year-old Chabal had charged across the top of the dinner table and tackled her older brother—inadvertently sticking a fork into his cheek—leaving him writhing and screaming on the floor, while Chabal had gone back and calmly finished her meal. A true tomboy, Chabal had smashed her mother's plans for dress shopping and tea parties, a teen who would rather watch *Die Hard* than chick flicks.

The older woman finally came to the counter with an Agatha Christie novel, carefully counting out the correct change and taking her leave just as the phone rang.

"The Coffee Dog Bookstore. How may I help you?"

"Chabal? It's Richam."

"What's happening?" she asked, perhaps a bit too forcefully.

"Easy there, girl, remember I'm stuck behind same as you."

"I'm going crazy here," Chabal replied.

"You're the command center," Richam said soothingly. "Everybody is depending on you for information, and I do have something for you. Langdon has become a person of suspicion in the death of Chief Guyton Lefebvre."

"What? The chief is dead? What's Langdon got to do with it?"

"He told me that he went out to the chief's house and found him dead. He said it was obviously a suicide, but somebody reported Langdon at the scene of the crime."

"Can't he just go in and clear his name?"

"He thought it would take too long. He also thinks that the license plate from the Jeep might have been spotted, and that Shakespeare has connections inside the police department, which makes him even more dangerous if he has access to their resources."

"How are the kids holding up?"

"Will has been a bit quiet since the run-in with Shakespeare yesterday, but Missouri and Tangerine are having a blast. This place was made for them. We're going to have a kickball game in a little bit." Richam sighed. "But, I don't know what to say to Will. I had to face things like that at his age, but I hoped that he never would."

"Can you see the bookshop from the window?" she asked, thinking that she could wave to them when she left in a little bit to go home.

"Yeah. I can see your building from here," he replied. "As a matter of fact, I'm looking at your storefront right now." Even though it was dark, the lights on the building and the streetlights illuminated the Coffee Dog's entrance. "What's more, I think you're about to have visitors."

"What's that?" The cold fear from Shakespeare's morning visit gripped her throat.

"The police. Two cruisers just pulled up out front and four officers are approaching the store. Call me back when they're gone." He read her a number and made her repeat it twice. "Don't write it down. Let me know what happens."

Chabal stared at the phone in relief, for the police were certainly better than a visit from Shakespeare.

~ ~ ~ ~ ~

Langdon climbed back out of Lord's small bathroom window and onto the fire escape, scraping his back in the process. When he reached the bottom tier of the steps, he heard voices and froze. He'd been about to drop down to the ground, but instead he flattened his back against the building.

Three boys came around the corner of the motel. They were about sixteen, local hoodlums taking turns slugging liquor from a bottle in a brown paper bag. They stopped just below him and stood, telling stories laced liberally with the F-word. The idea of dropping down from the fire escape into the middle of their clandestine drinking crossed Langdon's mind. He doubted they wanted it known where and what they were doing any more than he did. Better, he decided, just to wait them out. The alcohol couldn't last forever and the cold was a real and hard thing.

While he waited, Langdon let his mind drift over the case. It was clear that the chief had been blackmailed. Who was the woman in the picture with him? Why was Abigail Austin-Peters behaving so strangely, as if covering something up? Whatever Harold Dumphy had found must be the catalyst that started this whole train wreck in motion, so what did he find? Who was Shakespeare working for—that nugget of info might be the key to the whole thing.

As his mind mulled over just how many people seemed to be intent on thwarting them, his unease grew, sending a shiver down his spine. This wasn't simply taking pictures of Mr. Smith having an affair with Mrs. Jones, or catching Johnny dipping his fingers into the cash register at Cumbies convenience store. It seemed to go far beyond a simple murder investigation: this was possibly a conspiracy endangering the lives of thousands and involving a nuclear power plant, the chief of police, and possibly the governor of the state. This was the big leagues.

If there were problems at DownEast Power, who would benefit most from the plant staying open? The answer seemed obvious. Casco Bay Power. Langdon made a mental note to check in and see what Danny T. might have found out, as he'd been tasked with asking around about the chief executive officer, Johnson Halperg. He should probably push Peppermint Patti to search for him on the Internet as well, for Danny T. didn't even own a computer, his research done on the streets and not on the 'net.

Who else would benefit from keeping DownEast Power open? Or, to rephrase the question, who would be hurt most if the power plant closed? The people who lived in the town of Woolington, where the plant was located, would certainly be affected. For years since the 1960s, the population of Woolington had been paying next-to-nothing in property taxes as the plant's tax payments took up the slack. So, who were the larger landowners?

Several farmers would probably be put out of business if they suddenly had to start paying taxes on their huge tracts of land—but it didn't seem likely that a farmer had hired Shakespeare. The one other possibility was the ski complex, Mount Chamberlain, which spread across a large portion of Woolington. Langdon thought back to the night at Goldilocks a few days earlier when he'd caught a strange vibe and gone over to speak with Ellsworth Limington. The man owned Mount Chamberlain, as well as several hotels, restaurants, and other real estate in town. The closing of the nuclear plant would be financially devastating to him. Maybe that was what his meeting with Halperg at the bar was about. Again, Langdon kicked himself for not recognizing at the time that the 'John' he was introduced to was actually the CEO of Casco Bay Power.

Langdon was startled from his reverie by breaking glass. The boys had finished their bottle, smashed it on a rock, and were moving on with increased warmth against the cold evening and fresh bravado against a harsh world. With cold and aching muscles, Langdon dropped to the ground. He worked his way around back, thinking now of this young woman, Peppermint Patti. Her innocence reminded him of happier times before the disintegration of his marriage and subsequent absence of his daughter.

Langdon took a deep breath, and having had enough of bathroom windows, stepped to the door of her room and knocked. He had a key of course, but he figured the polite thing was to give warning he was there. When she didn't answer, he inserted the key and swung the door open. Peppermint Patti lay on the bed, at first glance naked until he saw the hotel bathrobe gaping open. Her body was posed awkwardly, with a stillness that proclaimed she was dead, as did the telephone cord wrapped around her neck and the blueness of her face. He opened his mouth as if to speak, realizing that he had no words, his head swirling with sudden and intense pain, grief, and anger at the wanton destruction of this vibrant young woman. His feet carried him mechanically into the room.

Blackness swirled around Langdon, the floor tilted and he leaned forward, clasping his knees, forcing himself to take a deep breath. After several gulps of air, his mind began to shut out the shock. He stepped over to Peppermint Patti, laying his fingers on her throat, and then her wrist, feeling nothing but a coldness that was just now beginning to invade her body. She hadn't been dead for long, and with horror, he realized that she was quite possibly being killed as he had sat in Lord's room.

Peppermint Patti's legs were twisted like a pretzel, and he was unsure if she had been molested before her death. Around her neck and spotting her bare breasts were red marks that would soon turn to mottled yellow and purple bruises, indicating a struggle. Her red hair billowed out behind her on the white sheets. A bit of dried blood dotted her chin from a cut lip, and there was also clotted blood in her nose. Her eyes were open and bulging, staring at Langdon in accusation and betrayal. She was just a kid, and he had gone and dragged her into this violent maelstrom.

Langdon pulled the sheet up and over her body. He noticed for the first time the eyeliner and lipstick, and the faint scent of perfume. And then he banished the image from his mind, for others depended upon him for their safety, so he needed to move, gather what evidence he could, then get the hell out of there. There were some papers scattered on the floor and Langdon picked them up without looking at them, sliding them into the leather bag Peppermint Patti had brought with her. The table lamp lay broken on the floor, and a damp towel lay by the bathroom door.

In the bathroom, he found a tape recorder still recording. It was wrapped in a towel, presumably to keep it dry while Peppermint Patti spoke into it. Langdon could picture the scene, the young lady with a towel wrapped around her body, another coiled around her hair, applying makeup and scent to her body to prepare for dinner out with a man she'd just made love to.

Langdon hit the rewind button. Peppermint Patti's clothes hung from the back of the door. The tape clicked as it reached the beginning, and he pushed the play button. Peppermint Patti's voice filled the motel bathroom. "May I speak with Ms. Austin-Peters, please?" Langdon hit the fast-forward, the recorder whirring in the deathly silence. "What I don't understand is how..." He hit fast forward again. Peppermint Patti had recorded her phone calls, and while this content could be invaluable, he wanted to reach the time when the murder had occurred. Finally, after several more attempts, the summary tone of voice of Peppermint Patti caused him to pause and listen.

"What we have so far is, one, Abigail Austin-Peters has agreed to meet with me privately tomorrow at noon for an off-the-record interview." Her voice had a buoyant and joyous tone. "Two, the press secretary for Governor Truman said he was unavailable until the middle of next week, and three…" the sound of a knock on the door could be heard in the background.

With a chill, Langdon was transported to the savage events of what appeared to have happened just minutes earlier, seeing in his mind's eye the events as they unfolded, present as a witness, but unable to help in any way.

After he had finished vomiting in the toilet, he looked up and saw that the screen to the bathroom window was gone. The killer had entered and left the room the same way as Langdon had entered Lord's room, perhaps at exactly the same time. If he'd only not sat talking to Lord in the other motel room for so long, or if those teenage boys hadn't come along, maybe, just maybe, he could have saved Peppermint Patti's life. Or been killed himself, he thought grimly, but either one would have been better than the anguish ripping at him right now, for what had happened was his fault.

He was sitting on the floor next to the toilet, his back against the tub, breathing raggedly. He made himself review what he'd just heard. On the tape there were two men who'd called each other Elwood and Stanley. They had been sent to scare Peppermint Patti, nothing more, but when they came upon her fresh from the shower, libido had taken over, a sick combination of perversion and power gripping them. Attempting to rape her, they had killed her. They may have been the authors of the murder, but Shakespeare was, he suspected, the one who had set this particular chain of events in motion. Several times they had referred to the boss, the last time in fear when they realized they'd inadvertently killed the young woman they were just supposed to put a scare into.

Langdon's cell phone rang, startling him, and he pulled it from his belt, muttering a silent hello into the device. The reply was hurried. "The police are out front with the night manager," Lord said into his ear. "You'd better get out of there."

A sharp knock at the door drove this message home.

"Police." The loud voice jolted Langdon back to the present.

Langdon rose and went into the bedroom and grabbed Peppermint Patti's bag with the notes from the day, shoving the tape recorder in it as well. He was climbing through the window when the door opened and he sprawled forward into the accumulated snow, which muffled his exit. There was no pursuit, the two officers gaping at the dead body, one of them stepping to the bathroom window to see Langdon disappearing into the shadows. He'd been seen leaving the murder scene and his fingerprints were all over the room.

Langdon guessed that he looked pretty guilty. He wasn't sure why he had run. But run he did, for the second time that day.

Chapter 16

After Richam had alerted her to the police paying her a visit, she'd hung up the phone and waited, relieved that it was the police dropping in unexpectedly and not that creep, Shakespeare. She'd puttered about, straightening spines and tidying shelves, wondering what the heck was taking so long. Finally, two patrolmen walked through the door.

"Hi Gary. Max. Looking for a mystery?" Chabal smiled gamely at them, knowing both men fairly well.

"We're here on business, Chabal." Gary Stout was a young man, new to the force, fresh out of the academy. He'd grown up in Brunswick, where he'd been a star athlete at the high school, always well-mannered, and at the moment, uncomfortable with the task at hand.

"Is Goff around?" Max asked with a little less sensitivity. He was a veteran of twenty-five years and carried the extra fifty pounds around his middle to prove it. Not the sharpest knife in the drawer, he'd hung on to his position because he knew too many people—and their peccadilloes—and outlasted anyone who might have fired him. At the moment, unfortunately, his seniority placed him in charge of the questioning.

"No, I haven't seen him all day. What do you want with him?" Chabal replied to Gary, ignoring Max.

"It's serious," Gary said, looking down at his feet.

"He's wanted for murder," Max said, afraid that the rookie would steal his thunder.

"He didn't kill the chief," Chabal blurted out.

"You heard the chief was killed, huh?" Max asked, a knowing look in his eyes.

"Langdon is wanted for questioning in the death of the chief," Gary added.

"But he's also wanted for the murder of Patricia Smith," Max said sharply.

"Patricia Smith?" There seemed to be a whole lot of bodies dropping all of a sudden, but who in heck was Patricia Smith?

"Her body was discovered earlier in a motel room, and Langdon was spotted going out the back window and running into the woods," Max said in a clipped voice, giving out more information than he should, but pleased to show off.

"Peppermint Patti," Chabal said dully, as the name clicked into place for her.

"I know this is difficult for you, Chabal," Officer Gary Stout said. "But we're gonna have to bring Langdon in for questioning, if only just to clear his name."

"Looked like some kinky sex game gone awry," Patrolman Max Schilling sputtered. "Her all naked on the bed and…"

Chabal stared blankly at the two men, still in shock. "How did she die?" she asked, noting in some distant recess of her brain that a customer had entered the store and was walking slowly through the shelves.

"She was strangled with a telephone cord," Schilling replied.

"She was naked?"

"Yes," Stout said. "Well, sort of. Had on a skimpy bathrobe."

"What was her relationship with Langdon?" Schilling asked.

"Relationship?" Chabal repeated, tears welling up in her eyes.

"Ya know," Schilling said with a sleazy grin. "Were they doing the nasty?"

Stout glared at his partner. "Did they know each other intimately?"

"Peppermint Patti was doing some research for Langdon on a

case." Schilling's blunt crudeness shocked Chabal into being careful in what she said.

"What case?"

"I only work here in the bookstore. He doesn't generally gossip with me about his cases."

"So, you don't know why they were in a motel room on Pleasant Street?"

"No."

Schilling smirked. "It looks to me like the case he had was a case of the hots for her, is what it looked like to me."

The customer came to the counter with two books as another person came through the door. The man looked sideways at the two officers. "Is this a bad time?"

"We were just leaving," Officer Stout said. "Mrs. Daniels, perhaps you could come down to the station when you have the opportunity?"

Chabal nodded her assent as she mechanically rang up the sale of the books. The man followed the two policemen out the door just as the phone rang. "The Coffee Dog Bookstore. How may I help you?"

"Chabal? Is that you?" Jimmy 4 by Four said too loudly into the phone.

Still rattled by the officers' insinuations, she didn't notice the slur to his tone or the increased pitch. "Peppermint Patti is dead." The words came out in a rush, and she felt suddenly nauseous.

"*What?*" 4 by Four ask incredulously.

"Peppermint Patti is dead."

"Shit."

"The police were just here."

"What happened?"

"Someone strangled her with a phone cord. She was naked, sort of."

"Have you talked to Langdon?"

"They said he was in the room with her and fled when they arrived."

"Why would he run?"

"Probably because the police are already looking for him after Chief Lefebvre was shot this morning."

"Yeah, I almost forgot about that." 4 by Four was wishing he'd drunk less, his euphoria at their success in finding Jonathan Starling now dashed.

A lady came to the counter carrying a book. "Where are you?" Chabal asked, raising one finger to the woman that she'd be right with her.

"We're on our way back from Madison. We just passed through Augusta."

"Richam and Jewell are at the loft with the kids. Call this number," Chabal said, rattling off the seven digits. "I'll meet you there. It's almost closing time."

"We brought somebody with us," 4 by Four said.

"I have to go," Chabal replied. She hung up the phone and looked at the woman at the counter. Her eyes first went to the Michael Malone book she held, *Handling Sin*, a rare departure of the store from the mystery genre which Langdon stocked simply because he had greatly enjoyed the novel. She looked up and realized with a start that it was Amanda, Langdon's wife.

"Hello, Chabal."

She had changed in the past six months. She was not the Amanda that Chabal remembered. Her eyes, having lost some of their youthful innocence, were wiser, harder. Her hair had changed from a sandy blonde to jet-black, cut short, with bangs tumbling over her eyes. A beautiful silk scarf of pastel colors was wrapped over her hair and tied below her chin, and even though it was dark outside, designer sunglasses adorned her face.

"Chabal? Hello?"

"Amanda," Chabal replied. "I'm sorry, my head is elsewhere. How are you?" Inside, her words were not so calm, as she wondered what the fuck this woman was doing, showing up here, swooping back in, most likely thinking she'd pick up Langdon's broken pieces and take them back to her lair for repair.

"Better than last week," Amanda replied. "I got a mysterious message from Jimmy 4 by Four that I should come get my daughter, but I haven't been able to get a hold of him or Langdon. Do you know where they are?"

"Missouri?"

"Do I have another child?"

"She's with Richam and Jewell right now, I think."

"I stopped by their house but they weren't there. The living room was all stove up like a tree fell on the house, very strange."

Chabal thought of Danny T. driving the car into the living room and all that had happened since.

"What's going on, Chabal?" Amanda had been doing a good job staying cool and collected, but she was beginning to feel an inward tide of rising panic. "Where is my daughter? And my husband?"

"Missouri is fine," Chabal assured her. "Langdon, on the other hand, is in a bucket of trouble." So, Langdon had called her to come collect Missouri, Chabal rationalized, trying to quell her inner anger. She was not here to reclaim her husband. She was not here to twist and turn Langdon around her little finger.

"Where is my daughter?"

"Let me lock up," Chabal replied, going to the door and sliding the closed sign down and turning the key, and then hastily checking over her shoulder to make sure somebody else wasn't in the store, but they were, indeed, alone.

"Missouri is with Richam and Jewell and their kids in a loft studio in Fort Andross," Chabal said.

"Why?"

Why are you here? Chabal wanted to ask. Instead, she said, "It's a case Langdon is working. Yesterday," was it just yesterday, she wondered in amazement, "a man beat up Jewell, and then Langdon, and even Coffee Dog, before leaving when Danny T. drove into the house."

"Is everybody okay?"

"Yeah, well, no." Chabal started crying. She did not want to cry in front of this woman, but it was all too much.

"Tell me," Amanda commanded.

"The police just came through and said that Peppermint Patti is dead." The tears were now rolling unchecked down Chabal's rounded cheeks.

"Who the hell is Peppermint Patti?"

~ ~ ~ ~ ~

By the time Chabal got Amanda up to speed on the events of the past few days, they were on their second glass of wine. Amanda had suggested they get a drink, once she'd ascertained her daughter was not in immediate peril. They had walked down to the Wretched Lobster. Chabal was probably the closest thing to a friend that Amanda had in Brunswick, even though they'd always maintained a certain distance. At first, Chabal hadn't really understood her own reticence, or that her feelings for Langdon went far beyond friendship, even though that relationship remained steadfastly platonic. As for Amanda, she'd been so busy hating Brunswick she hadn't been capable of making many friends. They were sitting on a plush couch, one of several in the corner of the lounge. There was low jazz music playing and seven or eight other people in the bar.

"So, Langdon is wanted in connection with the murders of Chief Lefebvre and of this Bowdoin College student?" Amanda asked, staring into her wine glass.

"Right." A few tears still streaked Chabal's face for the girl she'd only just met.

"And you think he's being framed because of the case he's working, the death of the security guard at DownEast Power? The one married to that slut?"

Chabal winced at such harsh words coming from a woman who'd

run off on her husband, but chose to not make an issue of it, saying pointedly, "The *slut*, Janice Dumphy, is the one who hired Langdon."

"And the villain of the piece is actually named Shakespeare? The guy who threatened my daughter and beat up my husband?"

Chabal nodded. It did all seem fantastical.

"What do you know about this Shakespeare fellow?"

"Well, first of all, he is a very gentle man unless pushed," Shakespeare said, sitting down on an armchair across from them. "But he does have his limits."

Chabal gasped and her hand fluttered instinctively to her cheek where the point of this man's blade had pricked her skin just that morning. "What do you want?" she asked.

Shakespeare's balding head seemed to glow a faint yellow in the gloom of the bar. "I was in for a pint and I saw you sitting over here with a friend and thought I might introduce myself, but it seems you've already done the honors. Lawrence Shakespeare," he said, holding out his hand.

"My name is Amanda," she replied, ignoring the outstretched hand but clutching her purse to her chest in an odd way. Her face had remained impassive, but her eyes were darting around the room, looking for the fastest way out.

He lowered his hand. "Mrs. Langdon? What an honor. I heard you were out of state, making me believe I might need to go in search of you, but now look? Here you are." He bit through each word, suggesting a temper simmering just below the surface. "Do you know where your husband is by any chance?"

"We are separated, and not very amicably," she replied. "Did you say your first name was William?"

"Lawrence," he said stiffly.

She turned to Chabal and half-whispered, "I see why you said he was such a fop!" And then swiveled to face the reedy, vaguely threatening man. "What is it you want with my husband?"

"Being around him seems to be downright deadly," he said with a chuckle devoid of mirth. "Have the police spoken with you about him yet, Mrs. Langdon?"

Amanda's smile grew sweeter. "As a matter of fact, my good friend, Jackson Brooks of the state police is supposed to meet us here any minute. I'm sure he'd be anxious to hear of our present predicament, and the uninvited psycho—probably with a knife in his boot and an unregistered gun in his glove compartment—harassing his friends?"

"I have nothing to hide from the police, Mrs. Langdon," Shakespeare said, inwardly seething at the accuracy of her guess.

"I suppose I should have said Lieutenant Colonel Jackson Brooks," Amanda said sweetly. "He is the head of the incident management unit."

"You seem to know this man very well," Shakespeare replied. "Is this something you should be sharing with your husband?"

"He is a friend of both Goff's *and* mine," she said icily, and perhaps too quickly.

"Maybe you should share the whereabouts of your husband with this copper you're so fond of, as he *is* wanted for two murders."

"Goff is an upstanding member of the community with many friends, while you are a stranger in a place that doesn't like people from 'away.' As a matter of fact, if you're done here, we were having a private discussion." Amanda turned back to Chabal.

"There's just one more thing," Shakespeare said. "I was wondering if you'd paid a visit to your daughter since your arrival?" He was not going to let some housewife have the last word, even if the impending arrival of a state trooper did make him a bit uneasy. If that had been a lie, well, the words had come rather glibly.

Amanda leaned forward and pinned him with her eyes, her hand now inserted in her handbag and holding it at an angle. "The man who sold me this rig," she moved the bag up and down slightly, always keeping it aimed at Shakespeare. "He gave me a tip about women protecting themselves. He told me that I shouldn't bother pulling it out of my purse, but just shoot right through the bag." She raised her eyebrows and leaned forward. "Do not mess with my daughter, Larry. Just so you know, my husband is a cream puff next to me. If you fuck with me or my family, I will shred you. Do you understand?"

Shakespeare held her hard gaze before looking a bit anxiously at the people around them, some of whom had begun to stare. How, he wondered, had this spur of the moment decision to put a scare into a couple of bimbos backfired so badly? He nodded curtly and got up to leave.

"Once Jackson Brooks hears about your late night rendezvous with Governor Truman," Chabal said to his back, "well then, I do believe the state police may decide to open an investigation, don't you? It's a bit sketchy for him to be having some punk like you to the house, particularly a punk with a record a mile long."

Punk? The word goaded Shakespeare like a cattle-prod to the proverbial bull in a china shop. He stopped at the words. He took a deep breath. "I don't know what you're talking about." He tossed the words over his shoulder, then paused, seeming to have made a decision. "Remember who is in charge here," Shakespeare said. "You both should be more concerned about your families." He was visibly shaking in anger. "Consider the consequences of your actions. Good evening." He turned to go and ran smack into the chest of an enormous man.

"Is there a problem here?" The man wore a Bowdoin football sweatshirt and stood four inches over six feet and must have weighed 250 pounds. He was already a few drinks into the evening with a couple of friends, and had been eyeing the two attractive older women when the slippery little snake of a man had come in.

"No, no problem," Shakespeare replied, stepping to the side to get around the wall of a man.

The Bowdoin offensive tackle reached one mammoth paw out and grasped his shoulder. "Not so fast," he said.

Shakespeare slapped his flat palm into the student's barrel of a neck, and then reached two cupped hands to clap the stunned football player's ears. He shrieked and slumped to the ground, and then lay there gasping for air.

Shakespeare eyeballed the football player's two friends, a current of red-hot energy electrifying his body, wanting—*begging*—for more, a human bolt of destruction ready to level everyone and everything in sight. The two friends carefully stepped out of his way. Shakespeare paused at the door and looked back, casting a savage and unhinged glance at the two women before exiting.

"Are we the only two in here that just saw that?" Amanda asked in a quavering voice, having lowered her "bag."

"I think so," Chabal responded.

"Do you have a gun?" Amanda asked Chabal, both women shaken to their core, Chabal for the second time of the day.

"Not with me."

"If there was ever a time to carry it with you..." Amanda began.

"I know, I know! I should start carrying it, I suppose. That's what Richam told me this morning."

"Speaking of Richam," Amanda said, rising to her feet. "I would like to go see my daughter now."

Chabal rose on shaky legs. "I should call my husband." He had been expecting her home over an hour ago. She called from the payphone at the front of the bar, having given her cell phone to Langdon, wondering what she might say as she dialed. "I'm going to spend the night with Jewell," she said, once he'd answered.

"Does this have anything to do with Langdon?" he asked.

"You mean am I sleeping with him?" The words had just slipped out, and she gasped as she registered the implications of what she'd just said.

"Yes. That is exactly what I'm asking."

"As a matter of fact, I'm standing here with his wife, and we are both going to visit with Jewell right now."

"So, you won't be seeing Goff tonight?"

"I don't think so," she replied, thinking of Langdon on the run from the police and the criminals chasing after him. She envisioned him in the woods, his teeth chattering as he tried to build a fire against the cold. She realized she'd missed what her husband had said. "What's that?"

"I want you home immediately," he said.

"I have some things to work out, and they don't involve you," Chabal said. "Can't you just give me some space?"

"So you can sleep with your boss?"

"I'm standing next to his goddamn wife," she said. Inside, a part of her couldn't help resenting that "goddamn wife," because Chabal was realizing how desperately she needed time alone with Langdon. But now with his wife back in town? Perhaps she should just do as her husband told her and go on home, otherwise… what?

"If I have to come over to the Denevieux house and drag you home, I will. Your place is with your husband and your children."

"Go for it, but I won't be there." This was said with more venom than she intended.

"I thought you said you were staying at Jewell's?"

"I said with Jewell. She isn't at home."

"If you're not home in twenty minutes, I'm packing the kids up and leaving."

Chabal sighed. That was probably for the best anyway, to get them safely away from whatever violence had descended upon her safe little haven of Brunswick. She reached the receiver over and hung up the phone.

"Whew," Amanda said. "Sounds like your marriage is in the shitter same as mine. Did I hear him ask if you were sleeping with my husband?"

"If I'm not at his beck and call, he suffers from a lack of confidence," Chabal responded, picking up the receiver, dropping more change in, and dialing the number she'd memorized earlier, unaware of Amanda's piercing gaze at the back of her head, her eyes hard as nails. "Jewell? Can you let me in the back entrance in about five minutes?"

Chabal and Amanda left the Wretched Lobster, peering out the door before stepping onto the icy sidewalk. There were no pedestrians in sight, only cars traversing Maine Street.

"How can we be sure that Shakespeare isn't watching, and we're not leading him right to them?" Amanda asked. She put her hand in her purse and grasped the butt of the gun again, one finger curled around the trigger guard. She had bought it down in Florida as protection when her boyfriend started hitting her.

"Follow me," Chabal replied, striding across the street and into the video store. They took just a few seconds to look through the plate glass windows to see if anybody was following, and then went out through the back door into the parking lot where Chabal had parked her car. In seconds, the yellow Volkswagen Bug was zipping away into the night.

"Other than this whole mess, how has Goff been?" Amanda asked, turning to look at Chabal. The very fact that she had to ask this question implied an intimacy she really did not want to acknowledge, but she pushed the thought aside.

"You mean since you left him?" Chabal tried to keep the malice out of her voice.

"Yes."

Chabal snuck a look back at Amanda, impressed that she seemed to be accepting responsibility for her actions, and not blaming Langdon, his friends, the town, or anybody else for their issues. "Not real good," she admitted.

"Has he been drinking a lot?"

"Like a college student."

"I think marriage and parenthood made us feel trapped." Amanda was reflective, trying to put her thumb on something elusive. "We were the first of our friends from college to have kids. As a matter of fact, most of them still aren't married, much less parents. It was hard to see all their freedom and not want some too, I guess."

"I can vouch for that," Chabal replied, thinking of her three children, and of her husband fuming at home. The grass always seemed greener on the other side of the fence. Married people wanted to be single and single people wanted to be married.

"I got a chance to think over a lot of things while I was gone," Amanda said.

Chabal realized that Amanda packing up Missouri and fleeing was exactly what she was contemplating in her own life—except that it was her husband who was threatening to move out with the kids. "Yeah, what things?"

"Marriage is sort of like a career. It's a job you have to work at every day, and there are some days better than others, but you can't just give up, not until the work is done. Which it never is."

"It seems to me that most people dislike their jobs," Chabal replied. "My husband, for instance, works long hours doing something he detests just so we can vacation in Mexico, or maybe so he can go fishing a couple weekends in the summer."

"Do people really hate their jobs? Or do they just always want what they don't have?" Amanda asked.

"Are we still talking about jobs here, hon?" she asked lightly, then shook her head as if to shed herself of the thought. "Yeah," she said after Amanda had given her a strange look. "You're probably right. Most people bellyache, but truth be told, they like their jobs. What they don't like is being told they have to do them. My husband loves numbers and putting things together like a puzzle, but he can't go around bragging that he's an accountant."

"So you're saying most people like their jobs, and married people like being married, and single people like being single—but everybody likes to complain?"

"That's what unites us," Chabal agreed. "We are all an equal mix of bellyaching and envy."

"Living with Goff isn't exactly easy, and being a parent is certainly no walk in the park, and surviving the winter in Maine is nothing short of a miracle. I looked around at my single friends and thought they had it made, doing whatever they wanted whenever they wanted. And perhaps that's right for them, but I rather enjoy the hard work of making my marriage a success and raising a brilliant young lady, and while the winter is cold, the summer down south sucks even worse."

"So, for you, married life with Langdon and sharing a child together is far superior than spending your time on the beach in Florida with a Greek god?" Chabal was beginning to have an inkling that this conversation was circling back to her.

"Goff is ten times the man that Alan is," Amanda said. "And did you ever read any mythology? Greek gods can be real assholes."

Chabal laughed, but it was a dry rasp without mirth. She understood that she was being told to back off. "So, you're coming back?" She had parked in the back lot of Fort Andross, turning the lights and car off, staring straight ahead into the cold darkness.

"If I'm not too late?" Amanda cocked her head sideways at Chabal. "And if that stubborn cuss of a man will have me, yeah."

"That's a lot of ifs," Chabal observed dryly, realizing that her life had just gotten a lot more complicated.

Chapter 17

Langdon went back down over the bank behind the motel in an awkward tumble, first slipping, and then going ass over teakettle, finally coming to rest at the bottom of the hill. He came to his feet missing his hat, and broke into a shambling run through the snow next to the train tracks, his mind racing at what he had just seen. Peppermint Patti was dead. He was running from the police. Would they get dogs to track him? Probably. Why was he running? Where was he going?

A half-moon had risen in the sky, faintly discernible through the trees to the right side of the tracks, giving him just enough light to see as he fled into town. Too late, he realized that he should have gone the other way, back to his friend's vacant house and his car. He could have hidden out there, but to turn around now was to invite certain arrest. The bookstore? No, the police would most likely look for him there. He would not be safe at any of his friend's homes. He couldn't spend the night out in the cold. That left Danny T. as his only option.

Langdon doubted that Danny T. would be on the radar of the police searching for him. The man had an apartment on Swett Street, a run-down neighborhood not too far from where he was. He left the tracks at the lumberyard, working his way past the buildings and through the parking lot. He had to risk a brief stint along Spring Street, which hopefully would muddy the scent for dogs tracking him, cut across Pleasant Street, and into the small park on the other side. If this were a movie, he thought, he would go all the way to the river and wade along its banks to put the dogs off his trail. But this was Maine, and the water would be freezing, he reflected. "Fuck it." He headed straight for Danny T.'s.

Danny T. lived on the second floor of a home, with his own staircase to the apartment carved out of the house to provide additional income to its owner. Langdon took the steps two at a time and opened the unlocked door without knocking. Danny T. was sitting in a dilapidated armchair in his underwear and a t-shirt, a plate rounded over with two burgers and a pile of macaroni salad on his lap.

"Where's my plate?" Langdon asked.

~ ~ ~ ~ ~

Chabal went to get out of the car, but realized Amanda hadn't moved, so, settled back into her seat. "This is the part where we go inside," she said quietly.

"Tell me something, Chabal. Do all of Langdon's friends hate me?"

"Hate you?" Chabal said, but the fact that she referred to them as Langdon's friends and not 'their' friends was telling.

"You know, all of it. He brings me back from college and parades me around town. And then the way I left, running off with another man, taking our daughter with me, leaving a note on the kitchen table…"

"You never gave Brunswick much of a chance, did you?" On the drive, both women had been silent, lost in their respective thoughts. Chabal had come to the reluctant conclusion that, even if her own marriage appeared to be crumbling, she wasn't going to be responsible for another's demise, however shaky it might be. Also, she had to admit she was warming up to this more thoughtful Amanda, who had matured from the leggy blonde that she'd never gotten to know in the years she'd lived here. Still, that was not to say that Chabal was ready to let her off the hook entirely. "I mean, you were gone for three weeks before I even realized it, and that was only because I asked Langdon where Missouri was."

"Y'all were polite enough when I showed up on Langdon's arm like some trophy he won at the fair, but that's not quite the same as being friendly."

"We welcomed you into our homes," Chabal protested.

"Sure, but I noticed the raised eyebrows at my accent, and early on when I asked the waiter if they had crawdads? The people at the table were laughing at me and not *with* me. Don't tell me people didn't make fun of my fur coat and my city slicker boots that were more like skates on the ice than Bean boots?" Amanda grimaced, thinking back to the countless times she'd been made to feel like an outsider.

"Well, you didn't help your cause that first time we all went to Popham Beach, and you showed up in a bikini that barely covered any part of your gorgeous body," Chabal said with a rueful grin. "So, okay, maybe you were a bit different, and beautiful, and maybe we resented you a bit."

"I'm not here to cry on anybody's shoulder," she said. "I suppose I did show up in Brunswick thinking I was better than the local yokels. I mean, the culture consisted of going to Hog Heaven for a greasy dinner and then maybe to the movies, which, by the way, were usually teenage sequels like *Mighty Ducks 2*."

Chabal nodded her head. "Well, girl, I am truly sorry if you felt I never gave you a chance. If you come back to live, I promise to invite you to my next Tupperware party."

Amanda wasn't sure if this was a joke or not, but was touched all the same. "Thanks," she said in a dry whisper.

"We'd best be going inside before Jewell gives up on us."

"Do you love my husband?" she asked out of the blue, staring straight ahead at the brick building in front of them.

"Why do people keep asking me that? First my husband, and now you. I work for Langdon, and he is a friend."

Amanda processed the answer, realizing that it had not quite been a denial.

At the door, Chabal knocked, and it was immediately opened a crack. "Halt, who goes there?" a British voice asked.

"It is I, Arthur, King of the Brits, traveling with a band of brave knights in quest of the Holy Grail," Chabal answered.

"What's your favorite color?"

"Purple, no, yellow."

Jewell opened the door with a smile, her eyes widening at the site of Amanda. "What brings *you* back?"

"Hello, Jewell. I got a call to come pick up my daughter, as Langdon's apparently in deep trouble."

"She's been talking about you all day."

"Sounds like it has been a tough few days," Amanda said.

"I don't quite understand why Langdon brought her home in the middle of this mess," Jewell admitted.

"Try going without your children for a few days, and then imagine a few months, and then you'll understand better." Amanda surprised Jewell with her defense of Langdon's actions.

"So, you're just grabbing Missouri and taking off? Where are you going?" Jewell asked.

"You can't go home," Chabal said. "Not after our run-in with Shakespeare. He'll be looking for you, and that's the first place that sick bastard will check."

"You had a run-in with Shakespeare? Again?" Jewell asked.

"Maybe I'll spend the night here and see what tomorrow brings," Amanda said. "If that's okay with everybody?"

The hallway to the elevator was poorly lit. A fixture on a hanging cord had one dim bulb under a dusty glass cover. It swayed in the rush of cold air from the open door, projecting eerie shadows across the floor and walls. At the end of the hallway were double cast iron doors, which Jewell swung open on creaky hinges. These were the doors to the old-style service elevator where Jewell raised the elevator's equally screeching gate so they could enter. Amanda pushed the metal grate back down and Jewell depressed the lever for the third floor.

They emerged in a long hallway lined with locked storage spaces, holding the possessions and secrets of various citizens. Chabal gazed at the mysterious cubicles, wondering what each held that was so important to keep but not important enough to have. At the end of the corridor, Jewell turned to the right and opened one side of ten-foot-tall double doors with a key.

"Mommy," Missouri yelled, her tiny legs running across the wide expanse of floor, leaving a kickball game behind. She ran straight into Amanda's legs and was hoisted into a huge hug. "Do you like my new home, Mommy?" Coffee Dog had followed the young girl over and was now dancing around mother and daughter in circles.

It was, indeed, quite a home. An enormous open expanse the size of a football field with twenty-foot ceilings stretched out before them. A baseball diamond was laid out, usually purposed for whiffle ball but was currently hosting a kickball game. A basketball hoop and backboard adorned one massive pillar, the rectangular half-court painted in wild, art deco colors. Gigantic canvases painted in equally vivid colors hung from the walls. Chabal thought they looked fairly similar to her children's work at home stuck to the fridge by magnets.

"It is beautiful," Amanda said, surprising even herself by not pointing out that this was just a temporary home until things got themselves sorted out, if they ever did.

"Do you want to play kickball?"

"Sure, honey, just give me a minute, I'll be right there." Amanda set Missouri down and looked around.

Their interruption had led to a break in the game, and the pitcher, who was a stranger to her, was now lying in the middle of the floor. Richam was huddled together with his kids, Will and Tangerine, whispering in their ears. Bart stood at first base glaring at her, making no attempt to hide his animosity. 4 by Four came over and kissed her on the cheek, his hand on the small of her back, both actions a bit too friendly, but perhaps better than hatred?

"Amanda! Great to see you," 4 by Four stepped back at arm's length and looked her up and down. His words emerged with the telltale slur of someone who had been drinking more than a tipple or two. "And Chabal, don't let me forget you." He turned towards her, but she sidestepped his hug and kiss.

Richam stepped in between with the practiced grace of a bartender and the disgust of a friend. "4 by Four, maybe you better stick to weed because drinking turns you into an idiot."

"I got into a bar fight today," 4 by Four said out of the blue. "Well, sort of. Before I could hit him, Bart grabbed the dude and knocked him cold."

"If I have to hear this story one more time, I'm going to give Bart the okay to knock *you* out," Richam said.

"Chabal, come meet our new star witness," 4 by Four cracked up at his own joke, while Richam winced, and Chabal and Amanda were left wondering at what was supposed to be so funny.

"Who?" Chabal asked.

"What?" Amanda asked.

"Jonathan *Star*ling," 4 by Four said, pointing at the pitcher who was now prone on the floor. "He used to be law partners up in Madison with Governor Truman."

"Are you building a case against Harper Truman?" Amanda asked.

"He's got to be involved somehow," 4 by Four replied. "Why else would he be having late night meetings with Shakespeare?"

"The man we just met?" Amanda asked.

"You just had another run-in with Shakespeare?" Richam asked.

"Yeah, he scared the bejesus out of us," Amanda said.

"And he's working with the governor," 4 by Four said.

"I think you're getting ahead of yourself," Richam said. "We have a rumor that the governor's young nanny saw him talking with Shakespeare. Even if it's true, so what? It could be any of a million things. Maybe they went to college together."

Chabal turned to Bart, who had ambled over. "What do you think, Bart?"

"I'm not so sure that Governor Truman would commit a crime for money. He seems to have plenty," Bart replied.

"What else could it be other than money?" 4 by Four demanded belligerently.

"Power." Bart held their attention now. "Truman is stealing uranium or nuclear waste as some sort of terrorist tool."

"That was Peppermint Patti's theory," Chabal said. Just saying the dead girl's name made her blood run cold. The others were quiet as well, remembering the lively spirit so suddenly snuffed out.

"Power?" 4 by Four asked with disdain. "You think the governor is a terrorist? He goes from being an environmentalist to threatening the world with radioactive fallout? You just think that everybody wants to be powerful, but mostly people want to be happy, and money is their conduit to happiness."

"You didn't mind me saving your weak-ass back when that punk was going to rearrange your face, now did you?" Bart asked. "Maybe I should have let him beat you senseless, and then you could have sued him for all the money he doesn't have?"

"Would you children stop your bickering?" Chabal asked in the soothing voice she used with her own kids. "I have to go with 4 by Four on this one. I think it's a bit of a stretch to think that the governor, the founder of Flower First, is orchestrating a nuclear meltdown."

"Unless it's just a bluff."

They all froze, looking at one another, unsure where this voice had come from.

"It's the same thing as tree spiking, really." The voice was coming from the prone figure of Jonathan Starling.

"What do you mean?" 4 by Four asked the immobile figure.

"Spiking a tree doesn't actually hurt the tree," Starling said, propping himself up on his elbow. "And then you notify the paper company that you've spiked one, or several, or many trees in a specific tract, whether you've spiked them or not, and suddenly they're too scared of the liability to go in and cut them down."

"Because some dumbshit working man might bounce his chainsaw blade off the spike and split his head in two," Bart said.

Starling looked grim for a split-second, and then plunged on. "And even if that happens, what's the big deal? What is one casualty when you're fighting a war to save Mother Earth?"

"What's the big deal about killing somebody?" Bart asked.

"I think we're getting off topic here," Richam said. "How does this relate to DownEast Power?"

"It's the fear that counts," Starling said. "Not the actual accident."

"What's that supposed to mean?" Jewell asked.

"Let's suppose that a potentially disastrous situation occurs at DownEast Power, but is averted at the last minute. Whatever it is doesn't really matter. It could be attempted theft of nuclear waste by terrorists, a close call with a complete meltdown, or a total breach of security—the crisis doesn't matter—not so much as what the public's reaction would be."

"People would go apeshit," 4 by Four said.

"Like cats and dogs playing in the street together," Chabal said.

Richam shook his head at her attempt to lighten the mood with a *Ghostbusters* quote. "The memory of Three Mile Island is not too far distant."

"Or Chernobyl," 4 by Four said.

"I know how Truman thinks, because we were both mentored by the same person," Starling said, lying back down and speaking to the ceiling. "It's the spike thing all over again, but on a much larger scale. If news of a problem at DownEast Power leaks out? The place would get closed down in a heartbeat—and then maybe we would have a lot more green energy, or at least a power plant that ran on natural gas."

"What a feather in the cap of Flower First," Bart said quietly. "All without hurting anybody."

"Except for Peppermint Patti," Chabal said.

"And Harold Dumphy," Jewell added.

"What's two casualties when you're trying to save the earth?" Starling asked.

"Hell, if Truman recognizes the issue at the plant and takes steps to avert a disaster?" 4 by Four looked around the circle of faces. "He'd be a goddamn hero!"

"You know what the saying is, don't play with fire if you don't want to get burnt, though," Amanda said.

"Boom," Starling said, and then broke into a cackling laughter. "Either way, there would be no more DownEast Power." He rolled to his knees and struggled to his feet, going off in search of his bottle, or the bathroom, or both.

This seemed to signal the end of the confab, and people wandered off to various corners and niches of the space, the kickball game seemingly over to the chagrin of the kids.

Chabal followed Jewell to the kitchen area of the room. Around an insulated column was a refrigerator, a stove, and a double sink set into a stretch of counter.

"Why'd you bring her here?" Jewell asked.

"Because her daughter is here and Langdon is wanted for murder," Chabal replied.

"It's not bad enough we have a drunk lawyer and a cop showing up with some wino, but now you bring that two-timing spoiled shirker along? I'm not sure I signed up for this particular tour."

"Shirker?"

"You don't leave a four-year marriage behind with only a note. And you don't take a little girl from her daddy who loves her more than anything in the world! That's just plain irresponsible, not to mention unforgivable. So, yes ma'am, *shirker*."

"She was in a bad place and didn't know how to handle it, so she ran." Chabal said, defending the actions of the woman who, just a few hours earlier, she would have castigated. It was not the apology, nor Amanda's subdued, almost apologetic manner that had won Chabal's sympathy, but the fact that she had just taken the first steps down that same path, pulling out of a marriage with kids.

"Not all marriages can be salvaged, and God knows that those two aren't a good fit for each other," Jewell said. "But you don't put a little girl in the middle of your personal failings, and there are some things that you can't forgive. Ever. I wonder if she's thought about that?"

The silence grew between the two women. Chabal was sorely tempted to ask why Jewell didn't think that Amanda and Langdon were a good fit for each other, but she somehow lacked the will to speak. Instead, she said, "I thought that once the kids get to bed, we could have a group update."

Jewell glanced at the small bistro table where Tangerine's head was resting precariously close to a melted Popsicle. Will was kicking a ball against the opposite wall with a vengeance, suggesting that the events of the past few days were certainly a burden upon his frail shoulders. "I'd say bedtime is a good call."

As if he'd been reading their lips, Richam ambled over, happy to leave 4 by Four and Bart's bickering behind. "What say we put our little monsters down for the night?"

~ ~ ~ ~ ~

Missouri and Amanda were sitting in a wooden swing set by the windows overlooking the town of Brunswick. The rocking was gradually putting both of them to sleep, a gentle interlude in the midst of chaos.

"Is Daddy going to be all right?"

"He'll be fine," Amanda murmured into the top of her head.

"What does murder mean?"

"Where did you hear that word?"

"I heard Uncle Richam telling Uncle 4 by Four that the policemen want Daddy for murder. But, I don't know what that means."

"Your Daddy did not murder anybody, honey, it's just a mistake."

Missouri frowned, her face wrinkled in thought and sadness. "Is murder when you hurt somebody?"

"Yes," Amanda replied gently. "But your Daddy didn't hurt anybody, not even a little."

"I know that." Missouri picked her head off Amanda's shoulder and looked into her mother's eyes. "But shouldn't somebody tell the policemen that? Then he can come back and see me."

"Tomorrow, honey," Amanda said, hoping it was not a lie. "We'll do that tomorrow."

Missouri was sufficiently reassured, her mind slipping into the rhythm of bedtime. "I brought *Goodnight Moon* with me. Jewell said I could, and so I did. Can you read it to me?" She popped down from the swing and ran across the room to retrieve her favorite book.

Bart was about fed up with 4 by Four, who'd been claiming all day that he'd been about to tear the kid in the bar apart when Bart had intervened. The truth was that the drunken lawyer been standing there, frozen, with his eyes pressed shut, probably about to burst into tears or have a heart attack or both. Bringing Jonathan Starling back "to be a key witness," as 4 by Four kept saying, was more a dream than a reality, the other reality being that they couldn't just leave him passed out on the bar. The sound of Bart's beeper going off reminded him that he'd missed several earlier messages, and he walked away from 4 by Four in mid-sentence to check them.

The first number was the police station, and he called it, reluctantly, though it was his job. They wanted him to come in because he was Langdon's friend, and he promised to be there an hour later.

When he called the next, he recognized Danny T.'s voice. "Whatcha want?" he demanded, and when the man merely stuttered nonsense, Bart guessed the reason. "Just put Langdon on the damn phone, and quit your whimpering."

~ ~ ~ ~ ~

Twenty-five minutes later, Langdon found himself in Fort Andross, summarizing aloud what he knew so far before the others weighed in with their discoveries. The children were fast asleep on the far side of the room. He'd kissed Missouri's forehead as she lay sprawled on the bed, but avoided looking at Amanda, wondering at her presence here when last he knew she was in Philadelphia. He assumed that 4 by Four's message had reached her, and she was merely here to take his daughter away, perhaps waiting until morning.

Langdon wasn't sure what he wanted, but her presence certainly put him into a quandary. She was beautiful, and they'd had many good times together. There had also been an increasing number of hard times leading up to the moment she walked out. The other bitter truth was, she'd been having sex with another man for the past six months, and Langdon didn't think he would ever be able to get past that. But she was also the mother of his daughter. How could he be part of creating a broken home for Missouri?

Amanda, for her part, was fine with keeping a distance. She knew the rawness that her presence created not just in Langdon, but the entire group. She wanted to make it work, *needed* to make it work. Time, after all, was the great healer, not that they had much of it, given the pace with which events had outrun their reality to make sense of them. She knew, however, that keeping her presence low key—just a mom taking care of her daughter—might ease the reconciliation, if there was to be one. She had no intention of leaving in the morning. Six months with an asshole had made her realize that she had had it pretty good with Langdon, even if it was in Brunswick, Maine.

"Peppermint Patti recorded everything from today," Langdon said, standing in front of a semi-circle of friends, one employee, one sort of wife, and a stranger lying in the middle of the floor. "There is a good deal of information from her phone calls for the day, but she also recorded her death." Langdon stopped, sucking in his breath abruptly as if to stop the rush of feeling at the memory of her ravaged body. "I would guess that she was just out of the shower. She'd wrapped the recorder in a towel to keep it dry, which is why the killers didn't see it. This muffled her voice a bit, but you can still get the gist of what happened." He stopped talking and looked across the room at the black windows, his thoughts drifting back to what he'd heard. "And all she had on was the motel bathrobe."

"Tell us," Jewell said. "We need to hear it."

"She's summarizing her calls from the day when you hear a knocking faintly. After a few seconds, you're able to hear her voice from further away, presumably by the door. She was," Langdon choked up, took a second, and continued, "she was asking if it was me or Lord, and then there was a rustling noise closer by. I think this was the second man climbing in through the bathroom window."

"Goddamn it," Bart muttered.

"I, um, don't think I can tell you what happened next, but you need to hear it. Believe me, it's not pretty, but I'm gonna play the tape. If you don't want to listen, maybe now is a good time to walk away?" When nobody budged, he hit the button and the recorder began to whir:

"Who is it? Lord? Is that you?"

A rustling could be heard and then a thump, followed by breathing. A creaking indicated footsteps across, presumably, the bathroom floor.

"Langdon?"

"It's the manager," a man in a high-pitched voice said. "I need to check something in the room."

"What do—," the words were abruptly cut off, followed by a muffled yell of terror.

"Don't make a sound," a man in a deep voice said. "Or I'll stick the blade in your neck." There was the sound of a door opening and closing.

"Put her on the bed," High Pitch said.

"Sit down," Deep Voice said.

"What do you want?" Peppermint Patti asked. Her voice was choppy.

"Shut up," High Pitch said.

"We want you to go back to your dorm room and leave all this behind," Deep Voice said.

"I was just making a few phone calls," Peppermint Patti said.

There was the sound of a slap followed by a cry of pain.

"I don't think you do understand," Deep Voice said.

"Okay, okay, just don't hurt me," Peppermint Patti said. This was followed by a sudden flurry of noise, cursing from both men, and then more blows.

"Sit your ass down, bitch," Deep Voice said. He was breathing heavily.

"Jesus Christ, Stanley, would you look at her tits?" High Pitch said.

"Cover yourself up," Deep Voice said. "Leave it alone, Elwood. The boss won't care for that sort of thing."

"Do you suppose the carpet matches the drapes?" High Pitch asked.

"Leave it, Elwood, the boss won't like this," Deep Voice said.

"Don't touch me, you pig," Peppermint Patti said between sobs.

"Ah, come on Stanley, I just want to take a peek and see if her cooter has a red scarf on it," High Pitch said.

There was a rustling, the sounds of a struggle, and heavy breathing.

"Get your filthy hands off me!" Peppermint Patti yelled.

"Shut your mouth, you filthy bitch," High Pitch said. "Shut her up, Stanley."

There was the sound of several blows being delivered and Peppermint Patti yelling out in fear and pain.

"Jesus Christ, wrap the phone cord around her neck," High Pitch said.

A yell from Peppermint Patti was cut off in the middle then and reduced to a slight gagging noise.

"That's better, now open your legs you bitch and show me your cooter," High Pitch said. "Grab her arms," he added. The bed was creaking, followed by the sound of more slaps.

"You grab her arms," Deep Voice said.

"You're getting me excited now, girl. What's that they call you? Peppermint Patti? I always wanted to fuck a Peanuts character," High Pitch said. His voice had gone several octaves higher to a feral whine and he was gasping for breath. "Hold her still."

"She's strong," Deep Voice said.

Faintly, one could hear a gagging, choking noise.

"Open your damn legs," High Pitch said, followed by a sound that may have been a punch. "Son-of-a-bitch, she scratched my face." There was the sound of more blows, interspersed with muttered curses.

"Take it easy, Elwood," Deep Voice said. "The boss ain't gonna like this."

"Ahh, that's better," High Pitch said.

"Shit, Elwood, I don't think she's breathing,"

There was the sound of the bed creaking and heavy breathing.

"We best get the fuck out of here."

"The boss is gonna be pissed."

Footsteps grew louder as the two murderers, as the noises suggested, jostled back through the bathroom and climbed through the window.

"That's it," Langdon said, turning the recorder off. "There's nothing for the next ten minutes, not until my knock on the door."

"Was she… raped?" Chabal asked.

"I don't think so," Langdon replied. "She was a tough cookie, Peppermint Patti. Maybe too tough. I don't believe they meant to kill her, just scare her, but when they found her almost naked in the motel room…"

"Elwood and Stanley," Richam said.

"Bastards."

"Why were they there and how did they find her?" Jewell asked.

Langdon shook his head. "I don't know. Clearly, it had something to do with her calls that day."

"I thought Lord was keeping an eye on her room?" Bart asked. "Where was he when the guy was banging on the front door?"

"I believe…" Langdon turned away from the gathered group and stood with his back to them for almost a full minute. Nobody said a word. Finally, he turned back around. "I believe that Elwood and Stanley showed up while I was distracting Lord form his duties. I tapped on his bathroom window, crawled into his room, and was bringing him up to speed on the day's events when we remembered we were supposed to be watching her room."

"You don't know that," Chabal said.

"It could've happened when Lord was taking a piss," Bart said.

"Any way you look at it, I brought her into this mess," Langdon said. "And I have to live with that, but I can promise you that the guilty parties will pay for what they did."

"She chose to be there," Jewell said.

"Who had she called so far? Do we know that?" Chabal's face was shiny with tears.

Richam had set up an easel and rested a large format sketchbook on it. Langdon walked over to it, turned to a blank page, and picked up a black Sharpie. "She set up a meeting with Abigail Austin-Peters, was brushed off by an aide to Governor Truman, left a message for Johnson T. Halperg at Casco Bay Power, and had plans for coffee with Ellsworth Limington III tomorrow afternoon at the Lenin Stop." He wrote the four names on the paper.

"So one of those four must have sent the two goons to shake her up," 4 by Four said.

"But instead, they then tried to rape her and, in the process, killed her," Chabal added.

"So where does that leave us?" Richam asked.

"If we find out who murdered Harold Dumphy, then we find who sent Elwood and Stanley to Peppermint Patti's room, too. It all comes back to DownEast Power, as far as I can tell," Langdon replied.

"It's a cluster-fuck," Bart said, shaking his head. "What do we know so far?"

Langdon wrote a capital A and Harold Dumphy under the names of the four people already listed. "A, we have the murder of an employee at a nuclear power plant, one Harold Dumphy. B, this murder is covered up, and the case is closed on the orders of Chief Lefebvre. C, a man named Lawrence Shakespeare threatens and bribes me so I won't take the case, starting before it is even offered to me."

"I was wondering about that," Chabal said. "How did he even know that Janice Dumphy was going to offer you the case? It would seem that there might be a connection between the bad guys and the widow."

Langdon nodded, and wrote down Widow Dumphy with a question mark next to C. "Good point, let's come back to that. D, we have a public relations director for DownEast Power who, at best, is acting very oddly, and at worst, is guilty of something. E, just when we discover that the chief is being blackmailed, he commits suicide, and an anonymous tip sends the police to the house and I am spotted leaving the scene by a neighbor. F, while at the chief's house, I discover a partially burned blackmail note threatening the chief with exposure of an affair, but the identity of the woman is not revealed, either in the photograph, or the note." Langdon cleared his throat. "And G, after a day of digging into DownEast Power and others associated with them, including the governor, Peppermint Patti is attacked and killed in her motel room."

"Do you have the blackmail note with you?" Bart was curious about the note, yet nervous of its contents. He'd worked for years with the chief. Even though they hadn't always seen eye to eye, he had, up until this case, always respected the man.

Langdon reached for Peppermint Patti's leather case, where he'd stashed the note and photo, and carefully took out the crumbling paper. Bart spent several minutes inspecting it before handing it to 4 by Four.

"And here's the photograph that was with it." He handed it to Bart.

The note and photograph made the rounds of all, except Jonathan Starling, who was now snoring loudly on the floor.

"I think it was a set up," Langdon said. He'd reached this conclusion on the train tracks before reaching the motel. "As you know, I often do this kind of work, and it's not all that easy to get a photo of people having an affair. When people are cheating on spouses, they pull the curtains. They don't go naked into the hot tub or make love in public like steamy movies would have you think."

"This picture makes it looks like they're posing," Amanda said, holding it out to the others.

"Exactly," Langdon said, part of his mind straying unwillingly to Amanda's unfaithfulness. He certainly hoped there wasn't a vengeful ex out there planning to upload a sex tape for all to see.

"It does look like he was having an affair with a married woman," Chabal said, the note in front of her. "This refers to her as Mrs."

"Too bad her name is missing," Bart stated the obvious.

"What I'm wondering," Richam said, looking over Chabal's shoulder. "Is why would the pictures be of interest to the police in a recent murder investigation, like the woman is a suspect?"

"The only murder investigation in the area for the past few months would be Harold Dumphy," Bart said.

"So the woman in the picture is somehow connected, or a suspect, in the murder of Harold Dumphy," Jewell stated.

"Do we think the woman in the picture is Janice Dumphy?" Chabal asked.

"Why do you ask that?" Bart walked over to where Richam held the photograph to look again.

"Well, for starters, it would be of great interest to the police if the chief was having an affair with the wife of the murder victim, don't you think?" Chabal replied.

"There's no evidence she was sleeping with the chief," Langdon said.

"Hasn't she slept with every other man in town?" Amanda asked. "Why not the chief?"

Langdon held back a sharp retort. "Okay, I wondered the same thing. But if you look at the picture, you'll realize it can't be Janice Dumphy.

I've met the Widow Dumphy, and the lady in the photo doesn't have…"
He trailed off, unusually embarrassed in front of the others.

"Huge hooters," 4 by Four yelled triumphantly as the realization
came to him. "That boob on the chief's head is half the size of the
widow's."

Chabal looked like she was about to object, but looked at the
picture again and began to nod slowly. It was obvious that it was not
Janice Dumphy.

"So, where does that leave us?" Bart asked.

"Nowhere." Richam replied. "We have two 'suicides' and a murder,
and Langdon is wanted in connection with two of those. There is
no real evidence of shenanigans at DownEast Power other than
what Shakespeare let slip to Chabal, and nothing to suggest there
is a cover-up other than a charred note and a photo of a woman
without a head. For all of this, we have put our lives in danger, and
our children's, too. Thanks a lot, Langdon."

"It's not his fault," Chabal jumped to Langdon's defense.

"Well, whose fault is it?" Jewell asked in a low voice.

"I'm sorry that I got you into this," Langdon said. "But I don't
know how to safely extricate any of us at this point."

"So, we best get to the bottom of this whole thing if we want things
to return to normal," Bart said, a finality in his voice.

"I'm sorry," Richam said. "I just hate worrying about my kids." The
others nodded in agreement. "So," he said, "what's the plan?"

"I think we start with the people Peppermint Patti talked to. She
obviously touched a nerve with somebody," Langdon said, his voice
grim. "With the stand-outs would be the governor's press secretary, a
representative of the Flower First Party, Janice Dumphy, and Abigail
Austin-Peters." He needed to listen to the recording again, he knew,
because it had been hard to focus on the facts while at Danny T.'s
apartment.

"Who are our prime suspects in hiring Shakespeare to kill Harold
Dumphy?" Bart asked.

Langdon turned a page on the sketchpad. "I think right now we have to look at Harper Truman, Abigail Austin-Peters, Ellsworth Limington, and Johnson Halperg."

"Are we certain Shakespeare killed Dumphy?" Richam asked.

"It's a definite maybe at this point," Langdon replied.

"So, what now?" Chabal asked. While the others seemed a bit put out, she had to admit that this was better than sitting at home watching *Wheel of Fortune.*

Langdon contemplated all the complexities that faced them. "4 by Four, do you think you can get Ms. Austin-Peters to meet you for lunch, like tomorrow, and with you sober, please? You can say that you have been retained by Janice Dumphy to bring legal action against DownEast Power for wrongful death. That should stir things up."

"For sure," 4 by Four replied. He had stopped drinking before he'd gotten back to the loft and was now working on water.

Langdon turned to Bart. "When do you go back to work?"

"I was supposed to be at the station an hour ago to answer questions about my relationship with you," Bart said. "Just an interview, not to work, but I should probably still hit a little mouth wash and the shower before I show up." His eyes were beet red, his clothes reeked of cigar smoke and beer, his breath would have felled small game, and his clothes were dotted with food stains. He walked over to the sink, rinsed his face, wet his hair, and ran it through with a small black comb he pulled from his pocket. He straightened his pants, tucked in his shirt, and dabbed at a few of the worst of the stains.

Langdon had followed him over and observed the disheveled man. "Hey, friend, not that this isn't a good effort," he said, gesturing to the comb, "but I really think you need to head home and hit that shower, get a change of clothes?" Bart looked at him, puzzled.

"Anyway," Langdon continued, "I had an interesting conversation with Danny T. before I came over here," he said. "He came across a tidbit of information that might be something important. I didn't want to bring it up to the group because we have enough red herrings already, but I thought you might be able to check into it."

"What'd that dirt bag find out?"

"He was asking around about Johnson Halperg, the CEO of Casco Bay Power, and somebody mentioned that he'd been at Bates College with Ellsworth Limington back in the day."

Bart whistled. "The guy who's buying up the entire town of Woolington?"

"That's the one. What's more, when the guy was talking, he referred to him as L, which I guess is a nickname his mates use for him, probably based on his last name."

"Which, unless the rest of the name was burnt off, is how the blackmail note appeared to be signed," Bart said slowly.

"You got it," Langdon replied.

"Shit," Bart said, leaning back against the wall.

"You be careful and watch your back at the station. It seems that someone has the fix in there, maybe into every powerful person and institution in the entire state. I wouldn't trust anybody, if I were you."

Bart nodded, his brow furrowed, and then walked out the door.

Langdon returned to the others. "Anybody got any other ideas?"

"I know the governor's wife fairly well," Chabal said. "I can track her down tomorrow and maybe shake the tree a bit, ask about Shakespeare?"

"If Harper Truman is truly involved in this somehow, then he's not going to let his wife within a hundred miles of you," Langdon replied. "And I'm not sure I'd want you anywhere near his orbit, especially if he's been meeting with that creep who has it in for you."

Amanda looked at Langdon and then Chabal, seemingly judging the vibe, but neither one of them noticed, caught up in each other.

"First of all, not all men run their women," Chabal replied. "But also, dumbass, you're assuming that they ever see each other. The last time I saw them together in a restaurant, they spent the whole time ignoring each other. As far as I can tell, the only time they are together is for photo events."

"Okay, then." Langdon turned to look at Richam. "You working tomorrow?"

"I'm on the ten to four shift, but I was going to make a few calls, get coverage," Richam replied.

"You should go in to work," Langdon said. "If there's any gossip to be had, it will either be at the diner or the Wretched Lobster." When Richam nodded his agreement, Langdon looked again around the circle of faces. "Anybody know what's going on with Lord, Nick, or that other fellow?"

"Lord got picked up by the police at the motel when Peppermint Patti was killed," Jewell said. "When the cops showed up, he came running down to see what the hell was going on, and they took him into custody, probably just because he's your brother. When they searched his room and found a rifle with a scope by the window facing Peppermint Patti's room? Well, that was that, and off to jail he went."

"What's the charge?"

"I think he's just being held as a person of interest," Richam said.

"I can get him out first thing in the morning," 4 by Four said. "Afternoon at the latest."

"And Nick?"

Chapter 18

One by one the group dissipated into the corners of the artist studio to curl up and grab a bit of sleep, until it was just Amanda, Langdon, and 4 by Four, who was snoring away in a beanbag chair.

"Did you come to pick Missouri up?" Langdon asked.

"Maybe," Amanda replied.

"I guess you got the gist of the whole mess."

"Sort of. Chabal filled me in on… a few things."

Amanda was sitting in a chair that looked like a bad mushroom trip. The fabric had been painted over in wild and haphazard colors. Langdon stared intently at the chair to avoid looking at his wife, and the wild patterns made him think of a Curious George book. It's the one where the monkey, George, is a window washer, and when he sees some painters leaving an apartment for their lunch break, he climbs in through the window and paints a jungle scene complete with a monkey. Langdon smiled at the thought, but this made him think of his daughter, and then of Peppermint Patti.

"Penny for your thoughts?" Amanda interrupted.

"I feel like Curious George," he replied after a moment. "Like I make a shambles of everything and I don't quite know how to get out of it. And I don't think there's any Man in a Yellow Hat coming to fix things." His voice was husky, and his eyes glistened with unshed tears.

Amanda stared at him wondering what he was talking about, but then realized how much like Curious George her husband actually was. He somehow got pulled into the complicated puzzles of life and banged around making a mess trying to figure things out, not realizing the repercussions of his actions. "That fellow Shakespeare paid me and Chabal a visit at the Wretched Lobster earlier," she said.

"What?"

"I told him that we were meeting Jackson Brooks."

"Were you?"

"Of course not, but I thought mentioning the imminent arrival of the state police was a good idea at the time."

Langdon nodded. The weight of the day had finally begun to settle on his shoulders, and he was finding it hard to focus, much less make meaningful conversation.

"Maybe I should actually give Jackson a call? He doesn't wear a yellow hat, but it might be a good thing to get some help on this one."

"Can I ask you something?"

"Sure, anything," Amanda replied warily.

"What is Jackson to you? You were spending a bit of time with him before you took off with the golfer."

Amanda shifted uncomfortably in the mushroom chair. "He was a good friend to me, somebody to talk to when I was confused."

"So, just to be clear, you never slept with him?"

There was a pregnant pause, a silence that was a bit too long, and too heavy.

"You had sex with Jackson?" Langdon did not sound surprised.

"Just once," Amanda said desperately. "I was mixed up, and he was comforting. It was a mistake and meant nothing."

Langdon went to the bar in the game room and poured himself a Jack Daniels, neat. He slammed the shot down, poured a second, thought about it, and put the bottle back. It wasn't like he hadn't known. But, yes, it was that he hadn't *known*. He'd guessed, surmised, even assumed, but he had not known.

Amanda came over and sat down on a barstool. "I'm sorry. I don't know why," she stifled a sob, "but everything was just all mucked up."

Langdon stared at her, trying to decipher her words, but realized that his thoughts were on Peppermint Patti, who'd been killed just hours earlier because of his actions.

"I should have told her we didn't need her." Tears began streaming down Langdon's face. He made no effort to wipe them away.

"What? Who?"

"Peppermint Patti. She's dead because of me."

"Did you have a… thing… with her?" Amanda asked.

"No, but I think Lord did, just this afternoon." Langdon tipped the glass up and took a shuddering gulp of the burning liquid. "God, what have I done? My brother is in jail? Peppermint Patti is dead?"

"Do you want to talk about it? About her?" Amanda asked, seeing the faraway look in his glistening eyes. "The girl, Peppermint Patti."

"Her name was Patti Smith," Langdon said. "We called her Peppermint Patti." A ghost of a smile creased his face as he thought of the shy girl who'd approached him in the Bowdoin library just a few days earlier. He shared all he knew of the twenty-year-old from Texas with the sharp wit, but long pauses haunted their conversation, the skulking remains of abandonment and the raw confession of cheating.

After a bit, a reassuring smile began to tease the corner of Amanda's mouth, a mouth that Langdon loved for its full, pouty lips set delicately under high cheekbones, sparking the memory of a shared moment, which threatened to restart the waterworks. It was strange how this image came to him all of a sudden—the two of them coming down a narrow canyon that opened unexpectedly into an expansive pool of water fed by a small waterfall. They'd taken a siesta there, with the burble of the falling water as background music, and made languid love in the shade of the only tree in all of Arizona, or so it seemed.

Was it too late to go back to those days? He wondered.

~ ~ ~ ~ ~

Langdon woke after just a few hours of sleep to a quiet sobbing in the cavernous silence of the old mill building. Earlier, he and Amanda had found one blanket left, and had little choice but to share it, their bodies touching, but no more. He carefully slipped from the warmth of cover and body and clambered to his feet. Missouri was crying, half-awake, and Langdon lifted her, sleeping bag and all, and moved over by the window away from Will and Tangerine.

"It's okay, honey," he whispered into her ear.

"What does 'dead' mean, Daddy?"

Langdon understood immediately that this might be one of those life-forming conversations and hoped he was up to the task. He decided to take the straightforward approach, believing that the truth, however simplified, was always preferable.

"Dead is when somebody is gone for good," he replied after a long moment during which he stroked her hair gently.

"So Peppermint Patti's gone for good?" Missouri looked at him, her eyes wide and innocent.

"In some ways, yes, Peppermint Patti is gone for good."

"I don't think I want to die if it means leaving you and Mommy."

Langdon pulled his daughter tighter into his embrace. "You're not going anywhere, honey," he said with all the power of his being.

"Where has she gone?"

"Nobody is quite sure. Some people think that when you die you go to heaven to be with God."

"Is heaven a nice place?"

"That's what people say."

"I hope Peppermint Patti went to heaven. Do you want to go to heaven, Daddy?"

"The way I see it," Langdon struggled to find just the right words. "I don't think that heaven is a place that you go, but it is actually right here. I believe that Peppermint Patti lives on in the memory of her friends and family, and that who she was, and what she did in life, will continue to affect everything and everybody who knew her. Like me. I only knew her for a few days, but in that time she made me smile, made me laugh, and made me feel good about myself. Because of that, Peppermint Patti lives on in me, but also in so many other people as well. Her spirit is all around us."

"What is spirit?"

"It is who you are. It's the thing that makes you cry and laugh and be angry."

She looked puzzled, and then her face cleared. "Can I have a snack?"

Langdon realized the conversation was over. She was only three and so her attention span was limited. Still, he was pretty sure his words were carefully stashed in that curious mind of hers, and would be processed, emerging as more questions when she'd had some time to think.

He made them each a peanut butter and jelly sandwich, along with a glass of milk, and they sat down to this 3 a.m. feast in the silent warehouse building in Brunswick, Maine.

"I was having a bad dream, Daddy," Missouri said through a mouthful of sandwich.

"What was it about?"

"Monsters were trying to make me dead."

"Monsters are scared of daddies, so you have nothing to worry about."

"No," she shook her head earnestly. "These monsters *eat* daddies."

Langdon did not know what to say to that.

"But Gasoline saved me."

"Gasoline?" Langdon was often stumped by the creative and fertile place that was the mind of his daughter. She filled him in on a few details while she finished up her sandwich and milk. Gasoline, it seemed, was the name of the winged dragon that protected her in her sleep, a gentle creature of immense size and power, who banished nighttime ogres back to the holes and closets from whence they crept.

~ ~ ~ ~ ~

Once Missouri had fallen back to sleep, Langdon realized that, while it would still be dark for several more hours, there was no chance of him getting any more rest. The bathroom had a shower—really just a bathtub with a curtain pulled around it—and a saucer-shaped showerhead dangling from the ceiling, but the water felt great, washing away the grime of the day. As he washed away the accumulated actual and cerebral filth, he felt as if a weight were lifting, some of his grief at Peppermint Patti's passing momentarily assuaged.

He found shaving utensils and turned on the radio that was on a shelf next to the sink. It was an old fashioned shaving kit—a brush, a tub of stuff that looked like cool whip, and a straight razor. Langdon made a mental note to buy one for himself once life returned to normal, for the process was somehow more satisfying. Maybe he'd just keep this one, as the author probably wouldn't want it back now that Langdon had used it, he thought. The radio, tuned to a local station, droned in the background, the latest news, of course, being Peppermint Patti's grisly murder.

Police are still searching for the man seen at the scene of the murder in a Brunswick motel. The woman, now identified as Patricia Smith, was a sophomore at Bowdoin College. She is the daughter of Senator Harding Smith of Texas. Senator Smith could not be reached for comment, but a spokesman for the senator said that he was devastated and had insisted upon a full-scale investigation into the events surrounding the death of his daughter.

Peppermint Patti was the daughter of a senator? Langdon realized how little he actually knew about the girl. Who was she, other than a generous and kind soul? He padded his way out of the bathroom wrapped in just a towel in search of fresh clothes. He found a closet filled with tasteful attire, even if not quite his size. A short sleeve polo shirt made his biceps look massive, and he flexed several times in appreciation. The waist of the Brooks Brothers pants was a great fit, but the cuffs hovered four inches above his red Chuck Taylors. Still, they smelled better than what he'd been wearing, so he stuck with the new wardrobe until he could do a wash or stop by his apartment to get some more clothes.

He went to the kitchen, his instincts leading him straight to the coffee, filter, and pot. For the next few hours he worked his way through almost the entire pot writing down everything he knew about the case so far. The more he considered the various pieces to this complicated puzzle, the more he realized that its key lay in uncovering the governor's connection to DownEast Power, a link that consisted solely, to date, of Shakespeare's rumored nocturnal visit.

"You writing your memoirs?" Jonathan Starling appeared across from him, snapping him from his musings. "Okay if I have that last bit of coffee?" He poured half a cup and then topped it up with the bottle of Jack Daniels in his hand. As he went to sit, his shaking hands sloshed hot coffee, and he cursed under his breath.

"Just trying to untangle something," Langdon said, and then looked at the alcoholic former lawyer with the glint of a thought. "You might actually be able to help me out with it."

"How's that?" He raised the cup to his mouth, quickly covering the territory between table and lips to avoid more spillage.

"I don't know how much Bart and 4 by Four told you, but it seems that an ex-law partner of yours might be involved in some cover-up at DownEast Power," Langdon said. "And is likely responsible for the death of three people." He knew no such thing, but sometimes the pot had to be put to boil a bit to see what would happen.

"She was always prone to being a bit violent," Starling said.

"She?"

"Jordan Fitzpatrick. That's who you're talking about, right?"

"Jordan Fitzpatrick is a she?" Langdon had quite forgotten that there was a third partner in the firm, and realized that he'd—all of them—had just assumed that Jordan was a man.

"That I know for a fact," Starling said with a leer that spoke of past intimacy. "But she could be as mean and tough as any man, and the way she put away the Wild Turkey was a sight to see."

The words tickled the edges of Langdon's mind, but he couldn't quite make the memory he was reaching for take definite form, so instead he just dumbly repeated Starling's words. "Jordan Fitzpatrick is a woman, and she has always been violent?"

"Took most of the skin off my back one time," Starling cackled with delight in the memory. "Ripped the shirt right off me, she did, first time we met. It was at some charity event for the spotted loon or some garbage like that."

"I wasn't asking about the bedroom," Langdon said.

"Sex was the perfect example of her tendency towards violence. Not only did she like it a little bit rough, she used coitus to get what she wanted and then moved on, like that insect, whatchamacallit. The praying mantis: she attracts the male, mates with it, then sucks the life out of it. She sure sucked the very life out of me, and left the husk that you see sitting here in front of you." Starling tipped a bit more Jack into his cup without the distraction of coffee this time. "And to tell you the truth? If given the chance, I'd do it all over again. There was something about that woman that seeps into your soul and squeezes in a painfully pleasant sort of way. If given the chance of having my old life back or one more night with her, I'd take the debauchery in a heartbeat."

Langdon understood the unhappy choice that life sometimes presented in the form of a delicious apple, and which, while you knew you should say no, you were powerless to avoid. He, himself, had been considering adultery. "What did she want from you?"

Starling looked surprised, like it had never crossed his mind. "Power, I suppose," he said after a pause. "I brought her legitimacy, joining her when she had an organization but no clout." He shrugged. "Or so I thought. Now I think that I was little more than a foot soldier in her army. She did have fantastic recruiting skills, though."

"Her army?"

"She was out to save the earth at any cost, no matter who got hurt, and she seduced people into doing her bidding."

"How so?"

"Sex was her major tool and weapon."

"Where is she now?"

"I suppose she's out on the front lines somewhere fighting The Man. Maine was too small for her once she spread her wings." Starling took a slug of the whiskey. "She started Flower First back when she was in college and took on issues all over the backwoods of Maine, but she always had national aspirations. Somewhere along the way, a more militant sect of the organization started up. They called themselves Terror First and Flower Second."

"Harper Truman joined Flower First?"

"We both did. I told you she had amazing recruiting skills. I couldn't take it and dropped out, but Harper, he was the golden child. She used to talk about taking him all the way to the White House. I mean, look at Reagan or Jimmy Carter or Bill Clinton—heck, a lot of Presidents started out small-time."

"So, is it about power or saving the earth?"

"Jordan Fitzpatrick would do anything to preserve the environment. *Anything.* But she thought the best way to make real change is to be the person holding the reins driving the horses, this particular buggy being one headed for Pennsylvania Avenue. She was never that hippie on the street corner holding a sign. She always thought that kind of thing was for amateurs."

"You and Truman were both romantically involved with Jordan?"

"She slept with everybody and anybody," Starling replied. "You could say she was an equal opportunity employer. She used sex as a weapon to hurt those standing in her way, as a tool to get what she wanted, occasionally an amusement to pass the time. I don't think romance was ever part of the equation."

"The three of you had a law practice together?"

"Harper and I were roommates at Maine School of Law down

in Portland. He had put a sign on the bulletin board saying he was looking for somebody to share an apartment with, and I answered it. Next thing you know, we were living right off of Deering Oaks on our way to becoming best friends. We had similar ideals in that we wanted to save the environment from civilization. And what better battleground to face creeping urbanization and pollution than right here in Maine, where there's something left to be saved? What's more, the enemy is out in plain sight, the paper companies clear-cutting the last bastion of virgin trees on the whole East Coast."

Langdon could sense the energy and passion that had once been Jonathan Starling, if not in his eyes, at least in his words. They both sat quietly, one drinking whiskey, the other thinking about drinking whiskey. "And then what?" Langdon prodded.

"When we graduated law school, we moved up to Madison and rented a house, right downtown. The front was our office, a converted living room with a partition for a conference room and our desks in opposite corners. We slept in the back of the house, but lived and worked in the front. Truman and Starling Law, our sign said, and we did everything legal—maybe a few things pushing it a bit—to stare 'em down, make 'em blink, so to speak." He smiled, remembering. "Man, we were a pain in their ass, that's for sure. We were right in their heartland in Madison. The mill was going full-speed ahead, and we fought them face-to-face, but we were still close enough to Augusta to lobby. We worked day and night. We took any case opposing the paper companies on any grounds whatsoever, zoning, permitting, emissions, groundwater pollution, and endangered species. Hell, we once sued 'em for violating a local noise ordinance. We fought and struggled and starved and loved life. We weren't in it for the money. We had a cause and that was enough. That was how it was at the beginning, anyway."

As he spoke, Starling's voice grew raspier, if that was possible. Langdon doubted that the man had spoken this many words in the past year. The cold December sun had now risen in Brunswick, and the light came flooding through the windows of Fort Andross, illuminating Starling's face, stripping away the wrinkles and mucus in his eyes, glinting off his brown, cracked teeth. Langdon almost broke into tears imagining the man that had once been while seeing before him the ruin that man had become.

"We had just won an important case," Starling continued. "I don't remember exactly what it was. We blocked a vote that would have opened up even more land to be clear-cut, or something similar. Harper and I decided a celebration was in order. We attended a fundraiser, for a change not to push the environment, but rather, to enjoy the booze and food that were part of it. We were tying it on real hard, me and Harper, and then there were three of us drinking, laughing, and giving high-fives to each other. Somehow, Jordan Fitzpatrick became part of our victory. We'd never seen her before, but it was like she was always part of us. I already told you how we ended up in a motel room madly ripping each other's clothes off and screwing on a table, but what I didn't tell you, is that Harper had the same exact experience. Mind you, I didn't know it then, and only found out months later. Jordan seduced both of us that night, and we both fell in love. It was only a matter of weeks before she became a partner in our law firm. We thought she was a fantastic addition. What we didn't realize was that she was driving a wedge between the two of us, pitting us against each other, unknowingly at first."

"Women can do that to best friends," Langdon said dryly.

"We vied for her attention, almost coming to blows on several occasions. For a while I thought I was the victor. That she had chosen me. The sex was magnificent. We agreed to not tell Harper we were fucking so that he wouldn't feel like the odd man out. But then, one night when Jordan was out of town, me and Harper had it out. In the middle of our argument, it came out that I was sleeping with her. Harper looked at me and called me a liar, a fucking liar, actually because *he* was the one sleeping with her. We just sat there looking at each other like stupid fucking idiots."

"So, how is it that Harper Truman ended up as governor and

you ended up, well, like this?" He gestured at the coffee cup.

"I can only guess at what decisions Harper Truman made, but I can tell you exactly when my descent into oblivion began."

"If it's not too much, I'd like to hear it," Langdon said.

"There was no official policy change, no change in the mission statement of the law firm, but at some point, I realized we'd become more aggressive in the way we went about saving the environment. Instead of using the law as a shield for Mother Nature, we began to use it as more of a weapon, attacking, often not legally, and in any manner we were able. This happened so gradually that I wasn't even aware of it at the time, but since then I've had plenty of time to go over it in my head. I wasn't very proud of the man I'd become, even less so then, than now."

"That happens to everybody in this life, at one time or another," Langdon said gently, trying to provide a bit of solace for this obviously tortured soul. "We start out thinking we're going to change the world. Then we realize that we're just pawns in the larger game of life, and it's hard enough just trying to pay the bills. Before we know it, we're middle-aged and jaded."

"I think I'm a little past jaded," Starling said wryly. "Let me finish the story, and then you can pass judgment." He spoke with the patience of one who had waited years to unload his story and now had a willing audience, and he meant to make the most of it. "Our law office became the meeting place for the radical hippies that Jordan was inducting into Flower First. One by one they crept up on us, until one day I realized there were a total of seven extra people sleeping in our house. The place reeked of marijuana, and at any given time of the day, I could find two, sometimes three, of them having sex in my bed. They were into free speech, free love, freedom from government interference, and militantly opposed to corporations. I didn't know it, realize it, at the time, but they were Jordan's strike force, an offshoot of Flower First that was nicknamed Terror First." Starling buried his face in his hands, the images obviously still quite powerful.

"Take your time," Langdon said, looking around the room to see if anybody else was stirring yet.

"I came home at the end of a particularly long and difficult day to find them holding a meeting in our law office. The objective was to block the clear-cutting of a pristine and beautiful forest. I've thought about the events of that night thousands of times since. It was a Friday. The paper company was set to start cutting on Monday morning. I'd already used every legal means I could to prevent them, and failed." He took a deep breath. "The meeting had been convened to discuss illegal means to block them from destroying yet another beautiful woodland. I think Jordan knew I'd be coming home frustrated, and that I was meant to walk in on that meeting in the state of mind I was. Someone suggested we pour sand in the gas tanks of the skidders, shoot the tires out, and spike the trees. I fought them for hours. I argued that we couldn't fight the beast by *becoming* the beast. I went so far as to threaten to turn them in to the authorities if they followed through on these actions, especially spiking the trees, which I knew could prove fatal. Finally, we called an impasse, and I stumbled off to bed. Before I fell asleep, my door opened, and Jordan slipped in. I can still remember her figure, illuminated slightly by the moonlight streaming through the window as she got undressed. She was so exquisitely gorgeous. She climbed into bed with me for the last time, and for the last time, rocked my world."

Langdon knew what was coming. The things men did for sex. The pieces of their soul they parceled out was a tale as old as time, yet they seemed unable most times to resist. "It's not your fault," he said, but both men knew it was.

"When I woke up in the morning, the planning was already in the action stage, and I realized I'd cast my vote of consent the night before. And to this day, I'm sure I'd do the same thing again. I was no match for Jordan, and the thought of her still makes my insides jelly and my lips dry."

"What happened?"

"We vandalized the skidders to slow them down, but we knew that was only a temporary delay, and they increased the security detail for the new ones. While they were at that, we were in the forest spiking the trees."

"You helped?"

"Yes," Starling replied. "A man I knew…" Starling poured a half-cup of whiskey and slammed the entire four fingers back. "Donny Leblanc found the first spike. His chainsaw kicked off the thing and embedded itself into his forehead."

"Dead?" Langdon almost remembered reading about something like that.

"Did you ever see a logger's Husqvarna? Those chainsaws, some of them are five feet long and with blades so sharp you can take a finger off even when they're not turning. 'Course he was dead."

"And then you fell apart?"

"I started drinking that very day, and it wasn't long before Jordan discarded me." He pushed the empty cup across the table away from him, his eyes watering either from the burning liquid or the memory, or both. "The day that Donny Leblanc stuck the chainsaw in his head was the day I became the man you see in front of you now."

Chapter 19

Lawrence Shakespeare banged on the front door of the restaurant. It was closed for the night, but he was expected. He had contemplated not coming. The notion of getting in his rental car and driving away had been plaguing him ever since those idiots had reported the botched events at the motel. Now, here he was, facing the wrath incurred by those mistakes.

The door swung open and a burly man stepped aside and gestured him in before locking the door behind him. The man went back to cleaning up the bar. Shakespeare let his eyes adjust, even after picking out the figure sitting in the corner. Finally, he walked gingerly to the table at which his employer sat.

The boss was eating a steak, carving the meat up methodically, his fork spearing the chunks and transporting them to his mouth. Every three pieces, he took a taste of the red wine by his right hand. He was about six feet in height and very thin, his Adam's apple bobbing prominently up and down, his hooked nose appearing enormous on his sunken face, and his ears jutting out from the sides of his head.

"What's this I hear about a dead girl at a motel in Brunswick?" he asked once the final piece of meat had disappeared from his plate.

"Elwood and Stanley," Shakespeare said carefully, "got a bit carried away."

"By 'carried away,' you mean they killed her?"

"They were supposed to put a scare into her, but she fought back, and one thing led to another."

The boss finished his glass of wine and wiped his mouth. "Do you know who the girl was?"

Shakespeare shrugged. "Some college student."

"That college student is the daughter of Senator Harding Smith of Texas."

"Senator?" Shakespeare was stunned. That chunky redhead was a senator's daughter?

"Not just any senator, mind you," the boss said. "He is the chair of Clean Air and Nuclear Safety."

Shakespeare wished he'd followed his instincts and gotten in his car and left, but what had kept him here still nagged at a spot deep in his consciousness. The smug look on that damn Langdon's face. His ire began to rise.

"You need to take care of the situation," the boss said.

"What is it you want me to do?"

"You've tried to bribe Langdon?"

"Yes."

"You've tried to scare him?"

"Yes."

"And neither of these things worked?"

"That is correct."

The boss stood and tossed his napkin on the table. "I shouldn't have to tell you what must be done, then, should I?"

~ ~ ~ ~ ~

The loft was beginning to stir as Langdon and Starling contemplated life and death. "What is it that you want?" Langdon finally asked.

"I want to forget," Starling replied.

"You can't do that, and you can't change the past."

"No shit."

"But, you can atone for past sins."

"How do I do that?"

"Well, you're going to have to lay off the booze, for starters," Langdon said. He stood and opened the fridge and found a package of bacon. There was a skillet under the counter, and the bacon was sizzling before he continued. "Of course, you'll need something to occupy your time, to give you purpose."

"My law days are done."

"How about you work in my bookstore?"

"I don't need your charity."

Langdon looked sideways at the man. "It wouldn't be charity. I've been needing to hire another person for some time, but my own life has been in a bit of disarray."

Chabal wandered over, looking especially sexy in the morning, her hair tousled and clothes rumpled, but a sparkle in her eyes of promised mischief. "You got the bacon started, but didn't think to make another pot of joe?" She went about preparing another pot of coffee, muttering under her breath, "men."

"I don't know the first thing about fiction books," Starling said.

"Mysteries, actually," Chabal said. "Did I hear you're joining our crack team at the Coffee Dog Bookstore?"

"I don't know if I can quit drinking," Starling said.

"Maybe first you get some help, do rehab. Then… what do the AA people say? One day at a time?" Langdon asked.

"Where would I live?"

"I suspect the Truman house might be coming up for sale soon. A distress sale, so to speak. Maybe I'll buy it and turn it into apartments. You can live with me until you find something, in any case," Langdon said. "I've got plenty of room."

"The Truman house?"

"Yeah," Langdon replied with a grin. "Once we get this mess cleared up, I have a feeling that Governor Harper Truman will be going away for a while on an extended vacation to Thomaston, if not some rougher federal real estate down south." Langdon thought he might have seen the hint of a smile on Starling's face at the thought of his former law partner going to prison.

A sudden pounding on the door made Langdon pause—and just as suddenly remember that he was still wanted by the police in connection with two murders.

"Fire escape over there," Chabal leaned her head toward the window. "I'll watch the bacon."

It seemed to Langdon that he'd spent plenty of time on a fire escape just yesterday, but he dutifully ambled off in the suggested direction. Richam had roused himself and went to the door, and 4 by Four dragged himself from the beanbag chair, looking slightly green around the gills.

"Open the damn door," Bart's muffled voice boomed through the cavernous room. Langdon paused halfway out the window and came back in, leaving the window partially raised behind him.

"Oh no, the police are here," 4 by Four said, and then walked hurriedly to the bathroom.

Bart had brought donuts from Frosty's—a Brunswick institution—and they made good appetizers while Langdon finished cooking a breakfast of bacon, eggs, and home fries. Jewell, hair crazy on her head, stumbled over for a cup of coffee and a donut, sitting down next to Chabal, the two putting their heads together in conversation. Will and Tangerine came running over for donuts, and Missouri woke long enough to find her mother and curl up with her before going back to sleep. The two women in Langdon's life were not known for being morning creatures.

"What a sorry crowd," Bart said. He stuffed an entire donut in his mouth and went to the fridge where he found a beer to wash it down.

"Unlike the poster child for health and happiness *you* are," Jewell retorted crossly. "I wonder if you wouldn't mind not doing that in front of our children. Maybe set more of an example, you being the police and all?" Bart just stared dumbly back.

4 by Four came out of the bathroom in time to see Bart shove another donut into his mouth and tip the beer back to noisily slurp

down half its contents, and that was enough to send him stumbling back in to visit the porcelain god for round two.

"Breakfast is ready," Langdon said, sitting back down at the table. "Grab a plate and help yourself."

"Great, I'm starving," Richam said. "I hope you didn't put any funny stuff in the potatoes this morning."

"What's the word on Lord?" Langdon asked Bart in a rare moment when the cop's mouth wasn't full.

"They had him up all night questioning him, but he has a license for the rifle and didn't do anything wrong, so I think they're going to release him this morning. Probably even before his sorry-ass lawyer is done in the bathroom," Bart said.

"Do you have to go back in?" Langdon asked.

"Funny you should ask," Bart replied with a smile. "The new acting chief, Chief Bickford, suggested that I take some time off beyond what I'm taking now, a paid vacation so to speak, until this all gets sorted out. It seems he's concerned over my close friendship with the main suspect in two deaths. How he actually knows we're friends, even good friends, well, that's a good question."

Langdon made a face of mock disgust. "Imagine the gall! To think you wouldn't uphold your sworn duty and nab this dangerous suspect at the very first chance."

"I think he was also concerned that I would give warning and information to said suspect," Bart said.

"Also known as aiding and abetting, I believe. Why, the nerve of this Bickford. If you need me to come in and vouch for your honor, why, I'd be happy to come in with you right now."

"Would you two stop being men for just a minute and get back to the matter at hand?" Jewell snapped.

"Okay, okay," Langdon said, smiling from his face, his eyes glancing at Amanda who had wandered over looking for tea, and then went about heating a kettle. "Time for a game plan. It looks like we need somebody to fill in for 4 by Four who is obviously not meeting with

Abigail Austin-Peters at noon today, seeing as Romeo is in the bathroom throwing up, again. I agree with Bart. That man really needs to stick to pot."

4 by Four came out of the bathroom wiping his hand across his mouth, his face still an unhappy green cast. "I'm fine. I'll keep the appointment with the mysterious Abigail Austin-Peters."

"You sure?" Langdon asked, the doubt evident in his voice.

"Try not to barf on her," Chabal said. "Some women are offended by that sort of thing."

"Make fun all you want," 4 by Four retorted. "But I believe she is the key to this whole case, and by this afternoon, this whole mess will be put to bed."

"Do me a favor and just stay away from the Wild Turkey, okay? She drinks like a fish, even at lunch, apparently," Langdon said. "If you can't get back here after you meet with her, at least call and give me an update. How about the governor?"

"I got that one," Chabal said. "I told you I'm pretty friendly with his wife, Karol. I'll drop by and pay her a visit and do some digging."

"Okay, but be careful," Langdon said.

"What's that supposed to mean?"

"What?"

"You didn't tell 4 by Four to be careful. Is this some sort of sexist thing?" Chabal grinned mischievously to show she was joking.

Amanda caught the exchange and didn't appear to much care for it. "I'll give Jackson Brooks a call and try to get together with him for coffee or a drink and pick his brain about this whole thing."

"Do you think he'll meet with you?" Langdon asked, but refrained from asking if she also planned on sleeping with the man again. The image was hot in his belly and mind, and he began to doubt that reconciliation with his wife was possible.

"Yeah," she said, giving a shrug. "If he's around, I'm sure he'll be agreeable to getting together." Amanda gave Langdon a cool look and then looked over at Chabal, who was still looking raptly at Langdon.

"Great," Langdon said. "Ask him what he knows about Flower First, any problems at DownEast Power that he might have heard. Maybe he has the goods on Halperg or Limington, wrongdoing past or present. They're both rich bastards, and you don't always make a fortune without breaking a few rules."

"Got it," Amanda snapped. "If you're done being a bossy man, why, I'll just take my pretty face on out of here so I don't distract you."

"And see if he's heard of Lawrence Shakespeare," Langdon added, oblivious to the irritation in her tone.

Amanda glared at him.

Langdon didn't notice and turned to Bart. "How about you check in with Janice Dumphy? I need to follow up with her, but not over the phone. And me going out in the bright light of day is probably a bad idea until the cops figure out I'm not a double murderer."

"Sure," Bart said.

Langdon stared at him in wonder. Bart had never, ever agreed so readily to anything as long Langdon had known him. Perhaps the gruff bear had a soft spot for the widow? "She gave me…" Langdon was going to say a list of men that she'd cheated on her husband with, but chose softer words looking at the cop's tired face. "She told me she'd had an affair with Ellsworth Limington some time back, so maybe you can ask her more about that, and anything else her husband might have said before he died."

"I will give her the full interrogation," Bart replied somewhat facetiously.

I bet you will, Langdon thought. He turned to Richam. "Ask around the bar about our four suspects, see what you can dig up."

"Don't forget about Shakespeare. He was in there yesterday and almost killed a man," Chabal said.

"That reminds me, has anybody heard anything from Nick?" The only reply was heads shaking in the negative.

As if on cue, the phone rang and Jewell answered it, and then held out the receiver to Langdon. "It's your brother."

"Hey," Langdon said into the phone.

"It's Lord. Nick just picked me up. He left Larry with eyes on Shakespeare. What's the latest?"

"How are you?" Langdon asked.

"Been better."

"I'm sorry about what happened to Peppermint Patti."

"Me, too," Lord said. "But not nearly as sorry as the motherfucker who killed her will be, soon as I find him."

"Where's Shakespeare?"

"That fancy hotel down in Freeport." Lord could be heard asking the name of the place in the background. "The Bernard."

"Don't approach him," Langdon cautioned. "We need to see where he leads us."

"I'll do my best. What do I need to know?"

Langdon quickly gave Lord the highlights.

"Okay, so the two goons who killed Patti called each other Elwood and Stanley. We can't kick any ass until Shakespeare leads us to whoever is pulling the strings. Got it. Anything else?" Lord spoke in the clipped speech of a man barely controlling his anger.

"That's it. Stick with Nick and Larry. Keep eyes on Shakespeare, but from a distance. We don't want to spook him. I need to know if he meets with any of four people: Abigail Austin-Peters, Governor Truman, Johnson Halperg at Casco Bay Power, or Ellsworth Limington."

"I'll see if we can dig up some pictures of them, otherwise I'll only be guessing."

"Yeah, well, if he goes to DownEast Power, Casco Bay Power, or the Blaine House in Augusta—you should be able to figure it out."

"Got it." There was a pause on the phone. "I'd left her room less than an hour before you went down there. That means she was killed while we were gabbing away, not paying attention."

"It's not your fault," Langdon replied. "I'm the one who pulled her into this. I'm the one who pulled you away from your post by knocking on your bathroom window."

"Well, brother, maybe we can share the blame. But somebody else has to pay."

"Check in when you know something."

"Will do." The phone went dead.

Langdon looked up at the circle of eyes staring at him. "Okay, my brothers have Shakespeare in their scopes, so we'll have some warning if he's coming to get us. If he makes a move, that will be the end of him. But don't forget we have a few more bad guys out there." He clapped his hands twice. "Let's get busy."

Chapter 20

Bart grabbed a beer from the fridge, stuffed one last donut into his mouth, and headed for the door. It would be good to see Janice Dumphy again. He'd met her a few times over the years when she'd come to her husband's bowling league night, and he had had a bit of a crush on her from afar. She was obviously a woman who did what she wanted and to hell with what anyone thought. Bart had a great deal of respect for that approach to life, as it was one he practiced. He'd thought about asking her out for a drink after her husband died, and what better time than now?

The hallway was silent as Bart passed by the storage spaces, but then a man got off the elevator with a flatbed cart loaded with boxes destined for one of the wire cages. Bart pulled the metal gate down and pushed the lever down, wondering at the ease with which he broke the law, this time by not arresting a friend he knew to be innocent. Over the years, he'd acted as judge and jury a few times, and never once had experienced a twinge of regret. As far as he was concerned, the law was about doing what was right. Sometimes it just took a while to work things out.

An hour later, freshly shaven and showered, and dressed in clean clothes, Bart was knocking on the Widow Dumphy's door. The door opened suddenly, almost as if she'd been waiting for just this intrusion into her life. The two of them stood staring at each other for a long ten seconds.

"Hello, ma'am. My name is Detective Jeremiah Bartholomew. I'm with the Brunswick Police Department." Bart flashed his badge at her. His face was flushed with excitement, almost like when he'd gone to his senior prom. His hair, what little was left, was combed neatly. He had on a black Brooks Brothers overcoat over a tweed jacket and sharply-creased khakis fresh from the dry cleaners. "You are Janice Dumphy, correct?"

"Yes, that's me," she purred. She was dressed in a pink halter-top so tight that it must have made it difficult for her to breathe, a man's white dress shirt over it, unbuttoned. Her pants were a shiny vinyl material and her feet were encased in large fluffy slippers that might have been cats. "Would you like to come in?"

"Thank you," he said, stepping past her into a living room that was too small and delicate for his bulk. "Do you mind if I ask you a few questions about the death of your husband?" he asked.

"Let me take your jacket," the widow replied. "Make yourself comfortable."

Bart gave up his overcoat and chose a love seat that appeared to be the sturdiest piece of furniture in the house and carefully sat down. "I understand that you have retained Goff Langdon to do some investigative work into the nature of your husband's death?"

"Can I get you something to drink, Detective Bartholomew?"

"Sure," he replied. "What do you have?"

"I have orange juice, coffee, tea, water, but was just about to open a bottle of wine when you knocked." She looked at him with large brown eyes that melted his insides.

Bart looked at his watch. It was not yet 11 in the morning. He liked this woman more and more. "I'll have whatever you're having, Mrs. Dumphy," he said with a wink.

"Call me Janice," she replied coyly, turning to go to the kitchen and hiding the excitement that flushed her face.

"My friends call me Bart," he said, eyes pinned to her backside.

She turned around and caught his eyes sliding back up. "Do you mind if I call you Jeremiah? I do love that name."

"That would be fine," he said, his face now as flushed as her own.

She returned with two glasses, an open bottle of Riesling, and a wine chiller. "Will you pour?" She went back to the kitchen only to return with a board of cheese and crackers, which she set on the low coffee table, and then squeezed in next to him on the love seat. "To answer your question, I had hired Mr. Langdon to look into Harold's death, but that was before I knew what a dreadful person he was. First he shoots the Chief of Police…" She clapped a hand to her mouth, displaying bright red nails. "Oh, I'm so sorry. You were probably quite close to Chief Lefebvre."

Bart handed her a glass of wine, holding his own gently, afraid that the crystal vessel would crumble in his hand. "It looks like Guyton may have killed himself, Janice." He raised the glass to his lips and finished the contents in one swallow.

"And how about the other one, the college girl out to the motel on Pleasant Street?" She surprised him by not taking a dainty sip, but polishing off her glass of wine as well. "I saw it on the news last night."

"We just want to ask him some questions, but it looks like other hands might have been responsible for that as well," Bart said.

"So, you don't think Mr. Langdon is responsible for either death, Jeremiah?" She held out her glass for him to refill. He poured, and then topped off his own.

"No, we don't believe so, Janice. As a matter of fact, we are reopening the investigation of your husband's death after receiving information that Langdon dug up, and we would be interested in what else he might know."

"All right." She nodded, taking in this new information. "So what can I help you with?"

"Do you know Ellsworth Limington?"

"Yes."

"In what capacity?"

"What do you mean?"

"What is the nature of your relationship with him?"

The widow licked her lips and swigged from her glass. She turned away, as if embarrassed. "Ells and I see each other about once a month."

"Really? So you're good friends?"

"I don't know how to say this, Jeremiah, so I'll just be blunt. We have sex together. I go up to his hotel on Mount Chamberlain for a couple of hours once a month, and we pleasure each other."

Bart stared at her. Though he was gruff, he was actually more open-minded than most people thought, not one to negatively judge anyone for enjoying sex. Rather, he thought he might be falling in love with her straight-forward, no-apologies nature. "Did you tell Mr. Limington that you were going to hire Goff Langdon to investigate your husband's death?"

"I don't remember telling him that, but I suppose I could have. I believe I saw him the day before I hired Mr. Langdon."

"Think hard, Janice, it's important."

"I could call and ask him?" she suggested.

"That won't be necessary." Bart stood and went to the kitchen, found another bottle of Riesling in the fridge, opened it up, grabbed a pint glass, and returned to the living room. The widow had removed her dress shirt entirely and now sat quite unabashedly showcasing her flesh, her top half more bare than covered.

"I may have said something, but I can't be sure," she said. "I'm sorry."

Bart settled back next to her, resting his huge paw of a hand on her knee and giving it a squeeze. "It's okay. Don't worry about it."

"I did remember something I hadn't told Langdon, or anybody else for that matter." She leaned over as if somebody might be listening, giving him a clear view of her cleavage and intoxicating him with her perfume, her tongue almost flicking his ear. "It was Clayton Jones who tipped Harold off that something strange was going on at DownEast Power right under his nose."

"Clayton Jones?" Bart asked. "Who's that?"

"He's the personal assistant to Governor Truman." Janice nuzzled his ear, breathing in deeply. "I'd forgotten because it was at least two weeks before Harold was killed, and he just casually mentioned to me one night that Clayton was in asking a bunch of prying questions, and he'd thought that odd."

Bart was barely able to remember what they were talking about as raw, physical desire flooded his body. "Harper Truman's personal assistant?" He turned his head to face her, and their lips met, gently at first, and then with growing hunger.

~ ~ ~ ~ ~

Chabal emerged into the back parking lot of Fort Andross, the December day announcing itself with a piercing cold, the kind that hurts your face and makes every breath a stab in the chest. Right then, however, she welcomed this bite, her thoughts muddled in her head, and an edge to her nerves.

She'd called her husband who told her dispassionately that he'd taken the kids and gone to his parents. This was probably good, removing them from the immediate danger, but their absence left a void in her heart. His parents lived down in Cape Elizabeth, forty minutes south—far enough, she judged to keep them safe until she could retrieve them. But, she had no intention of just resuming the life she'd been living. She was done.

Chabal knew that John would accept her apology if tendered, and they could go back to the way things had been. But she wanted more. She wanted passion and love and excitement. At the same time, she wanted the kids, maybe not now, not in the middle of the shit storm she was currently in, but afterwards. At least shared custody, she thought, because children need both a father and a mother.

Chabal had been shocked to see Amanda walk into the bookstore the day before, resentful at her return. Then she had begun to feel sorry for her. Now that Langdon and his wife—and Chabal did have to recognize that they were still married—were talking again, where did that leave Chabal? Suddenly a hot mess, she wanted to weep, curse, and shout, anything but this feeling of waiting for everything to explode. And explode it surely would, because, what was that phrase? The center couldn't hold, and she sure as shit was that center.

The car turned over sluggishly, and she let it warm up while she scraped the ice from the windshield, leaving the back to defrost on its own. As she pulled onto Maine Street, Chabal asked herself aloud what it was that she wanted. A voice in her head clearly replied just one thing—Langdon. She'd known this for some time, had fought against it, but now accepted it. Pursuing it was another thing, for it would mean tearing her life apart as well as his own, even if she were successful, because she did suspect that the feelings were mutual. She sighed deeply and began to weep hot tears of anger and frustration. Finally, the waterworks stopped, and she wiped her face with one hand. Sometimes the best things in life are those that you cannot have, and it was quite possible that this desire of hers might just be that, something to contemplate deeply, to enjoy, but not to act upon.

The Trumans lived up behind Bowdoin College in an area known as Meadowbrook. The neighborhood was upscale, but just short of real money, many of the residents having lived there for generations. The house was an old but well-kept Colonial on about an acre of land with a three-car garage. It could have been a postcard, so picture-perfect was the house, a lazy tendril of smoke rising from the chimney, virgin-white snow covering the lawn, and the windows frosted over. Chabal was hoping that the governor was not home, but so what if he was? She went to the front door, raised the knocker, and whacked it three times.

Karol Truman answered, letting out the noise of bedlam from somewhere behind her that announced four children between the ages of two and eleven. It must be a teacher workshop day, Chabal decided.

"Hello, Karol."

"Chabal?" Karol said with surprise. Chabal was able to watch the emotions cross the woman's face as she registered the arrival of her friend who she'd not seen for some time. A friend who worked for Goff Langdon, the man who was currently wanted for murder. She shuddered unconsciously, then seemed to note how cold out it was. "Come in," Karol said, opening the door wider and gesturing Chabal into the cozy home.

"Thank you," Chabal said, stepping past this trim and athletic figure who just happened to be first lady of the state. She had short blonde hair and was dressed in a pants suit, looking to be no more than thirty, even though Chabal knew she had to be closer to forty.

"Let's go up to the study," Karol said. She led the way past a room of more than her own children, with Randi Petersen, her nanny, in the middle.

The study was a tasteful room on the second floor with bookshelves lining the walls, oriental rugs covering a warm wood floor, and two desks facing the two windows. Two old, comfortable-looking armchairs guarded the entrance, an archway opening somewhat grandly on a wide hall. Once they were seated, Karol looked expectantly at Chabal.

"It's about Langdon," Chabal said.

"I was mortified to hear that he was involved in the death of Guyton and that Bowdoin student," Karol replied.

"That's what I need to talk to you about. The chief committed suicide, and Peppermint Patti was Langdon's friend. He didn't have anything to do with either death."

"I understand," Karol said with the patronizing air of somebody who doesn't believe you. "The two of you are quite close, aren't you?"

Why wouldn't the woman believe her? Chabal wondered. But she had to try, and that probably meant sharing some information if she wanted Karol, in turn, to talk about her husband. "Langdon is being framed for the murders because of a case he's working on."

"Framed?" The disbelief in Karol's face was clear, though she tried vaguely to hide it. "This isn't some Hollywood movie, Chabal."

"It's true," Chabal insisted. "He was hired by Janice Dumphy to investigate the death of her husband, Harold. Before he even took the case, Langdon began getting threats, and the whole thing seems related to something bad happening at DownEast Power."

"DownEast Power?" Karol said dumbly. Her dubiety had been replaced by a creeping unease clouding her classic American features, so regular and pretty, like those of a model in an Eileen Fisher catalog. "Didn't the man commit suicide?"

"That was the police verdict, but the widow was suspicious, and so were the officers who worked on the case. It turns out that Chief Lefebvre abruptly closed the investigation, claiming it was a suicide, no questions—case closed. Except he told another officer the case had been taken over by the Feds. Which there is no evidence of..."

"But, why would Guyton do that? That doesn't make sense."

"He was being blackmailed."

"How do you know?"

"A photograph he was trying to destroy. Yeah, it turns out the chief was having an affair with some woman, and it was being used against him so that he would cover up that Harold Dumphy was murdered." Chabal was giving out more information than she'd planned, but she sensed that something she'd said had struck a chord, for Karol stepped back abruptly, one hand clapped to her mouth as if in shock. "Langdon had gone over to his house," she continued, "to speak with him about the Dumphy investigation, and that is when he discovered him dead. He'd set fire to some papers and pictures in his trash can, put his pistol in his mouth, and pulled the trigger. Langdon pulled the charred remnants from the waste bin and then fled the scene, realizing he was in the wrong place at the wrong time."

"He killed himself?"

"Yes. Langdon said it was quite obvious."

"You said there were pictures?"

"There was one that was only partially burnt. You can make out the chief, but not the woman he is with, just that they are both naked and intimate." Chabal stopped talking and waited. "What do you know about all of this, Karol?" she asked after a long silence.

Karol mumbled something that was inaudible.

"I'm sorry, what did you say?"

"I am the woman in the picture."

"*You?*" Chabal had not expected this, but immediately sized up the woman in front of her, comparing the figure to the picture in her memory, and decided that it was indeed quite possible. "You were having an affair with the chief?"

"My husband has been screwing a woman for some time now, perhaps for the whole time we've been together. He kept promising me he would end it, but there were signs, and I knew he never did or would, so I decided to get even."

"Why couldn't you just divorce him?"

Karol inclined her head. "I suppose the normal reasons. Kids, house, money, and the fact that my husband is the governor."

"Who has he been sleeping with?"

"That slut at DownEast Power."

"Who?"

"Goddamn Abigail Austin-Peters, that's who. I wanted to let him know that two could play at that game. Guyton had always flirted with me, so one night, after he and his wife were over for a dinner party we hosted, I brought him up to our room. While the others had cocktails downstairs, I… fucked him in our bed." She spat the last words out brutally, and Chabal could feel her anger, fierce and hot, at her husband's years of unfaithfulness.

"I had no idea," Chabal said weakly.

"Of course it did no good, as Harper didn't know."

"And then you continued? But what about the pictures?"

"It'd been going on for about six months, and Harper seemed oblivious, even though I was blatant, leaving obvious clues to my infidelity. And then one night, after too many drinks, I shared all with a dear, old friend."

Chabal waited, knowing Karol wanted to tell her.

"Ellsworth Limington," Karol said, as if far away. "He's been a friend since college, and when I told him of my dilemma, he suggested that he send a man he knows to take pictures of me with Guyton, and then I could slap them in Harper's face and see how *he* liked it."

"So you showed your husband the pictures?"

"Yes. He didn't care. He actually laughed."

"Somebody also sent those pictures to Chief Lefebvre with a blackmail note. They were pressuring him to drop the Harold Dumphy case," Chabal said quietly.

"Why?"

"I think there is a problem at DownEast Power, something so bad it could potentially close the plant down, and that Harold Dumphy found out about it. He was killed so it wouldn't get out."

"My husband wouldn't do that. He hates DownEast Power. He's always going around complaining about living right next to a nuclear time bomb. Harper has tried numerous times since being elected governor to have it closed. He would be ecstatic if a crisis were exposed and the plant closed."

"And that leaves who?"

~ ~ ~ ~ ~

Amanda Langdon walked up Maine Street for her meeting with Jackson Brooks at the Lenin Stop Coffee Shop. She was remembering just how much she hated Maine winters, the frigid air and biting wind. The scarf she wore was silk, not wool, the coat borrowed and two sizes too big. She had left her warm clothes behind when she'd fled her husband and the state he lived in, and thus was not ready for the elements, not that she would be even with warmer clothes, which she doubted he'd even saved.

Jackson Brooks already had a table when she walked in. He stood and offered to get her a coffee and a pastry. He was exactly six-feet tall with dark features and black hair carefully combed. His body was muscular and his eyes intelligent. They traded pleasantries, which moved on to her marital status, and carefully avoided the time they'd gotten naked together. Amanda knew his reputation as a ladies man, and thus she knew that he'd see her, if for no reason other than to get with her again. It wasn't that he was a bad man; he just liked sex.

"Do you know where your husband is, Amanda?"

"You know Goff isn't a criminal, much less a murderer," she replied.

"He should turn himself in then, and we can get everything sorted out."

"He can't do that," Amanda said, and then clarified. "He doesn't think that would be a good idea."

"Why is that?" Brooks' navy blue uniform brought out the blue of his eyes, eyes through which his intellect shone keenly as he questioned her. Amanda knew he was a good cop, even if a bit of a dandy, his uniform pressed perfectly, his shoes shined to a gleaming black, and his face always smoothly shaven.

"The other players in the game are too powerful," she said.

"What other players? What is going on?"

"It's a long story."

"Give me the highlights."

Amanda sighed. "Goff was hired to investigate the death of a security guard at DownEast Power. The police had ruled it a suicide. It turns out the chief, Guyton Lefebvre, was being blackmailed to shut the case down, and then he killed himself. Goff was seen at the crime. There was a Bowdoin student helping him with the case, and she was killed. Goff is also being blamed for that."

"Why?"

"Goff's theory is that there might be safety problems at DownEast Power. He thinks that these are being covered up for some reason, endangering the lives of thousands of people."

"And you think the chief and the girl were killed by the same person?"

"Yes. Well, no. The chief killed himself, but because of being blackmailed by this guy. He's a real hard ass. And he was probably behind the murder of Patti, but that was done by two men," Amanda said, her thoughts all discombobulated. "He's been going around threatening people. Lawrence Shakespeare, he calls himself. As a matter of fact, I saw him almost kill a man last night. He did it partly, I think, to show Chabal and me what he is capable of, to reinforce his warning for Goff to drop the case and leave town."

Jackson Brooks had been about to take a sip of coffee, but he paused, and set the cup down. "Lawrence Shakespeare?"

Amanda shrugged. "It's probably a fake name, but yeah, that's what he calls himself. Goff thinks he must be working for somebody else. He says the man's just a hired gun."

"So who's paying him?"

"Goff has a short list—Harper Truman, Johnson Halperg, Abigail Austin-Peters, and Ellsworth Limington."

Brooks whistled softly. "That is a powerful lineup. Who's the woman?"

"The public relations director at DownEast Power."

He nodded, intent on his cup of coffee. "I had some reasons a few months back to do a little digging on Ellsworth Limington," he said after a minute, raising his eyes to meet Amanda's. "He moved to Maine about ten years ago from New York City. It was more of an exile than a love of the snow that brought him here. He was being investigated by the FBI for shady business practices and had also rubbed the mob the wrong way."

"What sort of shady business practices?"

"He was not above using intimidation to deter competitors. The FBI arrested several men suspected of working for him. The charges against them ranged from criminal threatening to murder. Not one of them turned on him, though, and he skated free. He'd still be New York's problem if he hadn't gotten on the wrong side of the mob. Appears he quite wisely thought it best to get out of Dodge."

"Wow! Wait till Goff hears about this." Amanda whistled softly. "Fast 'n' loose in his business dealings, someone who hires others to intimidate, comfy with violence—Limington's quite the nasty package, it seems." Thinking of how the group needed to hear this right away, she almost missed what Brooks said next, almost, but not quite.

"The man who was arrested for murder and suspected of doing it on Limington's orders got out of prison a couple of months ago. His lawyers cut a deal for manslaughter, and he served slightly less than ten years on a twelve-year sentence."

"What's his name?" she asked, but she already knew.

"Lawrence Shakespeare." Brooks nodded at her. "You don't forget that moniker. And," he continued, "if Shakespeare's running around these parts, I'm gonna go out on a limb here and suggest he might have some bosom buddies along for the ride. Goff sure can pick 'em."

~ ~ ~ ~ ~

4 by Four showed up at Goldilocks at five minutes before noon. He, too, was freshly showered and shaved. He'd tied his hair back into a ponytail and misted his body with cologne before climbing into black jeans, a white shirt, red suspenders, and a blue pinstriped jacket. He had sworn to Langdon that he wouldn't be able to drink due to his hangover, but was now second-guessing that decision. One, maybe two cocktails couldn't hurt. He rationalized that he'd only promised Langdon to not drink Wild Turkey, but that perhaps a nice glass of wine or a beer would be fine.

Two hours later, with a pretty good buzz on, 4 by Four stood outside room 17 at the Admiral Perry Inn fumbling with the key as Abigail Austin-Peters pressed herself tightly against his backside, her body writhing and twisting around his, one hand down the front of his pants, the other pulling on his ponytail as she bit his ear.

It was another two hours before 4 by Four collapsed backward on the bed for a brief reprieve. The woman was certainly good looking, he thought with relish, but it was the fervor that poured forth from her being, her eyes heavy with desire, her skin electric, and her touch pleasure itself. She was not only mysterious, but rather wild as well, he reflected. The scratches on his back stung and blood clotted his ear where she'd bitten him in the throes of passion. He wondered why his feet were sore, but it was with a deep contentment that he reviewed these aches and pains. The words "great sex" didn't even begin to cover it, he thought. Jesus, he felt like he was eighteen again, if somewhat battered. Abby had gone into the bathroom and turned the shower on, giving him fair warning that she was not done with him yet. He realized there was a foreign object digging into his back and pulled out the remote control to the television from underneath him.

He flicked on the set and Bob Walters and Kate Conley, the Channel Six Action News Team, appeared on the screen. They were talking about what Kate had done over Thanksgiving, and he was about to change the channel, when Bob suddenly interrupted her. "We have a story breaking right now on DownEast Power." As he spoke, old footage of the plant came on the screen, coils of steam rising from its cooling tower. "An anonymous source at the State House has leaked a report that the plant has such serious cracks in some high-pressure steam lines that it will shut down for years, maybe forever. Apparently, the Nuclear Regulatory inspectors discovered a number of potentially hazardous cracks, and there seem to be quote-unquote irregularities in record keeping, testing, and maintenance procedures that could have contributed to this dangerous situation. DownEast Power has released an official statement that they will be having a press conference at five this afternoon to address what they have so far refused to confirm."

"4 by Four?"

4 by Four tore his eyes away from the news and to the very naked body of Abby as she emerged from the bathroom. "Did you know about this?" he asked, pointing at the television.

"Of course I knew about it. I'm the public relations director, aren't I?"

"Don't you need to be there for the press conference?"

She found her panties on the floor and pulled them on in one fluid motion, the lacy red material mostly see-thru. "No, not this time. Johnson Halperg and a team of lawyers are going to handle this one. I have a different assignment."

"What's that?"

"I am supposed to speak with Goff Langdon about retaining his services. He, after all, is the one who broke this story. If he hadn't been so..." she paused, searching for the word. "So stubborn, let's say, it never would have come out. So, the board has asked me to contact him about doing an investigation into the... issues at the plant. DownEast Power would like to hire your Mr. Langdon."

"You know he's wanted by the police?"

"I have it on good authority that he will soon be cleared of those bogus charges."

"I don't know where he is." 4 by Four was not sure that he should be bringing her to the mill. Whether it was the two murders, the blackmail, or who had the cash to hire Shakespeare, her name had come up far too often.

"You know how to contact him, don't you?" She rummaged in her purse and found her lipstick and a hand mirror. She began to apply it to plush lips that so recently had roamed his entire body, facing him in nothing but panties.

"I might know where he is," 4 by Four said. Somehow, desire had rekindled whatever flames still burned in his depleted body, and her return smile lit up his soul like an autumn bonfire.

Chapter 21

Langdon felt helpless. It was not in his nature to sit back and wait, but that was what he was relegated to doing. He had stayed behind with the kids, who were having an amazing time running around the writer's loft. Jewell had gone and stocked up on some provisions, sandwich materials and snacks for the children, and, reluctantly, a bottle of Jack Daniels for Jonathan Starling.

He'd conversed a bit more with Starling, but the man made increasingly less sense before passing out on the floor by the basketball hoop. Jewell, back from the store, was giving him the silent treatment for endangering her family, and Missouri seemed content creating a band with Will and Tangerine. Langdon decided that life on the lam was not as glamorous as they made it out to be in the movies.

Chabal was the first back, bringing news of Harper Truman's longstanding affair with Abigail Austin-Peters and Karol's own dalliance with Chief Lefebvre in an attempt to get even, an infidelity she was unable to stop once she'd initiated the fling. It seemed likely that Harper Truman or Ellsworth Limington were responsible for blackmailing the chief, but it was possible they'd passed on to others what they had discovered.

Truman was having an affair with Abigail Austin-Peters, and Limington was an old schoolmate of Johnson Halperg, so their list of suspects remained at four. Langdon tried to call 4 by Four to warn him to be careful, but his cell phone seemed to be dead.

Bart was back next with a sleepy look in his eyes and a smile on his face that was so unnatural to him that the others stopped talking and just stared at him. "What?" he asked, joining Chabal and Langdon at the table.

Jewell finally gave in and put down the book she'd been pretending to read and came over and sat down as well. Langdon said nothing as Bart told him of the ongoing affair that the widow had with Ellsworth Limington, and that she'd said it was entirely possible she had told him in passing that she was about to hire a private detective to investigate the death of her husband.

"Yeah, she told me that before," Langdon said.

"There's more," Bart said with a sly look that was completely out of place on his broad face. "She remembered what it was that first tipped Dumphy off to start poking around."

"He didn't just catch on to odd occurrences because he was doing his job as head of security?" Chabal asked.

"Janice said that it was Clayton Jones who first tipped him off. It was several weeks before his death, so she'd forgotten that he mentioned it one morning at breakfast, sort of like commenting on what somebody was wearing."

"Who is Clayton Jones?" Jewell asked.

"He is an administrative assistant for Governor Truman," Langdon said.

"And one of his main tasks is as a liaison between the government and DownEast Power," Bart added.

"So, that would suggest that Governor Truman knew something was fishy?" Jewell asked. "But it sounds like he was trying to expose it, not cover it up."

"If Governor Truman knew something was up, why didn't he just report it? Send in the troops, so to speak," Langdon said.

"And if he's not the person covering up the issues at the plant, then who is?" Bart asked.

"If Janice told Limington, it stands to reason that that was the reason Langdon was being threatened by Shakespeare before he'd even been offered the case. They must be working together," Chabal said.

"We don't know for sure that she told him anything," Langdon said.

"True, but it's at least a possibility," Chabal said.

"Janice actually thought it was likely she would have mentioned it," Bart said. "She just doesn't remember it specifically."

"Let's not forget it was Limington's idea to blackmail the chief. Even if Karol thought of them as revenge photos, Limington certainly could have been using them to force the investigation into Dumphy's death to be dropped," Langdon said.

"And Limington and Halperg are old school pals," Chabal said.

It was then that Lord called, checking in as promised. They'd been following Shakespeare all day, since he'd left the Bernard around 11:00. The most noteworthy stop the man had made was at Casco Bay Power. They were not sure that he met with Johnson Halperg, but it certainly seemed likely. He'd been inside the building for only about twenty minutes. Nick had been about to go inside for recon when the man came back out. He'd driven by Langdon's apartment, Chabal's house, as well as the Denevieux home, and had a late lunch at Hog Heaven. It seemed he was on the prowl.

Lord was calling just as Shakespeare pulled into the parking lot of the Admiral Perry Hotel down on Water Street, and Lord reported that two men and a woman got out of a car and into his, and now the four of them were just sitting there. Lord wasn't sure, but he thought one of the men had a scratch on his face. The rage in his voice was a palpable and living beast. Langdon cautioned Lord not to do anything rash.

They'd just hung up when Amanda swept into the room, her eyes bright with the news that Ellsworth Limington was a person of interest to the FBI, and that Lawrence Shakespeare had just been released from prison for killing a man, most likely on the orders of Limington.

"Sounds like that's our man," Bart said.

"I should call Lord back and warn him about Shakespeare," Langdon said.

"And tell him he's dangerous?" Bart asked. "He knows that. Your face knows that."

"What do we have to eat?" Missouri asked, her eyes level with the top of the table. Will and Tangerine stood at a distance watching, obviously having sent her to make this request.

"I could make sandwiches?" Langdon asked.

"What kind?"

A banging at the door caused Langdon to divert his direction from the path to the fridge. Chabal started to suggest he shouldn't be opening the door in case it was the police, but stopped, knowing it was useless to talk sense to the man.

It was Richam, laden with several plastic bags holding containers of macaroni and cheese, cheesy bread, steak tips, and salads from the Wretched Lobster. Langdon propped the door open with a golf club that seemed to be there for exactly that purpose and helped him carry the bonanza of food to the table. The adults gave up their seats to the kids and stood around the kitchen eating as well.

~ ~ ~ ~ ~

It was dark by the time 4 by Four and Abigail Austin-Peters emerged from the Admiral Perry Hotel. They had arrived in his Vanagon, which had suspect heat, but it was less than a mile to Fort Andross. His teeth were chattering, but she seemed impervious to the cold. There was a flake or two of snow spitting from the black sky, but it was too cold for any real snow, the temperature at zero and still dropping. They were unaware of the car that followed them, as was that car of the car that followed it.

"Langdon is hiding out in Fort Andross?" Abigail asked incredulously. "I have to admit that he has huge balls. Hiding in plain sight."

The back door hadn't yet been locked for the night and they slid into the warmth of the hallway. "They're up on the third floor," he said, leading her towards the elevator.

"Let's take the stairs," she replied.

He veered past the elevator to the exit sign and the stairwell, and he tried to take her hand, that is until she pulled it roughly away. She was the ice queen again, having shed the flirty, sex kitten persona now that they were back out in public. 4 by Four was breathing heavily by the time they reached the top floor. They went past the storage units to where the door to the artist studio was cracked, showing a sliver of light from the door still wedged open with the golf club.

4 by Four led the way through the entrance. The kitchen table was in the center of the enormous room. The three children and Amanda were sitting there, while Jewell and Richam stood behind their two kids, huddled in conversation. Bart was leaning against a pole drinking a beer, while Chabal and Langdon were heating something up at the stove. Bart was the first to see them when they were just twenty feet away.

"Yo, hippie, I don't remember extending any invitations to strangers."

Langdon looked up, his eyes freezing. What had he done with that pistol? No matter, now. "Hello again, Ms. Austin-Peters. To what do we owe the pleasure of your company?" His phone, or rather, Chabal's phone, buzzed in his pocket, but he ignored it for the time being.

All conversation ceased. "Hello, Mr. Langdon." Her eyes swept the kitchen area, noting that Bart most likely had a pistol in a shoulder holster, but was probably the only one armed. "I thought I should congratulate you. Your questions the other day caused us to start an internal investigation. You may be right that there are problems with the plant, and what's more, the cover-up seems to be leading us straight to our own CEO, Johnson Halperg."

"What sort of problems?" Langdon asked. The three kids had returned to eating.

"Cracks in steam lines, problems that would cause DownEast

Power to be closed down, possibly permanently."

"And what do you want from me?"

"We're concerned about transparency, the public trust. Any internal investigation of Johnson Halperg we do will be compromised. I would like to hire you as an outsider to run a separate, completely independent inquiry, maybe with lawyer-man," she gestured to 4 by Four, "helping with the legal and regulatory angles."

"This doesn't have anything to do with the fact that you are having an affair with Governor Truman, one of the original founders of Flower First? He's been trying his hardest to get DownEast Power shut down since being elected. Did he have you sabotage the plant?" Langdon asked.

To her credit, her eyes never wavered as she stared straight back at him. "Do you have any idea how difficult it would be to circumvent security and damage a nuclear power plant?"

"Hello, Jordan." Jonathan Starling had woken from his stupor and now stood off to her side, swaying slightly, a bottle in his hand.

She turned to look at him, taking in his aged face, dirty and disheveled clothes, and rank odor. "Hello, Jonathan."

"Son-of-a-gun," Langdon said. "Of course. Abigail Austin-Peters. Jordan Fitzpatrick. You are the same person. You've been sleeping with Harper Truman from long before he got married and became a father and the governor." He slapped his hands together and shook his head. "Why didn't I figure it out before?"

"You're looking good," Jonathan said.

"Sorry I can't say the same for you," Jordan replied.

"That all makes perfect sense," Langdon said. "So, of course, it was you that somehow sabotaged the reactor, but it's not you who is trying to cover it up, is it?"

"I don't know why the whistle hasn't been blown until today," she admitted.

"Maybe because the man you tipped off was murdered?" Langdon asked.

"Dumphy? He committed suicide, didn't he?" Jordan Fitzpatrick, her real name, appeared confused. "Between the stress of his job and his wife sleeping with the whole town? Enough to make anybody want to end it."

"Dumphy was killed," Langdon said flatly.

"I know nothing of that," Jordan said.

"Why are you really here?" Langdon asked. "All of a sudden you decide to fall in love with 4 by Four and next thing you know he leads you right to us. What's really going on?"

4 by Four felt his face burning, his body betraying his humiliation at his own behavior. "This is Abigail Austin-Peters," he said lamely.

"I don't know what her name is now," Starling said, swigging off the bottle. "But she used to go by Jordan Fitzpatrick who was my partner in law. And sex."

4 by Four took two steps over to Starling and jerked the bottle from his hand and took a giant slug of whiskey.

"What is it that you really want, Jordan?" Langdon asked.

"For DownEast Power to be shut down," she replied.

"*Did* you sabotage it?"

"Does it matter?"

Langdon licked his lips. "Probably to the police, yeah, it matters." If she had also ordered the murders of Harold Dumphy and Peppermint Patti, well then, that would be the least of her concerns. But Langdon didn't think so, even though he had to make sure. "Why did you send Shakespeare to threaten me?" he asked.

"Shakespeare?"

"The man you sent to threaten me. The fellow who most likely killed Harold Dumphy."

"We're the ones who tipped Dumphy off to the issues at the plant in the hopes that he would expose them," Jordan said. "Why would we kill him?"

"Who did you tell about Dumphy?"

"Johnson Halperg. We thought once he found out that Dumphy

was suspicious of a cover-up, the whole thing would blow up, but then Dumphy was found dead, having committed suicide, and nothing happened. The place is a ticking time bomb, and nothing happened. I don't know if Halperg is the one covering it up, but he certainly knows something."

"Harold Dumphy was killed by a man named Lawrence Shakespeare," Langdon said. "And then Chief Lefebvre was blackmailed to make the case disappear, and when the guilt got to be too much, he killed himself."

"I don't know a man named Shakespeare, other than the famous bard," Jordan protested.

"I don't think you do, but I do wonder if you know two fellows by the name of Elwood and Stanley." Nothing had been turned up in connection with the two men who had killed Peppermint Patti. Langdon thought he had the rest of it worked out, but who did those two goons work for? And where were they?

"You mean the Blues Brothers?"

"That's Elwood and Jake."

"I don't believe I have ever met a man named Elwood, or Stanley for that matter." Jordan had begun edging her way back towards the open door.

"Well, let me introduce you," Shakespeare's nasally voice grated across the distance from the doorway. He stepped through the door, allowing three others to step through. The two men moved to his left, and he indicated them with a nod. "Elwood and Stanley." The woman moved to his right, but he did not introduce her.

"What do you want?" Langdon asked.

"Want? Well, I can't say that I won't enjoy it, but it's more of what I *have* to do than what I want to do. You, Mr. Langdon, have been annoying the wrong people. You and your friends. Too bad all of you are about to perish in a senseless fire. But who will really care?" He paused, wagging a menacing finger at Langdon. "You couldn't let well enough alone, could you?" He turned to Jordan. "And what a bonus that the lady who leaked the news of the cracks is here to share your fate. My boss will be very pleased."

Langdon stared at the reed-thin, sallow man. The woman to his right was tall, hunched over at the shoulders, with gleaming eyes suggesting a bit of craziness. Immediately to Shakespeare's left was a short, chunky man who looked like he'd just walked into his own surprise party, so big was the idiotic grin plastered on his face. The final thug, all the way to the left, had a lanky build, his pale face marked by scratches, deep scratches that might have been made by a young woman fighting for her life.

Chapter 22

"And who is your boss, Mr. Shakespeare?" Langdon asked.

"Does it really matter?"

"Who *are* you?" Jordan Fitzpatrick asked.

"Let's just say I work for a man who is not about to give up a fortune because of a little shit like you," Shakespeare said.

"Johnson Halperg?"

"That little cheerleader? I just went over to see him and give him a gentle warning to keep his mouth shut, and I kid you not, the man shit his pants." Shakespeare roared with laughter at the memory.

"He works for Ellsworth Limington," Langdon said. He noticed Bart easing his way to the side in an effort to flank the enemy.

"Aren't you the smart one, Mr. Langdon? I'd give you a gold star but I gave my last two out to Elwood and Stanley for a little job they did for me."

"You're going down for this one. Again." Langdon spoke with a calm he didn't feel. "Just out of prison, and back you go. Do you really think Ellsworth gives a shit about you?"

"Mr. Limington provided me with the best lawyers money can buy," Shakespeare snarled. "I'm no snitch," he added.

"Fat boy!" the female assassin shouted. "Move another inch and you'll be the first to die."

Bart raised his massive arms in his best fat boy pose.

"I don't understand what this is all about," Jordan Fitzpatrick—or was it Abigail Austin-Peters?—said in confusion. She'd come here with the intention of steering the blame onto Halperg and away from Truman. Instead, she was now about to go down with all hands on a ship she hadn't even realized had left the dock.

"Perhaps we should lay all our cards on the table, just so everybody knows what's going on." Langdon tried again to slow down the events that teetered on the brink of an orgy of violence. He hoped that the earlier phone call had been from Lord warning him that Shakespeare had arrived at the loft. If that was the case, his brothers should be here shortly, and there was nobody he'd rather have on his side in a fight.

"You're the detective," Shakespeare said nastily. "Why don't you fill us in on what this is all about."

"Okay, I will," Langdon said. Where were Lord and Nick? "Let's start with the woman who, until just recently, we knew of as Abigail Austin-Peters. Her real name is Jordan Fitzpatrick, and she is the founder of an environmental group called Flower First, but this organization has a secret sect, a strike force if you will, called Terror First. I would imagine that her name change and granting of security clearance was greatly aided by her partner, Harper Truman, once he was elected governor." He looked over at Jordan, who gave a short nod that this was correct. "This probably occurred after Harper Truman realized that his position as governor was not powerful enough to shut the plant down, because the real power resides in big money, and not with politicians."

"That's the fucking problem with this country in a nutshell," Jordan said.

"When they realized Governor Truman didn't have the power to shut the plant down, they hatched a plan, a scheme which involved having Jordan become an executive at DownEast Power. This allowed her to stage the sabotage at the plant, a plan that was probably carried out by militants in her Terror First organization."

"We didn't do anything," Jordan said.

"What's that?"

"We had plans to create problems, but we didn't have to. Years of cutting corners and neglect had caused enough issues to shut the place down for good without us doing a thing. We just had to expose the problems and let the regulators do their jobs."

Langdon stared at her, wondering if this was the truth, or merely damage control in the unlikely event that she survived the current situation. "Whatever the case, neglect or vandalism, they leaked the issues to the CEO, Johnson Halperg. That gem of a man was thrown into a dilemma, because the plant being shut down on his watch would effectively end his career. He took his quandary to his old school chum, Ellsworth Limington, who told him to sit tight and he would fix everything. I'm only guessing, but I'm pretty sure if you check who owns the most stock in that power company, you're going to find Limington's right up there on the list."

"Go on," Shakespeare said. Langdon was putting together puzzle pieces even the hitman hadn't known about, and he was filing them away, perhaps for future use if things went south.

"When Johnson Halperg didn't blow the whistle—and I'm going to guess some of those inspectors probably bought that new car or took the wife on the dream vacation, anyway, when things stalled— Jordan and Truman decided to have Clayton Jones, who was the go-between for DownEast Power and the governor's office, tip off the head of security, Harold Dumphy. I would guess that Dumphy not only found proof of the problems, but also incriminating evidence against Johnson Halperg, for they meant him to be the scapegoat in all of this."

"Who are 'they'?" Chabal asked, eying her pocketbook on the counter. She'd stopped home after visiting Karol Truman and picked up her pistol.

"Jordan and Harper, of course," Langdon replied.

"None of this matters. DownEast Power will be closed down. No matter what happens here, I have won," Jordan said.

"What Jordan is just now discovering is that there are other players involved in this game, namely, Ellsworth Limington III." Langdon looked with compassion at the radical environmentalist who had gotten in over her head. "Limington could not afford for DownEast Power to be closed down, because that would be financially disastrous for him. Sure, there are his now-worthless shares. But he's also deeply invested in the area—and deeply invested in having that place make his life easier. Come on, with no power plant pulling Woolington's train, the higher taxes alone on his property interests in the Mount Chamberlain Ski Resort and associated hotels, restaurants, and businesses would bankrupt him, not to mention the closing of the largest employer in the area eating away at his customer base. This isn't the first time Limington has been forced to play hardball, as a matter of fact. Ten years ago, he escaped New York City just before his fitting for either handcuffs or cement shoes because of his penchant for using acts of violence to perpetuate his business."

"I don't know how you know all that, but you're right on target," Shakespeare said almost with admiration. His face had the surprised look of someone shocked to be out-thought by some backwoods bookshop owner. "Go on." He did not appear to be overly concerned, most likely because he thought the situation was well in control.

"In New York City, Limington had his hired gun, one Mr. Lawrence Shakespeare, kill a competitor. But this backfired and the FBI caught him in the act. They couldn't prove anything against Limington, as Shakespeare refused to snitch. But the mob had become increasingly unhappy with his business practices, so Limington divested and moved to Maine and bought a town. When his man got out of jail last week, Limington sent for him, knowing that he was the perfect stooge to again take the fall if the police or FBI got too close."

"Shut your mouth," Shakespeare said, this next little not-so-subtle dig at the thug changing his tune. His jaw was quivering and spittle flecked his lips. "Mr. Limington needs me."

"You're right," Langdon replied. "He needs you to take the fall, just like you did in New York City. You went to prison, and he brought a boatload of money to Maine and has been living like a king. Hell, irony of ironies in our little scenario, he was even regularly bopping the first victim's wife!"

"It's not like that. Limington and me, I mean."

"But it is, isn't it?"

"I'm going to kill you, Langdon, but first I'm going to kill your sweet little daughter while you watch." Tremors ran through Shakespeare's body from head to toe as he fought the notion that he was being played, directing all of his anger at Langdon instead. Limington had gotten him out of the institution and given him respect and would never turn his back on him. "By the time you die, you will be begging me to end it."

"What you are going to do is lay that gun down at your feet and take three steps back with your hands over your head." Lord Langdon stood just inside the open window to the fire escape, flanked by Nick and Crazy Larry.

Elwood and Stanley turned their pistols towards the new threat, while the female assassin kept her weapon trained on Bart. Shakespeare held what looked to be a Beretta in his hand loosely pointed at Langdon.

Nick, carrying a large rifle, started to walk to an open space, spreading out the field of fire. The female assassin swung her pistol to cover him. "Stop. Don't take another step." She spoke in a clipped tone, a dangerous light in her eyes.

"Calm down, honey," Nick said in a soothing voice. "You sure are a pretty thing. What are you doing when this is all over?"

"Roasting marshmallows over your burning carcass," she hissed.

Crazy Larry pushed his coat back with his elbows to reveal the twin-holstered pistols.

Bart drew his pistol from his shoulder holster and pointed it towards the woman, while Elwood and Stanley, weapons drawn, looked dumbly from face to face. It was now four guns to four guns—a real Mexican standoff—and one that was just one spark short of exploding into a massacre.

Langdon raised his hands and stepped forwards towards Shakespeare. "Looks like you better lay your guns down and throw yourself on the mercy of the courts. The FBI would be happy to cut you a deal if you serve up Ellsworth Limington on a platter to them. Is he really somebody you want to die for? Or go back to prison for life?"

"Shut your mouth, Langdon."

"Or better yet, how about you just back out of here and walk away? No harm, no foul," Langdon said. The goon with the scratches, he was a different story, though one whose ending might best be continued another day.

Langdon suddenly felt his legs grabbed from behind. "Daddy, I'm scared," Missouri said, burying her face into the back of his knees.

Langdon reached behind him and tousled her hair, and when he raised his eyes, all of his love and weakness must have been on display for Shakespeare to see.

"Whatever happens here, I'm going to kill that little brat of yours," Shakespeare said with a demonic chuckle.

Langdon knew that he meant it and that the time for talking was done. The room around him slowed down. One by one everybody dissipated from his consciousness until there was just him, his little girl, and Shakespeare. The ugly black anger that had been brewing in the base of Langdon's spine, boiling in the pit of his stomach, tingling in his arms, and clutching at his heart solidified into a molten ball bubbling in the base of his skull.

Shakespeare raised the pistol like a duelist, standing sideways and aiming it at where Missouri's head poked out from behind Langdon.

Langdon turned his head and whispered to Missouri, "When I count to three, you lie down on the floor, and in a minute I'll be back to get you. Ready? One, two, three."

As Shakespeare's finger tightened around the trigger, Langdon charged forward, careful to keep himself between the man and his daughter. All the savagery and battle lust of his Viking genes roared forth, and he bellowed, a guttural blast of anger that reverberated throughout the cavernous space in Fort Andross.

He drove his body forward, intent on one thing, every bit of his being focused on Shakespeare's scrawny neck. The first bullet hit his thigh, just about where Missouri's head had been a split-second earlier. The entire room erupted into a crescendo of gunfire, but Langdon didn't hear any of it. His adrenaline driving him forward, he launched himself at that leering face.

The female assassin shot at Nick, the bullet an angry bee buzzing by his ear. Before she could pull the trigger a second time, Bart shot her full in the face, her features disappearing in a mist of blood and bone fragments.

The short chunky man turned his pistol at Bart and shot him in the side, the bullet a clean in-and-out, the lead later to be pried out of the wall behind him.

Lord aimed to shoot at Shakespeare, but his older brother charged forward, blocking his line of fire.

Nick shot the short chunky man in the shoulder, who dropped to the ground, causing Crazy Larry's shot to go over the mark. The man scuttled on his stomach to the door and slipped out as the melee continued behind him.

Amanda shot the tall lanky miscreant, the .22's bullet merely smashing his elbow, causing his own shot to miss. Lord turned his hunting rifle towards the man with the scratched face and blew a gaping hole in his groin, before tilting the powerful weapon up and shooting him full in the chest.

4 by Four went to grab Abby, or Jordan, or whatever her name was, but she pivoted away from him and then swung a roundhouse kick that broke his jaw and knocked him to the floor.

Langdon took a second bullet in the meat of his arm, and then a third glanced off his forehead just as he reached Shakespeare, driving the man backwards to the floor. He wrapped his hands around the neck of the man who had threatened his daughter, his one thought to cease forever the breath, even then labored, that he could feel through his fingers. And then there was nothing.

Epilogue

Langdon opened his eyes to a white room with a solitary vase of purple flowers resting on a small table beside the bed. He knew he wasn't in heaven, for he'd never in his entire life done anything to merit admittance.

There was a dull ache that was his body, and a pounding that was his head. He shifted his neck and was rewarded with a shooting pain that made him gasp. His eyes picked out Amanda asleep in a chair. She was dressed in black jeans with a baggy, white t-shirt. Even as careworn as she looked, she was indeed a beautiful woman.

The events of earlier came sifting back to him like snowflakes spinning slowly down from a frozen sky. Where was Missouri? Langdon shifted to look the other way and again gasped in pain.

"Goff?" Amanda was immediately at his side, her black hair tousled, the exhaustion smudging her eyes, and sadness in her face.

"Missouri?" he croaked.

"She's fine," Amanda said. She laid her hand on his forehead. "Everything is okay. Hey, let's get you some water." She reached to the counter along one wall and handed him a cup with a straw in it. He drank deeply, sighing.

"How about... everybody... else?" he asked finally.

"Everybody is doing okay. Bart had a bullet slice through his side but was drinking a beer as the paramedics led him off to the ambulance. Nobody else was even scratched. Well, that's not true. That woman? Jordan Fitzpatrick? She broke 4 by Four's jaw and escaped."

"How about the others? Did any of them get away?"

"Let's get a doctor in here," Amanda said. "You've been in a coma for the past three weeks."

~ ~ ~ ~ ~

Langdon had broken Shakespeare's neck with his hands. The paramedics had had to pry his fingers from the man's throat so that they could get him onto an ambulance stretcher. He'd lost a bit of blood, and the final bullet had glanced off his skull, leaving him in a coma. None of it was enough to kill him. The female assassin had been killed in the gun battle along with her tall companion, the short guy getting picked up by the police in the parking lot. Jordan Fitzpatrick had disappeared into thin air and had not been seen since.

The three children had been seeing a therapist, who seemed to believe that they were a resilient lot and would be fine.

Langdon was in a hospital in Boston, having been airlifted there by helicopter. He was a bit disappointed to have no memory of his first helicopter ride.

The death of the chief had been officially ruled a suicide. Dumphy's, a murder.

Elwood, the short guy, had confessed to killing Peppermint Patti along with Stanley, who was quite dead. He admitted that Shakespeare had hired them for the job, but that it was Ellsworth Limington who was the real boss.

Harper Truman had been arrested for his part in the potential sabotage and cover-up at the plant and was awaiting trial. He'd since resigned the governorship while his wife had announced their divorce.

Johnson Halperg confessed that Limington had counseled him to keep DownEast Power open while he tried to sort things out, and was cooperating fully with the authorities.

Ellsworth Limington had been arrested and refused bail.

DownEast Power had begun what would be a years-long march

to final decommissioning. Jordan Fitzpatrick had accomplished her goal, leaving more than a few casualties of war strewn in her wake.

Peppermint Patti's father, Senator Harding Smith of Texas, had been in town overseeing the entire investigation and had left a letter for Langdon before returning to Washington.

Dear Goff Langdon,

While I cannot absolve you of my daughter's death, I would like to inform you that the first time I had heard her happy in several years was right after she met you. There was no denying the lightness of her spirit when she told me of the case you were working on, and the strange ensemble of characters she'd met through you. You were a special person to her, and for that, I thank you. I do feel that it was very wrong of you to involve a child of twenty in a murder case. I cannot say that I forgive you, but you should at least know that you were a bright spot in her young and confused life.

Sincerely,

Senator Harding Smith

~ ~ ~ ~ ~

Chabal and Jonathan Starling had been running the Coffee Dog Bookstore in Langdon's absence. Starling was not, however, living in the governor's house.

Richam and Jewell had cut themselves off from the rest of the group as they tried to get their lives back on track.

4 by Four, embarrassed by his being duped by Jordan Fitzpatrick and unable to defend his actions due to his broken jaw, had taken an extended vacation and gone ice fishing on Moosehead Lake.

Later that day, with Missouri lying beside him in the bed, and his wife sitting in the chair next to him, Langdon was pondering: What was the next chapter of his life to be? Maybe it was time to write that mystery novel he'd always dreamed of writing. Maybe.

Now, enjoy Chapter One of Book Two in the Goff Langdon Mainely Mysteries, available December 2020 in ebook and paperback from Encircle Publications...

MAINELY FEAR

A Goff Langdon Mainely Mystery

Matt Cost

They're shooting baskets, amiably and mildly.
The noise of the basketball, though startlingly louder
Than the voices of the two of them as they play,
Is peaceable as can be, something like meter.
—From *Courtesy* by David Ferry

Chapter 1

The ice storm had already done most of the work. Much of Maine was still without power nine days after the freezing rain had ravaged the state, the thin coating of ice, initially turning the world into a glistening fairyland, morphing into a deadly menace as tree limbs broke and fell onto power lines, cars, and houses, and wide swathes of the state went dark.

Many people had fled their homes. Hotels were at full capacity. People moved in with family or neighbors with generators, or better yet, left the desolation behind for warmer climates. This presented opportunity for those not bound by laws.

The procedure was simple. Pick an isolated house that seemed without life and park just down the road. Stanley, because he was white, would go knock on the door. If somebody was home, Stanley would ask directions to an address down the street. If nobody proved to be home, however, then the looting could begin.

They took televisions, VCRs, stereos, jewelry—some people had even left money lying around. This night was the team's third in action, with a new element of wanton abandon added. Stanley had found several cans of spray paint and began to graffiti the walls.

REDNECKS, PERVERTS, QUEERS, he scrawled, that and worse.

What started as a simple act of vandalism unleashed something in the three boys that couldn't be stopped, and they began smashing china, furniture, mirrors, anything that would break. They took no joy in their actions, rather, the grim tightness to their eyes and their maniacal energy looking more like that of beings possessed.

It was in the town of Brunswick that a man came home to find his house trashed, having missed the vandals by about two minutes. He immediately called 911 and reported having passed a maroon van with out-of-state plates. The one problem with picking isolated homes meant a lack of escape routes, and it didn't take long for the police to locate the van.

The officer flashed his lights, and Maurice stomped down on the accelerator, which, on the still icy roads, proved one mistake too many. The next thing the three boys knew, they were in a ditch, the officer, gun drawn, ordering them to exit the vehicle with their hands on their heads. Maurice was angry. Stanley was terrified. Jamal was relieved.

~ ~ ~ ~ ~

"Langdon. Coffee Dog." Rosie was frantically working the cash register. The diner had been closed for the first three days of the ice storm, but the seven since had been a gold mine. It was hard to beat hot food and heat when there was so little of either to be found anywhere but downtown.

Langdon and his dog walked casually past the line of waiting people and over to an empty booth. They were regulars. Rosie worked hard to ensure that her regulars didn't have to wait. The increased cash flow created by the ice storm was certainly welcome, but it wouldn't last. Rosie understood the importance of taking care of the people who lived there, ate at her place—and would continue long after this storm was a bad memory.

The last few years had been bumpy for Goff Langdon given his ongoing separation from his wife, but the one constant had been breakfast every morning at Rosie's. He'd started going there his junior year in high school when he was trying to put on weight for football, and had missed very few days over the past 13 years, though only recently gained the distinction of being a regular. That wasn't bad, given that many old-timers didn't even consider you from Maine unless your lineage went back at least three generations.

Langdon was a mass of contradictions. He was a private detective, a bookstore owner, supported the environment, ate red meat, played football, and voted Independent, sometimes Democrat, but never Republican.

A police officer approached his table when he was most of the way through his bacon, eggs, home fries, and five slices of buttered toast. "You need a shave and a haircut," the cop said.

"Bart," Langdon greeted him. "Sit."

It was true that in the best of times, Langdon's hair was wild and unkempt, the dark red mop sprouting in every direction atop his head with little obvious effort to contain it. Shaving, well that happened when it happened, a matter of convenience, and there just weren't that many available time slots for such a banal activity. With the recent power outage rendering even the most mundane daily task unbelievably inconvenient, he now had twelve days of bristle on his face, a patchy mix of yellow, brown, and red shot through with gray posing rather unconvincingly as a beard.

"And have that mutt of yours think I'm moving in on his food? No way, partner. I know better than to get between Coffee Dog and food."

"Suit yourself." Coffee Dog was the gentlest of souls, but if he had one true calling in life, it was to eat ravenously and whenever possible.

"I just stopped in for a cup of joe."

"No donuts?"

Bart started a curt response, thought twice, and decided that might not be such a bad idea. "Thought you might be interested to know we caught those boys who were robbing and vandalizing all those houses."

"Yeah? Boys? How old were they?"

"Old enough to be tried as adults."

Langdon nodded. "How many were there?"

"Three."

"Local kids?"

"Boston."

"Damn creeping urbanization."

Bart nodded his head in agreement and ambled towards the door, or as much as a man seven inches over six feet and weighing in at over 300 pounds could amble.

Once he was gone, Rosie came over with a malicious glint in her eyes. "I need to talk to you about your dog."

"My angel?" Coffee Dog had grown bored waiting for Langdon to give him scraps and gone in search of easier game. His chin was currently resting on a table between a young couple, his mournful brown eyes imploring them to show just a bit of generosity.

"Had a customer complaint," Rosie said.

"How could that be?" Langdon smiled sweetly. "That would be like complaining about a giggling baby." Coffee Dog had now moved on to an elderly lady who appeared to be not quite finishing all the food on her plate.

"I know, but I have to take a stand somewhere."

"I could see if it would be okay for me to bring him to McDonald's from now on?"

"Goff Langdon!" Rosie cuffed him upside the head with the palm of her hand. "You know perfectly well what I told the customer."

He did know. On more than one occasion when a customer made the mistake of lodging a complaint with Rosie about the dog, her response had never once wavered. "I'm sorry about that." She would say. "Your meal is on me. Don't ever come back."

People from away who didn't know better might start to bluster, but even they caught on when they saw the look on her face. Rosie was only about two inches over five feet tall, but probably weighed close to 200 pounds. When she moved in close to stare grumbling customers in the face, they generally recognized the danger and quickly apologized. Most of them chose to stay in the company of the Coffee Dog.

The phone at his hip vibrated, and he answered the call. It was Jonathan Starling, his bookstore clerk, telling him he had a client waiting for him. Langdon slapped a twenty on the ten-dollar meal and whistled for Coffee Dog. They passed Danny T. on the way out, and Langdon, excited to have a client waiting for him, begged off the usual sports banter they engaged in.

It took Langdon just five minutes to get to The Coffee Dog Bookstore. The shelves were stocked with the best collection of whodunits in the entire state. Langdon was the owner, and under the bookstore name, there was also the inscription, GOFF LANGDON— PRIVATE DETECTIVE. Langdon had split his overriding passion for mystery into these two distinct businesses. The latter one in particular had significantly contributed to his marital difficulties and had almost cost him his life, yet he refused to step away from being a gumshoe.

"Good morning, boss," the man at the counter said with a grin. He was only about forty years old but looked sixty.

"Star," Langdon said. "How's business?"

"With the electricity out and all, it's like people have discovered reading all over again." There was indeed a crowd of people milling throughout the store. "If you're going to come sauntering in at any time of the day that suits you, then we might have to consider hiring somebody else."

"Or maybe just hire somebody with a little more energy than you," Langdon replied.

"Where else are you going to find somebody with my education to work for next to nothing?" Jonathan Starling had been a successful lawyer before running from his problems and hiding in a bottle of bourbon. Langdon was helping him get back on his feet, and in turn, the man had truly been a godsend in filling the need when Langdon had been laid up.

It was Chabal Daniels, with the help of Jonathan Starling, who'd taken over running the bookstore when Langdon had been in a coma almost two years earlier. Both the bookstore and the private detective business had been booming since Langdon had been shot in the head. He wondered why he hadn't tried it before. Being shot in the head, that is. It was, by far, the best advertisement he'd ever had, and it had cost him nothing except a hole in the head and a slight increase in his insurance rates.

"Is the potential client back in the office?" Langdon asked.

"Yep. Says she had to see you immediately. I told her you were on your way."

"What's she want?"

"Didn't say."

"She local?"

"Don't think so."

"What, then?"

"Nothing, boss. Just go on back and see her, she's been waiting long enough."

Langdon continued on to the back of the bookstore where a door led to his office. Not much more than a hole in the wall, the room had no windows and very little space. That was fine with him, because he could imagine Sam Spade in the same sort of dimly lit office.

As he opened the door, a woman stood and turned to face him. He noticed that she very attractive, but it was the anguish on her face that grabbed his attention. "Good morning, ma'am."

"Mr. Langdon?" Her eyes carried a palpable distress.

"The very same."

"Mr. Langdon, I have a problem and was hoping you might be able to help me out."

"I'm sorry, but I haven't even gotten your name yet?"

"Latricia. Latricia Jones."

"Would you like a cup of coffee, Ms. Jones?" He was trying to slow down the conversation, as he liked to get a sense of potential clients before making commitments, a lesson he'd learned the hard way.

"Yes, yes I would." She took a deep breath, and then exhaled. "That would be great. Thank you."

Langdon casually went back into the bookstore and grabbed two cups of coffee from one of the dispensers they kept filled all day long, the beans coming from the Lenin Stop Coffee Shop right across the street. Once back in his office, he handed her a cup and moved around her to his chair behind the desk and motioned that she should sit.

"Now, what seems to be the problem, Ms. Jones?"

"My son was arrested last night for theft, vandalism, and may possibly be charged with hate crimes."

No wonder the lady was jittery. "This happened in Brunswick?"

"Yes."

"How old is your son?"

"Jamal is eighteen, almost nineteen." Tears began to stream down her face. She made no effort to wipe them away or even to acknowledge their existence.

"Did he do it?" This was the moment when most clients got the chance to proclaim their innocence.

With difficulty, she nodded her head. "Yes."

Langdon tried to sort this out. What was he needed for if the crime had been done? It sounded like she needed a lawyer, and not a private detective. "Where are you from, Ms. Jones?"

She leaned forward in her chair. "Massachusetts. We live in Roxbury."

Langdon knew that most people within a thirty-mile radius of Boston would have replied that they were from Boston, especially if they were from Roxbury. Instead, Latricia Jones seemed almost defiantly proud to be from a rougher section of town. "And your son lives with you?"

"My son is doing a postgraduate year at the Molly Esther Chester Institute in Skowhegan." Latricia Jones stood up, unable to remain in the confines of a chair any longer and began pacing the small space. "Jamal is boarding there for the year, but he's been home since the second day of the ice storm."

"Your son is an athlete, Ms. Jones?" Langdon knew MECI, which served as the public school for Skowhegan, took private students from around the state, and boasted that it was one of the best postgraduate programs in the country for students looking to raise their prospects of getting into D1 athletics at four-year colleges.

"He is a basketball player, Mr. Langdon. A very good one."

"Just Langdon will do," he said with a smile. "Where does he want to go to college?"

"He was told by the basketball coach at Boston College that if he could bring up his SAT score by a hundred points and strengthen his math skills that he'd get a full scholarship." Latricia spoke as a mother proud of her son for his achievements, and not as the mother of a boy who'd recently been arrested on multiple charges.

"And where is his father?"

"He's out of the picture."

Langdon decided not to follow up on what that meant. "So, you think that your son is guilty of the charges?"

"I think he was put up to the whole business by somebody else. I think another person is using my son, and that Jamal will take the fall for that person. I won't have it. Jamal isn't a bad kid. His actions, what he did… that's just not normal for him." This single black mother of a star athlete from Roxbury with an iron will and the love only a mother could know stood in the dingy office of a PI in a small coastal Maine town, a single tear running down her right cheek. "Why?"

"Can't you just ask him?" Langdon already knew the reply.

"He would never *rat* on somebody else, not even to save himself. But it's more than that, something deeper, something I can't quite get to with him."

"What?"

"Since before Christmas vacation he's been withdrawn, brooding. That's not like him."

"Isn't that normal teenage boy behavior?"

"We have a very tight relationship, Mr. Langdon." She stopped pacing and fixed her intense dark eyes on his. "It is not an easy thing to bring up a boy all by yourself in Roxbury, and I couldn't have done it without us working together, my son and me. He's always been honest with me."

"Until recently." Langdon clarified.

"Just a few weeks ago he was home for break, and I knew something was up. I wish I'd dragged whatever it was out of him then. But now this? Of all times? When he has the world by the tail?"

"The world by the tail?"

"My boy was on the verge of leaving Roxbury behind for a better life. He was going to get a college education and have a shot at playing in the NBA. After eighteen years of steering clear of trouble on the sidewalks of Roxbury, he goes and does this? It just doesn't make sense." More tears ran in rivulets down her cheeks, but she made no move to wipe them away.

"What do you want from me, Ms. Jones?"

"I want you to find out who is responsible for ruining his life, and I want them to pay for it."

About the Author:

Matt Cost aka Matthew Langdon Cost

Over the years, Cost has owned a video store, a mystery bookstore, and a gym. He has also taught history and coached just about every sport imaginable.

During those years—since age eight, actually—his true passion has been writing. *I Am Cuba: Fidel Castro and the Cuban Revolution* (Encircle Publications, March, 2020) was his first traditionally published novel.

Mainely Power is the first of the Mainely Mysteries trilogy featuring private detective Goff Langdon. This will be followed by *Mainely Fear* (coming in December, 2020), and *Mainely Money* (to be released in March, 2021).

Cost now lives in Brunswick, Maine, with his wife, Harper. There are four grown children: Brittany, Pearson, Miranda, and Ryan. A chocolate Lab and a basset hound round out the mix. He now spends his days at the computer, writing.